No Lesser Angels, No Greater Devils

"Campbell's writing is poignant and riveting... seasoned speculative fiction readers will enjoy Campbell's atmospheric musings on death, divine retribution, and the afterlife."

~ Publishers Weekly

"A diverse collection of short speculative tales worthy of *The Twilight Zone*. Campbell spins tales that take readers into outer space, into haunted places, but especially into a realm that borders very closely with what might actually be out there!"

~ Beth Daniels,
Author of *How to Write a Funny Mystery* and *Muse to Manuscript*

"The title of the collection, *No Lesser Angels, No Greater Devils*, gives a hint of the overall intent of the stories: You can't really get away scot free with anything. Those who like dark stories will be delighted. Those who like the whimsical will, also... The occult, and seemingly occult, are represented as well, and there just might be a story or two which could lift your spirits."

~ Sue Sinor,
Co-author of *The Hunt for the Red Cardinal* from the 1632 universe
and avid reader

"Laura J. Campbell's collection *No Lesser Angels, No Greater Devils* has it all: prophetic dreams ("Just Passing Through") and... marathon runners ("The Horrible Mile"); alien conspiracies ("416175") and femmes fatales ("For the Love of Rachel"). But most of all, it has a heart. The stories are diverse in their style—from dark to humorous; and in their genre—from ghostly horror to science fiction. But they all touch the reader in profound and often unexpected ways. Beautifully written and deeply human, this is a collection for all lovers of speculative fiction."

~ Elana Gomel,
Author of *The Cryptids*

"No Lesser Angels, No Greater Devils is a riveting collection of the macabre, designed to keep the reader on edge, haunted by a subtly penetrating unease that torments the conscience with the suspicion that something is just not quite right. Ms. Campbell's brilliant attention to detail weaves mystery throughout the multitude of short tales, each of which stands out quite plausible, draws on into the oftentimes bizarre recesses of the mind, and concludes in a manner leaving just enough up to the imagination to keep the psyche awake at night, continuing the tale unchecked. Whether her well-developed characters are haunted, murdered, exploring space, running a marathon, or being chased by ashes of the recently departed, the pages quickly turn until a new adventure begins, just as eerily as the previous one ends. Brilliantly constructed; once you pick it up, don't put it down, unless, perhaps, you lock it in another room...."

~ Kirstin Holzschuh,
Owner of Bleepnwabbit Ventures

No Lesser
ANGELS
No Greater
DEVILS

A Beautiful Yet Haunting Collection by

Laura J. Campbell

From

Dark Owl Publishing, LLC

Arizona

Also From
Dark Owl Publishing

Anthologies
A Celebration of Storytelling
The anthological festival of tales.

Something Wicked This Way Rides
Where genre fiction meets the Wild West.
(Coming July 1, 2021)

Collections
The Last Star Warden:
Tales of Adventure and Mystery from Frontier Space, Volume I
Sci-fi pulp fiction at its finest by Jason J. McCuiston.

The Dark Walk Forward
A harrowing collection of frightful stories from John S. McFarland.

Novels
The Keeper of Tales
An epic fantasy adventure by Jonathon Mast.

Just About Anyone
High fantasy comedy from the twisted mind of Carl R. Jennings.
(Coming September 1, 2021)

YA Novels
Grayson North: Frost-Keeper of the Windy City
A totally cool urban fantasy adventure from Kevin M. Folliard.
(Coming December 1, 2021)

Buy the books for Kindle and in paperback
www.darkowlpublishing/the-bookstore

This book is dedicated to all of those who have encouraged me to write. To God, who has blessed me with this amazing vocation. To my parents, George and Pamela Sanger, who introduced me to literature and read Poe's "The Raven" to me as a bedtime story. To my husband, Patrick, who has listened to me lament story rejections and gush over story acceptances (and occasionally vice versa). To my children, Alexander and Samantha, who have inspired me and played while I sat on park benches, editing by hand. To my teachers and professors, who made it their calling to teach me to reason, read, and write. To all the editors and publishers who accepted my stories, and all those who didn't, who kept me moving forward in the pursuit of my craft.

Laura J. Campbell
September 9, 2020

Table of Contents

Introduction

One of the challenges of publishing short stories in the twenty-first century is that magazines and anthologies can go out of print. Electronic "links" to the tales can expire. In arranging my short stories for collection, I noted that several of the direct links to previously published material had disappeared. That made re-acquiring published material challenging.

In some cases, I have had to edit text from rough drafts, owing to an e-mail failure that saw many of my first thirteen short stories lost to the ether. It was time to gather the works together and present them as a volume of speculative tales.

I have made some edits, as some published versions have been lost to the sands of time, leaving me with only working copies to reconstruct. In addition, edits have been made to fit these stories into this collection.

I hope that you enjoy reading this re-collection of dark and quirky tales.

Laura J. Campbell
Houston, Texas
2020

Just Passing Through

"Just Passing Through" was the sixth story I wrote, written while living on Wyndale Street in Houston, Texas. I lived in an apartment built in 1946. The complex's original grandeur long behind it, it was like living in a time-capsule— children played outside in the courtyards, while we mommas cooked our diverse cuisines and rang a dinner bell for supper. We all kept an eye out and would yell to the collective children to keep them in line when they had their disagreements. It didn't even matter what language was used—that "momma" tone and look were enough to bring peace back to the kinder-kingdom.

All the psychic dreams were alike in at least one aspect: their temperature was simultaneously uncomfortably hot and disconcertingly icy.

JoLynne had them, these strange and oddly prescient dreams, ever since she was a child. As she grew older, their frequency had increased. She wasn't sure if their increase was a function of her age, her hormones, or the fact that as she grew older, she had known more people who had died.

For there was always a dead person in her special dreams.

The perished ones came to her, bearing emotions and vague visions. She had spent a lifetime trying to perfect a way to keep them near or to make the messages clearer. She was getting better, but apparently only angels could speak, for the dead were inconveniently mute. That left her with imperfect interpretations.

The dreams occurred in the deepest sleep. She was nearly impossible to awaken during their course. And the dreams were necessary. Without the psychic dreams, her energy levels dropped, her mood darkened, and her alertness faded. The world of waking became engulfed in fog and fatigue.

The dreams were vibrant: full of color, sound, and feeling—a place suspended outside the world. She could smell the scents around her, their fragrances and odors as abundant as in waking life. She could taste, and felt hunger and thirst in this semi-conscious world. Time had meaning. There was history and consistent geography to this realm.

She had other dreams, too. Regular dreams that faded with the embellishments of waking.

But the *special* dreams—the ones with the dead alive and the unreal real— always seemed to linger. And they always had some sort of meaning.

This particular dream dragged her down on a quiet afternoon, with the rain steadily beating outside her bedroom window. Her son was back in the United States, studying for fall finals, so she was alone and could abandon herself to sleep.

She was exhausted and everything ached. Her schedule had been too demanding and now, given the opportunity, her body insisted on oblivion.

Then she was in this special dream world. She knew it by its bright sunlight and clear open skies. She was on a street she used to walk, half a world away. Soft music drifted from a sidewalk restaurant.

She felt her son's little hand in her own. She looked down. He was much younger than he was now, in real life. He was four here, and his bright, round eyes shone excitedly up at her.

"We're going to see Daddy!" he said cheerfully, a merry step in his walk.

She did not reply. Daddy had been dead for years. That was why they had moved halfway around the globe. To escape memories like this.

"Daddy! Daddy!" Jeremy sang contentedly, his cheeks glowing like soft pink roses.

She heard the song again and walked toward it. "All the Little Ponies." She used to sing it to Jeremy when he was a baby, when she and Bobby were married and Jeremy was so very tiny. It seemed so many years ago, years longer than it really was.

It was a slow, mournful rendition of the lullaby, seeped in sadness. She and Jeremy walked into the building the song emanated from.

Bobby sat at a large round table, a glass of water in front of him. He stared blankly into space, his face registering nothing. He looked a little better than gaunt, his dark brown hair and dark brown eyes only making the pallor of his skin seem starker.

"Mommy, where are all the people?" Jeremy asked innocently.

JoLynne concentrated and lucidly injected a happy crowd of diners, the restaurant suddenly filling with wait staff, food, and patrons. Cheesy mariachi music played over a speaker system. She looked around. *Mexican food*, she noted. Bobby's favorite.

The dead, she had learned long ago, do better between worlds when they are in a familiar setting. That much she had learned how to provide. Bobby looked up at her, just as she remembered him from long ago.

Jeremy and JoLynne sat down. She had filled their table out with other relatives and friends. She needed life and movement to distract Jeremy and occupy Bobby's first thoughts. The visits were so tenuous that if the dead noticed their slipping into the living world, the connection would be lost.

It comforted JoLynne to be here, in this nonexistent place. *Mexican food!* It had been so long since she'd had good Mexican food. Romania, for all its emerging adaptations, had not gotten Mexican food down yet.

"Mommy, why is it so cold?" Jeremy asked, shivering slightly.

She put a sweater around his shoulders. Bobby looked up from his meal, regarding them both curiously. In the background, something moved. JoLynne saw two young men enter and sit down. Two men, yet three shadows cast behind them. She could not see a third companion. Had someone followed Bobby?

The interruption disturbed her lucid input into the dream, and suddenly the tables were empty, except for Bobby, Jeremy, and herself. The music had gone, leaving only the soft, sad lullaby in the distance. Bobby had been agitated by the appearance of the two men with their three shadows.

"Mommy, where has everyone gone?" Jeremy asked.

"They're closing for the evening, but the owners are being nice and letting us stay to finish our meal," she answered.

But the damage had been done. Bobby knew that he had crossed over, and that he needed to return. He looked at her, recognition and remembrance in his once-bright eyes. He held out his hand, but before she could grasp it, he disappeared.

She woke up, her body burning, her skin covered in goose bumps. She ran to the kitchen and drew herself a glass of cool water and placed two ice cubes into the glass. She was thirsty and disoriented. These dreams played havoc on her body, and she always awoke burning with thirst.

She went to her room and sat at the edge of her bed. She needed to reacclimatize to the world of the waking, the world of the living. She glanced at her cello, sitting in the corner. She would play in a few minutes and that ritual would help guide all her senses back.

But before she could do that, she remembered Bobby. Her eyes welled with tears, and she sat at the edge of her bed and cried. *Of all the people to visit, why did it have to be Bobby?*

***

The next day she walked the short distance to work. She had her own restaurant to open. The smell of fresh coffee brewing soon filled the air with its revitalizing scent.

She was still learning the limits of her ability. Her gift frightened her, and that diminished her ability to explore its boundaries. There were implications to communicating with the dead; she did not want to have her world filled with them.

In reality, she did not entirely trust the deceased, even those she thought she recognized. Phantoms could change faces—and their interest in influencing the world of the living seemed as disturbing as it did promising. There was no one to guide her as she worked on her ability. No teacher, no guru. Only three living people even knew.

The door opened and Mr. Georgescu entered, parking his bicycle in its spot just inside the door. He took out two bottles of *țuică*, homemade plum brandy, and placed them on her bar counter. He eyed her suspiciously. He was one of the few who knew.

"*Bună dimineața*, Doamna Russell," he greeted. He was being formal, which he always was when suspicious. He usually said a simple, "Good morning, JoLynne," his Romanian accent making the name sound more cosmopolitan than it seemed in English.

She turned around. "*Bună dimineaţa*," she replied. She picked up the bottles of brandy. Mr. Georgescu made the best *ţuică* in the region, and she was delighted he chose to sell it to her establishment. She reached into the cash register and paid him.

He pocketed the money and looked at her carefully. "You have had another dream," he noted. She had warned him a few years earlier of a faulty gas connection in his home and saved his life. JoLynne had dreamt a dream, visited by a little girl she did not recognize. The little girl walked JoLynne to Mr. Georgescu's house, throwing garlands around his faulty furnace. Without the warning, he would have died while he slept.

Mr. Georgescu waited for JoLynne's reply. He had survived the Nazis and the Communists, and he had learned a painful measure of patience. His family had not shared in his destiny. Not even his littlest sister, who had loved nothing more than weaving flowers into pretty necklaces.

When JoLynne arrived, nearly two decades ago, Mr. Georgescu had taken JoLynne and Jeremy under his wing and helped them acclimatize to Romania. He appreciated their motives for moving and the fact that her family had distant ties to the land.

"Bobby was in this dream."

"And?"

"I don't know what it meant. The message wasn't clear."

"But you felt something."

"You're too perceptive at times," she said, smiling. "Something is here, biding its time."

He grunted. "That is rarely a good thing."

The cook rang a bell, indicating that the kitchen was ready. JoLynne pointed a pretty waitress to the door, and she turned the Open sign around. The business day had begun.

"You will be busy," Mr. Georgescu predicted. "There were buses of tourists from America and Germany in last night. And a few loners as well. They are going to look for a good American breakfast, yes? Or one of your hamburgers."

"Tourists," she sighed.

"They come seeking something they have seen in the movies," Mr. Georgescu reminded her, "but they are good for our pocketbooks."

She nodded. The little farmhouses often rented small rooms to the visitors. Her own restaurant, offering its American fare, did well with tourists who were tiring quickly of trying new foods, if they were trying them at all. She listened to them as if she had never heard their stories and anticipations. For there was one major reason people visited Arefu, and that reason was in ruins at the top of a craggy hill.

JoLynne heard the street outside beginning to come to life. Visitors were conversing, many different tongues, all chattering about the same things in discordant voices.

People began to come into her small *cofetărie*, guidebooks clutched in their hands, cameras dangling from cords around their necks and wrists. In the cacophony of conversations, JoLynne could hear the one name pop up over and over again, like fat spitting on the grill. *Dracula*. Dracula this, and Dracula that. Because here in Arefu the local attraction was the decaying ruins of one of Vlad Țepeș's castles. That is what drew the visitors here, and as Mr. Georgescu noted, that coin is what kept dropping into the town's coffers.

***

Two young men sat at a table, university emblems on their shirts. They looked over a map and laughed between obscenities. Maria, the pretty waitress, had deftly placed two cups of coffee before them and moved on to her next customers.

One of them gestured his head in Maria's direction, behind her back. "Get a load of that," he said.

He was not referring to Maria's face, JoLynne knew, for Maria had a lovely, radiant beauty. Her hair was black, her eyes a beguiling green, her skin smooth and clear and pale. There was an exotic and innocent effect in her features. But then, there were her hands.

Maria heard their commotion and turned to see if they needed anything. JoLynne intervened.

"I'll take care of this table," JoLynne told Maria, in flawless Romanian. Maria nodded, and moved on. JoLynne recognized troublemakers.

The men were young and attractive, dressed in a carefully casual way designed to attract women. They bantered back and forth, language peppered with slang, obscenities used liked punctuation.

"Thalidomide," one said, almost sneering. "Guess she's lucky her momma couldn't have an abortion under the old regime."

The other one, blond and less shaven, nodded: "Freaky."

Maria's arms suffered from phocomelia, a deformity that left them stunted and underdeveloped. The name for the condition itself spoke volumes: Greek for "seal limbs." The cause had not been revealed to JoLynne. The young waitress's right forearm was stunted in growth, but she possessed two fingers and a thumb on that hand, sufficient for her to perform straightforward tasks. Her left forearm was almost nonexistent, and that hand suffered greater deformity; she had only tiny stumps for digits, save for a single, perfect thumb.

Still, she had mastered skills beyond expectation under JoLynne's guidance, support, and love. Those who had lived under communism considered JoLynne's adoption of Maria, fifteen years ago, good luck. JoLynne considered it one of the reasons Providence had drawn her here.

The young men looked at JoLynne. "More coffee," one demanded. "At least you make a half-decent cup. This part of the world seems to excel in dreck."

"Then why visit?" she asked.

They were taken aback by her perfect English.

"I'm an American," she said.

"We read in one of the guidebooks something about a place like this. Guess it's your place," the brunette one said. "Loser place to end up."

"I chose to emigrate," JoLynne replied, refilling their cups.

"You got a criminal record or something? Can't get a liquor license back in the States?" the blond one asked, a self-satisfied sneer playing around the corners of his mouth.

"Not exactly," JoLynne replied, although they were curiously close to the truth. Bobby's death had been the subject of several crime dramas and forensics shows so constantly in vogue in America. She did not want Jeremy growing up in the shadow of an infamous and highly publicized murder. So, she had taken them halfway across the globe, to a home only her genes knew.

"Why are *you* here?" she asked, feeling a brush of wind pass her back.

Another set of customers—German tourists on an organized jaunt—entered and sat down.

"Hey, check it out—Krauts," the brunette observed as the other tourists came in. "We'll have to avoid that mob if we really want to experience the castle."

"Are you planning on going up alone?" JoLynne asked.

"Sure are," the blond beamed confidently, knocking knuckles with his cohort. "Just us two and little old Dracula. We're here and we're gonna conquer."

"Vlad Țepeș has been dead since 1476. I doubt he'll give you much of a fight."

"But there are all sorts of spirits in this area, right?" the brunette asked excitedly. "Vampires, werewolves, all that old world stuff."

"Creeeepppy," the blond said, making fake booing noises.

"You are in land that has seen all sorts of real evil," JoLynne chided them. "Huns, Magyars, Mongols, Turks. More recently Nazis and Communists. And you come here seeking a make-believe person, a fictional character?"

"History doesn't interest us," the brunette said sharply. "It's boring."

"You haven't learned any history, then," JoLynne replied.

"We know what we want to see," the brunette snapped. "Something scary. Can't go back empty-handed after putting up with this dismal little country."

"It will be difficult for you, I suspect," JoLynne said, smiling. "Trying to find something you probably won't recognize when you see it." She picked up two menus from their table, writing down the orders they gave her, as they talked in overeager anticipation of their journey.

She placed the order with her cook.

"I'll walk them up," Mr. Georgescu whispered in Romanian as JoLynne passed him. "Make a little money, make sure they don't tear the landscape up. Perhaps these two are why Bobby warns you. They seem adept at rousing the unsavory. I will give them the grand tour, at least get them up to the castle remains."

"*Da, mulțumesc.* These two are the type trouble follows."
Then she shivered for no reason, as if her body sensed something unseen.

***

The climb up the mountainside was more arduous than the young men had planned. In their minds, prior to scaling the steep hillside, they had envisioned a leisurely walk up a well-defined path.

Mr. Georgescu laughed as he propelled his aged body up the incline. He babbled in Romanian at them, animating his language with gestures. He spoke English well enough to communicate with them, for JoLynne had taught most of the village enough of her native tongue to understand the busloads of English-speaking tourists who visited Arefu.

But he wasn't about to waste his education on these two. They seemed satisfied that they knew everything, anyway.

The trees grew straight and tall. Birch and oak intermingled with pine and spruce. The dirt roads were dry and the temperature pleasant. It was a perfect afternoon to walk, and the many miles from the town to the castle ruins could not have been attempted under any more favorable conditions.

Mr. Georgescu could have told them a lot of history, a lot of stories, but they were not interested. Usually his tourists were better mannered. These two were not interested in history, or culture, or the local flavor. They had come with their own script and were determined to stick with it.

He gathered that they planned to spend the night in the craggy castle ruins, armed with a video camera. They wanted supernatural selfies; "Me with the Monster" moments to post to their social media accounts.

Mr. Georgescu had met many monsters in his time. He had never had the desire to be photographed with any of them.

He gauged their intentions. They didn't talk about carving their names into the bricks and seemed to be planning no mischief or vandalism. Nor did they seem maliciously interested in the hydroelectric plant in the valley below the Castle of Arges.

Romania had only recently had copies of Stoker's novel available to them in Romanian. Now many tourists arrived, eager to climb the wooden bridge and steep steps to the castle. Romania was happy to oblige them in searching out the country's most infamous—and profitable—son.

He did tell them, mostly in Romanian, about the historical figure Vlad Dracula. He paused before saying the name, watching the delight in their eyes. They mocked his language, repeatedly saying "da" with an overdrawn accent.

He left them midway up the steep, mountainous walk, and collected his money. They had a map outlining the area and seemed to know where they were going.

He walked back to town.

As he approached JoLynne's *cofetărie*, he saw her standing outside her back door over two dead birds. They were long-necked corncrakes.

Their chests were stained red with little holes in them. A few feet away lay their tiny avian hearts.

She looked up. "I just found them like this, a few minutes ago."

"An omen?" he asked.

"A tangible presence." She frowned. "Shadows don't move on their own. They are creatures born of light and matter. Something is moving around us."

"This something can kill birds," Mr. Georgescu noted sourly. "Things I do not see are of some concern. Things that tear out hearts, these worry me more."

"Two birds, two boys," she replied, raising an eyebrow.

"You think those two brought it here?"

She shrugged. "Spirits wait, I think. After all, they have all the time in the world."

"Why these birds? Why warn you?"

"It knows I know," she thought aloud. "It senses my gift. This is a warning shot, to tell me it can hurt us." The thought chilled her. She had always thought herself invisible among the dead, as invisible as they were among the living. She looked again at the mutilated birds. "Corncrakes. *Crex crex.*"

"*Poftim?*"

"Their name is like their song—*crex crex*, in the night. Like two sticks being rubbed together."

"Two sticks. Like to light a fire?"

She shook her head. "Like a broken cross."

He grumbled.

JoLynne thought of the two boys and their plans. "Those two went up to the castle ruins for the night?"

"They are filled with Dracula," he replied. "I didn't think I could talk them out of it."

"*Ei nu ascultă niciodată*," she said. *They never listen.*

He grunted. "Vlad Țepeș is something of a hero to us Romanians. He fought the Turks, was an adversary to Mehmed, the despoiler of Constantinople. But the Dracula they seek is a story, not even a real person."

"It is easier to fight something that is fictional. You get to write your own victory," JoLynne offered. "And your guys always win."

He shook his head. For he knew, as did JoLynne, that real monsters were always around. Sometimes even in pleasant faces. As for JoLynne, she had a gift. She could direct the spirits that Mr. Georgescu intuitively knew were always in attendance.

He was wary of her gift, uneasy with the bridge she provided between two worlds that perhaps should know nothing definitive of one another. In his youth he had thought the world to be a place of logic, the next world a domain of memories. But just as he had learned that events in the living world were not always open to explanation, he now had to consider that the next world was capable of forethought.

She paused, listening in the descending nighttime. "Do you hear anything?" she asked.

"*Eu nu aud nimic.*" He replied, for he heard nothing. Not even the noises the night usually offered.

"Things always come, when victims present themselves so perfectly," she sighed.

"You are thinking of your Bobby?"

She nodded, acknowledging his intuition.

"Don't. He would have left anyway. He was seeking something that exists only in dreams, and no reality would have satisfied him. His wife and baby were boring and predictable. The viper he brought to his chest was of his own choosing."

"I should have been able to warn him."

"You did not know that future. His new woman had increased the insurance on his life, which you did not know. No one knew." He paused. "And that her first husband had also died by what at first appeared to be a tragic accident—she kept this hidden from everyone."

"At least she's in jail now. No more widows."

Mr. Georgescu shook his head kindly. "Bobby deserted you. When the second woman killed him, he had lost his claim to you as his wife. You are not a widow, JoLynne. Just a good woman who raised a strong son and brought up a forgotten little girl."

Mr. Georgescu was one of the few people she could talk with about the murder. Perhaps because they were kindred spirits in that regard.

"Do not dwell on the past, JoLynne. The love we have today needs that energy to thrive, and love that has passed lingers without the need to recompense."

"I am glad my family had roots here, to bring me back."

"Sometimes we must leave the Devil behind to find our way back home," Mr. Georgescu said. He looked up into the mountains, the sun beginning its descent. "I feel a cold breeze. You will be up late tonight."

"Is it a gift that I have, Domnule Georgescu? This strange sense of things unseen?"

"It is your gift, God's way of letting you stay away from your own demons by battling those of others." He looked very tired for an instant. "This gift I know myself."

She nodded, and walked back to her small home, where Maria would be reading or sewing, her little deformed hands knowing more industry than many fully developed ones.

Mr. Georgescu was right; it was going to be a long night.

***

Brian's hips ached from sleeping on the hard ground. He woke up and looked at Kalen. Kalen was sleeping, bundled up against the cold.

It was colder than they had anticipated, and Brian pulled his hat closer down around his ears. Cold winds circulated around him.

He sat up, noting that the fire was abysmally low. He reached over and put a few more logs on. The flames feebly regained some strength.

It was terribly quiet. Kalen mumbled and opened up his eyes.

"Dude, what time is it?"

Brian checked his watch. "Four a.m."

"Man, it is freezing!"

"Yeah, I know. Do you want to head back down to the village?" A warm bed and a hot cup of fresh coffee tempted him.

"No. We told the guys we'd stay up here all night. If we go back before morning, we'll lose the bet with Rat and the guys."

"Who cares about Rat? I'm freezing," Brian said. "It wasn't supposed to be this cold. And," he added bitterly, "this is one of the most boring things I've ever done."

Another cold wind whistled past them.

"Must be like a canyon wind," Kalen noted. "Did you notice that these winds funnel down here past us?"

"Maybe the castle wall?"

"Like skyscrapers in a city? Causing a wind pattern?"

Brian looked at the wall behind them, the fire throwing their dancing shadows between its old stones. "Should we move?"

"I still think the wall is more protective," Kalen said. He checked his hiking thermometer, attached to his jacket. "It says thirty-eight degrees Fahrenheit."

"No way! It was eighty this afternoon!"

Kalen shook his head. "They said the temperatures can be extreme in the mountains."

"This bites," Brian said. "Nothing here but old rocks and a bunch of tour groups getting suckered in during the day. And you know what? We're suckers, too. We should have stayed in Prague with those hot chicks and some decent brew."

"Hey, we do this and we're out of here," Kalen said, standing up and shaking off the cold. He walked a few yards away to gather more of the logs they had brought for their campfire.

They had found a small, enclosed area to set up camp, inside the castle walls proper. The old stones, remaining since the dreaded keep had been destroyed, made up three walls of their open-air room. The fourth wall was made of wood, with a gate installed. It was a modern creation, put in to help corral the visiting tourists while guides recited the history of Vlad Dracula.

Brian and Kalen were as familiar as they wanted to be with the stories of Wallachians fighting Turks.

That Dracula's reputation had gained extra infamy through Bram Stoker's vampire story would have probably suited Dracula just fine. The Wallachian prince would have appreciated his monstrous notoriety, for he was savvy to the two primary objectives of propaganda: to gain support from one's own people, and to strike fear into the heart of the enemy.

But Vlad Dracula had been buried elsewhere and his castle here was destroyed. Brian and Kalen had stopped by another castle on their way, Bran Castle. They considered it a tourist trap, because Dracula had only stayed there briefly and now it was a museum.

This was their real destination, living up to their end of a drunken wager. Spend the night in Dracula's Castle, or what little remained of it, and their cohorts owed them beer. A full night's worth, and the party to go along with it.

"Hey," Kalen said, as he picked up the logs. "It's not so cold over here."

Brian grumbled. "What do you mean?"

"I mean, it's okay. A little chilly, but not freezing."

"That doesn't make any sense," Brian said, as he adjusted his cap over his blond locks. He stood up and approached Kalen.

It was true. The temperature was warmer.

"Weird," Brian said. "The sooner we're out of this bizarre little place the better."

Kalen nodded, picking up a few logs. As he straightened up, a cold wind rushed between the two men. It swirled around them and the temperature dropped precipitously.

"What the..." Brian said, shivering. "This bites. I hate the weather here."

They moved back to the fire and placed the logs on. Again, Kalen paused. "Now it's okay here," he said, perplexed.

"Freaky old place," Brian complained.

It was very quiet, no noise to be heard. Brian felt compelled to say something, just to fill the silence. "Wasn't there a bunch of things making noises earlier on? Birds, frogs, whatever?"

Kalen nodded. The wind picked up again, and rushed past them, pushing the temperature down.

Brian fanned the flames. "Is this going to go on all night?"

"I don't know. I never studied weather patterns like this."

"You think it is natural then?"

"What else could it be?" Kalen replied. "You don't believe in the stories the locals are selling, do you? I mean, they're just in it to make a Yankee dollar. Hocus pocus for greenbacks. Don't believe anything you can't prove. All magic and miracles are just science we don't understand yet."

The temperature was uncomfortably cold.

"We must be some sort of weather foci," Kalen guessed. "Our body heat must be attracting some sort of weird weather phenomenon, associated with the mountainside and the rocks."

Brian nodded. He took out a metal kettle, filled it with bottled water, and placed it over the fire. "I'll get some coffee going. Only a few more hours to dawn anyway, then we're out of here. I'm going back to that little farmhouse we're bunked in and sleeping all day. Then we can grab burgers and beer for dinner at that crazy American broad's place."

"Wonder why she's here?" Kalen asked, just to keep the conversation going.

"Probably can't handle competition," Brian said bitterly. "No chain restaurants here, no other Americans. She has a sweet little monopoly."

"Must have been fun, getting permission to open up here," Kalen said sarcastically.

"They were probably just happy she gave a job to the chick with the freaky hands." Brian moved his hands and fingers in a mockery of Maria's deformities.

When they were not talking, the air was quiet, cold, and still. Then, there was a rustling of noise outside the tall wooden wall.

Both men were on their feet. "Who's there?" Kalen asked.

Brian took a pocketknife out of his pocket. "Probably locals just playing up this spooky old dump," he said, anger in his voice. "I hate people like that." He stood tall, his small knife clutched in his hand. "Go away, we're not buying!" he snarled.

The rustle grew in intensity. Kalen listened closely. The sound was low in the bushes outside and had a scampering quality. The noise seemed to crawl toward the old castle.

Brian cursed. "I should have learned enough Romanian to say, 'Go away!'"

Kalen listened to the noise pace back and forth outside the gate. It had gained in energy, as if its source had gained in number. He was happy to see the gate seemed sturdy and securely closed, holding them safely in the corral. The wind picked up and rushed around him, going toward the gate, as if to carry their scent to whatever moved around outside.

"Go away!" Brian called out. Clutching the little knife, he smiled. "English should be good enough for them." He chuckled.

The flames on the fire flickered, and the water was beginning to boil. Kalen considered the scalding water's potential as a weapon. These could be criminals, out to roll them over, rob them, and who knew what else.

The noise settled down and Brian approached the gate. Kalen tried to hold him back, but Brian was confident of the gate's security. They had closed and fastened it from the inside. There was a place by the gate, beside its two doors, that took the form of a small ramp. It was really a false hill, constructed over a storage shed in which props were kept for educating the tour groups.

Brian approached, driven by curiosity and bolstered by bravado. The manmade hill provided a means to safely peer over the top of the walls and gate, to see what lay outside the gate itself.

Brian motioned for Kalen to keep quiet and crept methodically up the little hill. Kalen edged back toward the fire and their nearby gear. There was a small axe in his kit, and he felt it prudent to retrieve the instrument, even though it was designed for chopping wood and not as a weapon.

As Brian inched noiselessly up the little hill, the rustling noises below grew restless and little twigs could be heard snapping beneath the weight of whatever prowled outside.

Brian positioned himself and motioned for Kalen to join him. The cold wind whipped around them, swirling dead leaves into the air and over the walls at haphazard angles.

Kalen climbed quickly to the top of the hill, hearing the noises grow to a low rumble of quick patters and crackling vegetation.

"Ready?" Brian asked, when joined by his friend. He held a high-powered flashlight in his hands, ready to view whatever lay below.

Kalen nodded, finding comfort in the axe in his hands.

They lifted their heads and Brian turned the flashlight on. A dozen sets of eyes turned their attention upward, blazing in the night. The air erupted with the angry yelps of hungry dogs and wolves.

They jumped at the walls, their claws falling far short of their quarry, their yelps filling the night with terrible shrieks and hardened barks. Teeth snapped at the two men on the parapet; the mass of canines tried to climb up the wall, scratching and snarling.

Brian and Kalen jumped back, fully behind the wall, the cacophony of howls and beastly cries filling the air around them.

Brian dimmed the light.

"Looks like they're looking for dinner," Kalen noted.

"I'm glad we opted for the enclosed campground," Brian noted. The noise was nearly deafening, the gate shivering as the canine creatures threw themselves in frenzied assaults against the entrance. "You think it will hold?"

"I think so," Kalen said. The cold air was back again, cloaking around them.

"I really, really want to get out of here," Brian stressed.

The cold air rushed away from them and swirled around a tree just outside the castle grounds. It struck the tree with the force of a small microburst, and a substantial branch clattered to the ground.

The wolves rushed towards it, yelping to the feral dogs. Teeth bared, the dogs obeyed. The group barked and snarled, and when the wolves stepped back, the dogs grasped the branch in their teeth and in concert dragged it to the base of the wall. Propped up against the wall, one of the wolves ran up its length, snarling at Brian and Kalen's position. It was still significantly short of them, but the pack below had gained a few feet of advantage they had not enjoyed a moment before.

The cold breeze danced and swirled around the men once more. It darted out of the compound, striking another tree. This time the branch it selected was shorter, but sturdier, than the first. The dogs, yelping and froth dripping from their maws, ran excitedly toward it, and started to move it toward the first branch.

"What...?" Kalen exclaimed.

Brian shook his head. "There's no way those mutts are doing what I think they're doing..."

"They are!" Kalen cried. "They're building a ladder!"

The cold wind was back, enjoying the panic that was beginning to fill the air. It circled around them. With increased velocity it began to pick little things up from the ground: small stones, wood shavings, whatever shrapnel of convenience it could locate. Whirling, it aimed the small pellets at the boys, opening small cuts on their unshielded faces.

The smell of blood on the wind enraged the dogs, their yelps gaining in fury. They started to move more underbrush, snarling and spitting as they smashed their scaffolding up against the outside wall.

Brian looked dismally at the small dimensions of his knife. "We are in serious trouble if they get in here," he said. He put his fingers to his face and the little speckles of blood sparkling black in the dark night.

"No kidding! Any plans?"

"We have no way of calling for help. My phone won't pick up a signal here."

"Mine neither. These are the only weapons?"

Brian nodded. "Hopefully that thing about animals being afraid of fire is true. Let's make a circle for ourselves."

"One of us should stay up here to keep an eye on the mutts." Kalen looked at the snarling mass of fur and teeth, the bright eyes glaring in the darkness.

Then he heard something odd beyond the clatter of barks and snarls. A soft melody in the distance.

At first, he hardly recognized it, thinking that the noise of the dogs and the wind's rustles were warping the sound around him. But then he listened closer, subtracting out the cold breeze and the animals' howls. It was a cello, playing somewhere out in the night. A lullaby, one he recognized from overhearing it play at his gym's nursery. "All the Little Ponies."

The music glided gently into the ruptured night air.

He felt the wind brush by him again, rustling his brunette hair. But this time it was back into the castle grounds, away from the trees and their branches. The dogs looked up and one whimpered slightly. The alpha wolf snarled and turned its enraged head toward the music.

"What's going on?" Brian asked, finishing a circle formation of flames that he considered satisfactory to shield them from the wolves and wild dogs should they scale the wall with their inspired embankment of twigs and branches.

"I don't know," Kalen said. "I hear music."

Brain listened, the dogs' noises subsiding enough to afford him hearing. "Where's it coming from?"

"I don't know." Kalen paused. There was a new threat. "Bro, you better get up here. I think something's coming!"

"What?"

"I don't know, man! It's just something!"

Brian walked briskly up the small hill, flashlight in hand. He joined his friend at the top of the wall. He looked over the edge.

The dogs were quiet, the wolves glancing around themselves nervously. Through the trees, through the long shadows thrown by the large moon, there was a sphere of red light dancing in the woods.

"What the heck is that?" Brian asked.

Kalen shook his head. "I don't know, but it looks like it is coming here. I don't like this one bit!"

The sphere looked about twelve inches in diameter, glowed a subtle brick red, and floated amongst the trunks of the trees.

Brian's mind raced to come up with a rational explanation. "St. Elmo's fire?" he asked.

"No. That's blue and occurs in stormy weather. Glow discharge. There's not a cloud in the sky."

"Calcite?"

Kalen raised an eyebrow. "Glows red under the right light conditions. Ultraviolet, fluorescent. I forget. It's found in Bavaria, not too far away, but the light here is natural, and calcite doesn't float on its own."

"Is someone out there screwing with us?"

"I don't see anyone, and the movement is erratic. It would take a mess of wires to make it move like that, and we came up that path yesterday. I didn't see any wires."

"Some sort of scattering effect?"

"This isn't a physics lab," Kalen scolded.

Brian bridled. "I don't see you offering any explanations."

The sphere hovered silently between the trees, and then it rose above the treetops. It seemed to swivel, as if it had eyes that stared directly at the two men.

"I think it sees us," Brain said, nervous agitation creeping into his voice.

"And you know what? I don't think pocketknives are going to help."

The light considered them; it moved slowly in their direction.

"It's coming!" Brian exclaimed. There was fear in his voice even he had never heard before.

Kalen braced himself against the wall. He looked down; the dogs and wolves snarled up at the two men, then ran off into the woods.

"Let's get into our ring of fire," Kalen urged, signaling Brian to follow him. They quickly made their way down the little hill, inside Brian's feeble circle of flames.

The light raced up toward the castle and stopped at the top of the wall. The boys eyed it with queasy anticipation.

It hovered for a few minutes.

To the boys, the time it hovered seemed longer in the silences and the dwindling darkness. There was a hint of rose to the horizon, the Earth slowly turning towards the sun.

"Morning!" Brian said. It was early dawn, and he was glad for it.

The sphere paused, perfectly still, then it sipped down and away from the old craggy castle walls.

"Is it gone?" Brian asked.

"I think so." Kalen replied. "Whatever it was."

"No one will believe us."

"I'm not going to stick around here long enough to tell anyone. We're on the bus out of here tonight, right?" It was an agreed-upon order.

***

JoLynne sat alone at the table, a glass of water in front of her. Mr. Georgescu entered silently, taking a seat opposite her. He placed a bottle of his homemade *țuică* in front of her.

"For you," he said.

"I suppose I did the right thing."

"Sparing them from something they did not understand? Perhaps one day they will learn. For now, they have fear. That is a valuable thing until you learn more."

She poured him a cup of coffee.

"You think this is what you sensed?"

She nodded. She had spent the evening in meditative prayer, playing her cello, watching the moon rise and set. She had lit a red votive candle beneath her home's Infant of Prague icon, and sensed something move through the night. A sharp breeze had rattled her windows, trying to break her concentration, but the music helped her chant the prayers. When the morning broke, the ominous sense had left.

"I don't know what it was," she explained. "Just something that knew they were isolated out there, waiting for something to happen. So it found them. It is gone now."

"Perhaps they will not think that they know everything now."

"*Cu cât știm mai mult, cu atât ne dăm seama cât de puțin știm,*" she mused. *The more we know, the more we realize how little we know.*

"I doubt they will be that wise," Mr. Georgescu said. "You are still thinking of Bobby? Of how he died? It was a very long time ago. I do not like how this episode has brought those memories back so vividly to you. Leave the old scar alone, JoLynne, it has healed."

"He thought he had love, and that would be enough." She remembered sitting at the back of the church with little Jeremy, as Bobby took his new bride. This second wife was so beautiful, so perfect. Everyone hovered around her, except for Jeremy and JoLynne, who took the first opportunity to leave the lavish reception. Jeremy had cried the entire way home.

"Bobby had let go of love," Mr. Georgescu observed. "I do not speak ill, JoLynne, only the truth. When we lose sight of love, all monsters can overwhelm us. We are safe from none of them." He smiled weakly. "I know this. Many things have been taken from me, but never love."

He paused, carefully choosing his words. "You must let him go, JoLynne. You must let him move on."

"But when he comes to me…"

"*Ti-e greu*—it is difficult for you, but you cannot change the past. He does not come to you, JoLynne—*you* call *him*."

She felt suddenly ashamed but let the feeling ripple through her. Bobby's sullen, speechless face in her mind. *She called him?*

Mr. Georgescu changed the subject, back to the events of the previous night. "Who answered your call to fight whatever stalked our two guests?"

"A brother from the monastery, recently passed. He had a routine, still reverberating here on Earth. Every moment dedicated to faith and obedience. He could be called back, to help, by God's will."

"You feel guilty?" Mr. Georgescu asked, sipping his coffee.

"I made the good brother take a detour on his journey. I had no right." *And no right to impeded Bobby's journey, either.* She felt a part of herself stepping aside. A gentle breeze filtered through the *cofetărie. A physical, real, thing*, she noted. *Like the birds. Like the shadows.*

"You have vocation. You have duty. These are things God gives to us only when we can bear them. Sometimes, we do not recognize it ourselves. You need to take care of yourself. You have two children who will want to see no tears in your eyes. And I'm sure the good brother understands."

She nodded. The transformation from being mirror to being a door. She was guard and greeter, watcher and watched, listener and leader. It was time to embrace the trust.

"And there are more tourists," he smiled. "They will need you, too. Even if just for coffee and those fatty cakes you make."

She was oddly comforted by his words.

"JoLynne," he added. "In this world, we are all just passing through."

He got up, put on his coat, and walked out into the new day.

And she was alone, in her restaurant, with her glass of water in front of her, waiting for whatever guests might arrive.

Old Graveyard Magic

"Old Graveyard Magic" was my second completed story, also written in December 2003 while I lived at the Parkwood Apartments, at 1906 Wyndale #2. I penned this piece as a response to a humor contest call, entering the final story draft on December 1, 2003. It didn't win. It would take seventeen months to find a home. On April 21, 2005, "Old Graveyard Magic" was published in a small literary journal. I also read this story on air in February 2019 during a broadcast of So What's Your Story? *The show was on the radio station KPFT 90.1 with hosts Greg Audel and Hank Roubicek. It was my first foray into writing humor. Humor is without a doubt the most difficult genre for me to write.*

*B*yline – Hades

While his brother may ride a pale horse, Death's youngest sibling prefers a John Deere.

Here in the heartland, Azrael-Bob—or "Bubba" as his friends call him—enjoys a simple life. His brother's high stakes career in death has brought fame to the family, but it hasn't spoiled Bubba. He prefers to reap corn, not human souls. And his favorite tool is a state-of-the-art combine, not an old-fashioned scythe.

"My brother is the traditional type," he explains as he sits on his front porch. "There's no changing his mind once he's committed to something." He laughs softly. "Yeah, we always said that he was the Grim Reaper and I was the happy one."

It was while sitting on another porch last year, at the family's annual reunion, that Bubba had his inspiration. "We were talking about all the commotion my brother brews up when I thought, *Well, why don't I brew up some of my own?*"

And that's what he did—literally.

"I went from the still to microbrewing in about a week," Bubba recollects fondly.

Soon he was producing a distinct, handcrafted beer. And he named his custom suds "Old Graveyard."

He confesses that being Death's younger brother has helped open some doors. "Old Graveyard is brewed using water from the River Styx," he explains. "The deepest natural source of spring water you'll ever find!"

But Bubba gets back to business quickly. "Seriously, I'm adding a lite version of the beer next spring. Not many people have an appreciation for how important better health is like I do."

And why a beer?

"It's not entirely original," he concedes, "but if there's one thing being in this family has taught me, it's that old fads never die."

The brewing takes place offsite, but Bubba runs the business from home.

"You have to watch your head in this business," he says. There is a wide grin on his face most of the time, emphasized by the four-tooth gap in his upper jaw. He keeps the books in a small office set up in an abandoned shed, by a rusting old muscle car set up on blocks. He affectionately calls the area "Camaro Alley." Sunlight streams through spaces between the shed's boards. And all that sunlight, he reckons, will only make you thirstier.

He also hopes that his brewing business will regain respect for him from his family. He points to a two-headed dog running after its own tail in an overgrown corner of the lot.

"That dawg got me in trouble with my big brother," he sighs. "My Mississippi hunting hound got a few minutes alone with Cerberus and there's the puppy they had. My brother didn't talk to me for months after that."

"On top of that," he adds, "my old repo business failed. My folks thought I was some kind of loser—my brother can claim lives, and I couldn't even reclaim a Honda Civic."

So next time you have a hankering for something that will knock you out—but not permanently—you could reach for a cold Old Graveyard. Azrael-Bob will thank you, and maybe he'll even put in a good word for you in return. And that's something we could all drink to!

Concerning Edward Sweetly

"Concerning Edward Sweetly" was based on a dream I had one hot summer afternoon, while I was pregnant with my daughter, Samantha. Written while residing on Wyndale Street, the story was completed in the summer of 2003. It was placed after eleven submissions, finding its home in the October 2005/Halloween Issue of The Sword Review. *It has a touch of Southern Gothic. I have numerous drafts of this story, but no full copy of the published form, which was in electronic format only. This version is derived from the revised version I sent to* The Sword Review *after entering their edits.*

It was dark when she entered the room. A bit darker than usual. The cheap foam-backed curtains did their job, solidly blocking out the sun.

He sat in the middle of the room, in a heavy old chair, quietly staring at a muted television screen. "Did you get your groceries?" he asked.

"Yes," she replied softly, putting two brown paper bags on the table. "I'll have to drink my beer now, 'cause we don't have a refrigerator to keep it cold." She paused. "I got you some of that tomato juice you like—the spicy kind. I don't think it spoils too quickly."

"I got a call," he informed her.

"Really."

"From an old friend," he replied. "She married wealthy, but it seems she's gotten bored with her old man."

Deena sat down at the small wooden table, etched with the graffiti of a thousand previous temporary tenants.

He stretched slightly in the dusty chair. "She says she can make us rich," he turned his face to her in the darkness, the amber color of his eyes lit by the barely visible light.

She considered his words, although the word that interested her most was "rich." They had always gotten by, somehow. Rich, though, meant never having to worry about how the next sack of groceries was going to be paid for, or paying for another room with crumpled single dollar bills while the desk clerk looked at you like you were less than nothing.

Deena responded with some apprehension. "How?" she asked.

"She's in a shabby marriage," he said. "She wants out, but he had legal papers made that prevent her from getting anything if she leaves. Only way for her to keep her house is for him to die and leave it to her." He paused. "He left her only one way out. He's got to go."

"Go?"

"Die."

"Oh."

He studied her face. "He's a healthy old man from the sound of it. I doubt that he's set to die on his own anytime soon. That's where we come in. We're going to help him get an early departure."

Deena looked at him, not sure if he was joking or completely serious. Matthew Lamd had a dark sense of humor. It was one of his quirks. He had always provided for them financially, although she knew that the money he had was running out. He only asked that she do odd chores for him, provide companionship, and not ask questions.

"We need the money," he stated flatly. "My friend would make us wealthy enough to not have to worry about money again this lifetime."

"Is it safe for us?" she asked. What she was really asking was, *Will we get away with it?*

How she hated considering the rapidly dwindling supply of cash, the prospect of uncertainty again in her life. All she had before Matthew entered her life was a wealth of futility. She had never had much, never been promised much, and, it seemed, would never have much. Matthew gave her a purpose, put a roof—however many of them there were—over her head, and gave her a sense of security. Other men before him had hit her, lorded over her inadequacies, and isolated her. True, Matthew had isolated her, but he did not have the former vices.

"Can we trust her?" Deena asked.

"She is an *old* friend," he stressed, longevity implying loyalty.

Deena thought for a moment. Nothing else in life had worked out for her, no matter how honestly or how hard she had tried. Except for Matthew Lamd.

The money would allow them comfort; it would stop the empty gnawing in her belly that told her she would never amount to anything. Matthew made her feel so worthy—and he *depended* on her. She wanted to let Matthew know that he had not chosen badly when he chose her. She wanted to make him happy.

"Okay," she acquiesced. "I will help you."

Matthew Lamd smiled broadly. "Thank you," he said, seemingly relieved.

She smiled in return, trying to not dread whatever she had just agreed to do. *Everything was going to be all right,* she told herself. And that alone justified anything.

***

Even with the windows down and the wind blowing through her hair, the Dixie day was uncomfortably hot for Deena. It had been relentlessly hot for a while, even for early July. The funnel cake vendors and traveling carnivals were setting up their Fourth of July booths in the town square. She sighed. The local traffic was going to be bad, with the increased flow of visitors and the constant presence of roadwork.

This is a pretty city, she thought as she looked out her car window, holding back the loose strands of her hair as they whipped in front of her face. It was hot and sticky, and the heat rose off the asphalt in watery ripples. Deena did not know much about the city except that there was a doughnut shop, a motel that had seen better days, and the house where Matthew's old friend lived.

It almost surprised her that Matthew had an old friend. He kept mainly to himself, only occasionally venturing out. His clock seemed to be off-time with the world. He slept most the day, sitting in darkened rooms at dusk. His infrequent ventures out were nocturnal and only sometimes did she accompany him. He ate little and he drank little. He once mentioned that he was abnormally sensitive to light and that exposure to the sun would trigger a disease. Among the things she provided for him was simple caring—she would rub antiseptic smelling ointments on his cool skin. She ran all errands that needed to be run during daylight hours.

He sometimes mumbled strange fears in his sleep.

It was such a small price for a companionship that did not involve pain.

The drive from the motel was not very far. Matthew's friend, Veronica Sweetly, had given them neatly typed and very precise directions to her home. Deena's mission was simple: locate the house, gas up the car, and purchase a few supplies on the way back to the motel.

At first the destination appeared to be an abandoned lot. The fenced-in land spit out tall, overpowering trees, and heaved with dense vines and brush. Ancient ferns carpeted the property, and tall oaks spread long arms across the driveway. Pines struggled to reach the sky, their needles browning from the recent lack of rain. A clean metal fence topped with concertina wire surrounded the property. A tall gate inscribed with an ornate letter S stood sentinel at the entrance. It had been left open, so Deena drove in slowly, as she had been instructed.

The small private road leading up to the house was well-maintained, with a neat, furrowed ditch on either side to collect drainage. Field horsetail grew in the ditches, creeping brown roots foraging into small puddles of water. Fire-flowered canna lilies thrived at the edges.

The car had been overheating recently, and only by driving within a narrow range of speeds could Deena keep the engine's temperature reading just below the red line. And, if they broke down, Matthew had told her, there would probably be no one who would stop to render them aid.

That thought only intensified the constant, creeping despair in her heart that nothing was ever going to work out in her favor. *Matthew*, she thought, Matthew and this one sordid source of income might be the only opportunity she would ever have to bridge the gap between her present unceasing struggle and a comfortable future.

There was a short turn in the road. Emerging from the vegetation, Deena could see a grand old mansion appear. The house had a portico, lined with thick, sturdy marble columns. An occasional vine climbed up one or two of the columns, gripping the cool smooth stone as best as they could; a few dead vines dangled listlessly on other columns, oddly more successful in their lifeless grips than their living cohorts.

The house was two stories tall, a perfectly symmetrical square building, crowned with a simple, sloping white slate roof. Neat rectangular windows were spaced evenly on each story. Deena noted that the windows were preternaturally clean, even those on the second story. It was impossible to see inside the house.

"It's beautiful," Deena whispered to herself.

Why is it that everybody else always gets the beautiful things in life? She thought bitterly. *Like this grand, old, beautiful house.*

To Deena, the house appeared cut off from all the world's challenges and sadness, a stiff defense of concertina wire and its beauty sparing it from the wretchedness of the world.

She drove past the house and out of the open back gate. She had accomplished her mission for the day. She felt urgency to get back to Matthew.

He would be sleeping fitfully in their room, relying upon her to have verified the location of the target residence. He had asked her to purchase a few things on her return trip. She felt the crumpled currency in her pocket, knowing that they were running dangerously low on money. Matthew's reserve of cash, once plentiful, was approaching depletion.

She had never asked him how he had acquired the previously substantial supply of paper bills. And although she had always been slightly curious, she would never ask him. He had promised he would take care of her for the rest of her life.

That would have to be enough.

***

It was past midnight when he left. Deena was sleeping soundly. The noisy window air conditioner was supplying just enough cool air to stave off the resonant heat of the day.

She had done everything he had asked, as usual. He was pleased with her.

He had told her he was going out, but that he would be back soon. He kissed the top of her sleeping head as he left.

Matthew drove the old car to an icehouse filled with cigarette smoke and Stevie Ray Vaughan songs playing on an old juke box. The mournful guitar music filled the air, the low steady beat of the bass guitar pulsating through the building. Bottles of domestic beer were being drunk by the patrons, the empty bottles accumulating in plastic trash-bag lined bins. Every so often the distinct clink of another bottle being discarded accompanied the sound of the music.

Veronica Sweetly sat, as she had told him she would, at the back of the bar. The counter behind her was open to the outside, the sticky night air swirling around them. Matthew joined her, ordering a beer for each of them.

He had been lying to Deena, a necessary lie, by his calculation. In reality, he had known Veronica less than a year. Their friendship was more a case of common affliction than affection.

"I wasn't sure that you would come," she said, greeting him.

"I wasn't sure either," he confessed. "This isn't the way I like to make my money."

"But you've made it this way before," she intimated.

He nodded grimly. The beers arrived and he paid the waitress in single dollar bills. He took a sip of the cold brew.

"I don't see why you find it so offensive," Veronica pointed out. "We live off of mortals in so many ways." A haze of smoke drifted between them.

"And your husband? He supports you well. And he's a mortal."

"The problem with Edward is that he isn't mortal enough for my tastes. And you are correct—he has enough money for both of us."

"Why don't you do this yourself? Why involve me?"

"The wife is always the first suspect, Matthew. And I want to keep the house for a while longer. You may do all right, running around in that old jalopy of yours. But I like to put down roots; stay a while. At least for a moment."

"That's a dangerous want," he reminded her. "Sooner or later a lot of roads will start to lead back to you. Regardless if Edward Sweetly is in residence or not."

"That's my problem. Your problem is cash flow. As in you not having much cash left flowing."

He ignored the remark. "So, we do in your old man. We get paid and disappear. You sit back and prey on this pretty little town a while longer."

"I like the music here," she replied. "So, you trust your companion enough? To do this with you?"

"A good companion is invaluable."

"Now there is a road that will lead straight back to you," Veronica replied. "*They* are not like *us*." She looked around the room, for emphasis.

"I trust her."

"I get that message. Why does *she* trust *you*?"

"She wants security." Matthew finished his bottle of beer with a final gulp. "I find that security is a better motivation for a companion than lust, or power, or glamor. Those motivated by those reasons will start to crave their independence again. That's when they can turn on you."

Veronica Sweetly smiled, no glow in her pale cool face. "I prefer ignorance." She handed him a wrapped stack of twenty-dollar bills. He quickly concealed the cash in his jacket pocket.

"Get yourself another beer, Matthew," Veronica urged. "My treat. Be seen talking to some other women, so your conversation with me doesn't stand out. I'd say look a little desperate, but you already do. The house will be unlocked tomorrow night. I will be at a charity function, giving myself an alibi. The old man sleeps in a big, oversized chair in his room every evening after dinner. There will be nobody else there."

"How do you want me to do it?"

"I don't care," she replied. "Involve your companion. Being an accomplice will forge even stronger a bond between you than just having her relying on you for security. Right now, she doesn't *want* to leave you; tomorrow night, make it so she *can't*."

Veronica turned and left, making her way through the crowd. As she left, Matthew caught her smell, the faint odor that all like them knew one another by: the subtle scent of death.

***

Matthew and Deena stood in the expansive foyer, next to an antique mirror hanging on a beige marble wall to their left. There was a sturdy granite table in front of the mirror, supporting a large ornate agate vase overflowing with cut flowers and fragrant eucalyptus. The floor was made of white marble, perfectly polished, with a large ivory-colored woven wool rug. The rug was rimmed in an elaborate oriental-style border rendered in gold, russet, green, and peach.

They stood facing the grand stairway. The entire house was cool and quiet. The soft noise of the outside traffic was absent. Deena felt as if she had stepped into a place that was miles away from anything.

The night air was still hot and humid, not much different than the fiery day, just darker. It was the Fourth of July, and all around them were fireworks displays seen though the windows, celebrating Independence Day.

Deena found some cold comfort in the irony. *Was it their independence day? Finally, no more worries? Freedom from constant, aching want?*

Matthew had said nothing the entire trip to the house. He said nothing now as they stood noiselessly in the silent, cool, white foyer with its antiseptic fragrance lingering in the air.

He had hinted that there was more peril in failing Veronica Sweetly than in failing at their mission. They were now committed to their miserable task.

It was so *very* silent. Deena shivered. There was a terrible clarity to the outlines in the house, everything so still and unrepentant.

Matthew Lamd silently motioned for her to follow him up the white wooden staircase. Her feet made no noise on the steady, solid steps.

There was sufficient light to see by. In addition, her senses were heightened to a sickening level of observation. She noted with an odd sense of concern that the bannister was dust-free and the staircase sparkling clean. She took extra care not to disturb anything; she kept her gloved hands off the bannister, holding them close to her chest as they ascended the barren staircase.

They arrived at the landing, and Matthew motioned for her to stop as he listened.

The landing, Deena thought as she remembered Matthew's outline of their plan. *We'll pause at the landing and listen to hear if the old man is sleeping, like she said he would be.*

Deena heard a low rattling sound. *The old man is snoring. Good.* That would make their job easier. She gave herself a quick mental re-briefing: *I just have to grab a few things while Matthew is... while Matthew is taking care of the old man. To make it look like a burglary. Then we are gone. We pick up the rest of the cash and no one will ever know.* She soberly noted that *she* would know, but that was a worry for the future. *My mind will be clearer when I have had time to think*, she thought solemnly, presuming the comfort of those days ahead.

They turned right silently, Deena keeping close ranks with Matthew.

He pushed open the door to Mr. Edward Sweetly's bedroom. It moved without a sound, making only the very softest thud against a rubber-ended doorstopper. The room smelled fresh and clean; there was a hint of scented bleach fragrance to the air. A vase of freshly cut roses rested on the dresser, their dark red petals almost black at the edges. In a large chair, with his back towards them, sat a sleeping Edward Sweetly.

Matthew and Deena could see his hand resting serenely on the armrest, the outline of the top of his head against the back of the chair.

Matthew pulled out a small rag soaked in chloroform. He held the cloth in his strong hands, nodding to Deena and gesturing towards the dresser. Mr. Sweetly's expensive watch, a diamond pinky ring, and a money clip stuffed with cash sat next to the long, sharp-thorned roses in the vase.

Deena turned quickly and quietly towards the dresser, averting her eyes from Matthew approaching Mr. Sweetly. She knew what was about to happen but did not want to witness the crime to which she was already an accomplice. She glanced outside the clean dark bedroom window, looking into the heavy canopy of trees that stood outside. Through the branches she could see occasional flashes of light from the Fourth of July fireworks, imagining their booms.

As she picked up the money clip, embedded with diamonds set into the form of a glittering figure eight, she detected a dart of motion out of the corner of her eyes. In her peripheral vision, she saw a heavy shadow launch itself and engulf a lesser form. The shadow had moved swiftly and silently, illuminated only briefly by the glow of a large red rocket exploding in the nearby sky.

This time Deena, her senses horribly heightened, heard the muted echo of the firework's boom. She instinctively turned towards the location the shadows had occupied; she was searching the room for Matthew.

In a sudden, heavy moment, she realized that she could find neither Matthew nor Mr. Sweetly. Both were gone.

Mr. Sweetly's armchair was empty. The faintest outline of his body lingered as an imprint in the cushions.

Matthew had simply vanished, leaving only the faint sweet smell of chloroform in the air, mixing with the aroma of the fresh roses.

Deena was drawn to the overstuffed chair and gently touched the cushions where Mr. Sweetly had sat. They were unnervingly cold to the touch.

"Matthew?" Deena called softly. It seemed senseless to stay totally quiet now; obviously *something* had happened. "Matthew?" she asked the quiet air again, a bit more urgency in her voice.

As she stood, she became aware that there was something dark and solid behind her. Something reached out of the darkness; something wiry and forceful wrapped around her wrist. Slender, steely fingers gripped her arm. It twisted her around with a sturdy jerk. She dropped the money clip, the diamond figure eight reflecting the final barrage of the nearest fireworks display coming to its climax. Deena fought for a scream, but her larynx was closed.

She felt herself being dragged from the room by an incredibly powerful hand. In the dim light of the hallway, she could see Matthew being dragged off in the opposite direction by a shapeless form of intense energy.

She felt something sharp stab into her shoulder; the pain did not register through the adrenalin that roared in her veins.

Then the hand that restrained her inexplicably relaxed.

Deena did not care why.

In those fleeting microseconds of opportunity, Deena broke free of her attacker, bolted down the staircase, and past the elegant eucalyptus filled vase. The door was open; she fled mindlessly into the hot evening air. The shadows of the trees fell sharply across the driveway.

Deena could feel the weight of a calm evil staring into her from the house as she scrambled into the car. She fumbled fretfully with the keys; in a moment of inspired panic, she turned the engine and raced down the driveway.

Watching Deena leave, Veronica Sweetly stood regally at the top of the staircase, her mouth dripping red with the blood she had stolen from Deena's shoulder.

"Ah, Matthew," she whispered to herself. "There is your problem with security. It does not bind. At least with power and glamor you buy some selfish loyalty."

***

Veronica pulled the rug back down over the carefully scrubbed floor. She was meticulous with their cleanups, never sure if modern science would somehow defeat them through forensics. She was concerned that if the house were ever sprayed with luminol and viewed through an ultraviolet light it would light up every inch with a ghastly glow. Still, the blood-soaked cleaning water seemed to help the cannas in the front driveway grow exceptionally well.

The last of the fireworks, stray rockets launched by individuals throwing their own after-parties, were wrapping up. Veronica could see the distant shards of light explode across the early morning sky. It had not taken her long to clean up this time, she noted with some regret. She had gotten very efficient at this.

Edward Sweetly entered the room, dressed in his luxurious bathrobe. He had finished eating and then showered. He sat in the big chair across from his wife and considered her with a critical eye.

"Was the man one of us?" he asked.

"If you have to ask," she replied calmly, "he wasn't much of one of us."

"The girl wasn't. That much I knew for sure. She escaped?"

"She was lucky," Veronica replied. She stood up and removed her cleaning gloves.

Edward Sweetly looked at her disapprovingly.

"She isn't going to say anything," Veronica assured him. "She was an accomplice to murder. Who is she going to talk to? She would be branded a criminal or insane, depending on if she was believed or not. Besides, she has enough money to keep herself for life."

"How very convenient."

"You think that I let her go?"

"I am not sure what to think, my dear. Perhaps you even hoped that the man would actually destroy me."

Veronica demurely cast her gaze downwards.

"It was too elaborate a scheme to secure dinner," he further chided her. "You are like me now. Your quaint human ways can be forgiven for a short while, but do not test my patience."

She stood silently before him, aware of the power he had in moments of tranquility, and afraid of the power he had in moments of wrath.

Edward Sweetly stood up. "It gets easier with time, sweet Veronica. Your sympathies will change. Although I do not know what Lamd saw in that mousy little companion of his. His sympathies should have been more established. He did not even make her one of us." He started to leave the room. "I am going to get dressed. I suggest that we go out on the town tonight, to see and be seen. Just in case the girl starts screaming to someone. We need to look our most reputable. And our most unscathed."

"Love," Veronica said flatly.

"What?"

"Love," she replied. "Matthew loved her. As best he could."

"And it destroyed him," Edward reminded her harshly, fierce light dancing in his black eyes. "Love is a sin for us. Remember that from now on."

As he walked away, she considered his words: *Love is a sin for us.* And a voice from her not-so-long-lost past bubbled up from her mind: *And all sin is misdirected love.* Was it Augustine who had said that? She could hardly recollect anything of the saints now. She could not even say, "Saint Augustine." It burned her tongue and it hurt her mind to consider the holy.

"Put away your cleaning, Veronica," Edward called from the next room. "You have to look splendid tonight. We still have time to celebrate. We will rest, then go out."

She headed towards her room, where she would dress, apply makeup to her cold skin, and fuss with beautiful hair that no longer grew.

And she thought briefly of Deena, hoping that the girl was long out of town. Hoping that the girl would start over with new wisdom to guide her. Hoping that the girl was now free of all the contagions that had claimed Veronica.

The Horrible Mile

When I am not writing, I have other leisure-time pursuits. These include attending rock concerts, visiting museums, working out at the gym, and running. I have finished three marathons (26.2 miles) and two ultra-marathons (30.1 miles). Having experienced those events, I sauntered into pondering a horror story set during a long race, when the mind grows weary of the physical pain that accompanies long-distance running and has exhausted its supply of thoughts and worries.

Seven minutes! There was no way he was ever going to lose so much time in a race again. Seven long minutes while he sat and poured water over his hot scalp and watched the other runners run pass him by. He had a sudden headache during the race and was forced to let the wave of nausea pass over him.

He had a horrible finish in that race.

Not this race! He had spent his life living in the shadow of physical inadequacy, hearing the snickers behind his back. *There goes Tubby,* the kids had said, all during his childhood. That was when they were being kind. He had finished college, graduating with honors, the guy that all the girls "wanted just as a friend."

He was large, nicknamed "Whale," and considered unattractive even by comrades who wore pocket protectors.

Now he had lost the weight, dramatically starving himself. His skin boasted loose rolls, his flesh marked with enormous stretch marks.

But he was in shape, beneath the debris. And now he could prove it to all those people who had taunted him with remarks about his weight. *Fatso. Lard butt. Butterball.*

He was going to run his first marathon.

He had intended to run a few long-distance races in preparation—some half-marathons, a few others delineated by kilometer length, rather than miles. 10K. 20K. 25K. 30K. He had never really mastered the metric system, so the numbers were meaningless. Six miles. Twelve miles. Fifteen miles. Eighteen miles. That Ty understood.

But he hadn't run much since the horrible 10K, the race with the headache and the nausea, six weeks ago. Still, he was in the best shape of his life and committed to the ideal of 26.2 miles.

He had been training himself, just as he had supervised his own dramatic weight loss. Eighty pounds banished in the last three months. That was when he started training for this marathon, when it had taxed him to walk around the block a year ago. But his work schedule demands had eaten into his self-devised training schedule. He had not had much time to run in the last few months.

Ty looked over the crowd at the starting line. There were men and women of all ages. They all fitted themselves along the asphalt road, according to what they seemed to think their time per mile was. An older woman, probably about fifty-eight, stood confidently in the ten-minute mile group. A young man, hair as black as a raven with a crooked arm stood in the ten-and-a-half-minute mile group.

Ty was mentally psyching himself up, preparing his speech for his approaching five-year college reunion, crafting it in his mind.

Where's Whale? they would ask.

Whale is dead! Ty would smile, *I lost the weight, and I've hardly eaten a carbohydrate in the last twelve weeks! I even ran a marathon. How about that?*

He had determined to stand at the ten-minute-per-mile starting position. It was faster than he had ever run, even for short three-mile races.

In reality, it boiled down to that was the speed he *wanted* to run.

An older man, perhaps in his late forties, stood beside him, stretching muscles carefully. Ty inwardly questioned if the older man should be in that time designation, or if he was just trying to get a better starting position.

The chatter in the line died down. People committed themselves to a last stretch, and checked their race numbers, carefully pinned to clothing. A few made sure that their time recording chips were securely attached to their shoes. A quick, ecumenical prayer was offered, inaudible over the murmured din of runners. Then they stood at attention, anticipating.

The starting gun fired with a sharp crackle. A cacophony of chirps and buzzes emanated from the mat, as the elite athletes and the quickest amateurs broke out across the starting line.

It took a few moments for movement to ripple back towards him. The crowd around him was like a solid animal, energy flowing through its body. They walked briskly at first, as if a pleasant mob out to march with no particular message. The chip on his shoe buzzed as he crossed the mat. He could not run yet; the mass of people around him was too concentrated. *His time was slipping away, and he was still walking!* It infuriated him. He needed a good finish, to show them all that he was a new man.

Then the pace quickened. He began to run, uncomfortably close to his cohorts.

It was a beautiful day. Too beautiful. The sun was out. It was humid, which made it harder to breathe. The air moved like soup.

The crowd had quickly dispersed, some advancing, some falling back. The forty-something man ran with his feet turned out, like a duck waddling a ten-minute mile pace.

Ty ran a little quicker, just to get past the man. To get away from the disturbing view of the man's supination.

Ty felt good. He was dedicated to the ideal of a superb finish. No seven minutes would be wasted this run for dizziness, his fingertips tingling as the on-course medics made him drink water and diluted electrolyte solution. There was shame in doing less than he expected of himself. It wouldn't happen this time.

He passed by the first mile marker, then the second. He was aiming for brisk marathon, something he considered respectable. Four hours, twenty-one minutes for the 26.2-mile course. Perfect ten-minute miles, easy to keep track of in his head. He had worked out the numbers on his computer's calculator the night before.

At mile 3 he heard the pace-keeper check a stopwatch and holler, "31:54!" at him. He was a little behind. *It had taken too long to reach the starting mat,* he grumbled inwardly. He determined he had to shave off a few seconds per mile. He could skip some water stations, which would help make up the time.

The crowds cheered him on. *Hoopla.* Flags waved and tables were out with electrolyte drinks and small pieces of fruit—bananas, apple slices, and orange sections. The run would take him around the city and form a large loop. The Wall, that quasi-mythical stretch where body and heart felt they could give no more, would occur on a city street in an affluent neighborhood.

There was a well-maintained lawn on the right of way at the stretch most people agreed the Wall was located, and people flocked there to sit there and cheer on the runners. He expected a few old college buddies and a couple of people from work to be there. They had told him to look for them at Mile 20. He had to look good for them. This was the inauguration of the new Ty.

By Mile 13.1—halfway—his official time was two hours, twenty-six minutes. He did the math quickly. He was running worse than eleven-minute miles! His heart sank. How had he lost so much time?

By Mile 15, he had improved slightly. His body burned. His head was hot and dry. He cursed his legs, for their lack of swiftness. He had never run this far before.

Both the old lady and the boy with the spastic arm passed him. The old lady sipped contently on a water pack she carried on her back.

There was no way an old lady and a partly crippled boy were passing him! He was lean now and in far better shape. His excess weight was gone, along with all its complications. He was going to live better, live longer. There was no stopping him. He had promised himself so much for losing the fat.

He noted that his mouth was dry, his forehead hot. He would stop at the next water station, then skip the next two. That would make up for the time he was losing.

At the water station he drank half a cup of water while jogging and threw a cup over his head. It was getting hotter and the humidity irritated his lungs. His leg muscles were beginning to feel like concrete and a sharp pain periodically jabbed in his side. His arms, he despaired, were tiring of their constant rhythmic swinging back and forth.

At Mile 17 he began to search the crowd. There was a sea of faces, and he thought he saw someone wave at him. It was a hand, raised at the back of the cheering mass. He heard his name. "Ty!" It drifted towards him. He searched the faces. None were familiar, although the lilting voice challenged his memory.

There were clouds beginning to drift into the sky, their dark bellies full of rain. *A little rain would be nice*, Ty thought. *Cool me off a little. It's hotter than they said it'd be.*

As he hit Mile 19, his time was holding steady, perhaps a little improved. The pace-keepers with their stop watches and pace books had called it out, along with words of encouragement like, "You're doing great! Way to go! Only a little way to go!" Ty disregarded them. His time was still off, and there was over seven miles before him. His skin was hot and dry. His knees ached and his jaw was sore from the repetitive rattling of bone on asphalt and concrete.

He stopped running, his lungs aching too much. He walked, despairing as each runner passed him. That was one more person who would finish ahead of him! He watched them, even unhappier that quite a few seemed to be heavier than him. How could they command more speed when he had so much to prove? He had to finish well, to be able to say with confidence that he had outrun people who had always been thinner. Those who had called him Fatso and Whale.

He saw the Mile 20 banner in the distance. And he smelled an offensive odor. Cigarette smoke. *What idiot is smoking at a marathon?* he thought.

It was a strikingly strong odor, but the other runners didn't seem affected by it. Ty looked around and followed the scent. It led his sight to an aging man, sitting by a tree in the back of the crowd.

Shit! he thought as he ran past, barely catching the old man's features. The man looked *exactly* like his Uncle Jim. *What a coincidence.* Uncle Jim was the type who would have congratulated Ty on anything successful he did. Uncle Jim had been like that, straight up and full of the right words, be they of encouragement or admonishment.

Except that Ty knew it wasn't Uncle Jim, just a guy who looked like him. Uncle Jim had lost a battle to lung cancer, his wasted body buried five years ago.

There was a light sprinkle of rain. Not enough to cool anything off, just enough to raise the humidity. Sheets of mist evaporated off the hot black topped road. Not only did the rain fail to alleviate the heat, but it mingled with the residual oil on the roads, making slippery ribbons on the track.

There was a water table at Mile 21, but Ty passed it by. He was already behind schedule.

He looked at the faces of the volunteers passing out electrolyte drinks and water as he passed. They all seemed vaguely familiar. Perhaps his alma mater had sponsored a table. They were familiar in that way. Like people he had passed by frequently, but never gotten to know. The last girl in line plaintively held out an extra-large cup of electrolyte drink. He shook his head and passed her by. He could have sworn she whispered his name as he passed. He looked back, a few moments later, but the rotation at the table had changed, as volunteers relayed with each other to get more refreshments for the runners. He could not see her.

He ran a few moments, before having to walk again. His mind was temporarily distracted from the pain that was wrecking his body, trying to remember the girl. *Vicki?* he thought, suddenly recollecting her face. Vicki had been a lithe little freshman in the English 101 class he'd taken, a monstrosity of a course with 400 students poured into an auditorium and lectured by teaching assistants. But she had buckled under pressures unknown to him and committed suicide over Spring Break.

This city's full of doppelgangers.

Ty's vision was blurred.

His fingers tingled, feeling heavy and hot. He patted the residual raindrops off his face with the tuft of his shirt. It was becoming uncomfortably warm and his lungs rattled. There was a searing headache beginning to form between his eyes. It was making him feel dizzy, nauseous.

Not again! He cursed. The fire in the pit of his belly spurred him on and he forced his legs to run again.

Mile 22 passed, and he picked up pace. About four miles to go. *A 5K is 3.1 miles*, he rationalized, *and four miles is just over that. And I've run a 5K or two.* His optimism cut through the pain. He passed the older woman and the young man with the crooked arm.

So much for passing me! He chuckled to himself, inwardly. Not that he could have said the words. His breathing was far too labored for speech. His pulse was rapid, weak. His vision blurred to black, his skin on fire. He felt his legs buckle, his feet stumble; his vision faded for a moment. He blinked, then opened his eyes to regain purpose.

The water stations were now at every mile, but he passed them by.

He was nearing the finish line, and his time at Mile 22 had indicated that his efforts to run faster were paying off. He just needed to concentrate on the goal and pour on the speed.

He felt oddly refreshed.

He looked for his friends from work. They had said they would be here, and he had not seen them. As he looked around, he saw so many people who looked like people he had known.

At Mile 23 there was a scrawny little kid, playing ball on the sidelines, who looked just like Danny Duggan, who had died in a car accident when Ty was eight.

There was an old lady at Mile 24 who was the spitting image of his old neighbor, Mrs. Guillen, who had passed away of complications due to diabetes and kidney failure when she was eighty.

And at Mile 25 he heard himself being cheered on by a handsome young man in sporty clothes. The man was the spitting image of Rex Illione, who had worked out at the same gym Ty did. Rex had died of AIDS-related complications a few years ago, emaciated and riddled with the purple blotches of Kaposi sarcoma all over his handsome, chiseled features.

Ty shook his head. Perhaps all the jogging of his brain had made him see the faces of phantoms projected onto the figures in the crowd.

Still, he was annoyed that his buddies weren't there, especially as he was picking up speed.

Since Mile 22 he had been doing great. He had found a hidden font of energy and speed, and the pace-keepers were confirming his joy. He had been running the last three miles at a swift pace.

He flew past the other runners, hearing the cheers of the crowd in his ears. He occasionally heard his name but did not slow down to survey the yelping throng. His buddies must have taken their seats at later mileage markers than they intended, he thought. His body felt a jolt of energy rush through it, like electricity fueling him. He just looked straight ahead.

He saw the prize he had worked so hard for. *The Finish Line.* This is what he had pushed himself through pain and delirium for.

He applied every ounce of energy and ran like he had never run before. He crossed under the large digital clock: four hours, twenty-four minutes, and a handful of seconds. Elation welled up inside of him. His body felt free and light.

The runners funneled into lines at the end of the race. Cups of water and bananas were handed out. Race numbers on the bibs were marked with a bright pink marker, indicating they had finished and were entitled to the finisher's goodies. The lines emptied into a large convention hall for the post-race party.

Ty was directed into an empty chute and walked through a set of doors into the building.

There was nothing inside. It was empty, a searing white light blazing in an impossibly large, vacant room. There were no fellow runners, no volunteers, and no band on stage. There were no boxes of raisins on the tables, no carts of free bagels to replenish the body with.

He could hear whispers, coming towards him.

Then shadows began to fill the room, people arriving. With bananas, drinks, and a crystal glass etched with the word "Finisher." Ty stood in stunned silence. Here was Uncle Jim, and the girl from English 101. And Danny, and Mrs. Guillen, and good old Rex. They circled around him and patted him on the back.

"Goodness, what speed." Mrs. Guillen beamed.

"You really broke all out. Didn't stop for anything!" Rex acknowledged. He smelled fresh and just showered, like he always had.

"The last mile was the best mile *ever,*" Vicki said, duly impressed.

Ty silently took the offerings. Uncle Jim, smelling of his favorite brand of tobacco, started to walk him towards a distant door in the large empty building. The group moved him along with them, chattering about old times, about Ty's race, about things that didn't make any sense to Ty.

He could hear other whispers in the background as he left.

"Did you hear about the guy at Mile 22?"

"Yeah! What happened?" A mature man, a man who supinated when he ran, asked.

"Heat stroke. He didn't make it to Mile 23. Kind of scary, when you think about it."

There was an older woman's voice. "I was running right behind him. He'd just passed me. He just dropped! A young man—he looked so in shape! But I guess he just pushed it too hard. It was horrible!"

"Yes," a young man's voice agreed. Ty could hear the man beginning to massage his sore, hard worked, disabled arm. He, too, had just been passed by Ty. "Horrible what happened to him."

Ty was still perplexed, as he was guided ever farther away.

Mile 23 had been his best mile ever.

Something That Knows Your Name

"Something That Knows Your Name" was based on a true event. In my youth, I spent quite a bit of time tending to my "threes:" Snakes, spiders, and spirits. If somebody had one, they would sometimes call me, and I would relocate the critter. So, I would collect spiders in plastic dishes, capture coral snakes while wearing welder's gloves, and assess "haunted" locations. Most locations were not haunted, no matter how much the requestor wanted them to be.

"This," Maya said, opening the door to the professionally decorated bedroom, "Is the room my son refuses to sleep in."

The other women in the party smiled politely.

Except for Jamie.

To her, the room moved, like an unseen river flowed silently through it. Time and place were mere eddies at the edge of deep, swirling invisible water. Jamie kept quiet, allowing her friend the luxury of showing off her grand new home to new, upscale acquaintances.

The room, like the whole house, was brushed with an interior decorator's magic.

"It's a new house," Maya told the entourage. "We finished building two months ago. There was nothing here before. But Harrison swears he heard something call his name out one night, and now he refuses to sleep in here."

"Well, you did just remarry," Irene noted, enjoying both envy and scandal. Maya's new husband was a decade younger and a million dollars richer than Maya. "I bet Harrison wanted to sleep with you and Barry."

"For one night, claiming he was scared, but he seems happy in the guest room now." Maya opened the door to that room, decorated with similar over-elegant flourishes.

Harrison's baseball bat and mismanaged school bag looked out of place in the contrived opulence.

Jamie peered into the room. It was still and regular, in the way most places on Earth are.

"Of course, it helps having *two* guestrooms," Maya beamed, opening another door, to a familiar scene of wallpapers, paint, and heavily-fringed fabrics. The scents of electrical outlet fragrances battled in the air.

At the end of the tour, Maya led the ladies down the sweeping staircase into a large room. A bartender stood at an open bar, already preparing fashionable mimosas, margaritas, and cosmopolitans.

Jamie grabbed a beer out of the cooler, feeling oddly underleveraged for the crowd. She sat by herself on the patio, not really knowing couture and cotillions satisfactorily enough to engage in conversations about them.

"Knock, knock," Maya said, slipping away from the party. She stepped gingerly on to the patio. "Someone once mentioned to me that you were *sensitive.*"

Jamie raised her eyebrows. Maya made it sound like it was a disease. Jamie hated people knowing that she *knew* things.

"Could you check Harrison's room?" Maya asked quietly.

"I thought you didn't believe him."

"Just in case. You never know." For an instant, Maya was a worried mom, not just a carefully poised caricature of what she thought she should be.

"For what it's worth, I wouldn't sleep in there, either. The place has a creepy vibe."

"That I don't understand," Maya said. "It's a brand new house. It wasn't like this place was an Indian burial ground, or an abandoned cemetery, either. You know, they have to disclose stuff like that. But if they lied, you could sense that, right?"

Jamie's ability to sense things was like enhanced sight, visualization beyond the normal range of vision. She could see odd curvatures in time and space, hinting at the invisible things they bore. It was akin to the difference between seeing a very good photograph and seeing something in real life; no matter how good the three-dimensional quality of a photo, it was still just an image. Being there, with an object, it had undeniable depth, something the mind perceived as reality.

Most people saw only the photograph. Jamie was transported to the place, seeing the figures of those not entirely bound by the laws of three dimensions, those who had somehow slipped between the fabrics of one dimension and another.

Maya coaxed Jamie up the stairs with a genuine, "Please help me. Harrison said he distinctly heard something call out his name. He seemed so sincere, and he doesn't complain at all about sleeping in the guest room."

Maya opened the door to the sparkling new room with its overbearing decoration. Jamie felt instantly queasy.

Something very fixed met her gaze, disconcerting her. Light bent around it, refusing to touch its form.

It crawled along the wall and disappeared into a corner.

Jamie hated moments like that, seeing things other people were blind to.

"Can you sense anything? Can you do anything about it?"

Jamie sighed. If someone did not believe, she was considered crazy. If someone did believe she had advanced perception, it usually went from asking for her observations to requesting an exorcism in one statement.

"I'll look around," Jamie offered.

Maya hugged her, in that quick posturing way socialites hug. Perfunctory in appearance, calculated in execution. "I have to get back to my party. They'll miss me. Please, keep this quiet."

Jamie secretly wondered if she had only been invited by her old friend to attend to a troublesome paranormal defect in the environment: that she was there as a friendly, preternatural groundskeeper. Jamie felt like an uncompensated supernatural maid, there for the sole reason of cleaning up the paranormal mess.

She moved from Harrison's room, with its localized malevolence, to the guest room he preferred. It was clean and fresh, with no hint of any disturbing presence.

Jamie pursed her lips, then reentered the queasy room.

"*Jamie*," an unseen man whispered to her.

She stepped back, startled. There was no one there, except the barely perceptible shape that quivered where light was repulsed. The presence had listened, she realized, learning her name. It must have learned Harrison's the same way, overhearing his mother or stepfather call him.

Jamie methodically moved to examine the other guest room that adjoined Harrison's original room. Intelligence that did not need to fear substance was a frightening prospect.

A sickly sensation was barely perceptible in the wall of the guest room, the wall the two rooms shared.

There was a barrier to the presence's domain, so the presence was defined within a scrap of reality. Three dimensions formed boundaries on what it wanted to be endless. Whatever it was, it was tethered to this wall.

"It's a new house," Jamie thought. *Large and featuring an open floor plan, part of an over-planned community. Brick façade, siding, and energy efficient windows. The house was located down the road from sparkling swimming pools, a private golf course, and a strip mall outfitted with the trendiest of businesses.*

Jamie stood in the hallway, staring at the wall. Feeling a dark presence wiggle inside wooden beams.

She started praying, inwardly, for guidance. For courage. The thing moved away from the words she mouthed.

The house is not tainted, the ground is not tainted. Jamie reasoned. It occurred to her, as she considered where the evil was confined: *There must have been tainted wood used in the construction. Wood used in beams that constructed the common wall. The wood probably faced Harrison's room more; it could exert its malevolence more vividly there. The guest room also featured a painting on the wall: Michelangelo's "The Creation of Adam."* The painting was there purely as decoration, but its theme was sufficient to prevent the force in the wood from penetrating into the guest room.

Jamie's mind allowed her eyes to see, to follow images to the place from which the wood had been harvested. She opened her mind to see dark, thick forest, and feel oppressive swampy humidity.

A man in an old suit hovered in the air in front of her. His back was towards her, his attention on someone in front of him. He was flanked by a few other figures of varying degrees of anger and pride.

"*We know your name, boy,*" the man said coldly to someone Jamie could not see. "*If the judge doesn't believe in hanging you, that's okay, because we do.*"

Justice at the end of a rope.

Jamie shook off the images, realizing that the man did this many times, to many people, for many reasons. He relished being the final arbiter of vigilante jurisprudence.

He was the lynch master, Jamie realized, *and this wood was cut from his hanging tree.* Who knew where? Lumber was shipped all around the country. Its history could lie anywhere.

"Your tree is chopped down," Jamie said, focusing on her here and now. Rooting herself in a place where the laws of physics and man still held sway. "Go back to its stump. That's where your justice lies. I cast you out in the name of Elohei Mishpat, God as justice."

The entity twisted, as she spoke its terrible secret. There was a witness against him, and he had to flee, lest his own justice catch up with him.

The thing wriggled out of the timber, slipping into nothingness. Scattering in the imagination of its own dark heart.

Jamie heard footsteps on the stairway.

Maya came up, her cosmopolitan cocktail surreal in her hand. "Everyone's wondering where you are. You *have* to come down. Before anyone asks any questions." She paused. "Is it gone?"

"Whatever was here is gone," Jamie assured her.

For a moment, Maya was Mom again, relieved her house was completely clean.

Then Maya bounded back downstairs, Jamie in tow. "We're watching *Court TV*, and the bartender is mixing up the best drinks," Maya explained. "I don't know what juries are thinking nowadays. And those lawyers, getting people off on technicalities."

Jamie shook her head, letting the last dust of the presence drip to the ground. The lynch master barred now from anything with form. *I can't imagine why he thought he'd be welcome here*, she thought sarcastically.

The echo of her name said on his dead tongue still crawled around in her skull, as she rejoined the pretty party, full of people she had never met before, and would probably never meet again.

But she was oddly happy that hardly anyone there knew her name.

From the Garden

Sometimes a place can breathe a story into my mind. That was the case with this story. I grew up in the El Lago/Kemah area, back when astronauts were in residence and you could still buy shrimp straight off the back of the returning shrimp boats. "From the Garden" was inspired by a small stretch of reportedly haunted beach; I found that area more peaceful than restless. I incorporated settings I knew into this story—the chicken restaurant I worked at, the university I attended when I received my Bachelor's degree in Biological Sciences and my Master's degree in Chemistry. In that year, 2006, submissions were still paper manuscripts, sent through the mail with a stamped, self-addressed envelope. That meant standing in line, or using kiosk machines, at the post office to get the return postage correct. And waiting for that envelope to come back in the mail: It took months. About a decade later, almost everything is electronic. There are online submission services, and files are simply attached and sent off. Sometimes replies come back within a day. It makes one wonder where we will be in another decade or two.

The restaurant closed at eleven. Kelly, ever the gentleman, walked Amelia to her car. His night was still going strong, late hours meaning little to his youthful years.

Amelia drove home, navigating the dark, quiet roads.

The April night was cool and sweet. The wind blew faithfully off the Bay.

Amelia went down Todville Road quite a distance, spacious homes gracing the street, some putting brave faces towards the Gulf. True, it flooded from time to time, and hurricanes occasionally crossed this path, but the street remained grand and enviable.

She turned past the El Jardin subdivision, onto the hidden plot of land her husband, Peter, and she called home.

The pebbled driveway crackled beneath her tires, rocky popcorn noises filling the air. A small string of Malibu lights guided her car, like a short, narrow runway. Crawdads built little chimneys in the ground, pushing up the grayish brown clay as they excavated. Cicadas sung in the trees. Large golden orb weavers slung webs between trees, their spotted yellow bodies suspended in space.

The perpetually lit porch light gave off its garish glare. The high-powered outdoor spotlights illuminated the ground immediately around the house.

Inside the lights were off, leaving the house itself a pool of darkness enshrouded by the circle of light.

Once inside, she flipped on as many lights as she could quickly illumine, as if radiance alone was her protector.

Peter was not inside.

She went through the house and then stepped out on to the little square, barren concrete patio. It was the last logical place to look.

Peter sat in the lawn chair, staring at ten rocks he had collected. They ranged from a pebble to a small rock, organized in increasing size.

"Peter?"

He looked up at her, eyes vacant and unfathomable. "How was work?"

"Fine. What are you doing out here?"

"I found the stones."

"What stones?"

"The ones that are singing to me."

It reminded her of a long-gone past.

Once upon a time, Peter had looked vacant and contemplative a lot. But in those days his eyes had been reddened with marijuana smoke.

Tonight, his eyes were sparkling clear.

"These rocks sang to you?" Time had taught her patience, indulgence, and non-judgmental listening.

"The pebble sings about when I was just born. Things I don't remember. Things I never knew." He leaned forward slightly. "Did you know that my mother used to sing to me when I was a baby? She had a pretty voice. She made up the songs as she sang them. Never sang the exact same song twice." A wince crossed his countenance. "God, I miss that woman."

Amelia approached to comfort him, and as she got closer, she gasped.

Peter's body was covered in bites. Mosquito bitches had made him their blood meal, seeking to lay their eggs later in the shallow puddles of dank water that littered the area. His skin was covered in the raised, reddish welts of the wheal-and-flare reaction to the insects' bites.

"Peter! You've been eaten alive!" she said. She grabbed an arm, pulling him off the chair and into the house.

She secured the doors and doused him in calamine lotion, turning his skin chalky pink.

He looked outside, at the line of rocks.

"I really had it made when I was a kid."

"Most of us did," she replied. "Have you eaten? I'll fix something to eat."

"Thanks. But I'm not hungry. I think I'll just go to bed. I want to dream while my memories are fresh."

She watched him climb the small staircase to the second floor.

"Good night," she said. He didn't seem to hear her.

***

Peter slept soundly, which was rare. Whatever lullabies he had heard dragged him down into a deep slumber.

The next morning, he was up before she was, which was even rarer. Ever since his accident at the petrochemical plant years before, he slept in late. With nowhere to go he had lost interest in getting up early to not go there.

Amelia readied herself for work and made coffee. Peter sat outside, gazing into the woods, his finger tapping the beat of a song she could not hear.

"Do you want some coffee?" she called out, a big mug of milky brown java already prepared for him.

"No."

"How about some breakfast?"

"I'm not hungry," he said. "I'm fasting. It cleanses the mind, cleanses the soul. There was a local doctor who used to recommend fasting as a frontline treatment for just about everything. Did you know that?"

"No. Where did you hear that?"

"One of the rocks told me."

She put the cup by him. "I'll leave it here in case you change your mind," she said. "You have to eat something. And put some sunscreen and bug spray on. Do you itch?"

"No."

"I work ten to eight today. I'll bring you something back."

She started off for work. As she drove it dawned on her that she had stopped offering to bring food back years ago. He usually asked. She usually resented the reminder that she was the sole breadwinner.

At work she concentrated on her duties, temporarily forgetting Peter and his sudden odd obsessions. Kelly was there, working with the garden in front of the restaurant.

Kelly was tall, red-haired and muscularly wiry in that way only Southern boys seemed to be.

Landscaping suits him, Amelia thought, not feeling her age for a fleeting moment.

He struck the soil at the base of a trellis, making sharp little cuts in the soil with the edge of a shovel. The purple flowers of the vine that climbed the trellis trembled with every stab. He came inside when he was finished, mopping the sweat off his brow with the back of his arm.

Amelia watched him pour himself a large Delaware Punch, the sweet red liquid filling the cup.

"What were you doing?" she asked, making conversation. His scent filled the air. *He smells like a healthy man should*, she thought. *Like Peter never did.*

"Root pruning. It makes the wisteria think it's dying. It blooms better then." He finished his drink. "Excuse me, ma'am. I have mulching to do before it gets too hot. No sense putting off what can't be done later."

Amelia watched him as he went back outside.

Kelly worked throughout the afternoon, catching the eyes of the ladies as they went by. To get a better look, they stopped by the small restaurant, ordering fried chicken, mashed potatoes, and diet sodas. *Saving calories where I can*, more than one explained. Amelia understood that philosophy; she practiced it herself.

Her mind drifted to Peter as she worked. Imagining him sitting at home, hearing rocks and stones singing to him. She figured it must be old drugs, being freed from fatty tissues. His latest delusion.

Her family and friends had stopped coming around after they eloped. No one wanted anything to do with Peter. He was rough, and his drug use dissuaded gentle company. After his accident, his discretionary funds evaporated. He went cold turkey from the drugs, and any acquaintances he had from that lifestyle moved on to better paying friendships.

Amelia dropped out of college to support them. She had always promised herself she would go back to school one day, get her degree, qualify for something other than a minimum wage job, but it had never happened. That goal was always something that would happen next year. It was all she could do to pay the bills with what she earned.

All the outside contact she had now revolved around her job at the little chicken restaurant, and that complement of contacts was forever rotating as the younger kids who worked there moved on to better things.

Kelly quaffed down another mouthful of punch, taking a break. He pulled out a book from his workbag and began to read.

"What are you studying?"

"Psych," he answered. "It's an elective."

"What's your major?"

"Business," he answered. "Something that will keep me working inside an air-conditioned building. Not in the heat and humidity."

"I was a psych major."

"Really? What happened?"

"I got married. Had to support my man."

"I guess it was tougher back then," he offered.

Back then, she bridled. The past was not her excuse for dropping out.

"You doing the two-plus-two plan?" she asked. Two-plus-two was a common college route for the locals. Two years at a junior college, such as San Jacinto or Alvin, followed by two years at the modern, airy campus of the University of Houston at Clear Lake.

"I'm officially ending my junior year," he replied. "Where's your old man work?"

"He doesn't," Amelia anticipated the disapproval, adding quickly, "He used to work out at the plants. He had an accident and they put him on permanent disability. He suffered a head injury and back injuries in a fall."

Luckily, they had not tested him for drugs. He had gone to work high that day. Amelia later learned that in those days the hospitals only tested for drugs when ordered to. The insurance companies didn't pay when the patient had been drunk or stoned at the time of the accident, so it suited the hospital bill collectors to have a policy of not testing. Things would probably be different now.

"Tough break. You ever think about going back to school?"

"At my age?"

"Lots of older students, especially at UHCL," he said the school's abbreviation as "you-click," like many of the students did. "You still have time to get a degree, start a second career. *This* can't be where you intended to end up."

He read quietly for a while, and then put his book back. "Anyway, work calls. I'm off at four, so I can get to class on time." He winked. "No rest for the wicked."

She sat for a while after he left, finishing her diet cola. Thinking of Peter sitting at home, listening to ordinary rocks sing.

***

When she arrived home, Peter was sitting out back, with ten more stones before him. He had neatly lined them all up into two decades. His eyes were closed; he was softly singing.

> *By the shadows, I lay dreaming*
> *In the embrace of fog, I let myself go,*
> *All my planning, my abandoned scheming,*
> *Lost me to the me I'd hoped to never know.*

Amelia had never heard Peter sing before, much less attempt rhyming verse. She put some food—crispy chicken tenders and fries—beside him. The decadent food odors wafted into the air.

The cicadas began to buzz, high in the treetops.

"Food," she said.

"I'm not hungry," he replied, wearily opening an eye. "These rocks sing so beautifully. I wish you could hear them. They know *everything*."

"You need to eat."

"No, I don't."

"All living things need to eat."

"Am I a living thing, Amelia? I mean, really living?"

She was getting exasperated. It was like talking to a troublesome child. "Yes, you are. I made the food especially for you. The least you can do is eat it. That poor chicken died for you to eat it."

Guilt didn't work. He turned slightly towards her, both eyes dreamily open. "Do you know how old our house is?"

"No."

"It's one-hundred-and-fifty years old."

"The rocks told you that?"

"And do you know what? This house used to belong to a healing woman."

"A healing woman? Like a doctor?"

"Not quite. She cured people with what she called *The Fast.*"

Amelia didn't like the implications the reverent tone in his voice forebode.

"She took patients in, and fed them almost nothing," he explained. "Just tea, water, some broth. It drove the toxins out. Like a modern spa."

"They feed you okay in a spa," Amelia guessed. She had never been to one but had seen late night television programs on the spas celebrities visited.

"This is better. No pretense."

"I think the lack of food is making you delirious. You're losing weight. I think that maybe some of the weed and acid stored in your fat is coming out. You need to eat."

"Weed and acid." He laughed. "Do you remember those days?"

Yes, Amelia thought bitterly, *I do.* Her family and friends had abandoned her because of his habits. They had an intervention, threatened to wash their hands of her if she wed him. They had all followed through on the threat. It was the worst thing they could have done for her.

She suddenly missed people she had vowed never to miss.

"The toxins are coming out," Peter beamed, closing his eyes again, and starting to hum.

"I think you need professional help," Amelia blurted. "You're really messed up."

"Maybe."

She went inside to make a cup of coffee and give herself time to think.

She could hear him singing, his voice suddenly strong and sweet against the background of percussive cicadas, rhythmic crickets, and a chorus of frogs. Carried by the soft bay wind.

> By the shadows, I lay dreaming
> In the embrace of fog, I let myself go.

She caught her haggard reflection in the window. *Hadn't they been letting go all along?*

***

"Kelly," Amelia asked, cleaning up the cooking area, "you've lived in this area a long time, haven't you?"

"All my life," he replied. Grease, cool enough to work with, was draining from the big cooker into a large pot. When it finished draining, he scoured the heating elements, removing debris that had baked on during the day.

"What do you know about an old story about a woman who healed people with fasting? I heard she lived in the area."

"Dr. Edith Hunsler?" Kelly laughed. "Lady Hunger?"

"I don't know. That's why I'm asking you."

"She supposedly lived at the turn of the century, in one of the houses near the Bay. No one remembers exactly which one, since a fire in the courthouse burned all the old deeds. It may not even exist anymore. One thing's for sure: after she died, no one turned up claiming the old place."

"Why?"

"Bad juju. Lady Hunger used to say that fasting could cure all ailments. She had a few success stories. Probably people misdiagnosed. But plenty of people were never seen again after checking into her little hospital. The only way people really found out what was going on was when a farmer went out one night looking for a wayward cow and found a woman crawling through his fields. The woman was emaciated—almost starved completely to death. She'd dragged herself across the ground, unable to stand. She was desperate to escape the healing house. That brought on an inquiry. They hung Lady Hunger in a tree in her own back yard. Back out by the Bay. Supposedly her house is surrounded by the unmarked graves of her 'patients.' They say she used rocks as grave markers."

"I'd never heard that before."

"It's a local legend. It's used to scare kids into eating their dinner. You know, 'If you were at Lady Hunger's house you'd be happy for that broccoli.' Sometimes I wonder if it ever happened at all. Why do you ask?"

"I heard a story," Amelia offered quickly. "Are you done with your yard work?"

"For now. The wisteria is going to look gorgeous. You wait and see." He removed the pot of oil a safe distance away and lit a match to the heating elements. The residual oil lit up hot flames, burning away the dirt he couldn't get to. In moments, the flames died, having consumed their source of fuel.

He lowered the cleaned element, sealing the oil drain again.

"Careful of the fat," he said. "It's still a little hot. I'll pour it back in a moment." He paused. "You know, I just remembered something else about Lady Hunger. She used to sing to her dying victims as they wasted away. It's a creepy story to tell your kids, when you think about it."

Amelia had the sudden, awful thought that she knew exactly where Lady Hunger had lived.

Then she checked her imagination. Peter had grown up in the area: he heard the stories, too.

It's just the drugs, she thought. *The chemicals are seeping out of his fat. Making him remember the story. And his mother used to sing to him. He said so. Everything is getting all mixed up in his head.*

She poured herself a regular cola. She suddenly wanted the calories.

There are worse things than being shaped like an apple. She shuddered.

***

Peter looked terrible when she got home.

He had surrounded himself with ten more stones.

And he had sat out all day.

She could tell by the bright, blazing red of his skin. His lips were parched. Small salt trails crept out of the corners of his eyes.

"Peter!" she said.

He brushed her away.

"Peter? What's happening to you?" she demanded.

She fixed him some ice-cold lemonade and brought out the aloe vera gel. "You're burnt to a crisp! Have you been out here all day?"

He turned and looked at her with an icy stare.

She shrugged it off. "I brought you something to drink. You look like shit."

He stayed on the porch, silent, saddened, and still.

By midnight she was exhausted, so she went to bed, without saying goodnight to Peter. They had not truly shared their bed in years anyway. The accident had hurt Peter's brain and his spine. Although he was mobile, he had trouble processing information, maintaining attention, and maintaining an erection.

It had all become more bother than it was worth for them.

The next morning, when she awoke to get ready for work, he was still sitting there. The lemonade was untouched, except for happy mosquitoes engorged with his blood, laying their eggs on its tranquil surface.

"Peter!" she exclaimed, rushing outside. "Have you been out here all night?"

"You killed them," he said.

"What?"

"You killed them. The rocks told me. Yesterday. How could you do that?"

"Killed who? Peter, what is happening to you?"

"You killed my babies," he stated, a sad rage in his eyes. "When I was twenty-seven and again when I was twenty-nine." He pointed to the twenty-seventh and twenty-ninth rocks.

She thought back, doing math in her head, correlating years with long hidden events.

"How did you find that out?" she exclaimed, feeling oddly violated, shamed, and weightless all at the same time. She had never told him. She had never told *anyone*. There hadn't seemed much point.

"Two babies, you killed them both. A little boy, then a little girl."

She shook her head, disbelieving. She had the abortions not knowing the genders of the babies.

"We were in no position to have kids," She defended her decision, so long her own hidden secret. "You were dropping acid. I had no idea how healthy they would be. We were barely making it as it was—"

He cut her off, a sudden lull of queer tranquility crossing his sunburned face. "We would be doing the laundry our son brought home from college now, and you'd be shopping for a prom dress with our daughter. Now would be a great time to have had those kids."

"You were stoned all the time."

"Kids would have made a difference. I would have quit."

"You're talking about things you don't know."

"The stones know, Amelia. They told me. We wouldn't have spent our entire lives as plankton. Drifting along aimlessly."

She was suddenly furious. "I don't care about what you think you hear the rocks saying! I don't care! Do you hear me, Peter? You were a stoner, until you couldn't afford it anymore, then the drugs stopped coming to you. You'd still be dropping acid if you could. Don't tell me you would have changed. You were a fucking loser then *and you're a fucking loser now*!" She stopped herself, just as the words tumbled out.

He started at her blankly, like a statue with eyes. Hollow inside, an elaborate lawn icon.

She shook herself off. "I haven't had my coffee," she offered as an apology. "I have to be in early today. I'm working a double."

She dressed herself quickly while the coffee brewed, anxious to leave. Years of sadness and anger and doubt and shame stood on a precipice somewhere inside her, eager to jump off. She had to hold them back.

She poured her coffee into a travel mug and left. Peter was still sitting on the back porch, looking at the stones that he tormented himself with.

She cried as she drove to work. *Was this what I ran away for? Was this what I gave up my youth for? Was this all I really wanted?*

***

Her eyes showed that she had been crying, but no one asked if she was all right. It made her feel all the more discarded.

She would have lied, had anyone questioned, saying she felt fine. But in her heart, she just wanted someone to ask.

By the end of the day, twelve hours of labor later, she ached.

She drove home, not bothering to pick up food for Peter. She poured herself a Delaware Punch for the trip home, hoping that it would give her some of the youthful vitality that played around Kelly's face and gave him the energy to trim reluctant wisteria.

The lights at the house were exactly as she'd left them.

She could see Peter's form sitting outside in the weathered lawn chair, the moths flying into the porch light with gleeful abandon. He had gathered twenty more stones, arranging them in a perfect circle around him, like a fanciful compass.

She didn't bother going outside. She had no idea what she would say to him anymore.

The next morning, he hadn't moved.

She walked outside with some hesitation. She had tossed all night, composing various speeches to give to him. Some were kinder than others, some kinder to him, some kinder to her.

It had been days since she had seen him even take a drop of water.

That can't be good, she found herself worrying.

She watched him as she approached.

He didn't flinch as she moved in front of him, the bright golden sun of the dawn splashing clear, cleansing light over them both.

He looks so tranquil, sitting there, she thought, like being made of stone suits him.

She touched his shoulder, and felt his cold, rigid body beneath her fingertips.

She was surprised that she didn't jump back. She just stood there, realizing he was dead. For an instant she wondered when. *During the night? Before I came home?*

She left him there, not sure what to do.

At work, she was oddly calm and peaceful.

Kelly sat down across from her in the break room, after the lunch rush was over.

"How's things?" he asked.

"Fine," she said, not lying.

"The old man?"

"He's better now."

"You working late again?"

"I close. I open tomorrow."

"That's a lot of hours."

"I'm saving the money."

"Anything in particular?"

Amelia smiled. "I'm thinking of going back to school, to finish my degree."

"Congratulations! See, old dreams never die." He grabbed his drink and went back out to his duties.

She wiped one involuntary tear away. "Old dreams never die." *And old nightmares?*

She could only hope those perished in time.

***

She borrowed the shovel from the restaurant overnight, knowing no one would miss it.

The ground was made of clay, and difficult to dig, but she managed to make a deep enough, large enough hole for Peter's body.

The water table lapped around the bottom of the grave, the Bay lurking just beneath the ground.

Amelia buried his body quietly, knowing it was highly unlikely anyone would ever ask where he was. She piled the stack of stones he had collected on top of him.

She looked up at the tree that became his headstone. Wondering if that was the tree Lady Hunger had swung from. And wondered if she was the only person Lady Hunger may have ever actually saved.

Amelia let the fanciful thought pass. *Just children's stories*, she told herself. *It was just the drugs seeping out of Peter's dwindling fat.*

After work, she went out by the Bay, and sat on the edge of the new pier, watching children fish for crabs with little pieces of raw chicken dangling off lengths of string.

The old pier was just visible, its pilings peeping above the gently lapping waves. There were other parts of the old pier submerged nearby. You had to know where they were to avoid wrecking on them.

The wind ran its fingers through her hair, the stiff Bay breeze bracing her face.

She sat, in the twilight of her decisions, feeling not quite alive, not quite dead.

For an instant she understood the wisteria, with its roots stabbed, thinking it had one last chance to bloom before it died.

Then the gulls soaring overhead laughed at her.

As she stood up, preparing to go home, she thought she heard something.

She looked around. The children were down at the end of the pier. All that was near her were the rocks of the breakwater. The murky, green water splashed against them, muffling the sound.

She listened for an instant, remembering a music box her mother had bought her at the circus, decades ago. It was a memory she had forgotten, the sad song locked away in the recesses of her mind, suddenly awakened to awkward life.

Amelia shivered, and walked purposefully away.

Although, she would have sworn she heard the rocks of the breakwater singing:

> *By the shadows, I lay dreaming*
> *In the embrace of fog, I let myself go,*
> *All my planning, my abandoned scheming,*
> *Lost me to the me I'd hoped to never know...*

Within the Bricks

Every now and then somebody will say, "You should write a story about X..." In a few cases, I've gone right ahead and done that. This story is one. My son, Alexander, who was about three years old at the time, wanted a story about something that was fascinating him. "Within the Bricks" was a response to that fascination. It was accepted by a children's magazine. He took in a copy to read to his classmates.

"We should not have gone off on our own," Paul complained.

Nicholas frowned. He was tired of hearing Paul say negative things. Nicholas needed to hear positive thoughts; otherwise, he might also believe that they would not come out of the desert alive.

The sun beamed down relentlessly. It seemed directly overhead for an impossibly long time. The earth around them was baked and dry. The brown mud was riddled with cracks and crevices.

Nothing seemed to live anywhere around them.

In the distance, they could see the mountains, tan and russet in color against the fiercely cerulean sky.

"We should have stayed at camp," Paul added.

"Talking too much will dry out your throat," Nicholas whispered.

Paul moped.

Nicholas felt guilty inside. It had been his idea to explore the desert on their own. *Just a quick trip over the ridge, and we'll be back before breakfast,* he had promised Paul. Paul was five years younger than Nicholas. Nicolas, at fourteen, was wise in all things as far as Paul was concerned. He trusted his big brother.

But the desert was disorienting. Its barren landscape offered only distant features, and without any perspective to guide them, they had gotten lost before they realized it.

Turning to find the ridge they had crawled over, they realized that all the ridges looked exactly the same. The dry desert wind had erased their footprints, leaving them no trail.

Neither had bothered to pack a compass before leaving camp, so it was impossible to tell what direction to go.

All Nicholas could hope for was that Dad and the others were looking for the two lost brothers.

"I'm thirsty," Paul said. "Again."

"We'll drink in a few minutes," Nicholas replied softly. "We need to maintain discipline with our remaining water. It's all we have."

Not planning on becoming lost, they were woefully ill prepared. They had grabbed a water bottle each, at least knowing to always take water into the desert. But once away from the oasis of camp, they quickly became aware that they had not taken enough.

The heat was getting unbearable. Nicholas knew they needed to get out of the direct sun. They had to find shelter.

He scoured the landscape, looking for anything that might offer shade.

In the distance, he spied a small building made of mud brick.

"We'll go there," he suggested. "Until the sun goes over. Then we can figure out how we can make ourselves conspicuous, so that any search party can find us."

"What about anything else finding us?" Paul worried.

"Dad's group will already be looking," Nicholas said. He was glad to see the small dwelling. Human hands had built it. And he remembered the four things that indicated water in the desert: plants, animal tracks, birds, and signs of human civilization.

He just hoped that nothing was already living in the little mud brick building.

***

They cautiously approached the building. Nothing stirred inside; they were relieved to find it empty.

It was a small one-room building, just big enough for the two of them. But it had a corrugated tin roof, and that provided shelter from the overwhelming rays of the sun. It had one tiny window opening, made of a missed brick in the pattern. The bricks were obviously hand made from the dry river mud of the empty streambed situated near to the building.

Nicholas and Paul drank from their water bottles, Nicholas noting they had only about a liter of water left each. At one gallon of water needed per person per day, they were carrying about a quarter of what each of them would need in the next twenty-four hours. Nicholas had heard that you could dig up burrowing frogs and squeeze water out of them, but he had no idea how to find them, and he was not carrying a shovel. That meant he could not construct a survival water still either, even if he could find a spot he thought might offer some moisture.

"I have a candy bar," Paul said, pulling out a chocolate bar. "I can share it."

"Don't eat," Nicholas said. "Eating uses too much water for digestion. We can wait until Dad finds us."

Paul reluctantly put the candy bar away. "Now I'm hungry, too. Not just thirsty."

"Give me your socks," Nicholas said to his younger brother.

"Why?"

"They're red. We'll use them to mark this location, so they catch Dad's eye.

Don't worry, you can put them back on if we decide to walk anywhere."

Paul reluctantly handed over his socks, and Nicholas wedged them between two of the handmade bricks.

The two boys sat down, listening to the wind begin to pick up force outside. The stiff breeze filtered between the bricks, providing a crude form of air conditioning.

In the distance, they heard a roll of thunder.

"Is that a storm?" Paul asked.

"It hasn't rained here in ages," Nicholas said. "The drought has devastated this area."

The boom rolled in the distance. "That's thunder," Paul affirmed.

The sky overhead clouded dark gray with alarming rapidity. The wind tasted of moisture as it whipped through the roughly constructed building.

"It's going to rain! It's going to rain!" Paul celebrated.

Nicholas was more apprehensive. He checked outside the little building, noting that the scorched riverbed seemed to be located sufficiently away from them. He was worried about flash flooding, the rain engulfing the dry riverbed. They seemed to occupy high ground, no doubt a selection made by the person who had built the little building. Nicholas was very happy they had located the shelter and would not be exposed to the ferocity of the approaching storm.

The rain came quickly, falling in thick, heavy drops. It splattered little dimples into the bricks, softening them. Nicholas now worried about the sturdiness of the structure that was their refuge.

Paul sat close to Nicholas.

The rainwater quickly formed small streams and rivers, furrows in the dirt becoming the conduits for the rapidly accumulating water. Where no water had been a threat before, too much water could become an equally dangerous situation.

Sensing his younger brother's unspoken fears, Nicholas reached out and hugged him in comfort. The wind howled outside; the rain swept in through the little crevices in the wall.

"My socks are getting wet," Paul said softly, looking at his red socks getting drenched by the relentless downpour.

"Mine, too," Nicholas replied. There was water pooling on the floor of the small building.

Paul looked very concerned. "Nicky," he said, "I hear something."

When he listened, Nicholas heard it too. A soft rustling sound grated against the outer bricks.

The noise began to increase in intensity, a rasping, squirming sound that seemed to shudder through the building.

"What is it?" Paul asked. "Animals outside?"

Nicholas shook his head. The sound was coming from all around them, wriggling and scratching.

"Is it ghosts?" Paul asked again, more fear in his voice.

"No, there are no ghosts here." He hugged his brother. The noise was growing in volume. The bricks began to move.

We should not have gone off on our own, Nicholas thought again.

The rain began to soften the outer bricks, and they became muddy. Little holes began to appear in some of them.

Nicholas could see beams of grass and stone interwoven into the mud, holding the flimsy structure together. The storm seemed to be abating, passing on. Nicholas could hear water gurgling in the refreshed stream outside.

The bricks shuddered, making horrible gooey noises. Holes began to expand in them, being pushed out from within.

"There's something in the bricks!" Paul shrieked.

"Don't worry," Nicholas comforted, masking his own fear.

Things began to push their way out of the bricks, slender, snake-like things that dropped to the ground and wriggled.

"Snakes!" Paul screamed.

Nicholas held him. "Not snakes," he noted. "See, they have little appendages. I think they're fins."

The things squirmed, dropping around the two boys. The creatures looked slimy as they dug their way out of the bricks and flung themselves towards the water.

"Snakes!" Paul screamed again.

"No," Nicholas said, recognizing the creatures. "They're just lungfish." He recognized the creatures as they emerged from their death-like sleep. He remembered from zoology summer camp that the elongated creatures made themselves leathery cocoons out of mucus, breathing oxygen from the air through that mucus in a hibernation-like state called aestivation.

The little blue-eyed creatures squirmed away.

Paul watched them warily.

The rain subsided, becoming a light mist. Beyond the dripping of the raindrops, Nicholas could hear a steady whirring noise.

He got up. "I hear a vehicle!" he exclaimed.

Outside, he waved one of the soaked red socks, recognizing an all-terrain vehicle from their father's camp.

It turned towards them, their father's voice strong and loud over a bullhorn. "Nick! Paul! Stay there! We're coming to get you!"

Paul stayed very still. "Can I have some water and eat my chocolate bar, *now?*" he asked.

"Yes," Nicholas nodded.

They would no doubt have some explaining to do, but he was just happy to be around to be able to do that.

As the vehicle approached, a slimy body plopped onto his shoe. It moved its powerful, eel-like body away, into the steady little stream that now flowed in the once-dry riverbed.

I really should not have gone off on my own, Nicholas scolded himself, watching it as it swam away.

No Lesser Angels, No Greater Devils

This story concerns a man who is simultaneously fighting a battle on two fronts, and yet has no idea he is under attack on any front. Externus *denotes something on the outside or farther from the center;* Intus *means "within, on the inside, inside." The headings help guide the reader to know where they are.*

1. Externus

Tim Councilman hated his job.

As he drove to work, the sun was rising, fierce and blinding. Its sharp rays stabbed through the tree branches. He drove his car ploddingly through the streets, flanked with ancient oaks. Their roots had warped the street, breaking and buckling it. He hated the rough ride.

He was an assistant in the District Attorney's office, a very minor underling in the hierarchy of justice. Once had grand aspirations of putting felons away for life and keeping the streets safe from criminals, but his hope had eroded with the realities of the position. He had no real power, certainly no direct power. He had to answer to bosses, politics, and good press.

Today he had only a half-day of work, but even that was an unhappy prize. The first part of his day was a scheduled annual physical with his doctor. He hated the cold examination room, the invasive questions, and the dreaded snap of the rubber glove.

It was seven thirty a.m. *At least I'll be on time for my appointment.*

The traffic light ahead of him turned red and he stopped. The cars started to move in the lane that crossed his. A woman pedestrian began to cross the street at the street corner to his left, with the traffic. Her hair was a warm brown color, like molten caramel.

There was a left turn lane ahead that directed turning traffic across the pedestrian walkway, and an eager car turned sharply. The sunlight blazed into the driver's eyes, and Tim Councilman could see the driver squinting.

Then it happened.

The vehicle, heavy, maroon, laden with momentum, slammed into the fragile woman. She fell with a thud to the cold, sun-drowned pavement.

The noise was dreadfully final.

The car stopped with a short squeak of its brakes. Then all hell broke loose.

People stopped their vehicles, and a few burst forth from their cars. Cellular telephones dialed emergency numbers. A man in a tidy, expensive shirt with an elaborate silk tie and a neatly laminated nametag rushed to the woman. *A doctor*, Tim Councilman reasoned. The doctor shook his head, replacing his stethoscope limp around his neck. His lack of action betrayed her condition. The oddly calm body was dead.

There was a rapping at his window. He turned off his car and put his hazard lights on. He rolled down his window.

"Did you see what happened?" an odd little man asked.

"Not really," Tim replied. "I wasn't paying much attention. I was looking at the light." It sounded like an oddly hollow excuse, considering the fatality.

"Hmm." The man summarized. He was of average build, with graying hair. There was something dignified about him; perhaps it was his late middle age. He wore a strangely colored suit, russet and reddish brown. His tie was a plum color that almost became a red. He offered his hand through Tim Councilman's open window. "My name is Mr. Cinnamon," he said.

"My name is Tim P. Councilman." Tim replied. His mind was still processing the woman dying before his eyes. "I'm a lawyer. With the DA's office." He added the detail reluctantly, bothered by a capital murder case he knew was sitting in his in box at the office. His boss was talking death penalty. That meant intense legal work and unfriendly press.

Mr. Cinnamon laughed. "A lawyer, huh? Probably just as well you didn't see too much," he said. "They'd never take down the word of a lawyer."

The policemen were pulling up in their marked cars, a few of them getting out to take statements from the people gathered around the woman's body. The man who looked like a doctor was talking in earnest with the first police officer that had arrived. An ambulance had also arrived, the EMTs draping the woman's body with a graying sheet.

There were police cars blocking the roadway. Tim wasn't going anywhere. He stepped out of his car.

He fidgeted uncomfortably. He felt even more useless than usual.

"What are you thinking?" Mr. Cinnamon queried compellingly.

"I wish there was something I could have done," Tim replied.

"There," Mr. Cinnamon smiled wryly. "I may be able to help you."

"Unlikely." Tim said. He could see that the policeman had finished talking with the doctor. The doctor was making a quick call on his mobile phone. Probably to his office, explaining his delay.

"Oh, but I can," Mr. Cinnamon said. "Would you like to change what happened here?"

"Of course," Tim said.

"You can."

"You're crazy."

"Actually, I'm not," Mr. Cinnamon replied. "Hear me out. If I'm a loon, it's no loss of yours. If I'm right, you can claim your own miracle. It's a win-win situation for you."

Tim started to move away.

"Not even curious, Mr. Councilman?" Mr. Cinnamon asked. "So eager to get back to that dreary little office? Don't you want to *save* somebody for a change? Stop the bad thing from happening before it occurs?"

The unexplained insight into Tim's frustrations gave him pause. His ears were involuntarily open.

"How can I change events?"

"These," Mr. Cinnamon said, pulling two small gold capsules from his pocket.

"Now I know you're crazy."

"It's worth indulging me," Mr. Cinnamon goaded. "I mean, you try a little crazy thing, and it works, or it doesn't. There's nothing lost in the trying. No one will see you—you don't even have to risk looking the fool if you fail."

"Magic beans?"

"Not at all." Mr. Cinnamon laughed. "Little gilded capsules, filled with nothing more than cinnamon apple potpourri."

"I suppose the carnage will be 'scent' away?" Tim thought his pun was clever.

"No. The breaking of the capsule is all ritual. Just to show you believe. Like most rituals, really. Doesn't do anything, but means a lot. Shows you trust me and believe in what I say."

"So, I break a capsule, and then what?"

"Time can be manipulated into little loops. Relativity, Mr. Councilman. A small frame of reference—this accident scene, for example—can be sped up past the speed of light, and then projected into the future."

"You watch too much television," Tim chided. Mr. Cinnamon held out the two gleaming capsules. Tim picked them up to look at them more closely.

"They're just little containers," Mr. Cinnamon reminded him. "The physical frame of reference is very small. You'll have to stay here, close to the scene, when you use them. Good luck, Mr. Councilman."

He walked away, leaving the lawyer standing on the sidewalk.

Tim looked at the capsules and sniffed them. He could smell the fragrant potpourri inside. *But the crazy old coot is correct—no one else is around, and what if they work? I play the lottery, and never really expect to win. So what if I crack one of these little pills, and nothing happens? No harm, no foul. And what if it works? I could actually save a life. Beats going to the doctor and then accomplishing nothing at work. I could really make a difference. For a change.*

There was broken glass still sparkling in the gutter.

It was well past eight o'clock and he was now running late for his appointment. He morbidly appreciated the opportunity to miss the invasive examination.

He got back into his car and parked it in a small lot adjacent to the intersection.

The sense of purpose flooded his veins; that made him feel wonderful.

He took out one of the capsules, closed his eyes, and broke the little pill with his thumb and index finger. There was a little whiff of the potpourri, like spiced apple pie.

Tim opened his eyes. He was at the traffic light, in his car. The light was glaring red. He hated the new light bulbs they had put into the traffic signals. They were too bright for him.

He glanced at the clock in the dashboard: nine forty-five a.m. *Why is it later?* he wondered. *Shouldn't it be earlier?* He was significantly past his appointment time now. That irritated him a little, not so much for missing the appointment, as in the decision being taken away from him.

Out of the corner of his eye, he saw the caramel-haired woman. Remarkably, she was alive.

Perhaps I'm hallucinating, Tim considered. *Too little sleep and too many things to do.*

The woman stood at the corner, eying the crossing signal. The sun was lower now, and there was a mist in the air. Clouds had gathered in the sky.

There had been a light shower of rain. The moisture near the road's surface rose, further agitated by the traffic. Its low gray body made the road difficult to see, and the wetness was just enough to lift the film of oil off the streets. Tim could see the pink and green iridescence of the oil on the water.

The woman began to cross the street.

From around the corner, the vehicle that had previously struck her approached.

It was the same vehicle, Tim noted: maroon with bright chrome hubcaps. The man inside squinted, now trying to clarify the lines on the street.

He could hardly see the woman, and when he caught sight of her, his eyes opened wide.

She saw him, too, at what could have been her last moment on Earth. Her body jolted upwards in awkward surprise.

The driver frantically turned his steering wheel, overcorrecting as he desperately swerved to avoid hitting her.

The tires squealed in objection to the sudden gymnastics they were being asked to perform. One of them slipped on a small patch of pretty oil.

The car lurched, the driver turning the wheel both directions in an effort to correct its path. He was frantic, and with every movement, the car became more erratic in its motion. It slid sideways, and then began to turn around, as if pivoting on one front tire.

In a violent and ugly ballet, and the car careened around with a sudden twist. The driver's side smashed with a startling cracking sound into a streetlamp pole. The sound of metal crushing and glass shattering exploded through the misty air.

The car came to a sudden, unfortunate stop. Its left light blinked on and on, and the glass made a tinkling, almost chiming noise as it fell to the asphalt.

Tim looked on in horror. There were people stopping their cars and getting out. They were dialing on their cell phones, and there was the doctor again, in his neat, starched shirt. He got out with a small bag in hand and rushed to the car.

The woman, startled, was sobbing on the other side of the street. People were comforting her, a young woman taking her pulse and speaking to her soothingly.

The driver of the vehicle, a bald man, was sprawled ungracefully over his deployed airbag. His head was at a weird angle, his eyes fixed and unresponsive. It was obvious that he was dead.

Tim shook his head, and opened his door, screaming, "No!"

There was a hand on his arm. It was Mr. Cinnamon. "Not quite what you had in mind."

"How can you say that?" Tim screamed frantically. "A man is dead! This isn't what was supposed to happen!"

"The woman is safe."

"But not like this!"

"That's the problem with tinkering with appointed time," Mr. Cinnamon said soothingly. "It's not always as straightforward an exercise as one might hope."

Tim surveyed the scene, the police cars and ambulance again appearing to do their grim duty.

"You can make this better, still," Mr. Cinnamon soothed. "You have one capsule left. You failed this time. Perhaps the third time is a charm."

Tim hated failure. He felt the little golden capsule remaining in his pocket. *I can't believe I screwed this up so badly*, he thought, both frantically and bitterly.

"You seem better educated for your last attempt."

Tim's analytical mind, reminded of its education, threw an observation to his lips. "Why did time move forward?"

"I don't know," Mr. Cinnamon confessed.

"It just doesn't make sense that the woman was alive at nine forty-five when she died at seven thirty."

"You should have taken more physics. Then you would remember that you cannot assume there is an absolute significance to your observation of time; it is not necessarily independent of the state of motion of the body in question. I don't entirely understand it myself. Good luck, all the same."

He walked away, his cane tapping the ground happily.

Tim pulled out the last little golden pill and closed his eyes.

With a quick snap, he broke the brittle little shell. Apple cinnamon fragrance wafted around him.

He opened his eyes. It was eleven thirty a.m. He was standing by his car in the parking lot, getting drenched.

It was raining now, quite steadily. The traffic was picking up for the lunch hour.

Tim watched the woman approach the intersection. She pressed the crosswalk button and waited patiently.

The maroon car pulled up, the squinting driver looking briefly at Tim.

The crossing signal changed with the lights, the left turn arrow green. The woman walked out, and the man in the car regarded her carefully. She was safely across the road. The man cautiously navigated his car through the intersection.

Traffic moved unimpeded.

Tim got back in his car, soaked from the rain. There were no screeching tires, no soft thuds, and no breaking glass. No policemen were summoned; no ambulance came. He smiled. He had actually done something good today.

He called his physician's office. His doctor was booked solid and the doctor's assistant was suggesting an appointment next month. Tim declined.

If his doctor couldn't accommodate him, then perhaps he couldn't accommodate his doctor. He'd do his physical next year. What harm was there in waiting? He felt more or less okay. He had a few odd aches and pains, a little pressure in his abdomen, but that was probably just gas related to stress and his haphazard diet.

He had taken the day off to deal with the annual checkup, and today had gone very differently than originally planned.

There was too much to do at work with the new capital murder case sitting on his desk.

The clock read eleven forty-five. He could go into the office, grab some coffee and lunch. Do some work. Go home. He didn't feel as useless as he usually did.

Mr. Cinnamon sat on a bench hidden behind a tree and watched Tim drive away.

Mr. Cinnamon did not have any talent for foretelling the future, something that bothered him greatly. But he could read the past and was especially sensitive to the perils of the present.

Somewhere, hidden deep inside Tim's body, Mr. Cinnamon knew that something was going terribly wrong. *What was it Tim should have known? Didn't he want to be well?* Mr. Cinnamon bristled at the remembered words of his enemy.

Mr. Cinnamon liked Tim, though. Tim was an ideal human. Tim blamed others for his failings; he looked to others for his opportunities. Tim liked to be taken care of, in every way. *Sir, I have no one to put me into the pool when the water is stirred.*

Truth was, today would have been a very good day for that checkup. Putting it off was ill advised.

But then, Tim hadn't asked about any of that. And Mr. Cinnamon only answered questions he was directly asked. Anything else would be saying too much.

He smiled and walked away.

He loved his job more than life itself.

2. Intus

Deep in its warm, moist space inside Tim's body, the cell knew only that it was hungry.

If it had a purpose, that purpose no longer occupied its efforts. It did not matter what it had done or was supposed to do. It did not know if it had forgotten, if it had changed, or if it had never known.

All it knew was that it wanted to live. The urge to expand and fill this warm, lovely space obsessed its every mechanism.

But it knew that it was starving; and worse, it was accumulating dangerous levels of its own waste around itself. The tissue was turning necrotic, slowly blackening around it. Small, calcified nodules pressed up against it. Oxygen was getting more difficult to come by. Diffusion through the tissue was no longer an effective method of living. It knew that it had to move, or else it would die. And anything was justified to save itself.

The cell had seen the big white ghost cells squeeze amoeba-like between other cells. They seemed to come and go as they pleased from the big, fast red river.

It had observed, and the cell had thought as much as its reflexive chemistry thought. If it could get to the big red river, it could move and find better sustenance. Oxygen and glucose to fuel its designs with.

It could still make things. In fact, the cell could make anything it wanted. Its neighbors—neat and stacked like ordered bricks—did not seem to have that freedom. They could only make certain things, and some things they were forbidden to make at all.

And they died. The cell had seen it. Their centers grew dark and little packets of poison exploded within them. They seemed to consume themselves. Then new cells would arise, young and fresh. But even these new cells could only make the same things as their predecessors.

The cell held them in disdain. They were weaker, less efficient cells. The cell considered itself vastly superior to those obedient drones. The cell could make— or not make—whatever it pleased.

And it knew something wonderful about itself, something those other simple cells could not possibly comprehend. The cell knew that it would never die. It was immortal now.

But it could be killed. It had seen other cells like it, robust and challenging, try to take over the small space from the neat, organized cells. When the cells like it had made the fateful move to get more oxygen and food from the great red river, grayish ghost cells slithered silently out of the crimson waters.

The gray phantoms were drawn to the rebellious cells and destroyed them with chemical weapons. The cell knew that it would have to be cleverer than its previously destroyed cohorts.

The cell spent days running small molecules up and down its deliciously distorted strands of DNA, savoring the entire length of the code available to it. Then the cell found a key: a small sequence of nucleotides that encoded a protein that might solve the cell's problem.

If it was dangerous to go to the river, perhaps it could make the river come to it.

The cell made a protein it had never tried to make before. It packaged the protein neatly and pushed it gently out of its pores. Once free, the protein drifted towards the great red river.

At first nothing seemed to happen. The cell was growing desperate as the tissue around it sickened and died. It made another chemical—one it enjoyed—to comfort itself, bathing in the enjoyable chemical's transforming caresses.

Then the cell saw something. The cells that surrounded the red river like neatly interlocked sandbags were animated. They twisted slightly and seemed dazed at the delightful protein the cell was sending. The cell watched, and the sandbag cells copied themselves. In a short while, they made a small branch off the great river.

The cell was ecstatic. It was beginning to suffocate in the hypoxic, dying tissue. It warily watched for the ghost cells, which would assassinate the cell if it could not escape in time. Caught between starvation and predation, the cell anxiously watched the sandbag-like cells build a new riverbed.

The river was coming! The cell held on, feeding off the happy chemical. It watched, and the sandbag cells brought the waters of the moist, glorious red river to it. It drank deeply, feeling the rush of oxygen gird up its nearly exhausted strength.

Now it thought, *Now is the time to move.* Before the ghosts came.

The cell considered the little river before it. It enjoyed the rich nutrients it brought, but where the river flowed the ghosts could follow. It could not stay. It needed a place to hide, behind bulk that would shield it from the ghosts.

If the ghosts could slip in and out of the stream, the cell thought, why couldn't it? It recollected the ghosts' movements. At first it had looked like they passed through the solid wall of sandbag cells, but then the cell realized that the ghosts were corporeal. They were slipping between the sandbag cells, not through them.

The cell expanded and contracted the edges of its outer membrane, making itself blister. In time, it could distort itself at will. It approached the sandbag cells with some hesitation, but the sandbag cells were dumb and still. They offered no resistance.

It squeezed pseudopodia between two sandbag cells, feeling their jelly-like insides push away. Then the cell wriggled its way between them, pulling itself into the river. The sandbag cells popped back together after it had passed, oblivious to its passage.

The red river was warm and rushed towards the great undiscovered regions the cell sensed existed beyond its cramped home. It had some predilection for where it wanted to go, a yearning for a place it instinctively felt would provide safe harbor.

It kept itself quiet and shielded its skin with a layer of mucous and sugar, so that the ghosts would not see it. And it swam in the brilliant red river.

The mucus helped the cell tumble effortlessly through the little knotted mazes that popped up in the great river's course. They were infrequent, but the tangled little islands acted like sieves, capturing weaker cells and debris. The ghosts snaked through the convolutions of the islands. They went to the entrapped with a dreadful silence and embraced them with death.

Once the cell felt a ghost consider it strangely. The ghost nearly moved, but the polysaccharide coat that covered the cell seemed to answer the ghost's curiosity. It let the cell pass by unchallenged.

The cell followed an intuition it possessed yet did not comprehend. Something drew it from the main river, a sense of luxury and belonging. It drifted lazily along, homing in on the source of its delight.

The cell felt its home nearing and let itself be guided into a tiny red creek. It lined up behind the little red inner tube-like cells that swam so abundantly in the great red river. The walls made by the sandbag cells were thin here, and they were joined relatively loosely. The cell easily squeezed between the sandbag cells and stood on the banks of its new home.

It sent out little blasts of a chemical to break down the tough sinews of the bank and squeezed its way through the small hole it made. The cell was happy in this new tissue, shielded by bulk. It did not understand the configuration, but it sensed that this was the spot it had been yearning for.

The cell pulled shiny dense spheres of metal towards it, pulling them from the nearest trickle of the great river. It engulfed them and added ribbons of proteins, fluttering hypnotically around the spheres in magical twists and turns. These coaxed the minutest amount of the creek to the cell, and it grabbed some oxygen and some nutrients. It also relieved itself of the horrible gas that made it ache, a small red inner tube cell carrying the ill vapors away. Hopefully, the ghost cells would never venture this deep or find it in their mission to explore this insignificant little backwater.

The cell considered its new home with favor. Here was a place where its clones would thrive. The metastasis had been a very successful endeavor.

The cell felt stronger now, and more confident in its repertoire of proteins and factors. There was scarcely any limit to the catalog of chemicals it could produce. It would recruit some of the slave-like cells, coaxing them away from the employment they currently toiled in. It would inspire them to become lesser versions of its own majesty, and then they would also proliferate.

The cell nestled in, feeling the warmth and comfort of its hidden home. Yes, barring any extraordinary outside influence, it could expand its reign from this little spot.

There was no limit to how far it would grow.

By the time Tim would get to his doctor, it would be too late.

The time Tim lost could not be regained.

And thanks to Tim's choices, time was now squarely on the cancerous cell's side.

Desert Penguin Blues

This is my "writing challenge" story. My brother, George Sanger, handed me a list of about thirteen words and asked me to write a story incorporating these dissimilar words. This is what resulted.

Pierre was dictating as he drove. The little digital voice recorder paused and restarted with his voice. He was recording a memoir, an educational story.

There wasn't much else for Pierre to do.

He was in the middle of the desert, returning from a mission. The sands around him were white. Pierre remembered hearing that they were comprised of pulverized gypsum crystals. All he knew was they were nearly blinding.

His cellular communications were out. There was no signal in the wastelands.

He passed his time listening to his own voice. "After the warming period, the climate shifted, and the mini-ice age we are currently in began." He blinked his eyes. The glare from the sands was intense. The endless dunes were disorienting.

"Most of central North America is desert now, but not long ago it was fertile basin. We manage to make enough food to feed ourselves, but just barely. That is why population number is so critical." He paused. The recording would be broadcast over a school public address system. "That is why we look to you, our children, and know that our future lies in your decisions."

Pierre Plinge liked projects like this one. On one hand, the stories helped teach reverence to the young. On the other, they addressed the philosophical heart of his job; the story reminded him why he killed the lawless in the desert.

Pierre had helped kill forty people that morning, outlaws trying to hide their crimes in the desert.

His car went suddenly silent; the steering wheel refused to turn.

He sat for a moment, as the car stopped.

A panic filled his well-groomed mind.

He was suddenly stranded in the middle of nowhere.

***

Pierre Plinge hated the scavengers.

Two of them were stopped ahead, securing something to their truck. It was an old truck with an extended cab and a rusted bed and patched tires. It looked like it had an old-fashioned gasoline tank, along with a modern ethanol-biomass fuel converter. He wondered where they found the gasoline, if they did.

They saw him walking towards them.

The pitiful truth was that he was happy to see them. Lawless bands roamed the desert. His car was inoperable, many miles behind him. He had no communications. He was running low on water. He wouldn't make it much farther in the desert heat.

They eyed him suspiciously as he approached. One was a muscular African man; the other was an equally fit Caucasian male.

Pierre was flabby around the middle and was proud of the distinction that bore. He was well fed, while they probably barely survived in the desert.

He flashed the badge to make sure they knew they had to obey him. "I'm Pierre Plinge," he introduced.

"An Observer," one man noted.

"You're a long way from a killing field, or a desk," the other added.

"My vehicle broke down. I need a ride back to the city. I'm commandeering your vehicle."

"Your lucky day, then," the black man noted. "Finding us here. Desert gets hotter as the day gets longer, and you aren't carrying enough water."

"I didn't intend to get stranded."

"You always carry more than enough water in the desert," the white man scolded.

"Let's get going," Pierre commanded.

"We're waiting for our partner," the white man informed. "She's picking up a piece of scrap we saw as we drove by."

Pierre nodded. He looked at the truck, crudely stenciled with their company name: ESTUARY. *A strange name*, he thought, *for a desert-based business.*

The men had names sewn onto their shirts. The black man, "Edward." The white man, "Ellison."

"Emma is back," Edward reported.

"Into the cab, G-man," Ellison said.

Pierre took the seat behind the driver. It looked the cleanest. He watched outside, as a lithe figure emerged over the dunes.

A girl, perhaps seventeen years old, appeared. She was carrying a large hollow plastic penguin. The sort that used to be used as a lawn ornament. She was impossible to classify quickly. Blonde hair, dark skin, Asian eyes. She wore rings at every knuckle on her fingers, the gemstones reflecting the overwhelming sunlight.

She looked critically at Pierre, while securing the giant penguin model in the bed of the truck.

"Serendipitous find?" Pierre asked, as she sat down next to him. Her partners climbed into the truck cab, closing doors.

"Saw it sitting in the desert. Scrap is scrap," she replied.

"I like your rings. Bonuses?" he asked. She wore three to four rings per finger, all of them real precious metals and gemstones, some very expensive. Pierre counted. There were thirty-seven rings in all.

"We can keep what we want," she recounted. "You know the law."

"I'm not a regulatory agent," he assured her.

"Yeah, and you don't know any, either."

Pierre retreated from the conversation. He was accustomed to the fear his position inspired.

The truck was moving, and he was able to feign an interest in the passing landscape. Dune upon dune, expanse of white sand drifting into more white sand. The truck smelled of sweat and dust. A scavenger smell.

He tried his telephone again. Still no signal.

The scavengers were quiet. Pierre left them to their contemplation. He didn't like them, even though he recognized their duty. There was something unwholesome about free agents, sifting through the things death left behind.

The scavengers helped clear up material belongings. They were especially useful when whole communities died.

Without them the junk would heap up, and recyclables would go underutilized.

The scavengers could keep what they wanted and sell the rest. If something could be salvaged, it was. Nothing could be wasted; that was the mandate of their licenses.

Pierre was many stations higher. He was an Observer, sent to make sure those who *should* die died, whether they wanted to or not. Otherwise, the living would exceed the numbers the world could support.

Resource management, economic policy—everything was planned according to a population number. There was only a small margin for deviation.

His attention was distracted by a mechanical choking noise. The truck shook, and then stopped.

"Shit!" Ellison exclaimed.

"Is it dead?" Edward asked.

"Yes."

"Can you fix it?" Emma asked.

"Yes." Ellison paused, calculating. "It sounds like sand clogging something. I'll need some parts to get the work done."

Edward unbuckled his seat belt. "We have some parts back at base."

"You crazy?" Pierre asked.

"It's only a five-mile walk. We can make it before the afternoon sun. If we stay here, we're dead," Edward told him. "The outlaws could find us."

Emma opened her door and stepped onto the pavement.

"We have enough water," Edward replied, handing the Observer an insulated bag.

"Probably his bad luck caused the truck to die," Emma said.

"There's no such thing as luck," Pierre reminded her. *Superstition*, he thought. *Just like a stupid scavenger to believe in luck.*

"You seem to have pretty good luck today, mister. You found a ride. And we have extra water, so you won't die of dehydration," Ellison replied.

Pierre accepted the water. Emma picked her penguin out of the back of the truck.

"You aren't going to carry that, are you?" Pierre asked.

She nodded. "It's not that heavy, and I have straps. It can ride on my back."

"Why bother?"

"It's worth a lot of money. It's for the yard, and only the very rich have those. So, they'll pay top dollar for something their neighbors don't have in *their* yards. I'm not having it stolen."

"I guess it looks light enough."

"It's made of old plastic. There's a little sand in the base, to keep it from toppling over." She strapped the penguin to a backpack like device, securing it over her shoulders.

Pierre started walking with her, while her companions locked their truck down. She had a point. Very little arable land was available for something as frivolous as a garden. He himself lived in an exclusive high rise, which had a rooftop retreat. A garden hidden away stories above the crowded concrete.

Pierre and Emma walked ahead.

Ellison and Edward walked closely together behind them, carefully out of earshot.

"What are we going to do with the G-man?" Ellison asked. "He might see things. Figure things out."

"We couldn't leave him at the truck. I doubt he'd stay behind, anyway. We've been commandeered, remember?"

The quartet walked in the hot sun, the heat rising in waves off the reflective white sands: Three men and a girl carrying a large plastic penguin, trekking through shifting dunes.

***

The water almost evaporated between the mouth of the water bag and his lips. Pierre hated desert assignments. He wanted to move up in the ranks just to get assigned somewhere more hospitable.

He had been called in the very early morning to a commune. *What was it about crazy religions and deserts?* he wondered. *Those sects that still clandestinely preached individualism seemed drawn to the godforsaken sand.*

"You like your work?" Emma asked.

"Yeah, I like my work. Just hate the workspace."

"You don't like the desert?"

"No, I don't."

"That must suck."

He nodded.

There was still that limited arable land, but its use was preciously guarded.

That land was used for expensive agriculture and as a reward for the privileged. That was why the population *had* to be strictly controlled. Deserts and ice caps did not support much humanity.

"What are you thinking about?" she asked.

"An old man," Pierre replied. "He would have been ninety years old now. He was a veteran of one of the Arabian Peninsula Wars. I was a witness for the prosecution when they brought him in."

"Those wars were mid twenty-first century, before the great climatic shift," Emma said.

"Before modified ethanol became a viable fuel source. Eliminating the need for oil as a fuel source. Now that oil-producing part of the world is just sand and ancient anger." Pierre smiled. "The trial was about thirty years ago, early in my career. He'd probably be dead by now, anyway."

It was becoming very hot. He felt his skin beginning to burn, even though the intense sunscreen he wore as part of his uniform. *I really hate the desert*, he thought again.

Emma glanced back towards the two men, trailing them. She kept Pierre's mind busy. "So, what about the man?"

"He led a community, preached opposition to the population regulations. He said he believed in individuals, not governments. He'd forgotten who'd signed his paychecks." Pierre paused. "He had been in Qatar, said he'd heard a radio mufti telling the population that the individual was subservient to their culture. The old man proclaimed that he didn't like any system that suggested personal rights weren't indispensable. *Good of the one more important than good of the many* crap. I remembered him today when I raided a commune."

She became very quiet.

Pierre smiled. He enjoyed the fear he saw in her eyes, as she contemplated the nearly limitless police powers he enjoyed.

He looked back at the two men, then at Emma. "I thought scavenger units were usually family businesses."

She shielded her eyes from the sun. The reflected light made even her youthful skin look blotchy. "Not always," she replied.

Pierre eyed them critically. There was a similarity about them, not withstanding their racial distinctions.

Their eyes were similar, he realized, Oriental in shape. *They are siblings*, he thought. *The girl is the youngest, about ten years younger than her fair-haired brother.*

Three children to one couple went against sustainable repopulation laws. They must have had different mothers but share a common father.

One child per woman. That would be the only way they would have survived. The only way the community would have welcomed them. *Every child a wanted child, not only by family, but also by society.*

If he gained any evidence that any of them were the product of an unapproved birth, he could kill them here and now.

There was a small rocky outcrop in the desert, the sands shifted to reveal a little piece of desperate scrub and shade.

"Let's stop here to rehydrate," Edward called out.

Emma and Pierre retired into the rare shade. The girl took the penguin lawn ornament off her back. Ellison and Edward joined them.

"So, you're family?" Pierre asked.

"We're half-siblings," Edward said. He could sense the interrogation.

Pierre nodded. "And you live here in the desert?"

"We have claims, staked throughout. No one else wants this territory. I'm surprised we weren't called to clean up your site this morning," Emma replied. "We're the closest scavenger unit."

"It was a commune," Pierre reminded her. "They were an illegal operation, so everything escheated to the state. Nothing for you profiteers. The government will send out one of its own units."

Emma quaffed a mouthful of water.

There was a rustle in the sand, and a Pierre jumped back, pulling out his gun.

A sand viper peered up at him, tongue flickering wildly.

Pierre aimed.

Emma swung forward quickly and pushed his hand away.

He turned quickly and re-aimed the weapon at her. "*No one touches an agent!*" he proclaimed fiercely.

"You don't need to kill it," she said, staring at the gun. "It's just a snake. It doesn't use any resources we do. It's just trying to stay out of the sun."

"Hey, G-man, you're just thirsty. Put the gun away," Edward soothed. Edward offered the government man the small vial of *aqua*—water infused with nutrients and hydration factors. "Take a sip. The desert sun can make us all jumpy."

Pierre needed them to get him out of the desert alive. He returned the gun to its holster. "You're not dead because you're helping me," he informed her. Pierre drank the *aqua* down. The wrinkles on his forehead relaxed.

Emma placed a few drops of water into her hand, her palm forming a little cup. She carefully maneuvered her hand in front of the reptile. She placed down a small plastic cap, filling the cap with the water.

The snake slithered up to the water and drank the precious drops in. Quenched, it retreated into the shadows.

"It's not a protected animal," Pierre scolded.

"All the more reason its needs protection." She replaced the penguin on her back, securing the straps.

They walked back into the desert, Pierre keeping up with Emma. He noted her undisciplined mind. If he determined that she was a threat to the peace, Pierre had a mandate to kill her. Spare the world another mouth to feed. Another set of lungs consuming oxygen. Another source of waste. A node of dissention.

He smiled. *I might have the opportunity to shoot her after all.*

***

Pierre stepped carefully in the sands, following the path forged by the girl with the penguin.

The desert was populated with religious nuts, rebels, and outlaws. They didn't seem to mess with each other much. All of them seemed too content to hide out in the desert, thinking they were beyond obedience to the law. As if the desert itself was an aegis against authority.

The commune he had raided called itself the Salt Colony. He didn't understand the name, and he didn't care to.

There were ten women in the colony and eleven kids. Simple math, there should have been only ten children, maximum. *One child per woman.*

Pierre and the rest of the squad had shot the men of the colony first, then the women. Pierre had personally lined the women up for their execution.

A little two-year-old had run after his mother, grabbing onto her leg. Pierre had pulled the towheaded brat off, pushing him away. The child had run out again, screaming, "Mama! Mama!" As she reached for her baby, Pierre shot her.

An underling held onto the child while they killed the other women. It turned out two of them were pregnant. *That would have been thirteen brats*, he thought.

Pierre had spat onto the desert sand, the moist spittle evaporating almost instantly under the blaring sun. Then he shot the troublesome little boy, still crying over the bloodied corpse of his dead mother. The gunshots resounded across the arid landscape.

The ten children remaining would be relocated to the city, adopted into better-behaved families unable to bear their own biological child. There the children would be taught proper reverence.

It was an innate need, Pierre thought, *the need to revere something. To be obedient to it. That energy just needed to be properly channeled.* To serve society, not challenge it.

The scavengers stumbled towards a large bank of Barkhan dunes.

Edward motioned to a space of eroded earth, beneath a sturdy rock pedestal. "You guys can wait in the shade," he suggested. "I'll go get the tools. No sense wasting any more energy in the heat. It's getting hotter. And we still have to walk *back* to the truck."

Pierre shook his head. "No. I'll go with you. And the girl." He gestured towards Emma, wrestling the plastic penguin off her back.

"I can stay here," she suggested. "The penguin is getting heavy."

"You said you'd be all right," Pierre reminded her. "And we *all* go. I want to see your scavenger's nest up close."

"There's nothing to see," Edward replied. "Just stuff collected from suicides, accidents, other sites. Just junk, needing to be cleaned up before we try to sell it."

Pierre pulled out his gun, pointed it at Emma. "I thank you for the help and all, but my curiosity is now in an official capacity. I want to see your base."

Ellison scowled and nodded to Emma.

She picked up the penguin, holding it in her arms, her many rings resplendent in the intensifying sunlight.

They walked solemnly up the windward face of an oversized dune, following the direction of the windblown sand.

"We're nearly there," Ellison reported, attempting to put the agent more at ease.

Pierre motioned them forward with the gun. They sidestepped down the slidding face of the dune. Pierre's sight fell upon on their base.

It was larger than he had anticipated, arranged into a neat geometric order. Four large square buildings, neatly sitting in a grid with four equal quadrants. It was an obscene amount of space for three scavengers.

Pierre looked at the northwest corner of the base, where lines of yard statues were arranged in neat, ordered rows. They filled every description: Animals, gnomes, angels, and windmills. Made of plastic, resin, and stone. Sitting underneath the hot, searing sun.

Pierre pushed them forward, giving directions with his weapon.

They entered the base compound quietly, Edward going into the ground floor of the southeastern building. Pierre followed him, pushing Emma before him.

The large open space was full of tools and workbenches. Edward picked up a metal box, beginning to fill it with the accouterments of repair.

Pierre looked sternly at Emma. "Why do you keep so many lawn ornaments?" he asked. It seemed a misplaced luxury, in the middle of the abandoned desert. "I thought you said you sold them."

"Some are broken," she offered. "The better ones get top dollar. I repair the others as I can. I store them here until I can fix them up and find a buyer."

Pierre grunted, looking around. There was a workbench near him, with two portraits on it. They were family portraits. The woman was the same in each, an Asian. She sat next to a Caucasian husband in the first photograph, a small boy resting on her lap. In the second she posed with an African husband. The small boy from the first photograph was present in the second photograph, standing next to a little toddler with melanin-rich skin. A tiny, newborn little girl nestled in the woman's strong, gentle arms.

Pierre smirked. These were siblings—but born of the same mother, not the same father. The rule was: *One woman, one child.* She could have had only one child legally. Yet, here were her three offspring. That meant that two of them were his to kill. *He knew which one he wanted to kill first.*

He pointed the gun at Emma. "I observe that you are not legally a person," he said slyly.

Emma did not look at him with the fear he was used to. Her amber eyes burned into his.

Edward watched the agent carefully. He wrapped his hand around a heavy wrench.

Pierre motioned the girl outside. She followed the orders that flowed from the tip of the agent's gun.

Pierre stood with her outside the building, the sun burning high in the cloudless sky.

Emma looked straight at him, unwavering. Defiant.

He pointed the gun, readying his shot.

Ellison lunged out of the shadows of the building, grabbing the gun before Pierre pulled back the trigger.

"*I am judge, jury, and executioner,*" Pierre screamed. "*I'll kill you next—for assaulting a government agent! They'll give me a medal for killing you!*"

Ellison gained the advantage and propped the muzzle of the gun under Pierre's chin; he helped Pierre's forefinger choke down the trigger.

The sound of the shot was swallowed by the quiet, unhearing valley.

***

Blood and brain matter sprayed against the building as a fine raspberry mist.

Pierre's body slumped to the ground, the skin and hair crudely ripped off his skull by the bullet's exit. His eyes remained in their sockets, grotesquely large.

Edward stood at the doorway, surveying the scene.

"We need to clean up, before the blood dries and sets." He looked down at the Pierre's remains. "We'll take the body out to the wadi. Make sure we collect the shell casing. We need it for the scene."

Ellison shook himself off. "Do you think that will be enough?"

"The desert air will mummify him. It'll look like he chose suicide over dying in the desert. That's if anyone bothers to look." Edward gave Emma a quick hug.

"His car is still on the road," Emma noted.

"A car he abandoned while unprepared for the desert," Edward reminded his half-sister. "Come on, we have to repair our own hunk of junk. Then we'll move his car into the desert. The sands will swallow it."

"No scavenging," Elision reminded them. "That would be something to connect him to us. We have this one in our favor. No one in the city bothers about the dying or the missing; death is exalted there. And as it sits right now, even if anyone did find him, a mid-management G-man blowing his brains out in a godforsaken dry wash isn't going to have anyone asking why."

"He would have been the first to appreciate that," Emma said.

***

Edward and Ellison disposed the body in a distant wadi and drove back to the scavenger's nest.

Emma looked over the expanse of sand.

The others who lived with them would be back soon, after nightfall. They would come back from the shadow of the old fault line, where they had located a little fertile oasis.

The oasis bore fresh water that consistently bubbled in the deflation hollow. That supported fruit growing in a little orchard. Figs and sweet desert dates flourished.

No one in the government suspected how many people were in the desert; the satellites never bothered to swing overhead. They were more concerned with guarding the arable land and protecting the borders from invasion.

Ellison and Edward brought in the things they had scoured from the pantries of the dead in the truck: bread, canned meats, and powdered milk for the babies.

Emma took the penguin out to the neat rows at the northwest corner of the colony. She sat calmly on the ground and pushed away the hot sand. The cool hidden soil revealed itself. She took a small spade and dug a hole.

She toppled the penguin over, unscrewing the base. Inside there were fistfuls of little sealed plastic bags. Each was filled with ashes: Ashes and a small slip of paper with a name written on it. Sometimes, if the handwriting was small enough, there was even a short epitaph. Or a flower, drawn by a child.

She handled the ashes lovingly, gently placing them into the cool earth that lay beneath the searing sands. She started to sing, a lone hierophant whose voice was nearly lost in the desert winds.

This is what Emma and her colony did for hidden communities, bound together by their irreverence for the contrived lawfulness of the affluent cities.

It was the most dangerous of all missions: *burying the dead.* With land at its premium, burial was strictly forbidden. All remains were to be cremated, then scattered.

It was a vigorously enforced law.

But scattering the ashes left the earth nothing to remind it that its clay had been made magnificent.

I nearly died myself today, she thought. *My own ashes would have been lost.*

No such luck had smiled upon the Salt Colony. The agents had killed them.

She knew the agents would have burned the bodies.

Edward and Ellison would go to the remains of the colony, to collect the ashes and bring back whatever the agents had left behind.

The agents would not have found the hidden stores of spices and salt, the things the Salt Colony provided. Now someone else would have to assume those responsibilities.

Emma started to cry, abstract thoughts no longer able to guard her emotions. Her tears evaporated before they fell down her face.

She grabbed fistfuls of sand, letting the grains run between her bejeweled fingers.

She thought of the Observer, his body now providing food for animals that were not protected by his laws. *He had not been saved by obedience, he had not been saved by his duty to death*, she thought. *And every scavenger knew that you were not saved by duty to death, but by duty to life.*

She could hear Ellison beginning to hum on his harmonica, and Edward pick up his banjo. Their music began to fill the air.

Edward called out to her, and she went back to her home, to wash the graveside dirt from underneath her fingernails. The others were returning. They had mourning to attend to; by the morning, they would have to rediscover joy in these desolate sands that were their home.

Emma loved the desert; she knew why they were there.

Because in the desert, only the truth mattered.

Hannia's Dance

Hannia's Dance was inspired by a documentary about a man who was designing and painting a dancer's studio for his wife. While the documentary was sweet, the story takes a darker approach to the idea.

1. Hannia

There was little luxury backstage. It pissed Gregor off. Not so much for himself, as for Hannia.

He stepped out into the dimly lit hallway.

From the other end, *she* walked. Briskly, full of effervescent life. Her dancer's body lithe and lyric.

She grabbed him as she passed, looked around, and pushed him into a small closet. Her mouth fell hot on his, her kisses warm, deep. He could feel her blood pulsing through her.

His body ached. He pulled her closer.

"Hannia," he whispered.

"Shhh!" she warned, a slight giggle of panic to her voice. "They will hear us!"

Secrecy. How he hated it. He wanted the world to know about them.

They called her name, summoning her to the stage.

"I have to go rehearse," she said, pulling herself away. "I have my audience to prepare for."

He watched her walk to the stage. Her long brown hair pinned up in braids, her slender form encased in her leotard. He wanted to grab her, make love to her then and there. Especially in front of Jon. To show him whom she really belonged to.

Gregor then approached the stage himself. He worried that it would be suspicious if he, also, were late. He was only one of the coryphées, and his solo was short, but the divertissement he danced interrupted the scene Hannia was rehearsing.

The scene Hannia, and her husband, Jon, were rehearsing. The prima ballerina and the premier danseur.

Secrecy. Gregor hated living the most joyous part of his life in secret. But Hannia insisted. She still felt insecure in her genius; unable to comprehend how flawlessly she performed. She felt obligated to Jon, her husband and leading man, who had recommended her to the company.

Gregor wondered what time it was exactly. He had lost his watch—another irritation—and he needed to go on seventeen minutes after Hannia danced her piece.

He stepped towards the stage. Something moved on the dark, wooden floor. Little legs clicking on dry slats. Gregor looked down. A large cockroach. He crushed it underfoot, thinking of Jon as he did so. White meaty matter oozed from the insect. It was enough to put him off lobster for a while.

Hannia was practicing a *pas de deux* with Jon. It was an elaborate and flamboyantly choreographed piece, full of daring, acrobatic lifts. There wasn't much Hannia could do at certain points, save trust Jon's strength to carry her elegant frame.

Gregor settled back onto a stool standing in the wings.

The music picked up, quicker in tempo, its volume loud and furious.

Hannia danced, jumping a little at the beginning of the lift. Jon stretched out his arms and carried her up. There was a rush of wind, as she sped upwards.

Then Jon's arms retreated, failed, buckled.

Hannia went crashing to the floor, awkwardly attempting to correct her fall.

Gravity and momentum were not on her side.

She hit the ground with a sharp cracking noise. Then she screamed, howls of pain that shook the walls.

Gregor rushed to her, cradling her head in his arms. Crying, "Call an ambulance! Call an ambulance!"

2. Gregor

He liked to keep his workshop clean. It was one of the few things in life he could control.

Gregor looked up at the ceiling, high and fitted with long fluorescent tubes that gave the room an odd blue tinge. There were black, stringy spiderwebs beginning to fill the crevices of the ceiling again, he noticed. *Good. Spiders to kill*, he thought.

He pulled out a neat wooden box and caressed its carefully stained and polished top.

An hour to myself, he thought happily, awaiting the catharsis. *The witch will be busy entertaining herself for an hour. Perhaps she'll be dancing on that pathetic little stage.*

Hannia never disturbed him when he was in his workshop or his courtyard. She didn't like the smell of sawdust and congealing paints and varnishes. It was understood that when Gregor worked in his shop, she stayed away.

He looked admiringly at his space. The neat shop, with its tools and supplies, adjoining the little garden with its high rocky wall and two towering pines.

Fall was coming. He could smell it. He loved the fall because he loved the winter, and the former heralded the approach of the latter.

78

He thought of Hannia, dancing on her little stage. She could still dance, but it was like watching a very talented amateur. Her broken leg had never healed back to professional quality.

I was once a dancer, too, he rued, anger flushing his cheeks. Now he tended her stage, making scenery, painting backdrops, fixing lights, and repairing the old red and gold velvet curtain.

He opened the box. Inside, neatly arranged, were skulls. Animals he found dead by the side of the road. He picked them up when he found them and brought them home in a pail. There was a little wire box in his garden where he left the carcasses for the insects and small birds to clean. In a few weeks there was nothing but bones.

He recollected his epiphany, which had occurred after a disappointing night of receipts. Hannia howling that if she had a competent *corps de ballet* she would be a star again. The frustrated dancers stood and endured the tantrum, assessing the advantage of putting her still illustrious name on their resumes.

He remembered that evening, that poorly attended performance.

She had thrust a prop into his hands. A basket of wooden apples, painted gold. "They look cheap!" she complained. "They do not look gold—they are yellow like piss! Make some more, or repair these. People were laughing at them. I could see them laughing! How do you expect me to make a success of my theater when you provide me with trash like this!"

He painted them gold, again, as sparingly as he could. The gold paint was more expensive than the rest, and he did not have the budget for flamboyance.

As he went into his garden, to place the gilded apples on a ledge to dry, the bitterness welled within him. Hannia blamed him for her failure. She said it in everything she did.

But he had given up everything for her! Surely, she owed him at least a modicum of civility.

And as he stomped, carrying the props, he felt a snap beneath his feet. A delicious sound that broke the silence in the air. *Something that gave in to him.*

Bird's bones, brittle and aged. Hidden in the leaf litter.

The relief was so instantaneous, as if his heart had been momentarily purged of its shadows. He had found a remedy to his own emotions, as unspeakable as that self-discovered therapy was.

He smiled after remembering that epiphany, as he removed a squirrel's skull from the box. It had fallen from a tree, into the garden. It was dead when he found it, its eyes eaten out by the ants. Now it was nothing but cleaned, white bones.

He went outside and placed the skull on a small stump. Then he picked up a club, and with a mighty, heart wrenching swing, crushed the skull into a hundred bits of flying bone.

He listened, hearing the little bits of bones settle into the yard.

The pain was gone, even if he knew it would be back. And he had done no violence, really. His present anger against Hannia receded, like a raging tide swept underneath itself.

Now, he could work. Finish up some background painting for a themeless ballet Hannia wanted to dance. *No theme!* He laughed, his humor returning. *She thinks that dancing aimlessly will bring success.*

He moved the brush methodically. Up, down. Smooth strokes.

I used to be a dancer, too.

There was an echo of music in his mind. Building in tempo.

3. Hannia

The other dancers scurried around, backing away from Hannia's broken body, as if it were full of a contagion that would infect them.

Gregor comforted Hannia, letting her grasp hold of his hand. She whimpered now, heaving sobs occasionally rising and falling in her chest. She shivered.

He held her close.

"The ambulance is coming," the ballet mistress said. She crouched close to them, wrapping a blanket loosely around Hannia. "She is going into shock. You must keep her warm. And keep her head up."

The ballet mistress wrapped a towel into a wedge and propped up Hannia's foot. The one not attached to the grotesquely broken leg.

The répétiteur came over, applying a pressure bandage to Hannia's leg, trying to stem the flow of blood. His old face wore the mask of concern, not just for the extent of the injury, but what it forebode. He looked around. For the principal dancer. For Jon.

Jon finally approached, composed, stiff. "She must have slipped," he said, flatly, without emotion.

"It is a terrible injury," the répétiteur assessed. In his day, he, too, had married a fellow dancer. Now a widower, his life revolved around the little ballet company. He had always treated them all like family.

He kept pressure on Hannia's upper leg, the blood slowing, but still seeping out of the many wounds made by the explosion of bone fragments from her leg. "It will be many months before she dances again. If at all."

"She must get care," Jon agreed. He stepped in, sat down, took over the job of holding the pressure against the flow of blood.

Gregor looked on in dismay.

There were voices all around him, performers and crew whispering to one another as they witnessed the scene.

Two days to opening. Would they make it?

"We must go on," the director said. "We have investors."

"Gennifer can dance the part," the ballet mistress replied. "She has been a diligent understudy."

The director grunted. "Where the hell is that ambulance?"

As if summoned by his agitation, the theater doors swung open and two paramedics with a gurney entered the building. They wheeled their gear down the theater aisle.

"I will follow them in my car," Jon told the director.

The director nodded, breaking up the rehearsal. "We'll meet tomorrow morning," he announced. "Someone call the janitors to clean up this mess!"

Jon picked up his bag, retrieving car keys and pulling out street shoes.

He approached Gregor.

Jon pressed something cold into Gregor's hands. "You must have lost this," he said. "I found it in my bed." He spun around, walking towards the door.

Gregor opened his hand. He had, at least, found his missing watch.

4. Gregor

"I think we need a permanent audience," Hannia said. She was standing on the stage in an elaborate tutu. Extra money had gone into purchasing the indulgent fabrics that made it. Receipts had been picking up modestly.

"A permanent audience?" Gregor asked. He finished cleaning off a chair. Another row done.

"Yes," Hannia said. "Psychology. If you think other people are here, you'll be more likely to want to be here yourself. You could paint it, Gregor. You're good enough."

He did not reply.

"I want a variety of people—men, women—of all ages. *From* all ages. Joining the real audience. It would give the audience something to look at before curtain rise and between acts."

Gregor looked at the walls. The theater, as small as it was, still presented a challenge for such a scheme.

"Go, get some paint and start this afternoon. I think the novelty will attract people."

She walked off stage. Her supporting dancers followed her. Bryce, the man, and Gretchen, the girl. They were last season's additions to the company, presently learning the interpretive dance Hannia herself was largely choreographing.

She still has connections, Gregor acknowledged. She had been great in her day, expected to be among the best. That credit still was worth something.

I used to be a dancer, too. He assessed his body. It was older and less nimble.

Regardless of whatever he had done, his decline was Hannia's doing. She had been under funded, once her living expenses were accounted for. The theater was smaller, more run down, in a less desirable neighborhood than it should be. *Ballet!* He laughed, cynically. *Perhaps if she danced on a pole she would do better in this neighborhood.*

He sat down, resting a while, surveying the blank walls.

He began to imagine. The rows he would paint would mirror backwards, towards profitable oblivion. Opera glasses, feathers, fancy dresses with fake jewels. He could do this, he told himself, although the task was daunting.

And *she* would probably not be satisfied, no matter what the finished product looked like.

He had a bitter taste in his mouth. Anticipating the paint fumes, anticipating her displeasure. She was never happy with what was. She always wanted what was next.

The pianist started to practice, an oddly compelling piece, given its discordance.

"What are you playing?" Gregor asked, as he resumed cleaning the theater seats.

"'A Song for Athene,'" the pianist replied. He was a harried young man with wrinkles he did not deserve yet settling into his face. "The music is by John Tavener, the lyrics by Mother Thekla, an Orthodox nun. Hannia hates the way I play it."

She was never happy with the pianist, either.

"She says my timing is off," the pianist apologized.

It's her who's off, Gregor thought.

"It's beautiful." Gregor said aloud. "You play very well." He knew how little praise was allowed to anyone but Hannia. It was a satisfying dirty little sin, praising someone else.

"Thank you. It's a funeral song. You have to imagine an eight-part choir belting it out. It's magnificent then."

A funeral song. "Hannia will dance to it?"

The pianist shrugged. "Not something I would dance to, but she's choreographed something for it. Some sort of going to the graveyard bit. Nothing says art like romanticized mortality."

Gregor smiled. "Well, painters do better after they're dead. Why not dancers?"

The pianist laughed. He resumed his practice.

Gregor looked at the walls. If Hannia could dance at her own funeral, he would take care of her arrangements afterwards.

5. Hannia

Jon and Gennifer had danced very well together. Some said Gennifer was as good as Hannia.

Gregor visited Hannia every day in her hospital room. His own performances suffered from the time he spent by her side, and a new junior soloist was eagerly waiting in the wings for his spot.

At first, Hannia received many visitors, many flowers. In time, these dwindled, until all that was left was Gregor's self-destructive attention.

She progressed beyond expectations in physical therapy. It was prognosed that she could dance again, albeit never at the level she had before.

She was released on a cold gray day. Gregor picked her up.

"Home?" he asked.

She got into his car, pulled her coat around her. "No," she replied. "I really don't know where."

Gregor looked confused.

Hannia smiled weakly. "Jon has told me he knows about us. He has filed for a divorce. He says if I agree to his terms, he will not destroy me."

"It is all my fault."

"I cannot take the humiliation," Hannia replied. "I must dance again. And you—you, my faithful Gregor—you will make me a theater to star in. The people remember me. They are my public. They will come back to me."

"But the company..."

"The company? They put Gennifer on stage and say she is as good as me. She will never be as good as me!"

Gregor drove, aimlessly, but in some direction.

"Take me to the Hotel. When I am officially divorced, we will open our own company, and I will dance. My first dance," she paused, "will be *La Sylphide*."

She settled down, seemingly satisfied. "This will turn out all right, my darling, faithful Gregor. We will move on from this."

He drove toward the opulent Hotel she specified.

At least the world would know, at long last, that she was his.

6. Gregor

Gregor stood in his little garden. A cat's skull perched on the stump. He swung his club. It shattered the bones. He paused, letting the anger and the pain ripple out of him.

Hours before, he had sat in darkness. Waiting for *her* to arrive.

Gregor had sat in his car, in the cold night air, across from Bryce's apartment building. He watched Hannia enter.

Gregor knew that excitement in her eyes and that fire in her veins.

And now he knew Jon's feelings, also. *A bit late for empathy*, Gregor thought bitterly.

He watched their shadows embrace, like passionate Polynesian shadow puppets projected against Bryce's blinds.

At least I was smart enough to turn off the lights, Gregor remembered. Not smart enough to keep track of his watch, but that had fallen off him accidentally. Perhaps it was fate.

Fate! He snorted. *I'll give them fate!*

Gregor had happened upon the cat's skull quite by chance, a few weeks earlier, while driving back from the lumberyard. One of the businesses along his route had a marquee. The board complained about the small city's sanitation department. "Dead cat, one block ahead—two weeks, not picked up!"

So *he* had picked it up. *Doing a civic duty*, he remembered. It didn't smell as much as he had feared. He placed the carcass in his bucket and drove on.

It was a prize. He was glad he had it when he returned from seeing Hannia and Bryce. The two were no doubt presently in Bryce's bed.

Gregor's initial flush of jealousy evaporated as the bones shattered. Then he picked some of the fragments up. Considered them, bleached and lifeless in his hands. All its life, the cat's body had poured energy and calcium into knitting this bone. And now it was just spent shrapnel.

He was infuriated that Hannia had made Bryce her premier danseur, *then* her lover. Gregor she had unmade from the beginning. First her hidden lover, then her unloved husband, and finally not even a dancer on her stage. Jealousy at Hannia's new tryst was secondary; that he had been made little more than a footnote in Hannia's history filled Gregor with a queasy, vindictive rage.

A curse upon her! Gregor thought.

He held the bone fragments in his hands and spread out his arms. He twirled and released the bones from his fingertips. His body ached to be dancing again.

When the bones were dispersed, he stopped spinning.

He picked up the paint cans. *They could all go to Hell*, he thought, happy at the notion. *Hannia, Bryce, Jon, even himself. Where was it that illicit lovers went? The first level of Hell? Damned to fly about in some stupid circle for all eternity, caught up in each other's arms, getting in each other's way forever.*

Well, then, we'll dance on Earth as in Hell.

He had painting to do. A curse to put upon them all, to help the Devil take them in his time.

7. Hannia

It was raining, great drops of water tumbling from the sky. Hannia sat in the lobby of her hotel, her luggage by her side.

Gregor entered, his heart pounding. Hannia was beautiful, her long brown hair swept up elegantly around her head. She wore a lavender silk dress, her dancer's body radiant and firm. Amidst the sage colors and bamboo fixtures of the lobby, she appeared like an exotic flower in a secret garden.

He sat down beside her. "Well?"

"It is done," she smiled as she pulled a tri-folded set of papers from her purse. "I am a divorced woman."

Gregor opened his mouth to speak; she placed a fingertip on his lips. "Shhh," she said. "These are the terms." She opened the papers. "I am divorced. I have received a settlement, between Jon and the company, which is surprisingly sufficient. In return, I am to leave the company." She smiled brightly. "I can open my own company now!"

She posed herself on the edge of her chair. "Now you may ask me to marry you."

8. Gregor

Gregor started painting in the middle of the back wall. *Best seat in the house.* He smiled.

He was a good painter. Better than he had imagined he would be. Perhaps inspiration had something to do with it.

He wanted the first figure finished while the image of Hannia dancing into Bryce's arms still burned hot in his head. The rest would follow, centered around this character. Two, three rows deep. *She will have an esteemed audience*, he thought.

This first figure he painted sat in a large, regal chair. The figure wore an oversized coat and hat. *To hide his true form*, Gregor admired. He painted subtle shadows and highlights into the garments. Horns hidden by a hat, tail secluded under a long coat, cloven hooves sequestered in soft felt boots. *If the Devil is to pay for my troubles*, Gregor pondered, *I'll include the price of admission.* Lucifer, Angel of the Cursed, had a seat in the little theater forever.

Gregor was startled to hear soft footsteps.

Hannia? It sounded like her... before.

He turned around.

"You are a good painter," Gretchen admired.

Gregor felt suddenly embarrassed. Silly. Ashamed. "I'm okay at it."

She smiled. "I like the idea of a court," she said.

"Court?"

"Isn't it some sort of royal scene? With the throne and all?"

Gregor nodded, standing in front of the picture. "That was my idea," he said, stumbling over the words.

She paused, biting her lower lip. "Have you seen Bryce?"

Gregor's veins welcomed the return of ice at the sound of Bryce's name. It lifted his embarrassment. This scene was for Hannia and Bryce. Gretchen was not his intended audience. "No, I have not seen Bryce," he lied. And told the truth.

"Oh," she said. "He was supposed to run through some steps with me. It's okay. I'll catch up with him."

Her crestfallen face and tone betrayed her.

Gregor had told the same lie multiple times before, when seeking after Hannia. Long ago. When it was his arms she was falling into.

I might be the only person not sleeping with Bryce, Gregor thought.

Gretchen left quietly. Gregor knew her routine from his own heart. She would fumble around the theater slowly, hoping the lover would show up. Then she would realize that nothing was going to happen tonight. Fight dejection, go home. Feel empty. Dream about tomorrow.

Gregor felt sudden energy, a need to expand his creation. He started to sketch, penciled figures filling the false rows of painted patrons. Men, women. From all history. *Ancient Rome.* He painted in a contemplative Caligula, brow furrowed. *Forward in time:* Elizabeth Bathory leaned over to whisper in the ear of the Marquis de Sade. Murad IV glanced into a program held in his hands. Dictators, despots, murderers. Every nationality was represented. By their worst, dressed in their best.

Gregor took care to disguise them, ever so slightly. If there was a signature moustache, it was not painted. If there was an infamous uniform, the character wore a different outfit. Glasses went on and off in opposition to what had been worn in real life. He painted for hours without pause. The work progressed at an astonishing pace.

It was an infamous and sordid gallery that filled the walls. There to sit and watch Hannia dance.

Gregor stood back, pleased with his work. He doubted Hannia would ever recognize the figures. She would see only their furs and jewels and nice clothes.

He had brought the deeper levels of Hell up to see how they do it in the first level.

Let Hannia dance for them.

9. Gregor

Gregor stood in the shadows off stage, his club in his hand. He had rummaged through his boxes, finding nothing satisfactory to smash. He had to find something. Now he was scouring the backstage area, looking for rats caught in traps.

He was filled with unquenchable anguish. The police had called to inform the theater that they had taken Gretchen to the hospital. She had swallowed bottles of pills. Sleeping pills, tranquilizers, and anti-depressants. Washed them down with a fifth of scotch. Cheap stuff, not even worthy of her pantry.

Gretchen had figured out what was going on between Hannia and Bryce.

Gretchen was being worked on at the hospital, but they had told Gregor, as representative of the dance company, that it was unlikely she would make it. Even if she did somehow manage to survive, she would suffer terrible brain damage. She would never dance again, like she had. *Before.*

Gregor had cried. Cried like he never had before. Some of the tears had been held back for years, all the way from Jon's release of Hannia onto that cold stage floor. But the tears did not wash away the grief or the rage.

He *had* to smash something. Something to answer for the dying.

There was a sound at the front of the theater. Doors unlocked, opened, locked.

Footsteps in the foyer.

Bryce entered the theater clumsily. Gregor crouched in silence and watched.

Drunk. Gregor assessed. He could smell Bryce from across the room. *On good wine.*

Bryce took off his scarf and coat, laid them across the back of a chair.

"Gretchie!" he called out. He surveyed the dark theater with lascivious delight. "I'm sorry I'm late, my darling. I had things to do." He smiled, subtly.

Like Hannia, Gregor thought.

"Gretchen. I know you may be a little upset. After all, I laughed at your little marriage proposal earlier. But I can't be tied down right now. The ladies—the ladies in the audience want to fantasize, my sweet. They need to think they might have me. If I got married... Well, that would spoil the illusion. The only reason anyone comes here is to see me."

He looked piqued at the darkness. "Gretchen. Now come on. Come out of wherever you are." He sniffed the air. "It smells in here. Has that coddled old man been painting?"

He turned around; saw the figures, freshly painted on the walls.

Gregor frowned, but watched. He watched Bryce inspect the paintings.

Bryce went up to the first figure. "You're an ugly old fellow," he said "And you dress funny. But, got to admit, the old man did a good job painting you. You look almost real sitting there."

He reached out, touched the side of the painted figure. There was a small smudge of paint on his finger. "Not quite dry," he snorted, wiping his hand with a handkerchief from his pocket.

He looked at the figures, eyeing them all intensely. He began to look displeased. "What the Hell?"

He was recognizing them, Gregor suddenly realized. *Hannia would not have— but Bryce...* Bryce's recognition was not something Gregor had counted on.

But Hannia must dance for them!

"First," Bryce said, wine still fueling his tongue. "I'm going to find the old man, send him packing. It's time Hannia fired him anyway. Then Gretchen—our night is still young, my sweet. Are you hiding up there? I am coming to find you..."

He stepped up onto the stage. The backlights illuminated him against the darkness, making him a walking silhouette.

Gregor nestled in the wings, remembering the club in his hands. Panic flooded his mind. *How could he explain the club? No one would understand his habit!*

Bryce sauntered about, issuing threats to Gregor, lewd comments to Gretchen.

Gretchen, who lay dying mere blocks away, her flesh succumbing to the poisons she had embraced.

A curse upon us. A curse upon us. Gregor whispered. There was no outlet for his emotions. He could not purge this desperate fear and hatred from his soul. He tried to push the panic and anguish out with whispered incantation.

Bryce heard the buzz the chant made. He started towards the wing, where

Gregor crouched.

"A curse upon us! A curse upon us!" Gregor uttered the words, liberated by the sound they made as they were spoken,

The mantra filled Gregor with fire, a spell woven from sorrow and rage. Jealousy and despair. Rejection and loss. Vengeance and retribution. Yesterdays that should not have happened, tomorrows that should have been.

The buzz continued, Gregor's lips racing to keep up with the words. "A curse upon us. A curse upon us. A curse upon us."

Bryce followed the sound to Gregor's hiding place, seeing Gregor crouched in the darkness. "You crazy old man."

Gregor smiled, his hands embracing the readied club. Bryce approached. He would make a fine meal for the insects and the birds.

"A curse upon us."

10. Gregor

After he was done, Gregor stood, covered with Bryce's blood, upon the stage. He looked at the paintings and took his bow. He had been flawless in his execution, faithful to his emotions. It had been a magnificent performance.

After all, he had been a dancer, too.

He hid Bryce's body and cleaned the scenery. Then Gregor sat on the stage, rocking himself back and forth. Whispering over and over again: "A curse upon us. A curse upon us."

Basking in the sultry smiles of the damned.

Morgellons

The ultimate in nosocomial infections.

T he rain kicked up just as Dr. Lenore Keats made it into her office. She shook off drops of water as she walked past the reception area.

"Morning, Dr. Keats," the attentive receptionist said.

"Morning, Tricia."

"It's a real gully washer out there."

"Yeah," the doctor replied. "You got in okay?"

"I come in from the north side. The rain isn't hitting so hard there."

"Is Everett in yet?" Usually Everett Hayden, M.D. was in before her, but the rain had been heavier where he lived.

"No. Dr. Hayden isn't here yet." The receptionist looked at the young doctor; years of serving in professional offices had taught Tricia how to sense undue agitation.

"Everything all right, Dr. Keats?"

"Everything's fine. I'm just flustered from the traffic." She looked outside at the billowing, gray clouds. "What a way to start the day."

***

"You look happy," Everett Hayden said sarcastically when he saw Lenore. "You on decaf again?"

"I've had two cups of full strength this morning," Lenore said. "Traffic was bad."

"Traffic's always bad. What else? Something bothering you?"

"Did you talk with Tricia? She seemed to think I was off my game earlier, also."

"You're working something over in the back of your mind," he observed. He sat down, drinking a mouthful of coffee. "You crease your brow when you're thinking about something you're not talking about."

"It's a good thing I'm not married. I'd love to hear the advice you'd give my husband."

"Claire hates it when I give her advice—and she is unfortunate enough to be married to me," Everett Hayden replied, his blue eyes sparkling.

"I saw a woman at a bus stop on the way in," Lenore said, feeling that a quick confession would end the speculation. "She was covered in sores. She was actively bleeding from violently scratching her own skin."

"Was she homeless?"

"Yes," Lenore replied.

"We can't force people to seek treatment, and we can't force treatment on them," he reminded her. "I know the city is a little different from your circumstances back home. It will take time to adjust to seeing things that you want to fix, but can't, every day."

"She's probably schizophrenic. A little olanzapine might help."

"You can't just go around just giving antipsychotics to people—even the psychotics." Everett stood, his medium stature enhanced by his confidence. "Choosing to be ill is a personal right to some people. You just do what you can for those seeking to get better."

"I don't know why it bugged me so much."

"You're a doctor. You saw something broken and you wanted to fix it. Nothing wrong with that. In fact, if I remember your schedule today, you have quite a bit of fixing to do."

"You're probably right. The weather is crazy, and my day is booked solid. I guess I was just agitated."

"We have drugs for that." He smiled, leaving for his own patients.

"I'll stick to the caffeine," she replied.

***

Everett Hayden had one important appointment in the morning.

Joseph Vanner arrived with his expected punctuality, bodyguard in tow.

"Everett," Joseph greeted. He was dressed for the office, having already put in hours of work before most of his employees arrived. He sat down in a well-padded leather chair.

"Joseph," Everett greeted. "How are we feeling?"

"Fine, as a matter of fact." Joseph Vanner motioned his bodyguard out of the room.

"Ah, you trust me after all," Everett said, noting the bodyguard's departure. "I'd say you were paranoid, but a man with your wealth should have a healthy concern about his security."

"Paranoid or not, there are people after me," Joseph replied. "Or so my lawyers tell me." He paused, looking around. "I have a problem, Everett."

"What problem?"

"I have *things*. Things living inside of me."

"*Things*, Joseph?"

"Little worms. They crawl under my skin. I can see them sometimes, just beneath the surface."

Everett sat back, listening to his patient. "Do they itch?"

"Occasionally." Joseph Vanner's face became darkly serious. "I want you to do an experiment."

"I'm a clinician, not a research scientist. That's more along Lenore's lines."

"Of course. The new partner."

"She just joined my practice," Everett replied. "She has developed a small onsite laboratory in the backspace we weren't using. She's running some clinical samples for us, saving some money by keeping a few tests in house. But she has a research background."

"Then task her to figure out what's inside of me," Joseph said.

"You don't have anything with you? Any specimen that you may have captured?"

"No. And stop being condescending. This isn't imaginary. I've seen the tracks of the things. They move, Everett."

"Well, let me talk to Lenore."

"I'll be back this afternoon," Joseph Vanner said, getting up.

"But you and I are not done here yet."

"Yes, we are," Vanner replied. "Have Lenore clear her schedule—no doubt you have her seeing a hundred patients an hour. I want to talk to *her* when I return."

"Joseph..."

"Don't get too high and mighty on me, Everett. I'm the best thing that ever happened to you. I saved your ass. I pulled your practice out of debt when I paid off some substantial financial obligations you had incurred. You owe me."

Joseph Vanner walked out of the room, signaled his bodyguard, and the two left, disappearing into the approaching rain.

***

"Joseph Vanner wants to talk to *me*?" Lenore said. She was eating her microwaved lunch quickly before having to see her next patient.

"He insists. I'll take your patients while you talk to him," Dr. Everett replied.

"I don't feel comfortable talking to him."

"Even the richest man in town is made of flesh and blood. You're a doctor. Your job is to fix flesh and blood. You can't be intimidated by him."

"What's his problem?" she asked.

"Originally he came in for depression," Everett replied. "He reacted badly to his own success. His mind's way of coping with his achievements was to cripple him with overwhelming feelings of inadequacy and worthlessness."

"So why not just cut a check to charity?"

"That would mask the symptom temporarily, but not address the underlying issues. He knows that. He's one of the smartest men on the planet. I put him on olanzapine."

"And how is he now? Olanzapine is a good antipsychotic. We talked about it this morning."

"I think he has developed a delusional parasitosis."

"He feels things crawling on his skin?"

"*Under* his skin, actually."

"Olanzapine is a treatment option for delusional parasitosis. That symptom persisting while he is already on the treatment doesn't make sense."

"Which is another reason I'm letting him speak to you," Everett said. "I'm hoping that talking to you will shed light on what's going on with him. You could provide a fresh perspective. He and I may have too much history to get to the root of this one."

"Any sign of amphetamine abuse, or cocaine? He mingles with some pretty heady celebrities..."

Everett laughed. "No, not Joseph. He's not like your homeless woman from this morning, sitting on a park bench scratching herself to death courtesy of crystal meth or alcoholism or untreated psychosis. Or all three. Joseph is both more complicated, and in some ways, more fragile. He wouldn't be strong enough to make it as a homeless person."

"You're expressing some sympathy for the old woman. In your own odd way," Lenore noted. "I may get her in for treatment after all."

"Turning sinners into saints takes resources," Everett said. "*That* sort of strength Joseph has. He's given a lot of money to hospital buildings that both do and don't have his name on them."

"So, what's your initial diagnosis?"

"Have you ever heard of Morgellons?"

"They just did a news show on that syndrome. People think they have things growing inside of them, right? Didn't a bunch of people clamor into the local emergency departments claiming to have Morgellons right after the show aired?"

"Some of the people claimed to have things living in them, some claimed to have fibers growing inside them. Often they'll bring in little pieces of lint or debris, claiming it is evidence of their infection. Joseph didn't bring in anything he identified as evidence of his infection."

"No matchbox syndrome. Okay, send your man in. I've never seen a case of delusional parasitosis sitting right on my examination table," Lenore replied. "Truth is, the diagnosis has always fascinated me."

"Why's that?" Everett Hayden asked, regarding his young partner with curiosity.

"They say there's nothing worse than an itch you can't scratch; this is scratching you can't find an itch for. It may just be the only thing that is worse."

***

Joseph Vanner arrived early, placing his bodyguard by the door. "I have half an hour," he told Lenore sharply. "You good enough for that challenge?"

Lenore Keats, M.D. looked him over critically. "I'll get the exam done when the exam gets done."

"Quality over expediency?"

"Accuracy over malpractice," she replied bluntly.

He smiled broadly. "I can see why Everett likes your work. You'll keep him out of hot water. This time. Then I won't need to bail him out."

"Why did you bail him out the first time?" Lenore asked, setting up a few medical tools. Her curiosity was part genuine, part bedside manner.

She knew that a major malpractice lawsuit had nearly ruined Everett Hayden. He had told her that Joseph Vanner had paid for an expert attorney and salvaged Hayden's license and his practice.

"I am invoking patient-physician confidentiality," Vanner announced.

"Of course," Lenore confirmed. "I need to know what may be disturbing my patient."

"I'm in love with his wife."

"Claire?" Lenore asked, shocked.

"Saving Everett was the least I could do to keep her from becoming a failed doctor's wife. Now she's happy again. She has no idea about my affections for her. Neither does Everett."

Lenore didn't have a reply for that, medically or otherwise.

"Where do you feel the irritation?" Lenore asked. She wanted to find out where Joseph Vanner itched physically, now that he had revealed an emotional itch.

"On the inside of my right calf," he said. He lifted his pants leg up, revealing a red-orange patch of irritation.

He had obviously scratched himself bloody.

"I'll have to rule out ringworm, and a spider bite, in my differential diagnosis."

Joseph ran his fingertip over the rough erythema on his leg. The little purple blotches beneath the skin seemed to wriggle.

Lenore looked at the wound carefully, observing the unexpected movement in the wound with clinical fascination.

"Do you travel?" she asked.

"All the time."

"Anyplace exotic?"

"That depends on your definition of exotic."

She paused, looking him straight in the eye. "Don't BS me, Mr. Vanner. You know what I mean. Someplace tropical."

"No."

"Cleaned an attic? Own a cat? Sweat a lot? Been in a closet?"

"What are you trying to differentiate, my dear? My symptoms or my sexual orientation?"

"I'm doing my job, Mr. Vanner. When did your symptoms first appear?"

"About twenty-five years ago."

She stopped. "And you're just seeking treatment now?"

"I'll tell you the history of my infection," Joseph said. "It may assist you. I was in a business class, as an undergraduate. My professor was brilliant. He ran a Fortune 500 company by day and taught the not so privileged—like me—at night. He had a peculiar ring-like pattern on his cheek. I watched it. Over time it moved." Joseph Vanner paused, looking for the right word. "It *migrated.* One day it left his face. I saw it move beneath the skin of his forearm."

"And your point?" Lenore Keats was running her mind through contagious bacterial and fungal infections, trying to find a match.

"I was struggling in that class. Feeling overwhelmed. One day, I touched him."

"What?"

"On his forearm, placing my hand over his skin." Joseph Vanner smiled. "It was a subtle gesture, like a reinforced handshake. Given under the guise of gratitude for his service to those of us in the working class. But I placed my hand intentionally on that ring-like lesion. Soon thereafter, I never had trouble with business again. Everything became so easy for me. And now I run a Fortune 500."

"Have you been troubled by your success?"

"I have no trouble with success. I *had* trouble with losing. Before I got my worm. Then everything changed."

"You're brilliant, that's why you're a success. You're projecting something to make up for that—you really should talk to Dr. Hayden. This sort of thing is more his area of expertise."

"I don't want the help of the husband of the woman I love. Not for this," Joseph Vanner said. "I helped Claire, indirectly, when I bailed Everett out of hot water. I keep coming here to keep an eye on him. I don't want Claire going through that sort of humiliation again. No, Everett cannot help me, because I say he can't. This is something I want *you* to comprehend."

"What do you want me to do?"

"Look at these and tell me I'm delusional. Then tell me that Everett's voodoo can help me," Joseph Vanner said as he unbuttoned his shirt, carefully peeling it off.

His skin was covered in little ring-like lesions. They vibrated softly beneath his skin. Some unfurled and moved within his flesh.

Lenore gasped.

"Is it a delusion if you see them, too?" he asked her.

"Those aren't fibers," she said, peering closer. She pulled out a pre-packaged iodine swap. "Are you allergic to iodine?"

"Now you're interested?"

"I was expecting Morgellons."

"Something in my mind, manifested into a compulsive itching? No, Dr. Keats, these are very real."

"You've had them over twenty years?" she looked carefully at the writhing vermiform creatures in his skin.

"Not this many at once, dear doctor. I started out with one. But recently I felt a small eruption in the side of my neck. Then these appeared on my back. They move very methodically, down my arms, towards my hands."

"I'm going to extract one," Lenore said. "It looks subdermal—I won't have to cut deeply."

"And then? Examine it, publish a paper?"

"I've never seen *anything* like these. What other symptoms have you had?"

Joseph Vanner put his hand on hers. "I thought you thought my symptoms were delusional?"

She wiped his skin with iodine, coating it in the area over one of the worm-like lesions on his chest with a rich blanket of deep orange liquid.

"I'm going to administer a local anesthetic and then I'm going to gently remove one of these things. You may feel some pressure, and there might be a little blood, but you should be back at work in an hour. Let me know if the extraction site becomes infected or you get a temperature."

"So, I'll be what? A case study?" he asked. He winced slightly when the thin, stainless steel needle delivered the anesthetic.

Lenore Keats pulled out a sharp scalpel. "This is clinical, not research," she told him. "I need to know what this thing is. To treat my patient, not publish a paper."

"Are you sure the area is numb?" he asked.

"We'll find out," she returned. She steadied him, putting him in a position to best suit her spontaneous surgery.

"There is one strange symptom I forgot to mention," he reported to her, feeling the pressure of his skin yield to the sharp blade.

"Which is?"

"Once I got the worm, I felt like protecting it. I never want to give it up. It's a symbiotic relationship—it gives you an enhanced ability and you give it a home. Commensalism."

"You attribute your success to the infection?"

"You'll understand once you see it," he replied. "After I got the worm, my intelligence increased. My problem-solving skills were enhanced. I developed an instant sense for who was being honest with me and who was bullshitting me. For whom to trust, and for whom to avoid. For what projects were worth pursuing, and which ones were going to go bust. The worm made me a great success."

Joseph Vanner felt the organisms move, felt them burrow deeper into him, passing past skin and fatty tissues, and sequestering themselves in his deep anatomy.

"Damn!" Lenore exclaimed. "The thing wriggled away. It moved pretty fast."

"You'll grow to appreciate them," Joseph said. He felt her put a bandage over his skin. Reaching over, he picked up his shirt. "I'm glad you find them fascinating."

"Come in next week—we'll try again."

"I'll come in next month," Joseph Vanner told her. "That's when my schedule permits."

"But you're infested..."

"I know how to deal with these critters," Joseph replied, buttoning the last button. "Did I mention that about twenty of my business class went on to become very successful business people?"

"I don't see how that matters."

"Some of us are empty chairs, Dr. Keats. We just need the right being to fill us. To help us conquer our fears and depressions. To enhance our possibilities for success."

"Medication cured your depression," Lenore countered.

Joseph Vanner summoned his bodyguard. "My depression had nothing to do with my business acumen or my success. My depression was rooted in the love of my life being married to a doctor who couldn't be bothered to count his sponges. But *you*—I have more faith in *you*. With your calm, professional guidance, this practice will be very successful. That will keep Claire happy. She has a deep and enduring affection for this little medical office. And *her* happiness makes *me* happy. So, we all win." He paused. "By the way, those twenty odd classmates of mine—each and every one of them has the worm. We get together from time to time. To discuss future business opportunities. And philanthropic pursuits. Perhaps you can think of something to mention the next time I visit?"

He left.

The thunder roared as the next band of storms approached, and Lenore thought of the old woman from the morning, with no sure shelter from the elements. *Mentally unbalanced and homeless, where did the woman go?* Lenore wondered.

What happened to the empty chair, when it was filled with nothing but delusions?

***

The storms did not abate. Lenore went home, avoiding giving a report to Everett Hayden.

She was exhausted but filled with odd excitement.

The things that lived in Joseph Vanner fascinated her.

She fell into a fitful sleep, her mind filled with images of Joseph Vanner, his worms, the old woman on the park bench, and the sounds of the storm.

Lenore woke up at midnight. A profound itching radiated out of a small pinprick type hole on the back of her hand.

She examined her skin carefully, as the lightning illuminated her room, observing the subtle track of a small worm burrowing deeper into its new home.

Lenore did not gasp, which surprised her.

She would have expected surprise, anticipated revulsion. But something connected the worm to her psyche; the worm waking up her mind to the realization of possibilities she could not have comprehended before.

She let her worm take her down into sleep, where it began to fill her dreams, just as its brethren had filled the minds of so many before her.

She would call Joseph Vanner in the morning, to let him know he had been successful with his subtle handshake. He had passed his gift on to yet another.

She was not upset with him. He had done her a great service.

She was now happy to be one of those who *knew*.

By the Pond

There was a pond in the coastal area where I grew up; it was a popular spot for skinny dipping, swimming, indulging, and making out. There was a fence around the property, which would be put up, torn down, and replaced with regularity. This story was inspired by that secluded and forbidden place.

Robb Whelton was every girl's favorite kind of bad boy. Nice on the eyes, charming at first impression, and hinting at forbidden adventure.

Sunny was thrilled when he first called her five months ago. She told her parents she was going out on a date with a boy from school—another freshman at the local community college where she struggled to make good enough grades to transfer to what they called a "real school."

She didn't tell them her date was fresh out of his latest round of drug rehab.

Robb was blond, tanned, and taut muscles rippled beneath his smooth skin. His healthy physical appearance concealed a lifetime of smoking pot. And dropping acid. And getting high on mushroom tea. And ...the list went on. He swore it was everything "but never heroin," which was supposed to be positive personality trait. Sunny didn't even recognize the names of half the drugs he took. What she did know that most of the girls considered him one of the best looking guys around.

Robb had been clean their first date. He sparkled, brand new from twelve stepping and supervised living. They had dinner, went to a movie. Drove around. He spoke brightly of becoming a chef, loving art, thinking she was nice.

He also seemed responsible enough.

He sodomized her every time they had sex, to prevent her getting pregnant.

He had met up with an old friend, not long after he and Sunny started dating. Josh was brunette, tanned, oiled, and always smelled like tropical fruit.

Josh's folks weren't as well-heeled as Robb's. For Josh, there had been no rehab, no one around to just say no. Josh came with territory. *Robb's old territory.* Josh had met Robb at the mall. Offered him marijuana two minutes into the conversation.

One toke for old time's sake.

That ended the latest short stretch of sobriety.

Sunny wasn't ready to give up on Robb yet. She had seen him at his best; and figured she could wait out this temporary relapse.

She even tried to fit in. She stole a few of her mother's tranquilizers one evening, just to have something in her purse when they went to a party, in case any of his friends asked what she was into to. It was an absurdity that she selected the little blue diazepam pills because they accessorized well with her blue outfit.

Now it was late summer. Robb had plans for the humid Friday night.

He picked up Sunny while the daylight-savings-time sun still burned in the evening sky, then they got Josh. Robb talked about grabbing something to eat, going to a birthday party for someone Sunny had never heard of before.

The car, a Corvette, had been a present to Robb from his ever-indulgent parents. A gift for getting through rehab, for being clean longer than the last time. They had no idea how brief his latest wagon ride had been.

Josh retrieved a gaunt girl from a rundown old house in a neighborhood that smelled of cheap beer and sulfur. He ushered her noiselessly into the back of the car and slapped the back of Robb's chair.

Robb took a swig from a soda can and accelerated away down a lonely stretch of highway.

Sunny could smell the whiskey he had carefully added.

"We have time before the party," Robb told Josh. "Want to go skinny dipping?"

Josh laughed, pulling his tongue out of the gaunt girl's mouth. "Sure. You girls up for it?"

Sunny wasn't. "Where?"

"Pond, out by the plants," Robb said, running the fingers of his right hand up her skirt, under the elastic of her panties.

His fingers played in her. She went queasy, not thinking. "I don't have a towel," she complained. "I just put on my makeup and did my hair. They'd get messed up."

"You'll like it." Robb's erection pushed against the fabric of his jeans.

Josh went back to his girl. Sunny could hear slurping and groaning noises.

They drove past ever more squalid suburbs, until the distant lights of the chemical plants appeared beyond the abandoned cow pastures and the railroad tracks. A wash of red and gold painted the horizon, sunset enhanced by chemicals pouring into the thick hot air.

Robb pulled off the road, driving over a segment of fallen fence. He turned down a little dirt path for about a quarter of a mile. Tall grass, Chinese tallow trees, and a small ridge hid the area from the road. He parked the car beneath a dead tree near a small pond.

The pond was deep, blackish green, and square. Its surface shined like obsidian. Pampas grass grew around it wildly, silken heads gray in the light of the rising moon. Gulf muhly sprinkled the shoreline.

Robb lit and passed a joint to Josh. He offered it, in turn, to his date. The gaunt girl puffed obediently.

"We're lucky," Robb said, offering the joint to Sunny. "Usually the fence is up, and we can't get back here. But people tear it down from time to time. They say this is the best skinny-dipping hole in the area. No one can see you from the road."

Sunny declined her turn at the ganja bud. She had tried pot once. It made her lose all sensation of time. That disconcerted her enough to discourage future use.

Robb coughed happily, his voice squeaky from the weed. "Skinny dipping," he beamed, removing shoes, sports socks, and blue jeans. He picked up a soda bottle he had taken to the pond, hidden in the trunk of his car—a clear plastic two-liter size—filled with dark brown liquid. "Magic mushroom tea."

Sunny noted his car keys lying on top of his jeans. Stoned, he might lose them, and then it was a long walk home. She picked them up and secured them inside a zippered pocket on her vest.

Robb splashed into the dark pond, disturbing the salvinia floating on the pond surface.

Josh made all sorts of whooping noises as he joined his buddy.

The gaunt girl started to remove her clothes.

Something about her seemed mindlessly automatic to Sunny.

"Are you coming in?" the girl asked.

Sunny was shocked the gaunt girl had the assertiveness to start a conversation. "No, I don't want to get wet."

The gaunt girl neatly folded her t-shirt, placed it on top of her tired old jeans. "You know," she said, "You don't belong here. You're not one of us."

Sunny did not reply.

The gaunt girl continued. "You have a future. A brain. You can't seriously see this thing with Robb going on much longer. He's a total loser. I've known him nine years. Twelve tries at rehab. Sooner or later, you gotta realize that broken clock isn't even right twice a day."

Sunny was beginning to realize that: part of her was already losing interest in Robb.

The boys were laughing, talking trash. Saying "fuck" every three words, just to hear themselves say it.

"Water's fine," Robb splashed. "Get naked. Any other girl would already be in here with me."

Sunny declined again. The cool water had no doubt erased Robb's erection. She sighed.

"You think you can save him," the gaunt girl guessed. "The good girl rescuing the bad boy. Not going to happen. He'll drag you down with him." She paused, looking for convincing words. "Sometimes, you just got to save yourself."

The girl stood naked, except for a red headband holding back greasy hair. She walked away, picking a smooth path through the tall grasses, towards the pond.

Sunny heard her body glide into the water.

There was splashing and chattering. Marijuana smoke filled the air.

Sunny sat on the hood of the car. The mosquitoes were coming out, searching for victims.

She looked at the pond, imagining water moccasins and toxic runoff from the chemical plants in the murky water. She preferred swimming pools: turquoise, clear, and chlorinated. Ponds, by contrast, were covered in oozy green scum, although this pond seemed surprising free of grime and algae.

She heard a rustle in the grass.

Snake! Sunny feared, pulling her feet off the ground, onto the hood. She had heard once that there were fat timber rattlers hiding in the ridges of the sandy clay.

She took out a small flashlight she kept attached to her keychain. Directed the beam towards the rustling. An armadillo frantically scattered out.

Sunny let out her breath.

Watching it scamper away, her eyes fell upon something she had not noticed before. A dull, metal object, resting in the grass a few yards away. She slid off the hood, bored and needing something to do while the boys slugged back mouthfuls of drugged tea.

Perhaps the gaunt girl was right, Sunny thought as she walked carefully between the scrub bushes. She couldn't exactly see herself walking down an aisle and making babies with Robb. She couldn't imagine herself spending her life bailing him out of jail or visiting him in rehab. *Which his Mommy and Daddy will surely be sending him back to sometime soon.*

She walked towards the metal object, careful of her footing. The field was carefully maintained, despite being overgrown. *Someone* was tending certain spots in the area, while intentionally letting other parts of the property revert to their wild state. The property owner only seemed to keep the right-of-way tidy and maintained the no trespassing signs by the roadside.

Sunny was in an unkempt area now, the grass around her as tall as she was. Tallow trees, invasive and thriving, dotted the landscape in little groves.

She pulled back an arm's length of vegetation.

A car sat in the thick underbrush.

She approached it carefully, wary of any animals that might have taken up residence in the old vehicle. Its paint was faded, dull. The windows were down. It was intact, as far as she could tell. The hood was down, and the radio still inside. *Not stripped, not vandalized.*

There was a bumper sticker from a local high school's girls track team on the rear bumper of the car; two piles of clothes were thrown haphazardly on the passenger's seat. A ring of keys sat on top of them. Dust and rust covered everything, the calling card of elapsed time. Pollen blanketed the windshield.

There was a photograph in the front seat. A young man and a young woman. The girl's dark hair had a patch of white in it. Sunny reached in and read the back of the card: *Ian and Jess.* It was dated eight years ago.

She was intrigued by the find. The car appeared to have been driven to the skinny-dipping pond and then abandoned. The tags had expired years ago.

Eight years ago, Sunny noted.

Sunny looked past the car, suddenly aware that the grass was growing in weird patterns. Little islands of heavy vegetation were seemingly maintained amid cultivated ground.

She needed a better view, so she jumped up on the derelict car's roof.

Scattered throughout the field were at least a dozen more car bodies in various states of decay. Beyond them, she could see irregularities in the scrub, suggesting many more vehicles were out there.

There was no sign of mechanical distress in any of the cars she could see.

She shone the little flashlight beam at the next closest car. The keys dangled in the ignition. A Styrofoam cooler sat in the back seat, the ice long since evaporated. Unopened cans of beer and cola had settled on the cooler's bottom. *Probably still good,* Sunny thought.

She got off the car. Her first thought was an illegal dumping ground for cars, but the presence of keys in both abandoned cars she had looked at mitigated against that.

She could still hear Robb and Josh chattering and swilling their intoxicating brew in the background. Obviously, there would be no stopping by any place worthwhile tonight. The sun was beginning to dip low below the horizon, dark purples taking over the sky.

She moved back towards the parked Corvette, deciding to start getting them back towards town, so she could get home. Then she could watch a nature show on TV, snuggle down into her comfortable bed, covered with her plush animals. A multitude of toy zebras, given to her over the years by people who knew she liked those best.

The mosquitoes were still buzzing, and she hoped they'd provide a good excuse to get everyone out of the miserable dank pond.

Robb and Josh frolicked in the water, throwing handfuls of salvinia at each other.

The gaunt girl wasn't with them. Sunny had planned to ask her to get out of the water first.

Even stoned, women seemed to have more sense.

She didn't know Josh's girlfriend's name, which was a disadvantage, as Sunny didn't know what to call out. She was pondering options—*girl, girlfriend, honey*—when she noticed the girl's red headband wrapped around a little clump of salvinia, the little eggbeater like stalks holding it above the water that gently lapped around them.

The girl was nowhere to be seen.

Probably got out while I was walking around, Sunny thought. Practical things always filled her mind first, when she wasn't thinking with her G-spot.

Sunny looked around. The gaunt girl's clothes were still neatly piled up.

Sunny redirected her efforts to Robb and Josh, now both outrageously giddy. They were talking to the salvinia now, the full psychedelic effect of the mushrooms taking hold their brains.

"Hey," Sunny said, "Time to get out. The bugs are really beginning to bite. And I need to go to the bathroom. And I'm getting hungry."

She noticed a funny echo to her voice, as she called out. As if her voice hit something solid as it broadcast across the water's surface, bouncing oddly back at her.

She felt disturbed, as if something was watching her.

She shone the flashlight at the pond. In the water, just above the surface, two purple spots of light gleamed back, hooded by solid blackness. For a moment they considered her, and then sunk silently back down into the pond's dark waters.

Alligator? She wondered. It was possible, although the pond seemed too isolated and too small to support a decent gator. And alligator eyes glowed green. She had seen them before, taking a nighttime pontoon boat trip down a nearby bayou.

These were eyes glowing regal purple. They were also spaced more like human eyes rather than alligator eyes. But these eyes were hooded in a skull that didn't entirely match human dimensions.

She felt a calm urgency and backed away from the pond's edge.

"Robb!" she commanded. "Time to go!"

"Not yet, babe. I'm just getting my buzz going."

"I thought I saw something in there. Like an alligator. I think that you should get out. *Now.*"

Josh slung a mouthful of the tea from the bottle. "'No gators in here." He laughed. "Just a couple of snakes!" he reached down, grabbing himself.

Robb burst out into ridiculous giggles.

Their pathetic inebriation was grating Sunny's nerves. "I did see something."

"Probably Marta," Josh replied. "That bitch got all sulky on me. Hey," he took another swig of the drugged tea, "why don't you drive her back home? She's holding out on me, anyway. And Robb here says you'll give out enough for both of us."

Sunny felt sudden fire fill her cheeks. Robb looked suddenly ugly in the moonlight, promising Josh he'd pass her around like candy.

"I'm going in five minutes," she said icily, tapping her watch. "You have that long to get out, get your clothes, and get in the car. After that, you're walking home. I'll drop your car off at your house, Whelton. Five minutes. That goes for all three of you." *Freaks*, she added silently, as she turned back towards the car.

There was a gulp in the pond behind her, followed a watery gurgle. She turned around. *They're playing games, trying to scare me*, she thought, angrily.

Robb stood in the middle of the pond, on a little island of weeds and muddy clay singing and playing air guitar. His blond hair was silken in the moonlight, shadows outlining his body.

There was a *plop* and the empty two-liter plastic bottle bobbed up from beneath the water's surface. A small trail of bubbles briefly surfaced.

"Josh, stop being an asshole," Sunny called out. "I'm getting sick of this. I'm going to go. For real." She opened the door to the car and sat down in the driver's seat.

"One minute, and I mean it." *Why weren't these idiots responding?*

She closed the door, turned on the engine and switched on the lights. In the low beams she could see Robb, on his own island of reality, talking and gesturing to fans only he could see. Her hand was on the gearshift. She glanced at her watch. They had one minute.

The water moved.

It caught her attention.

The pond shivered again, and Sunny looked closer, peering over the steering wheel. A low shadow circled Robb, like something gliding underneath a carpet. Smooth and silent, barely disturbing the murky water's surface. It changed direction, moving towards the edge of the pond: *towards her.*

"Robb!" Sunny yelled out the window. "Get out now!"

There was a whisper in the breeze, as it came off the water's surface. *You do not belong here.* It was a coarse imitation of Marta's voice.

Sunny's fingers flew over interior buttons, raising windows, locking doors. Then she put the Corvette into reverse and backed up towards the little dirt road. She braked, moving the gear into drive, surveying the scene as she felt surveyed by it.

Don't go too fast, she whispered to herself, *don't wreck the car.*

She honked the horn. Robb ignored her. The water trembled, bubbling up at the edge of the pond.

She pushed the accelerator, mindful of the rough terrain. Her wits gathered about her in sober fear.

Steady! Steady! She reminded herself, as the car bounced over the rippled clay. She merged onto the little dirt path leading away from the pond.

In the rear-view mirror she could see the eyes, violet and blazing, rising above the pond's edge. They stopped, at the boundary between water and land.

Teeth smiled at her: a sick, knowing smile.

Not gator teeth, not human teeth.

Very sharp teeth.

Then the violet eyes sunk purposefully back into the depths.

The wake on the water began to approach Robb.

She hit the open road, finding herself in the only car out there. Sunny rejoiced as she finally hit a patch of road lit by streetlights.

Sometimes you just got to save yourself.

***

Sunny drove Robb's car to his house, just as she promised. Luck favored her, and his parents were still out for the evening. She would have to walk home, a trek of over five miles. But that now seemed like the most minor of inconveniences.

She dropped the keys in the front seat, wiping her fingerprints off the steering wheel, the buttons inside the car she had touched, and the keys.

She wasn't sure why, but she wanted to have some options for constructing her story.

When they asked, she would say that they drove back early. Robb dropped her off at home and then went back out with Josh and Marta.

No, she hadn't seen or heard from any of them since then.

***

She drove by the old, nearly empty stretch of road every month or so.

The small piece of fence alongside the street went up and down in a cycle. It would be down for a week, then up for six. She wondered about that. The property owner seemed to be maintaining the forbidden entrance in a cyclical fashion.

Sunny could not shake the vision of the thing with the purple eyes.

She sometimes questioned if she had even seen anything. There was comfort in doubt.

Probably a contact high created the sighting, she told herself sometimes, hoping she had not seen what she had seen. But she knew better. *She knew what she had seen.*

The worst part of her memories was that she somehow knew that the thing with the purple eyes was satisfied that Sunny had not told her story to anyone.

***

Robb, Josh, and Marta had illustrated their share of milk cartons, mass mailing flyers, and small posters pinned hopelessly to trees and power wire poles. The trio had not been seen or heard from in twelve months. Rumors circulated about a drug deal gone bad. The drug paraphernalia and weed in Robb's glove box supported that theory.

No one ever asked Sunny anything. It turned out that no one knew she was with them the night they disappeared. It was her secret to keep.

A year after the disappearances, Sunny drove by the stretch of road. It was a clandestine anniversary, to an event she could tell no one she attended.

A man was putting the fence piece back up. A woman was raking leaves up nearby.

Sunny's curiosity got the better of her. Despite the feeling in her stomach that told her to drive on, she stopped.

"Howdy," she said, getting out of the car.

The man eyed her sternly as he nailed the fence piece back up.

Sunny noted the fresh tire tracks that went under the now raised fence segment. Tracks that did not replicate their going in by coming back out.

The woman stopped raking. "This here is private property," she said.

"You the owner?" Sunny asked.

"No," the woman replied. "He is."

The man spat tobacco onto the ground. "You have business here?"

"Some friends of mine went missing a year ago. Last I saw them, they said were heading here," Sunny answered. There were too many details in the story she didn't want to have to explain to anyone. Not her parents, not the cops, not Robb's family.

"You never told anyone they were here, did you?" the woman asked, panic rising in her voice.

Sunny shook her head. "No. *Something* stopped me."

The man and woman exchanged knowing glances.

"Better to keep it that way," the man said. He tested the fence, making sure it was secure. He replaced a NO TRESSPASSING sign. "You saying something won't bring them back."

Sunny looked at the woman. The woman's dark hair was prematurely graying, but her hair had a distinct white patch. And she bore horrific scars. Terrible deep rips had marred her face, leaving disturbing welts across her cheek. Her hands and forearms were scratched and pitted, as if deep claws and razor-sharp teeth had torn into her.

About nine years ago? Sunny wondered.

"Are you Jess?" Sunny asked.

The woman froze.

The man moved forward. The woman motioned for him to stop.

"I'm Jess," the woman said. "How did you know that?"

"I found Ian's car," Sunny said.

"You must be mistaken," Jess replied.

"Purple eyes," Sunny said.

Jess looked away. "You never go back out there," she warned. "You come out once, you're luckier than you'll ever know. It won't make the same mistake twice."

The man spat at the ground again. He looked at Jess, pointing at Sunny. "If *she* had gone missing there would have been a ton of news people down here. EquiSearch, on their horses, looking for her. FOX News all excited about their next round-the-clock story." He looked at Sunny. "What were you doing here? It isn't a place for a pretty co-ed to be."

"I was at a crossroads, although I didn't know it," Sunny replied. "I saved myself."

"Keep saving yourself," the man ordered. "By saying nothing to anyone. *Ever.* Enough secrets in this ground as it is. You tell, people will be out here. Looking. Curious. A lot of them won't come back out. Maybe none of them. And that will be on *your* head."

"I've already covered evidence. Left people to die. I don't want anyone to know that."

***

Jess raked, trying to forget Ian's plaintive dying calls to her as she sprinted faster than she had ever sprinted before in any track meet, racing away from the pond: *Jess! Jess! Come back! Don't leave me here!*

But it had caught up to her anyway. Her only saving grace was that the thing was not as fast on land as it was in water; it got tangled in the vines and underbrush as its teeth and claws ripped into her. She had managed to free herself from its grasp, collapsing from the loss of blood by the roadside.

When she had woken up in the hospital, the old man was sitting by her bedside. Telling her she was a trespasser and an accessory, and that she needed to keep her mouth shut, for her own good.

Jess envied Sunny: Sunny had been spared hearing any screams.

***

The old man walked Sunny back to her car. "Your part is stay quiet and never come back by here. Then no one need know you left anyone to die. Agreed? Containment, young lady. We have containment. That's the best we can hope for. Trust me, we can't kill it. The damn thing won't die. We've tried. Ten carloads of men one night, armed with guns, bows, knives, flame-throwers, hand grenades— you name it, we were armed with it. You know where those cars rest now. You know where the bones of those men rest now. I was the only one who made it out. Used to be hundreds of people would go back there. Now, I have it down to about a couple dozen a year."

"We know what will happen to them," Sunny said.

"Way I see it, the people sacrifice themselves. They go someplace they're told they shouldn't go. They pay the price. And the thing seems satisfied to stay where it is. You, me, Jess—we know what that thing could do if it got out. Well," he rubbed the back of his head with a heavily scarred hand. "You *would* know. Except that you were never here. So, you don't know anything. Right?"

"I have no idea what you're talking about. I was just stopping by to see if you needed any help raking," Sunny replied.

The man smiled, a quick, sad smile. Nostalgic and grief-stricken. "We have it under control. Thanks for your offer, though. You have a good day. You're a blessed young lady."

Sunny nodded, starting her car. She wasn't ten carloads of over-armed men. She wondered how she had managed to survive. Much less emerge unscathed. Perhaps it knew she didn't belong there.

As she drove away, Sunny couldn't help but look past the tall wall of weeds and trees. Wondering what the purple-eyed thing dreamed of during the long weeks between its feedings.

***

At home, Sunny sorted out her plush zebra toys, placing them in a basket to donate to a local charity.

They were no longer her favorite animals.

Zebras forded rivers, thick with crocodiles.

The strong let the weak be eaten by the predatory reptiles. The healthy gave up the sick. Those in the prime of life sacrificed the old and very young of others, mindful only of their own survival.

It was enough to save themselves.

The zebras made her uncomfortable. They reminded her too much of herself.

There was now a new creature in Sunny's life.

Something that she needed to resonate with. *To elevate herself from prey to predator. To believe she was stronger than she was. Stronger than she had proven to be.*

She pulled a toy crocodile out of a paper bag.

She felt oddly kindred with crocodiles now.

They saw such carnage and said nothing. Lurking in their protected spaces, with the elements at their advantage, waiting for the hapless to wander too close. Knowing that the others in the herd would let them feed.

Using a pair of scissors, she pried the toy's eyes out. With a needle and thread, she attached sparkling amethyst beads into the empty orbits.

It was as close to the thing in the pond as she could get.

She had created a secret space in which she belonged.

She was saving herself.

Of Dust

A tired man takes on a lonely mitzvah, hoping to secure death for the dead.

When the Cloud came, it brought life back to those who ought not have it anymore.

So, when the Cloud appeared, Edwin Trace naturally headed off towards the cemetery. Where else would you go when you knew that zombies were about to be raised?

Edwin had three cans of free-flowing salt with him, seventy-eight ounces in all, not counting the handful of little packets collected in his truck's glove box from the drive-thru windows of various fast-food restaurants.

He hoped it would be enough. He said a little prayer, just in case. You didn't want to get caught with an insufficient amount of salt when the Clouds came.

Salt had taken on increased value again. In medieval times, salt was the delineator between the rulers and the ruled. A valuable commodity, salt was placed in the middle of the table. The rulers would sit "above the salt," and the servants below it.

Now salt formed a line between the living and the undead. *You definitely wanted to stay above the salt.*

Edwin Trace did not consider himself an especially religious man. He knew the Psalms—most of them—by heart, because his mother had sung them to him when he was a child.

"*Confitemini Domino,*" she would sing, as she washed the dishes after dinner, or walked the babies that came after Edwin. "*I shall not die, but live, and declare the works of the Lord. The Lord has punished me sorely, but he did not hand me over to Death.*"

His mother had been a hard-working woman who never enjoyed much luxury in her lifetime. After she became a widow, she had talked often about moving to the city and getting a better job; she would imagine the ease of her life, if only she had more money. But it never happened. Not that it mattered. She never seemed to mind not having luxury. She tended to her obligations and kept her nose out of other people's business.

Now, Edwin Trace was driving towards the small country cemetery where his mother's grave was located. The salt was secured in a box, buckled into the passenger seat beside him.

There was no way he was going to let his mother's body become a damned zombie.

He listened to the radio as he drove. The radio announcer talked about the location of the Clouds, inserting the updates between country songs. There was even a popular tune out currently, one in which the man's wife died, and he hoped she stayed dead. "*Although I want to see your blue eyes again,*" he wailed, "*I don't want to see your Tennessee smile replaced with an undead grin. You stay in Heaven, darling. And in my time, to you I'll come a'calling.*"

Somehow country music ballads and zombies mixed. Perhaps the two-step was so straight-forward a dance, even the zombies could master it.

The "Clouds" were officially "of unknown origin." Edwin suspected that somewhere, someone knew more about them than they were telling. Things like the Clouds rarely spontaneously generated themselves.

Like most evil, Edwin suspect, *human hands had probably created them.*

The Clouds, despite their ill-omen, were actually beautiful to look at. They were like lightning storms, best appreciated from a distance. They were almost lavender in color.

Majestic and large, the Clouds soared high into the atmosphere, as if they wanted to pluck the dead directly from Heaven. They rained a precipitation, but it was not just water. They rained a substance that was said to have no effect on the living. Those results were according to a study conducted with research grant money awarded from the tobacco industry.

Edwin took the reported findings with the proverbial pinch of salt. And a *literal* pinch.

Because while the effect of the Clouds on the living appeared harmless, the effect on the dead was much more notorious.

The substance that rained out of the Clouds seeped into the ground, much as any other water-based substance would. But if the water came into contact with dead human tissue, it would reanimate the remains. The dead would claw their way out of decaying tombs.

That was if they were lucky enough. Those enshrined in well-built or new secure coffins writhed inside their prisons. In the large corporate cemeteries, the groundskeepers would break open the cemetery seals and dig up the perished, just in case any of the precipitation had penetrated the graves. Then they would sprinkle salt on the corpses. In essence, killing them again. The zombies would slip back into the quiet sleep of death.

People were sprinkled with salt now, before being buried. "Seasoned embalming" was an actual term.

Television scientists postulated that sodium chloride interfered with the reanimation chemistry initiated by the Clouds.

Edwin had never studied much chemistry, so the analysis meant little to him. But he had seen garden slugs killed with salt, so perhaps there was something in common between reanimated flesh and slugs.

The bodies the Clouds summoned arose mindless, desperate, hungry, and in despair. The zombies were not hungry for living human flesh—that was B-movie mythology. The bodies hungered for something they no longer had. Something the body remembered, even with nothing human left inside the empty shell.

The zombies lolled around the Earth like wayward cattle. They were disruptive and frightening, but fundamentally harmless. *They were actually more like deer,* Edwin thought as he approached the cemetery. *But deer could be more dangerous than the predators that stalked them. More people died every year because of deer than bears. Only about one person was killed each year by a bear, yet twenty deaths were caused by cows, and fifty-two by other mammals. Other mammals like deer, which could cause fatal traffic accidents and other calamities.*

But even worse, by Edwin's estimation, were some of the living. They tormented the resurrected bodies, beating the corpses, using them for target practice, or indulging in even more vile acts. He heard the stories on the news stations, wondering what was wrong with some people.

Luckily, the Clouds that created the zombies were predictable. It was a weird new part of life, to keep up with the location of the Clouds. When they were seen, people would rush into action to stop the dead from being raised, or to place them back into death as quickly as possible.

Edwin Trace arrived at the cemetery, watching the Cloud approaching. The wind rustled through his thinning hair. He wore his old field clothes, made of closely woven fabric and fitted at the cuffs. He could smell the dusting sulfur on them, powdered over him to dissuade the chiggers from crawling up his limbs and biting him. If a thing could bite, it would try to bite Edwin. That included the zombies. He intended to prevent them from having the opportunity.

A monstrous Cloud was on the horizon. It tracked directly towards the graveyard, as if it knew the dead were there. It was like how some people thought that tornadoes targeted mobile home parks: the Clouds almost always went directly towards the dead. The more dead, the larger the Cloud.

That couldn't be a mere coincidence, he reasoned.

Edwin parked his truck by a low rail fence designed to keep vehicles out of the cemetery grounds. There had been problems with vandalism a few years earlier. Kids driving off-terrain vehicles between the graves, knocking over the tombstones and monuments. *It was a sleepy little town,* Edwin acknowledged, *but you couldn't figure out something better to do on a Saturday night other than tear up hallowed ground and spray-paint hate symbols over the graves of people who never did you any harm? What was wrong with people? Say what you will about the zombies; they seemed to have more common sense than some of the living.*

It had been Edwin who had constructed the little barrier, and it had been him who cleaned up the graveyard after the attacks. He got permission from the people who regulated the cemetery grounds and reconstructed headstones and patched together monuments. They really didn't care much about the cemetery; they were more than happy to let Edwin assume responsibility for the non-profitable ground.

Edwin even learned the difference between a cemetery and a graveyard: a graveyard is usually smaller than a cemetery and a graveyard was frequently associated with a church. This was a cemetery, out on its own, with no church near it. No parishioners to care for it.

He had planted fresh plugs of grass between the headstones and managed to raise enough donations to put fresh flowers at every memorial on All Saints' Day. *It is a blessing to do things for the dead,* his mother had taught him. *Because it is true altruism. The dead can't pay you back. And disturbing the sanctity of the final resting places of the dead? No good could come of that,* he thought.

The cemetery was small, abandoned by its original owners decades ago. Large conglomerate funeral homes and cemetery companies provided most of the burying services now. They had established large modern cemeteries located conveniently to the more affluent neighborhoods. The places all had welcoming names like Forest Meadows or Tranquil Acres, as if the living didn't know what price had to be paid to reside in such a pretty place.

Only a few people remembered this little old cemetery even existed. It wasn't officially taking new residents, but funerals happened from time to time. It was named Our Lady of the Resurrection Cemetery, even if there was no church associated with it. It seemed an ironic name now, as he watched the Cloud approaching, seeking to prematurely raise the dead. He wondered if anybody else would get there in time, to help him with his task.

The families and friends of those resting at Our Lady of the Resurrection sometimes helped tend the grounds and graves, assisting Edwin with his unpaid duty. Preachers still showed up every now and then, to inter dead. They weren't supposed to. But everyone in attendance at those burials was someone would keep quiet about the service. It was something special to be at a clandestine funeral, an event both wonderfully holy and earthly illegal at the same time.

The lack of government interest into the cemetery was going to be helpful to Edwin this afternoon: The bodies were not over-buried. There were no concrete seals. Just simple wooden coffins lowered six feet into consecrated clay. Here, dust was allowed to become dust again.

The cemetery's biggest adversary, prior to the Clouds, was an environmental group, concerned about decaying flesh adversely affecting the ecosystem. But they had moved on to other concerns, and the remote little cemetery in the middle of nowhere became a back-burner cause. *After all, death and decay are natural events.* Edwin thought scathingly. *Bears not only poop in the woods, they eventually die, are scavenged, and what remains of them decays in the woods, too. It was the natural order of things. What was wrong with some people?*

Edwin's immediate task was to toss salt over the graves. Even a few grains over each body was sufficient; the Cloud's precipitation would become just rain and the dead would continue to enjoy their tranquility unabated.

He stepped over the small fence and walked towards his family plot. While the Cloud moved slowly and deliberately, he had to apply himself purposefully to the task.

He stood over the graves of his mother, father, and his older brother, William, who had died in Vietnam just before the fall of Saigon. There was a fourth stone already in place, inscribed with the words *Edwin, faithful son and loving brother,* along with his date of birth and a dash. He almost regretted having that engraving done already. It was disconcerting to have two-thirds of the information pertinent to his passing already etched into the marble. *As if he was already two-thirds dead.*

He had other siblings, younger than him, but they had all left for the city. None of them ever visited anymore. According to them, there was nothing to do in the sleepy little town, unless you were into knocking over headstones and tearing up the grass that grew in sacred soil.

What was wrong with my brothers and sisters?

In their appointed times, Edwin reasoned, his other siblings would be buried in places with pretty names like Forest Meadows and Tranquil Acres.

Edwin sprinkled a scant handful of salt over the ground and around the family headstones. *That would be enough.* He wouldn't be distracted by seeing the bodies of his parents and brother crawling towards him.

The graves next to theirs were those of Mr. Witkins and his wife, Joy. They never had any children of their own, and Mrs. Witkins had spoiled the Trace children. She baked delicious, sweet fruit pies almost every day for William, Edwin, and their siblings. It was a tribute to metabolism of growing children that the Trace children had not been massively overweight.

Edwin threw pinches of salt over their plot.

He reasoned that three cans of salt would be more than enough for the entire grounds. He poured the salt into a leather-lined basket that he used for sowing seeds. Then he walked downs the rows of graves methodically, gently dispersing the white crystals.

In the strange light of the Cloud, the salt glistened as it fell, like a rainbow of tiny mauve crystal beads.

Edwin had heard that the salt could be used to subdue the risen flesh, but he did not want to test that claim. He had no desire to see dead bodies, moving or not moving. He had heard that the many of the bodies were like soap, thanks to the embalming process. Squishy, slimy, saponaceous corpses covered in the garish make-up the mortuary used. The very thought revolted him.

He moved to the edge of the cemetery.

Hidden in a grove of weeping willows at the border of the cemetery's property was The Garden, where the babies were laid to rest. Most of the grave markers bore only one date, making him feel ashamed he had discounted the gift of having two dates to inscribe on his own headstone.

There was an unfathomable sadness to the little garden. Stillborn babies and other infants who didn't make it very long were buried amidst little whirly fans, small toys, and little solar-powered nightlights. Mrs. Klinghoffer tended to this part of cemetery and was raising her daughter to take over the chore when Mrs. Kinghoffer herself became a resident of the cemetery's soil.

Mrs. Klinghoffer even performed the grisly task of scooping out the little bodies and severed limbs from the biohazard dumpster behind the family planning clinic. She would collect the sawed up little limbs and still-trusting faces, gently placing the bloody bags into tiny boxes. She would dig holes in the ground of The Garden, then place the bodies into cold earth that was kinder to them than human hands. She would give them names and laminate index cards she would place above their graves. It was their only identity on Earth, the only recognition of their humanity.

If the city council objected, they kept quiet. Because Mrs. Klinghoffer also helped bury the homeless, the Jane and John Does left unclaimed in the city morgue, and anybody else who happened to die or have unidentified remains discovered in the county. If their name wasn't known, she gave them a name, something to be remembered by. Even if just by her.

But the Klinghoffers were out of town, so Edwin knew it was up to him to guard the most vulnerable dead. He looked up to the Heaven, where the God knew all names.

The Cloud was nearly at the perimeter of the cemetery. It smelled like rotting citrus, moldy and tart. The Cloud began to approach more rapidly now, as if it somehow knew it was close to its target. Edwin sprinkled salt rapidly over The Garden. He did not want to see those innocent bodies rising from their tiny graves. He didn't even want to imagine that.

From there, he moved to a separate section in a much older part of the cemetery. In the misguided days of the past, segregation had seeped into even the society of dead. In the past, non-Caucasians were buried in separate sections of the cemetery. Edwin spread salt over the graves of the dead buried before the Civil Rights Movement had erased the odious practices of separation.

Pharaohs and paupers, his mother had taught him. *We're all the same once we're put in the ground. Skin color doesn't matter when the skin sloughs off of your bones.*

He placed a handful of salt carefully, lovingly, and respectfully over the graves of Sgt. and Mrs. Kirby.

Mrs. Mamie Kirby had been a widow by the time Edwin met her; she taught Edwin how to play the piano, filling him with the rapturous energy of Southern gospel music. Edwin's mother had sung while Mrs. Kirby played the piano out at the revivals. They were best friends, choosing love over the haphazard assignment of melanin quantity in their skin.

Ironically it was Edwin's mother who was always trying to change the amount of melanin in *her* skin. Every summer Edwin's mother had tried to get a tan. Every summer she ended up looking like a crawfish straight from the boiling pot. "God made you perfect as you are," Aunt Mamie would scold. "Don't get all wrapped up in getting a tan. You spend half the summer getting burned and having to slather aloe vera gel all over you."

Edwin's mother should have listened to Aunt Mamie. It was melanoma that killed his mom. Aunt Mamie was there at the hospital when Edwin's mother had died, weeping and holding her old friend's hand.

The Kirbys had two children before Mr. Kirby died.

Sgt. Sheppard Kirby had died in combat. The Army chaplain who had attended to Sgt. Kirby in his final moments had visited with Edwin, on this very spot, many, many years ago. The chaplain recounted those last fateful minutes. Mr. Kirby had lay dying, among so many others. The chaplain had made his grim rounds, giving last rites among the carnage. He had sat next to Sgt. Kirby, holding his bloodied, war-stained hand. At the end of the recitation, the pastor looked at Sgt. Kirby and said, "God bless you." Sgt. Kirby, with so few words left, grinned through the pain and grime and replied, "That's the first time a white man has ever blessed me."

The chaplain shook his head. "He was so covered in blood," he recollected, "That I had no idea what his skin tone was. All I knew was that there was a bloodied battered man, dying. Beneath the blood, son, we're all the same."

Sgt. and Mrs. Kirby should be allowed to rest in peace, Edwin thought, as the salt fell from his fingertips.

In short time, Edwin had covered all the graves with salt.

The Cloud had reached the edge of the cemetery with hastened purpose. Its strange rain began to splatter against the ground; the drops made little hissing noises as they encountered the grains of salt. The slightly purplish drops gave off little puffs of smoke, extinguished by the salinized soil.

Edwin started to head back towards his truck, a few tablespoons of salt still in the last remaining jar. It had been close, but he had figured the quantity necessary within a reasonable degree of accuracy.

Then he smelled it. An offensive odor, like burning hair.

Then he heard it. A rattling noise, like popcorn popping inside of rusty cans.

It wasn't a pleasant smell; it wasn't a pleasant sound.

He turned around. There was a columbarium, just off center in the cemetery. Little recessed holes in its structure housed the ashes of the cremated.

Edwin froze. He had not considered the ashes. Surely, they could not be brought back to life?

He started to move towards his truck; he would need more salt, and the little packets of salt in his truck's glove box were now needed.

The rattling grew more intense, little cracks fracturing the marble facings that covered the compartments in the columbarium. The sepulchral structure shuddered, a squealing internal wind ripping it apart. Ashes exploded outwards, congregating in the air. The mass hissed like a swarm of angry bees.

Then the ashes noticed Edwin.

He started to run, as fast as his aging legs could carry him. The mass of ash aimed itself towards him, hurtling itself as a corporate arrow. He realized he could not reach his truck in time.

He stood his ground, his last handful of salt in his hand.

The ashes swarmed, coming directly at him. He threw the handful of salt into the ash cloud, just as it was about to touch him. The cloud of charred remains shrieked.

The salt crystals convulsed inside the ash cloud; sections of the cloud began to fall out of the mass, in ordered succession. Individuals, he thought, the ashes of individuals together for one last time, attempting to be alive again, attempting to be human again. Each clot of ash had been someone.

In the end, one set of ash remained, suspended in the murky air, trying to reach him. He dusted the salt clinging to his palm from his hand and threw those remnants at the ash. It gyrated briefly, then fell to the ground.

The Cloud's mauve shadow largely dissipated, having found nothing to fuel it. A small fragment of it crossed over the silent graves, moving down the road. It was still seeking something.

Edwin was alone in the cemetery, with no witnesses, living nor undead, to what had happened.

He dusted himself off. He went to his truck and sat inside. He removed the small packets of salt from the glove compartment. He was now underpowered. But he needed to follow the small fragment of the Cloud, to stop what it was seeking from becoming undead.

It seemed wicked to bring despair back again.

But the little cemetery was still and quiet. The evening sunlight was painting the horizon a pretty golden color. Edwin knew he had work to do in the coming days, to clean the grounds and repair the columbarium. At least his work there would be done.

He had heard that once the Cloud had passed over, no Cloud would ever visit the same space again. It was as if the Cloud left a signature, indicating that the ground had been cleared.

He followed the remnant of the Cloud. It seemed to trace its way parallel to the lonely stretch of state highway, hovering low over the densely overgrown woods. Then it paused, beginning to rain.

Edwin stopped on the highway shoulder and got out of the truck. The Cloud, seemingly satiated with its hunt, disintegrated.

He walked warily into the thick underbrush, happy he was wearing his sulfur-powdered clothing. The birds chirped overhead, finding their roosts for the evening.

He heard a scratching noise, low and methodical.

Edwin tore open a packet of salt, making sure the other packets were accessible in his pocket. Something was moving. He just hoped it was a *singular* something.

There was a terrible odor. He looked at the ground, reddened fingers covered in black scorch marks gripping at the bed of moist soil and fallen pine needles. Its nails were covered in dirt and moss.

He covered his face with his left arm and threw some of the salt over the hand. It stopped moving.

He looked at the hand. It was a woman's hand. Chipped red nail polish still covered the fingernails.

He got into the truck and telephoned the sheriff.

"Edwin?" the law enforcement officer greeted. "You get out the cemetery all right?"

"Yes, sir. I took care of it. The place will be quiet now. Just like God intended."

"You're a good man, Edwin. Thank you for taking care of that. We had all of our deputies called over to Serenity Grove, that big cemetery close to Grovetown. Hundreds of people buried there. I doubt there's any salt left at the local grocery store. Bad night to be boiling up some pasta."

"I found a body, out by the state highway. You should send someone out when they're freed up. I already salted it. Poor woman. Her body's already gone through Hell at least once. *Requiescat in Pace.*"

"Crap. That's the second Jane Doe remains we've found this week."

"The body is in the woods a bit. I'll text you the location. It's a shallow grave. Only one there, as far as I could tell. Or smell. It was a woman, maybe in her thirties or forties. Probably had a rough life. Her hands were worn and bloodied."

"We've had five missing women in the last year. There may be more, we don't know. All in their mid-thirties to sixty years old. Since we found one, finding a second may be informative. You may have helped out a cold case."

"They say that's what the Clouds were developed for, right? Cold cases and such." Edwin asked. "I saw one of those programs. They said that some forensic scientists made up a batch of microbes that could change color to purple if they detected human remains. Like luminol for blood. But this was for finding hidden human flesh. Some sort of chimera organism. A bit of this, a bit of that. They used it in Argentina, after that earthquake, as a demo. To find the trapped people and the corpses. But then something happened. The microbes changed. Now they make the Clouds and make zombies. When will people learn?"

"I'll come over myself," the sheriff said. "*You* need to get over to the tavern. I'll buy you a steak dinner and some scotch. Least I can do to thank you for your service."

"Thanks, but I'll take a rain check. I need to get out to the cemetery early tomorrow. Start cleaning up and repairing the columbarium."

"Jesus. I forgot about the columbarium. Were there any problems?"

"Nothing I couldn't handle. Make sure the deputies spread salt in the mausoleum at Serenity Grove. The urns are inside a structure and the rain shouldn't be able to fall on them directly, but better to be safe."

"Cemeteries are too much a part of your life, Edwin. A living man shouldn't be so at peace with death. Stop by the tavern. I'll send a deputy out with you tomorrow, to help make the work go faster."

Edwin sighed. Perhaps he did need to spend more time with the living. *Perhaps that was what the raised flesh was trying to do in its frustrated, mindless way. Trying to remember what it was to be alive.*

He sprinkled a few grains of salt on himself. He wriggled his fingers. *Yes, he was still alive.*

"Okay," Edwin acquiesced. "What time?"

"You get over there now. I'll tell them you're on my tab. Tell them to turn the television station to some sports. Any sports. Girls Tiddlywinks if that's all there is. Just *not* the news."

"Any reason why?"

"A cloud passed over some celebrity's unsalted grave in California. I can't keep up with the living celebrities, much less the dead ones. The paparazzi stalked the reanimated body. I kid you not. They swarmed all around the resurrected corpse, flashbulbs exploding in the zombie's lifeless eyes. Some decent person came up and threw some salt on it. Himalayan pink sea salt. Only in California do you fight zombies with fancy gourmet salt. The news stations play the video every ten minutes, it seems. I've had enough of zombies for a lifetime. I'm having extra salt poured on me when they bury me. Just in case."

"Me, too," Edwin agreed. "We both deal with dead people too much, Fred."

Sheriff Fred Livingston nodded his head. "I'll call the crime scene unit on the body you found in the woods. No excuse not to get yourself to the tavern now, Ed. Your work is done for today. Detective Kirby will handle the details from this point on. That body will bring her out of that big city office of hers."

"I just poured some salt over her parents' graves," Edwin mentioned. "They were good people."

"They were the best," Fred Livingston agreed. "You, too, Ed. You're the best, helping us out like this."

"I feel like there's something wrong with me sometimes, Fred. Is it normal to care for the dead so much?"

"People should care about the dead. That's just plain old-fashioned respect. There's nothing wrong with you, Ed. Nothing that a whiskey and a sirloin won't cure, anyway. You're a good man, Ed. Never doubt that. Everything's all right with you."

Everything's all right with me, Edwin smiled, taking the turn towards the tavern. Those few words reminded him that he was alive. He felt lighter than he had in years.

So light he could almost imagine himself soaring into the Heavens, like a majestic purple Cloud, wishing that everybody could feel so alive.

Twins Without Moments

Stories about twins often feature the special bond twins reportedly share. This story is no different.

Mona didn't like the way the girls looked at her. It looked like they were sharing secrets about her.

The two girls were twin sisters with straw-colored hair, cut short so it bobbed around their chins. They wore school uniforms: even without the insignia showing, the uniforms screamed Catholic school. They wore tailored, neatly starched white shirts and pressed mock tartan skirts. On their feet they wore little black buckle shoes.

They stood close together, whispering and looking at Mona, reading each other in that peculiar way only twins can.

As they skipped away there was a peculiar urgency to their step.

They had seen something and were not going to share their vision.

Mona frowned; it was a rotten enough day without the strange encounter. She was upset enough, thinking about the impending days.

Marcos was coming home on Monday.

He had served his time and the stupid fucks were letting him out of jail.

In her hands, Mona carried a modest bouquet of flowers for her dining room table, not entirely understanding why she was sprucing the place up.

Marcos certainly didn't deserve it.

She walked with the flowers as if she were going to a grave, arriving at the Italian restaurant where she had agreed to meet a friend, Denise, for lunch.

Denise knew about Marcos.

Why did they have to be twins? Mona thought as she sat down. The little girls' penetrating gazes disturbed her.

A voice interrupted introspection. "Hi, frowny face."

Mona looked up. Denise, radiant as ever, sat down opposite her.

Denise picked up on Mona's sour mood. "Are you ready for Monday?" she asked, slinging her purse over her chair, opening the red, white and green menu.

"No," Mona replied. "The house is ready. But..."

"You're not."

"I can't believe I agreed to take him back in."

"He had no place else to go."

"Yeah," Mona chafed, "and whose fault is that?"

They placed their orders. Mona chose something with an Alfredo sauce, Denise opting for a salad. Mona was happy for that. She didn't want any red sauce on the table. Nothing that looked like blood.

"Are you scared?" Denise probed.

"No. I'm over five years old. Too old for him to kill."

Denise sensed an impasse in the conversation. Ordered a glass of wine. Merlot. Mona despaired. Red wine was even worse than red sauce.

The twin girls had unnerved her. Just when she thought she had it all under control. Maybe it was just her imagination projecting, remembering Marcos's crimes. Mona had always been more impressionable than she wanted to be.

"I have a gun. You can borrow it," Denise offered.

Denise was from Texas. Weapons always seemed so natural for Texans, like they had an evolutionary adaptation to bearing arms.

"A gun would be too quick," Mona replied. *Texas.* She thought wistfully. *They'd have stuck a needle in his arm in Texas.* Then he wouldn't be coming home.

A waiter brought them their drinks.

"You know," Mona said, fiercely squeezing a lemon into her iced tea, "They talk about victim's rights—that's fair. They talk about criminals' rights. They even give the families of the victims a chance to speak, to be recognized. But what about the families of the perpetrators? Wives, girlfriends, mothers, sisters, daughters, aunts, nieces. Good Lord, what about us?"

"I think most people would agree you're some sort of victims, too..."

"The Hell they would! We're pariahs. We nurtured the bastard, gave aid and comfort to the enemy. Turned a blind eye, perhaps. Washed their laundry. Fed them. Gave them a safe place to sleep and replenish their energy. I tell you what we are—we're the unconvicted."

Denise gulped down a mouthful of wine.

Once her tirade was over, Mona didn't bring up the topic again. The subject of Marcos's homecoming left unresolved.

That suited both of them just fine.

***

It was Sunday night and Mona couldn't sleep. She flipped channels on the television, hoping to find something that would distract her mind long enough for exhaustion to sneak in. She was tired, not wanting to watch the *E! True Story* of Hervé Villechaize. *Again.* But that was all that was on, except for the rotating weather forecast and inane infomercials. (*And how much would you expect to pay for all of this? If you call in the next twenty minutes...*)

Marcos was due in tomorrow afternoon, a taxi scheduled to carry him from prison gates to her front door.

It was a quiet evening. Cool, with winter just blowing in. The slight chill in the air was reminiscent of Thanksgivings and Christmases past. Those before Marcos discovered dealing drugs made him a quicker buck than any honest work he felt inclined to take.

She remembered falling asleep on the couch one Christmas evening, exhausted from the stress of getting everything ready for the holiday. Marcos had tiptoed to where she slept, left a teddy bear with a big red bow in her sleeping arms. The next morning, they awoke to a fresh blanket of snow, powdery and clean. The sunlight reflected off the snow's surface. They were so excited that they rushed out into it, throwing snowballs at one another with ungloved hands. When Marcos saw how much her hands hurt, pink with cold, he took her inside. He made three cups of steaming cocoa. One for her, one for him, and one just to warm her fingers.

Mona almost smiled, recollecting the old days. But then her mind fast-forwarded. Marcos was not that man anymore: a worm had crawled from inside his butterfly.

She vividly remembered the night they picked him up.

The cops banging on the front door, papers in hand, cuffs ready. Dragging a stoned and barely coherent Marcos off the couch, reading him his Miranda rights. Marcos screaming at her to bail him out of jail as they pushed his head into a waiting police car.

Law enforcement pressed into the house. A court had given them a search warrant, given them permission to tear the whole place apart. *Everything.* Even Mona's room and belongings, she quickly discovered. Apparently, the papers didn't cover putting anything back, and Mona had stood dazed in her pajamas, her neat home in shambles around her.

There had been no bail in Marcos's case.

His crime was too reprehensible.

When she heard the story, she was glad she couldn't bail him out. Even if she had all the money in the world, she would have been happy to let him rot.

Marcos's story splashed across the papers, and even now she knew the neighbors pointed to her house and retold the tale to newcomers.

Months before his arrest, Marcos had traveled with a fellow drug dealer to the remote home of a supplier. Methamphetamine producers who cooked the drug in their home kitchen. Surrounded by green fields and empty highway. Where the fumes of their batches dispersed quickly into fresh country air.

Something had gone wrong. Marcos's partner wasn't happy with the cooks. He expressed his displeasure by slitting both their throats.

It would have been bad enough, to stop the story then. But the police hadn't responded to a call about two dead meth maggots. They had been summoned to the location by the anguished calls of grandparents, who had gone to check on their grandchildren.

The meth maggots had kids. Three years old. Left with corpses for parents. They had tried to survive, little hands lifting drops of water out of the toilet bowl. Little fingers dipping into sugar, munching on their last cereal flakes. Trying to open cans, but not strong enough to work the lids open. Pouring what they could out of tiny holes in packets, little last drops of tomato flavored sauces. In the end, it wasn't enough, and they had starved, resting weary little heads on the decaying flesh of what had passed as parents.

They had been twins, little twin girls with golden hair that fell in pretty ringlets.

Mona had seen a picture of them in the newspaper, taken with grandparents a year before they died. Smiles beaming, cheeks flush with life.

Marcos turned state's evidence, cutting a deal. He'd only been the driver, he swore. He didn't slash anyone's throat; he didn't know about the kids. His lawyer negotiated a solid plea. And Marcos had served the time it called for.

Now he was coming home. Tomorrow. To Mona's quiet home in her peaceful neighborhood.

She sighed, watching the channels change.

Thinking of the twin schoolgirls from earlier in the day, with their piercing eyes.

Maybe it was just paranoia. That she thought the world judged her as well.

Her mind kept going back to the twins. The way they moved together, exchanged knowledge between them with a glance.

She had read somewhere that all twins had a psychic bond. A connection existed that allowed them insight into each other. Knowing what the other knew. Some sort of paranormal phenomenon that kept them on parallel tracks. Even separated, by time and space. Pursuing similar studies and goals, practicing the same hobbies and beliefs, marrying similar spouses.

Twins and twins, she despaired. How old would the little girls have been? They were three when Marcos left them to die.

The schoolgirls were about the same age the dead twins would have been now.

Mona stopped herself. It was a coincidence; one she was unusually sensitive to. The girls probably weren't even looking at her.

She felt sandy tiredness irritate her eyes.

She closed them and was swallowed into a dreamless sleep.

***

Marcos was home, the worm triumphant.

He had arrived; she had fed him.

He spent the evening in a sullen, restless mood. He did not bother to thank her for dinner or accepting him home. He retired to the couch with her remote control in his hands, flipping channels.

They did not speak much.

Mona noted that he had new tattoos. Prison had changed him. Not for the better.

He was more bitter and older. He glanced nervously at the telephone, like he was looking for an opportunity to use it.

She did the dishes and read a little. Eventually she announced that she was going to bed.

She locked her door. Afraid, even in her own house. *Again.* Just like the last night he was home. The night she found out.

She could hear him downstairs, talking on the phone. Loud outbursts interjected into his conversations. He shouted obscenities and spoke of plans.

Making his reconnections.

Mona lay in her bed, her hands on her chest. Thinking of the two schoolgirls. *What had they seen?* She worried.

It was a shame that the psychic visions twins shared couldn't be transmitted beyond them. That collective knowledge would surely benefit the world, Mona thought.

Then her mind turned, even as she fought its direction. To the other twins, the ones that had died.

Their blue eyes sparkling in a faded photograph, little bows in their hair. Sitting with grandparents, in a Christmas picture taken the holiday before they died. Before Marcos helped rob them of every moment the future may have held for them.

There would have been good times, holidays with grandparents, Mona thought, a tear slipping out of the corner of her eye.

Why hadn't the grandparents kept the twins? They could have saved them. Mona felt a twinge of pain within her, a dark, deepening well opening inside her.

Things were already unraveling. Marcos had only been home nine hours and she already knew that there would be no rest from the past.

Eventually Marcos turned off the television and went to his room.

She heard his body rest on the guest bed she had made for him, the box springs creaking slightly with his muscular weight.

When she was sure he was asleep, Mona went noiselessly down the stair. She heard Marcos snoring.

She went into the kitchen, looking at the table. Remembering him putting the cups of cocoa down. Kissing the top of her head. Snowflakes falling off her into the hot liquid set before her, melting in the steam.

She stood in the dark kitchen, wondering how Marcos had done the things he'd done.

Like lie on the stand.

Mona *knew* that he had killed the mother of the twins, while his partner slew the father. She knew that he had known about the babies and left them to their fate.

But no one ever called her as a witness.

She pondered these things in her heart. *Is this how it felt, Marcos, knowing that you were about to kill someone?*

She took a large knife out of the knife block and tiptoed to where Marcos slumbered. Where she was providing him lodging and peace.

Marcos was in a deep sleep, never noticing her as she crept into the room.

She stood over him and plunged the blade into his throat.

Blood erupted everywhere.

He snapped up for a second, as much reflex as reaction. Mona had severed the artery.

He collapsed into a puddle of warm red fluid. It kept pumping out of him, longer than she'd expected.

His eyes stared up at her. The worm twisted, accusing her as it died.

Then the massive blood flow stopped to a trickle, the afterbirth of trauma. There was no pulse to push blood through quieted vessels.

She paused, wondering how far violence could have taken her. If she had not practiced the self-control Marcos never bothered to master.

She turned the knife towards herself, knowing that she could never be like him. She could feel the worm move inside her, wriggling in dark delight. Tasting the blood she had spilled.

She sat on the bed, and dug the blade deeply inside her thigh, severing the femoral artery.

The pain and shock were more than she expected, and she contorted into a crumbled ball beside Marcos on the bed. Feeling the worm cry out in anger.

"We deserve this," she said to Marcos's body, as she felt her body succumb to violent chills. "We'll never kill again."

We deserve this.

Me for not stopping him then, she thought. *Him for what he did.*

And there were the future crimes he would have committed, she told herself. Some undoubtedly already planned, him sitting in her house, using her phone.

Knowing that gave Mona a sense of peace.

He was unrepentant. The psychic bond she shared with her twin brother had kept time with the violence in his soul, just as it always had.

Mona living in the shadow of big brother Marcos, born two minutes before her.

She wondered as she died if that is what the twin schoolgirls had seen. If they had sensed her resonant darkness.

Then Mona's mind heard it beginning to snow. Just like in all those Thanksgivings and Christmases past. The snowflakes melting before they could suffocate the ground, cleansing the earth of the stains death left behind.

Marie's House

I read an article on reincarnation. And I wondered, what if the baggage of the last lives were carried through to the present—and could not be discarded?

There was a dripping sound at the end of the hallway. Little droplets rhythmically hit the floor, their music resounding off the tiles.

Marie approached the noise cautiously, a baseball bat in her hands. She knew it would do no good, but it made her feel better.

The hallway was long, slender, and divided into discrete sections. The low-wattage recessed lighting did not provide enough lumens to illuminate the ends of the hall sufficiently. It was an unfortunate consequence of the design she had followed.

Little arched windows, set high, let in adequate light during the day. In the evenings, the windows were portals for the low light that burned inside; the long extension of Marie's house glowed like a shard of warm coal in the night.

Tonight, there were ripples of aqua and turquoise light on the ceiling.

Like water reflecting, she thought. There was a lovely deepness to the swaying pattern on the ceiling, the little drips falling like rain.

But there was no water in the hallway. Nor any source for it.

Marie felt queasy, success riveting her mind. Her hair stood on end.

She approached; one section of the hallway was distinct from the others. It glowed a soft blue, the sound of water trickling down the wall.

Marie stood at the edge of the blue light, not daring to enter. She gripped her bat, in happiness and fright.

At the far edge of the non-existent waters, soft shapes shivered. Shadows moved.

Marie's mind flooded with fear. Primal and commanding, it urged her legs to flight.

She ran back to the body of her house and slammed the heavy door to the hallowed hallway shut.

She trembled in horror and glee.

Her hallway had been designed to act as a trap, to capture spirits crossing over.

It had succeeded.

***

She slept, before she could summon the courage to enter the locked hall again.

In her dreams Marie remembered lost lifetimes.

She recollected memories of past lives, their imprints playing in her head. In this remembrance she was a lost woman, who just tried to keep thinking about the money she was procuring. It took her mind away from the man's touch, away from his probing. He was paying for his own pleasure, not hers.

Marie hated what she had to do but could see no alternative. She couldn't read, she had no skills. In the nineteenth century, education was not a luxury she had been afforded. Prostitution required no book learning.

Now no family would claim her; no man take her for a wife. It was a daily challenge for her to earn enough to eat for the day, to afford to share a small room with other women, a leaking, dirty roof over their heads.

The old city air was thick around them, as he got what he was paying for in the corner of an abandoned mill. The pulpy smell of old, damp paper blended with the fog, making the atmosphere smell like cheap paste.

He was paying rent on her body, using her as a more anatomically correct hand.

He was an odd one, though. She remembered noting that he looked around a lot. Most of the Johns kept their eyes shut, or they focused on something. Her breasts, the wall, their own hands. Something.

He was different. His eyes darted about nervously. And he did not get down to business quickly. Looking back, she should have known he wasn't interested in renting her body for sex. He was interested in stealing it forever.

His desires were carried on the blade of a knife. As many thrusts as most men used on her before, he cast with sharp steel.

She was dead before she had a chance to react.

The smell of paper still repulsed her, as her last sense from that life had been the particles of damp pulp trapped inside a nose that could no longer exhale.

Marie woke from the memory, in the soft gray moonlight.

She thought about the ghosts, trapped in her hallway, the azure watery reflection dancing on the ceiling.

Now that she had them, she would have to do what she had always intended to do.

Right her own wrongs because no one else would.

She poured herself a glass of cool water. It tasted good, the nothingness comforting as she felt the sharpness of her memories fading.

The dream had been of two lifetimes ago. When she had been the prostitute, left dead in an abandoned mill. Her blood formed a shallow black pool in the moonlight.

Her killer was never really pursued. Never caught, never punished.

I deserved better, she thought bitterly.

She had carried those scars into her next life. Recollections chiseled into her soul.

She remembered her last life, also, the life immediately before this one.

She was at a truck stop, running away from a boyfriend who battered her. She walked out of a diner and shop, after buying some supplies for the road.

It was nighttime, and she remembered the mill. Perhaps it was the moonlight; perhaps it was the smell of a truck parked there. The truck was carrying newspapers, the inky smell dissolving in the mist.

A man followed her out. She walked with a purpose and he passed her. Then, as she struggled with too many keys on a chain, he turned back.

He walked towards her.

She panicked as he approached, his big feet silent and slow. Like clown's feet. Floating towards her, eyeing her strangely.

She wasn't going to die again. She grabbed a brick sitting on the asphalt, her mind seizing on any weapon of opportunity it could identify.

As she struck him his skull cracked inward, like a large, hard-boiled egg.

The police report said she'd struck him nineteen times. She didn't remember any of them. All she could recollect was the feeling of the cold brick in her hands, then sitting next to his bloodied body, her hand shattered with the force of her own blows.

It turned out he was just going back to the truck stop diner. He had forgotten his wife's anniversary present inside. He was just going back for a gift.

She spent that lifetime languishing in jail. Eventually she died there, old and crippled. The state had been too frightened to execute a woman, especially one who seemed to suffer from a mental defect. Their prisoner was a woman who kept talking about her past life as a prostitute, who had been stabbed to death in an old paper mill.

And now she had two deaths carved into her soul.

***

The moon was still in the sky, even as the sun began to rise. The night was unwilling to yield to the approaching lightness.

Marie opened the door to her long hallway. Just inside the door stood a statue, reverently erected in an ornamented alcove.

It was a statue of the Nemesis, the goddess of revenge and retribution, the Guide of Souls. Marie placed a magnolia flower at the statue's feet. It was difficult to worship a lost deity.

Marie worried that she was merely imagining the rituals, making up the prayers herself.

In her heart she felt familiarity to the rituals, as if a lifetime from ages ago illuminated the rites for her. She was comfortable in the sensation that she had been a priestess in the temple of Nemesis, her service in the ancient temple faithfully serving her now, as she had faithfully served it.

There was no comfort for Marie in modern faiths. She had died a whore, died a murderess. She needed the priestess she had been to guide her now.

Marie's guilt sang in her, a siren's song, lighting her way back to the world of the dead.

Her hallway was her portal. Lined with columns that spoke of Grecian glory, dividing the hall into discrete sections. The hall was only sixty-six inches wide, but it stretched out for ninety feet.

Marie had bought up little plots of land, adding on to her hallway year after year. The city had even recognized it as an attraction. "The Long Hall," the city chamber of commerce called it. Her neighbors called it "Marie's Folly."

It was a poor imitation of the temple the shadows of her mind remembered. That temple had been carved into a long cave hidden in a hillside, excavated and fashioned by the faithful. Lined with flickering torches, resounding with the gentle cascade of water trickling down the cavernous walls. The cult of Nemesis attending to their devotions while the full moon washed muted light into the mouth of the cave. She remembered fasting while the moon disappeared into the maw of the night sky, the new moon a temporary eclipse that denied them the power of the goddess.

Marie had built this modern temple with money she had won in a game of chance, sitting in a giant, well-lit casino. Surrounded by statues of the Greek gods.

Praying to Nemesis, Goddess of Vengeance.

Vengeance. Modern faiths didn't offer that devotion much anymore.

Marie approached her destination in the long hall, the section that had become an ethereal pool. She watched the cerulean reflection play on the ceiling.

She peered into the murky light.

A shadow burst from the nothingness, directly in front of her face.

Startled, she jumped back.

She had forgotten that spirits could move as they wish.

The face was a girl's, perhaps twelve or thirteen years old, dripping with water. Her lips were frosted blue, her eyes sunken and dark.

A smaller shadow, the shadow of a young boy, clung to the girl's leg. His lips were purple, his blueberry cheeks glistening with cool water.

"Mom?" the girl asked. Her voice had no echo in hallway.

"No," Marie said. "I am Marie. I am here to help you."

"Where are we?"

"My Goddess's House. You are safe here."

The girl motioned for Marie to step over, into the undulating blue light.

Marie shook her head. "I have to find out who you are first," she said. "Spirits come in many forms."

If they were bad ghosts, Marie would draw a circle of sand and sea salt around them, allow the full moon to take them to Hecate's crossed arms.

If they were good, she had to arrange for their avenging.

Two spirits revenged, she thought, *will cleanse the dual stains from my soul.*

***

Marie quickly identified the captive souls.

A woman appeared on the evening news, crying crocodile tears, petitioning the return of her children. Marie recognized the girl in her hallway as the missing daughter from a photograph broadcast on the television.

The woman, named Ulrike, told a vague story of unlikely abduction, of her children gone and her car stolen.

Marie knew better. She prayed for strength and fortune.

A few days later, when the woman ducked out of sight of police and news crews, Marie tempted the woman into her car. The opportunity for privacy and secrecy that Marie offered worked well with Ulrike's penchant for subterfuge and covertness.

Once home, Marie overcame her quarry and wrapped the woman in ropes and duct tape.

When the full moon was high in the crisp nighttime air, Marie dragged the bound woman into the hallway.

The moon's rays filtered through the panes, washing the hallway in milky light.

Marie paused at the statue of her guardian. With a sharp knife she slit open one of the woman's fingertips, letting the blood drip over the goddess's feet.

The blood was black and still in the shadows.

The woman started to cry. Her eyes asked: *Who are you? Why are you doing this?* This time the pleading was genuine.

"How much were your children worth?" Marie asked. "A hundred thousand? A million? Was it just the insurance money? Or is there some man who didn't want them?"

Ulrike tried to say something through the gag of gray tape.

Marie dragged her down the hallway. Ulrike tried to throw herself to the ground, to impede Marie's progress. Marie was annoyed at the woman's squirming.

They arrived at the dancing blue light, the sound of gurgling water.

The shadows looked up. *They have been waiting all this time*, Marie thought, *but not as long as I.*

The woman's eyes grew wild and large. She tried to bolt away. Marie threw her to the ground, put her foot on the woman's back.

The girl floated over, her lower body little more than mist. The little boy followed his sister. He shivered, yet comforted himself with his sister's presence.

The woman struggled to free herself, then looked up and saw the ghosts.

Marie smiled, watching the girl's sullen expression, her blue lips quivering.

"Annabelle," Marie said, "I've brought you a gift. Something to free you."

"Mommy," Annabelle said.

The little boy clung tightly to his sister. He tried to look at the woman, but averted his eyes, filled with terror at the sight of her.

"Ulrike," Marie said to the woman, "Behold your children. You thought you had seen the last of them?"

The woman was sobbing, almost convulsing. Her body was tightening into a ball, like the little roly-poly bugs Marie had played with as a child.

Annabelle hugged her little brother. *Martin*, Marie thought, remembering the reward posters.

"Children," Marie said, "behold your mother."

The children had been reported missing, but Marie had figured out the truth. The phantom water that engulfed the children was a reflection of their tomb.

The mother had drowned her children. For profit? Out of desperation or depression? For a man? Marie didn't care about that woman's motives.

She had motives of her own. If the two children could avenge themselves by slaying their murderer, then Marie would be saved.

The image of Nemesis, standing in awesome, vengeful victory, filled Marie's mind. *These victims for the victim she was; this killer for the killer she was.*

"Annabelle," Marie said soothingly, "You remember, don't you? How she killed you? You and Martin?"

Annabelle knelt, her blue, cold skin transparent in the dancing shards of light. The phantom water trickled down her face, dripping off her youthful chin.

The woman was saying something underneath the tape, rocking madly.

"You can destroy her, Annabelle. Touch her, and she dies. She drowned you and Martin. Claim her life, for taking yours. Touch her with the chill of death."

Marie was wary of the hands of ghosts. Their touch, like viper venom, could be as deadly as they chose it to be.

Annabelle shook her head. "No."

"What?" Marie questioned, confused. "I brought you here for this special purpose. This is a temple, Annabelle, to avenge the powerless. You must do this!"

"For us? Or for you?"

"For all of us," Marie said, comforting and cajoling. "I deserve this. I *need* this. I can't take the memories anymore."

Annabelle hugged her brother. "We are going to leave this place," she said, "You cannot keep us here forever."

"I can! You are trapped."

"Soon the moon will fade, and when it is new, we can escape."

How had the girl come by that intelligence? Marie's heart skipped a sick beat. That was ancient knowledge, knowledge only the priestesses knew. Was the girl like her? A kindred spirit from lifetimes ago? Was that why she had gravitated here, her murder so close in geography, her spirit recognizing the temple's rough form?

"I need you to avenge yourself. You understand, don't you?" Marie pleaded. "This woman killed you! I've given her to you, to exact your revenge."

"To give her what she has earned?" Annabelle asked, "Just like you?"

"There's nothing wrong with that."

The girl looked up, her face moist with water, little streams of it falling from the corners of her mouth as she spoke. "Grace is accepting what you do not deserve. Good or ill. It is what allows us to move on."

"You need to destroy her!" Marie commanded.

"I am already beyond destruction," Annabelle replied. "And I have my brother to carry. My focus is to free us on our journey. I do not have to help you seek your vengeance."

The girl stepped back, disappearing into the murky blue light, the water that filled the space without being there. She motioned. "You may follow, if you wish. Where we go, all are welcome." She picked up her little brother, his face nuzzling into her neck.

Marie watched them retreat. Anger welled up within her. *The stupid girl is going to cheat me*, she thought bitterly.

The mother was writhing on the hallway, her eyes wide with terror.

Marie dragged her back to the house. On the way she paused by the statue of Nemesis.

Marie hung her head. "I have failed us, Goddess."

In the moonlight the statue remained: cold, unmoving, and mute.

***

Marie unbound Ulrike and dropped her off at a local hospital, along with a fabricated tale of finding the distraught woman wandering around her yard.

The woman was incoherent, and incapable of relating her ordeal. Marie was satisfied that anything she did say would be considered delusion. Ulrike's life was about to unravel, anyway.

As Marie left the hospital, she glanced at a television set. They had found Ulrike's car in the lake: two little bodies had been trapped inside it.

Marie felt her fury grow.

As she entered her home, an approaching storm gathered in the sky. The clouds covered the moon, concealing the silver shepherd's light.

Marie unlocked her hallway and entered.

The rain rattled the windows; thunder boomed close by, echoing down the marble hall.

There was no blue light in the hall, no reflection of phantom water. No shadows defiant in the clean, classical edges of the hallway.

The ghosts were gone.

"The moon is not yet new!" Marie cried out. But the clouds covering the lunar countenance had been enough for Annabelle. Even if she did not cling to them, Annabelle knew the ancient rituals. She had used the moon's blindness to escape with her sibling.

Marie sank down, sitting on the cold marble floor at the feet of her deity's statue. The lightning threw outlines of the arched windows around her.

Marie thought. *One day I will have my perfection. I will have my vengeance.*

She started to sing, to comfort herself.

Κάνε μον παρέα, Στά σχοτε ινά. "Kane mou paréa, Sta skoteená." *Keep me company, in the dark.*

Marie cried out to her memories of lifetimes long lost, crying out to a goddess only she knew.

It was Marie's cry to Nemesis, the Enemy, who reflected all the deep, dark mysteries that hid themselves within the complicated architecture of the human soul. The perfect mirror for the indelible memories Marie could not let go.

The statue remained still and unmoving in the moonlight. Marie's perpetual adoration could not sanctify it beyond the marble it was made of; to endure forever was not immortal life.

Marie felt the violation creeping back into her flesh.

Tikal

Inspired by tales of early Viking journeys, and of the true horrors that had been practiced by ancient religions, Tikal matches the power of man against the power of nature.

T he stifling jungle heat reminded Sweyn that the cool fjords of Scandinavia were an ocean away.

It had been years since he had been home, perhaps decades. With nothing but varying states of captivity to account for his life, his memory served him well by forgetting the passage of time.

The prolonged regional drought had forced his latest captors to seek fish and fruit far beyond the comforts of their own borders.

That he traveled with them marked the relaxed confidence they had in him. In exchange for a station above abject slavery, he provided them with his formidable hunting skills.

The natives were smaller in build than Sweyn; their foreheads sloped, artificially molded from birth with pieces of wood.

He was very different: tall and blond with eyes the color of the clear cerulean sky.

They had traded fistfuls of shells for Sweyn, buying him from his previous captors.

They understood what he already knew: alone in this unfamiliar land, he benefited from accepting servitude among them. Escape led nowhere.

He was with three other men and one woman in this foraging party. They moved quietly, wary of the ruling people of the area.

They told him terrible things, describing their neighbors as little better than devils.

Sweyn's own people had their own terrible past, distributing devastation and despair along the coastlines of Europe. But the Vikings had been careful raiders, plundering deposits of goods and coin and then departing, to allow the mark to refill its coffers again.

Around his neck, Sweyn wore the one item all his captors had miraculously allowed him to keep: a soapstone pendant. On one side the stone showed the cross of his Lord, Jesus Christ. On the other, the hammer of Thor, a memory of who his people were.

Not that he still adhered to the old ways. When Thorhall the Hunter had sung heathen hymns and soon thereafter whale meat for the colony appeared, Thorhall had bellowed: "Is not the Red-Bearded Thor more useful than your Christ? *This is my reward for chanting to my patron Thor.*" Sweyn had been among those who tossed his share over the cliff face. He was no longer a follower of Thor.

Sweyn touched the engraved cross briefly. Praying silently for safe deliverance.

The foraging party around him seemed especially nervous. He sensed they were not safe.

"Quiet," the woman said.

He had picked up words of the languages of the peoples he had encountered. He owed his life in part to the gift of tongues. The gift of even one word could elevate him from death to life. He had noted that a person who could not communicate, even when obviously human in form, could be killed so easily.

The men were anxious, hands clenched upon their spears.

Sweyn could hear the approaching enemy as they crawled through the thick jungle around them. Many feet, stepping in the shadowy soil, beneath the branches of the rainforest.

He and his group crouched low, trying to avoid detection.

The sound was all around them. It formed a grim circle, whose circumference shrunk ominously inwards.

Twenty men, armed with shields and spears, stepped into the clearing. The lead man, a man who painted his face blood red, motioned. He pointed out their small party, still trying to huddle in the underbrush.

The native men were separated out, the woman pulled forward and flung at the red-faced man's feet.

Sweyn had learned long ago when to look like a victim, and when to bear his people's pride. He stood up, his tall, fair frame standing in a column of light that fought between the layers of leaves and vines.

The red-faced man stepped back, the others in his party mumbling. He talked quickly. He pointed to the native captives. "*Ch'ak! Ch'ak!*"

His subordinates gathered the three natives together. They pulled out daggers with obsidian blades. Fearsome images decorated the handles, the visages of skulls and lustful serpents filling the spaces in gruesome decoration.

The blades were as fearfully effective as they were ornamented, and once drawn quickly across the throats of the captives, the men died with gagging, fluid sounds.

When they were dead, the blades were used to sever the heads, which were gathered up and delivered with reverence to the red-faced man.

The man bellowed something. He ordered Sweyn and the woman put into a line.

He proceeded to march them out of the steam of the viridian jungle. Brightly colored birds cawed high in the canopy.

Sweyn understood intuitively that the woman and he were being spared for something more elaborate than a simple beheading.

"*Mictizqueh,*" the woman, Cualtzin, whispered, confirming his fears. *They will kill us.*

Sweyn thought grimly about the new words the man with the red face used. Regardless of if it meant "kill," "behead," or "slit their throats," the term " *Ch'ak*" served as evil greeting.

***

They entered the city from the east. Sweyn noted the maize crop struggling in the fields, the incessant drought winning its battle against the wilting stalks.

Small, thatched huts dotted the landscape, farmers struggling as bitterly as their decaying crops. Occasionally a small stone building appeared, holding ritual items, pottery, and small stores of food.

Everything was threatened by the encroachment of the dense tropical rainforest.

As they entered the city, a small crowd had gathered to see them led in, cheering violently when the red-faced man proudly displayed the heads of his victims.

Sweyn looked around as much as he could, making careful observations. His own people had succeeded in their raiding and their settlements by having good intelligence and communication. Information was crucial in surviving the next challenge.

Sweyn was astounded. He had never seen a city like this before.

It rose out of the cleared jungle, a mighty stone metropolis. Buildings carved out of rock sat proudly on the ground, their façades painted with bright colors.

Some walls looked smoothed, but as he viewed them Sweyn realized that the stones in the walls were covered in an adobe façade. These were a people who maintained their temples, generation after generation.

Most of the walls were decorated with garish carved figures. Some depictions were recognizable as animals, but others were surely mythological beasts, comprised of reality and nightmare.

Patterned textiles gently billowed inside many of the buildings, reflecting the bright afternoon sun in deep reds, powerful yellows, and a delicate azure blue.

A large central building loomed over the others. It had the aura of a temple, built with three distinct layers. A small shallow pool of collected water sat at the bottom of the steps. Its precious liquid remained undisturbed, despite the oppressive drought, speaking of both obedience and fear on the part of the people.

The pyramids of the city were tall, bearing steep staircases on their faces. Numerous stone columns dotted the green grass lawns, inscribed with fearsome images of man-headed serpents and skulls.

Cualtzin shivered. " *Mimíhcatzitzintin*," she whispered.

Dead people.

She nodded to small pools laid in between the buildings. "The opening to the world of the dead, Xibalba," she said. "We are in Tikal, the City of the Dead. This is Yax Mutal, the First Prophecy. The Place of Tongues."

Sweyn looked at the imposing acropolis, ignoring the many eyes that regarded him with cruel ignorance. "A temple and a crypt," he acknowledged.

They were led into a stone building and taken down into a lower room, where wooden beams crossed the windows.

A prison looks like a prison anywhere, he noted.

They were unbound and pushed into the room.

The man with his blood hued face smirked, saying quick words in his native tongue.

Sweyn listened attentively to the unknown language: *Pitz. K'ux. Ah k'in. Chak.*

The latter word seemed ominously close to the order to behead.

Inside the room there were four more captives, apprehension etched into their tawny features. Two men and two women.

Sweyn noted that they looked like the other residents of the city.

He nudged Cualtzin. "These people are not from your tribe," he noted.

The other prisoners had shaped, sloped foreheads and copper colored skin, but there was something subtly different about them.

Cualtzin spoke to them, using their language.

The practice of enslaving and killing one another had yielded some comprehension of the other's languages.

The four spoke back, tumbling over one another's words. Sweyn noted their slight frames and thinning hair. The drought had brought troubles to the land, and malnutrition stalked those least able to bear it.

"They are the last members of a small city near the sea," Cualtzin reported. "The others are all dead, killed in sacrifice to the great rain god, Chac. A ceremony is planned, over the next few days. We will all be killed then, to bring water from the sky."

Sweyn looked outside. The sky was clear and blue, without any clouds. The sun glared high overhead, bringing as much death as life in its rays.

Sweyn remembered his journey across the vast expanse of boundless ocean. He longed for home, wishing to see it one more time, although his heart told him it was a foolish wish.

A soft breeze wafted between the sturdy wooden bars.

Sweyn smelled it, almost imagining he smelled salt water borne on its deceptive wings.

***

Night brought the need for fitful rest, a thankful diversion from the desperate sounds and awful smells of the dungeon room.

Sweyn had coaxed Cualtzin into teaching him some of the language, picking up vocabulary as quickly as he could. The words swirled around his mind as he settled into his guarded sleep.

Sweyn's mind fell into a dream, a memory wrapped in thought. He remembered coming across the great ocean with Thorfinn, seeking grapes and wheat in a new and open land.

He had joined a party that headed south, eventually founding a place they called Hop. There the game was plentiful, the fish abundant, and the grapes and wheat were delivered as promised.

Indigenous people visited, friendly at first, but soon the relationship soured. Perhaps the natives had taken offense that Thorfinn forbade Viking weapons be traded for local pelts.

The natives caught the Northmen by surprise.

Lady Freydis had picked up the sword of a fallen Northman and charged the attackers.

In the midst of a sky flooded with arrows, Sweyn had fallen wounded.

When he came back to consciousness, he was a prisoner of the natives.

They traded him for pelts to another tribe.

Over time, Sweyn had been blessed with continuing life, even although its definition was at times miserable.

Traded from people to people, he had eventually come far south to reside with Cualtzin's tribe.

Convinced that he would never see his homeland again, nor partake in the Lord's holy supper once more on Earth, Sweyn had resigned himself to making as comfortable a life as he could.

A nudge awakened him.

Cualtzin sat next to him.

"Listen!" she said nervously.

He heard drums beating outside, the sounds of people chanting. A crowd murmured below the ritual noise, observing and approving.

Sweyn peered out between the wooden bars of the cell.

One of the lower pyramids boasted a small stone altar. A man in a serpent mask ascended the staircase, accompanied by an entourage of dancing men wearing capes made of iridescent bird feathers.

Behind them, four small boys were led by a smaller group of men. The men who walked behind wore human skulls around their necks, painted brilliant reds and golds.

The chanting died down as the boys were led up the steep stone steps, the sound of drums pounding rhythmically filling the air.

Sweyn had seen how the peoples who lived in this region treated one another. They were embroiled in unending conflict, perpetually capturing one another for purposes of slavery or gruesome sacrifice.

The assistants on the low pyramid tied the young boys to the legs of the altar with vine ropes.

The ropes were a deep rusty red, stiffened with layers of blood that had dried in succession, layer upon layer.

Sweyn closed his eyes and started praying.

He grimly wondered about his own dismal future at the hands of these captors.

The boys were prodded with spears, and began to croak loudly, like a chorus of frogs.

"It is hoped," Cualtzin interrupted, "That their song will appease the Rain God, Chac, and will bring rain again upon the lands."

Sweyn opened his eyes, his prayer finished.

"Your god has no power here," she said coldly.

"My God is the one true God," Sweyn replied. "His power is far greater than the Devil who plays here."

"You have been abandoned. One man lost among many. Is this how your god saves you?"

"His ways are His ways, and not mine to discern," Sweyn replied.

The drumming increased in tempo.

The man in the serpent head mask raised an obsidian blade, hollering incantations to the clear sky.

Four men positioned themselves near the boys, each wielding a heavy club.

Maquahuitl, Sweyn thought, knowing the word for club.

The dancers picked up the pace, the drums rumbling in hideous frenzy. The men beat the clubs on the ground in time.

The man in the serpent mask jumped down, pausing solemnly in front one of the boys.

A man with a club let out a fierce cry, and with all his power, brought the club down upon the boy's face.

Small pieces of obsidian cut and sliced, as the weapon broke the bone and pulverized tissue.

The man struck the boy again and again.

The serpent-masked priest directed the next boy be killed, until all four were dead, pulped corpses mauled against the legs of the altar.

The red-painted man danced and raised his arms, calling to the still, quiet sky.

From the other side of the pyramid, another man approached, dressed in a jaguar skin. He wore a blue-colored mask, with a curving pendulous nose, and a wig of jet-black hair tied on the top of the mask's head. Vines tied and painted to look like snakes dripped from the corners of the mask's lips.

"K'ul ahau," one of the native captives in the cell said, watching with Sweyn and Cualtzin through the barred window.

"The supreme and sacred ruler," Cualtzin translated.

"Their king," Sweyn acknowledged.

The ruler sat on a small stool placed on the altar top. An attendant placed a small bowl beneath his spread legs.

The king accepted a sharp, short obsidian bladed knife from the priest.

Lifting his robes, the king held his penis in one hand. With the other hand, he brought the blade to his own flesh and cut a sharp incision into the exposed organ.

Blood dripped down into the bowl, while the priest and his attendants chanted.

The priest placed a new bowl beneath the king and lifted the bloodied one to the sky.

Cualtzin and the other captives seemed oddly calm, while Sweyn stood transfixed by the venerated violence.

She looked reverently between the bars. "Perhaps now it will rain," she said softly.

***

Sweyn awoke with a pounding headache. The captives had not been provided with much food or water, and dehydration was taking its toll.

"They will keep us alive just enough to sacrifice us," Cualtzin had noted.

Cualtzin had managed to get rudimentary information from the other captives. The two women were 11 Kimi 14 Sotz and Kib Yaxk'in. The latter was pregnant, Cualtzin pointing to the woman's small abdominal bump and saying, "*Cocozque.*"

The two men were 10 Chuwen 19 Kumk'u and 6 Men 3 Pax. Cualtzin told Sweyn the numbers represented dates.

There were others captive in adjacent cells, Cualtzin learned. Hundreds more, many of noble birth, spared immediate death for imminent sacrifice.

"Our captors have a precise knowledge of the heavens," she reported. She explained their intricate calendar to him, a system of counting based on twenty, and the accuracy with which they predicted the wanderings of the great god Venus.

She pointed to a carving on a stone they could see through the bars. A regal figure sat over a stack of papers made from fig tree bark, folded accordion style.

"Their scribes divine the stars," she explained, "telling the people when to plant their crops, when to make war, and when to make sacrifices to the great gods."

The fearsome visages of the gods themselves were engraved on the plaques of the *witz*, their word for pyramid.

"*Witz* is mountain," Cualtzin said. "Where the ancestors lived."

Her own people were a different people, she added. They were very similar, but different in ways that obviously mattered to her and their captors. The distinctions were lost on Sweyn. He saw them all as alike: caught in slavery, religious wars, mass sacrifice, and a gruesome obsession with the powers of human blood, flesh, and bone. They faced common problems, including overpopulation, drought, malnutrition, and disease, and constant waves of invasion.

Their solution was to kill one another in droves, to appease gods that seemed possessed of no happiness.

In the darkness, the jailors opened the door to the cell, two men with clubs removing 10 Chuwen 19 Kumk'u and 6 Men 3 Pax. Three other men motioned for Sweyn and Cualtzin to follow them, taking Sweyn and Cualtzin in a different direction than 10 Chuwen 19 Kumk'u and 6 Men 3 Pax.

As they were moved out of the building, Sweyn saw priests place bowls of the king's penile blood at shallow wells, chanting in the moonlight.

"They place offerings at the *cenotes*," Cualtzin said, "the mouths of the earth monster that lead down to the watery world of Xibalba, where the Lords of Death dwell and play."

Sweyn nodded, remaining quiet. He had begun to search the grounds with a discerning eye, noting where the perimeter of the city was guarded and where it was not.

He had no intention of handing himself over to such evil.

They passed an I-shaped courtyard with sloped sides. Rows of stone were arranged around the court like staggered benches. At both ends, stacks of human skulls and decaying human heads polluted the air with a foul odor.

"The ball court," Cualtzin said, noting his inquiring gaze. "The game will be part of the ceremonies."

They moved forward, into a small stone room.

Inside there was a portly man, so obviously better fed than most of his laity. Sweyn recognized him, even without the man wearing his serpent mask.

He babbled at them.

Cualtzin answered, Sweyn recognizing her translation.

"They want to know our birth dates," she said.

"Why?"

"They comprehend the great rhythms of the universe. Our birth dates are part of a pre-ordained order."

Sweyn stood straight, looked the heavy priest in the eye. "Thirteen August, in the Year of Our Lord, Jesus Christ, 990."

Cualtzin translated, although Sweyn noted she dropped his assertion of his faith.

The priests began to murmur very excitedly amongst themselves, one coming over and looking carefully at Sweyn.

Sweyn had a very unhealthy feeling about the examination.

They motioned for the captives to be removed, and they were walked back to their dank cell.

The women were sleeping, the men still missing. Four bowls of *atole*, a maize gruel, were placed inside, along with four cups of water.

Cualtzin started to devour her share.

Sweyn brought food and water to the sleeping women, rousing them. The pregnant woman looked at him inquisitively, and then quietly retreated with her rations.

Sweyn sat down, sipping the water and scooping the gruel up with his fingers. He paused, half his food remaining in the bowl.

"You should finish that," Cualtzin scolded.

"What about the other men? No portion was allotted them. When they return, they will be hungry and thirsty, also."

"A *tlamacatzintli*—a wise man—does not sacrifice his own strength for his weakened enemies."

"In my faith, *toteotahtzitzihuan*—our saints—do not abandon even their estranged brothers."

She laughed hoarsely. "Your little gods do not matter here."

Sweyn swallowed a mouthful of water. It tasted restorative and clean. "Why did they react that way to my birth date?"

"August thirteenth is the date of creation. They consider you a divinely sent sacrifice. You will be the last of us to die, the closing sacrifice to Chac. After your blood goes down to Xibalba, *quiahuiz*, it will rain."

She looked unnervingly relieved. "It will rain."

***

Venus rose in the morning sky.

The other men had not returned.

Outside the priests took a small statue of a beautiful, bare-breasted woman, with a unique curl in her hair, back into its daytime reliquary. Sweyn recognized the local image of the moon goddess.

It was a slightly shocking image, but nothing compared to the gruesome images of blood, brutally slain sacrificial victims, and the gods of the underworld. The latter spouted excrement in rivers from their bodies.

Cualtzin woke up, relieving her bladder in the corner. She approached the window.

"Today is the ballgame, a sacred rite. The ball court itself is an entrance to the underground."

"Every place here seems to be a portal to Hell," Sweyn noted.

As they looked out of the cell's window, four painted men appeared, pulling 10 Chuwen 19 Kum'k and 6 Men 3 Pax—both bound—behind them.

The painted men started to club the captives, taking care to aim for joints.

Blows descended upon their elbows and kneecaps.

Cualtzin seemed unaffected by the violence.

"They are getting ready for the ball game," she reported.

"You don't seem to care about the men."

"They are not my people."

"And when it is our turn?"

She looked him squarely in the eye. "You are not my people, either."

He ignored the remark. "Why play a game? It seems odd."

"The Hero Twins," Cualtzin told him, "were forced by the gods of Xibalba to play ball. Lord 1 Death ordered the brothers to kill one another."

The captives' blood splattered onto the ground.

"Hunahpu raised his axe to strike down his brother, Xbalanque, but it was Hunahpu who was beheaded," she recited the myth without any emotion.

"Xbalanque carved a squash to look like Hunahpu's head, then played, appearing to use his brother's head, while Hunahpu's head remained severed."

"A rabbit distracted the great gods," another woman's voice picked up the story. 11 Kimi 14 Sotz warily approached, her people's tale upon her lips. "Xbalanque sewed his brother's head back on, and then continued to play. But the squash broke, and the great lords realize they have been fooled."

The guards stepped away from the broken bodies of their victims, untying them.

Sweyn could see the hunger and thirst in the captives' eyes.

The maimed men were then forced onto their feet.

The door to the cell opened, and two men approached Sweyn. They carried spears and spoke strange words at him.

Cualtzin translated, Sweyn carefully following her words. "You are to watch the games. The king wants to show the people that he has obtained a special sacrifice for the gods. But you need to know the gods before they will be pleased, so the king will show you the rites. That way, the gods will not be offended by your ignorance."

Sweyn was led out, into the sun-choked day.

There were wisps of clouds high in the sky.

Sweyn knew the winds and the tides, navigating by them a lifetime ago, observing the position of the sun through a blessed fragment of rare quartz. Now he felt a familiar change, a pressure shifting in his sinuses, a smell of salt and bulky moisture, far away.

***

"*Amocualli*" was how Cualtzin's people said "evil."

It was how the people regarded Sweyn as he was led into the ball court.

The king sat opposite him, flanked by the high priest and the crimson-faced warrior.

The main plaza of the ball courtyard featured a stone pillar, inscribed with images. Sweyn knew that the pictures, along with symbols for consonant-vowel combinations, represented the languages of the region. The two forms of writing, rebus and logograms, were used to express the religion and history of the peoples of the area.

Or more importantly, those great deeds of the current king.

The stelae, or *te tum*, as he heard them called, customarily recorded the events of the king's life and reign. Arranged in patterns, the stone columns mirrored the trees of the forest and jungle that surrounded the cities.

Three stone panels were set into the court floor, carved shells embellishing them.

Sweyn understood the significance of three to these people, as Cualtzin's own tribe held similar beliefs. The three stones represented the three stones of creation. The three stars in the hunter's belt—Alnitak, Saiph, and Rigel—reflected order in Heaven as on Earth.

Sweyn preferred his own faith's Trinity. *Here*, Sweyn thought bitterly, *the Devil has many forms, as father, sons, and unholy ghosts.*

People sat on the hillside to watch the spectacle.

Two players, garbed in elaborate gear, entered from one side, passing by a stack of skulls. The crowd cheered wildly for their noblemen.

From the other end, the maltreated 10 Chuwen 19 Kumk'u and 6 Men 3 Pax entered. The crowd hissed.

All four players wore padding on one shin, one forearm, and at the waist. Sweyn surveyed the field, noting a marked area at the end of each court, and a stone hoop not much wider than the circumference of the ball at each end.

The ball itself was made of a hard, black rubbery substance produced by one of the great forest trees.

While the crowd's attention turned to the game, Sweyn surveyed the area, pondering ways to escape. He noted that the guards seemed primarily armed with spears, their concentration drifting towards the event.

Sweyn also watched the golden light of the sun disappear behind thickening clouds. He had seen their herald before.

A tremendous storm was approaching. His years of navigating the great oceans had provided him with keen meteorological instincts.

He imagined the growing storm, still out at sea, gaining strength from the warm waters, building colossal columns of cloud that soared into the heavens. The storm would be well formed by now, a dense disk of terrible energy and destructive force. If it was still this well-organized inland, the coast was already doomed.

To the people around him, the threatening clouds were an affirmation that their grisly rituals would bring rain.

The ballplayers took their places, and Sweyn watched.

The healthy players threw the ball into play. The two teams ricocheted it off their bodies, trying to score in the backcourts, using the padded areas of their body when possible. Hands and feet were kept off the ball's jet-black surface.

It fell into the court behind 10 Chuwen 19 Kumk'u and 6 Men 3 Pax.

The crowd cheered.

10 Chuwen 19 Kumk'u and 6 Men 3 Pax seemed unaffected by the score against them. Their broken bodies were intended to lose, a self-fulfilling prophecy to appease the gods.

They must know this is their last day, Sweyn thought bitterly.

An official pulled out a colorful tile. It held a symbol which represented a numerical value. He placed it down on a smooth stone.

Knowing the vigesimal method of counting used by these people, Sweyn considered that it most likely represented a factor of the number 20. The tile itself was beautiful, inlaid with shell, flint, and small fragments of royal jade. Bright hues painted its raised surfaces.

There was a painted stone next to the smooth tile. It was a carving of a giant bat, which wore a necklace of human eyeballs, the optic nerves still dangling limply from the orbs.

Sweyn shuddered. He had to get away from here.

The hometown heroes scored again, one player sharply hitting the ball with his shoulder.

In front of Sweyn, a woman handed a piece of brightly colored woven cloth to another woman. The giver grimaced, while the receiver smiled self-satisfactorily.

A wager, Sweyn noted. Probably based on the time for the spread in the game to be obtained.

A number of such maneuvers were performed over the course of the game, the tiles reflecting the increasing score against the captives.

In time, one of the conquering players ran towards the end of the center of the court. His fellow player hit the ball, using his forearm. The receiving player used his head to propel the ball up, and it ascended towards the small hoop.

The crowd silenced, watching the black sphere as it sailed through the air.

The ball hit the hoop, wriggling in its circumference. A moment later it dropped neatly down through the hoop.

The crowd exploded in thunderous approval.

10 Chuwen 19 Kumk'u and 6 Men 3 Pax were defeated.

The priest descended from the royal box, accompanied by several his underlings.

They rudely grabbed the losers and pressed their backs against the stone ground. The priest directed two men, dressed in brightly colored feathered cloaks, to show their obsidian knives to the crowd.

Sweyn noted the odd curvature of the blades.

The crowd became excited, focusing their attention of the spectacle below.

The knives descended.

The blades dug into the chests of the captives, but not directly into their hearts.

Sweyn suddenly comprehended the design of the blades with sickening understanding: the curvature of the volcanic glass blade allowed it to be inserted under the rib cage, cutting a hole in the chest cavity.

The rough blades carved *around* the hearts, while the men screamed in unimaginable agony.

Sweyn winced, as if only he heard their cries.

In a moment, the still beating hearts were ripped from the chests of the men and held aloft. The high priest collected them, and danced with them in a sordid jig, towards a small statue of a reclining figure holding a bowl.

A Chac Mool, Sweyn recognized.

Cualtzin's people also performed this grisly rite, although Sweyn had never personally witnessed it before.

He grimly reflected that this was likely his own fate, and that being useful at clearing large plots of rainforest for maize crops was not going to save him this time.

The priest put the hearts in the bowl, and the king stood up, saying rapid words of benediction over the crowd.

From his seat, Sweyn could see 10 Chuwen 19 Kumk'u's and 6 Men 3 Pax's heads severed from their bodies. The heads were held up, the priests grabbing them by the hair as a symbol of conquest.

Attendants at the sidelines encased the heads in rubber sheaths.

The victorious players stepped over to the other side of the court, while slaves cleaned the blood from the stones.

Two more players appeared, bandaged and horribly thin.

The scorekeeper approached the victorious players, giving them a new ball for the next game.

The new ball was not another black, rubber sphere.

It was the head of 10 Chuwen 19 Kumk'u.

***

In the afternoon, the clouds began to turn a greenish gray.

Sweyn had seen clouds like these on the oceans, meticulously avoiding them. These were the clouds that shepherded great storms, monsters of rain and wind that swallowed vessels and turned them into little better than kindling.

The population of the city seemed encouraged in their grim tasks, as if all 90,000 of them agreed their dark lords were hearing their blood-speeded prayers.

In the afternoon, the guards escorted Sweyn towards a large pyramid. It was not the largest, but it was an impressive structure in stone.

They were being gentle with him, but he sensed that was not a kindness. He was, he understood, to be the sacrifice without blemish: a perfect offering to the gods.

Inside the temple, priests and officials busied themselves, preparing for a nighttime ceremony. The penultimate sacrifice was approaching.

Sweyn realized he had less than twelve hours to live.

He was guided to an inner room. It was decorated in stucco relief pictures of skeletal death gods brandishing the heads of acceptable sacrifices by the hair. Brightly colored lintels depicted gory bloodletting rites. The men and women of the culture seemed queasily eager to draw their own blood to appease their deities.

"*Pib na*," one of the guards said, as they entered the sanctum. It sounded like he was introducing the room.

Layer upon layer of blood had dried upon a far wall, nearly an inch thick.

How many people had died in this room to make such a horrific testament? Sweyn wondered.

A woman was seated on the ground. Her forehead sloped sharply, a mark of great beauty among her people. She wore vibrantly colored, intricately woven clothes. Her garments marked her as noblewoman, likely the queen.

The king, richly appointed with jaguar and jade, stood over her with a flaming torch.

There was a terrible excitement in the room.

Priests put a bowl before the woman. Inside the bowl they placed a piece of bark paper.

Sweyn watched intently, noting that the guards were more transfixed by the prospect of witnessing so holy an act than on him.

Sweyn was across from the door, and his back against the wall. If he tried to escape, it would be difficult to navigate his way out of the room and down the steep steps without being recaptured.

The queen sat in front of the lintel, decorated with a two-headed serpent. A man armed with a lance emerged from one head; the other head spit out a skull.

The high priest entered and handed the queen a rope. It was impregnated with sharp thorns.

The auto-sacrificial rites disturbed Sweyn. People who were so willing to mutilate themselves could hold fearsome fates for those they did not care about.

The priests began a steady drumbeat, and the queen opened her mouth. She stuck out her tongue, and Sweyn noted a grotesque hole bored into the muscle.

She swayed, as if intoxicated, and inserted a smoothed end of the rope into the hole.

Then she began to pull the thorny rope through her tongue.

Blood erupted from the jagged wounds. The blood dripped down onto the bark paper.

In time, the guards took him silently back to the cell.

He was even more determined not to hand himself over to them.

He watched the storm clouds as they congregated in the sky.

They were not the messengers of life-sustaining rain.

Years of observing such storms instructed Sweyn. This storm would be massive, bringing devastation.

Sweyn calculated that the storm would arrive that night.

It was one more reason to get out of the City of the Dead.

***

There was loveliness to the way the light shone from inside the rooms of the temples and buildings. The vibrant fabrics that moved in the doorways and windows caught the light like textile stained-glass windows.

The wind was picking up.

Sweyn could feel the pressure of the air changing, indicating the ferocity of a storm the likes of which he had never felt before.

Cualtzin joined him at the window. "They will kill us when Venus is highest in the sky, when it crowns the great stone witz. Then Lord Chac of Rain and Lord

Wak-Chan-Ahaw who nurtures the maize will bring water and food to the people."

"I will be the last to die," Sweyn replied.

"You are obviously a son of Xibalba. You crawled through the jungle, a cast out one. We will send you back to Xibalba, a great joke upon the dark lords."

"And you will fare so much better?" he asked. "When is your time?"

She seemed to enjoy his predicament so intensely that she neglected her own peril.

"They consider me the lowliest. They will kill me first. I am not afraid; I am better than all of them. I will climb the great World Tree, with its roots in Xibalba, its trunk in our world, and its branches touching the sky."

Not a tree of the knowledge of good and evil, but a tree that is good and evil, he noted.

He looked at the pyramid, appreciating how the Evening Star seemed to ascend the steep steps as it rose into the night sky. A pyramid facing it seemed designed to track Venus as it appeared in the morning sky.

It must have taken great precision to design such buildings, he thought. The astronomers and engineers had worked diligently to keep every angle faithful to the mission of the building. With their limited tools, the chore must have proved extremely challenging.

Cualtzin pointed to the two women in the cell with them. "These two will die right before you."

"11 Kimi 14 Sotz and Kib Yaxk'in," Sweyn said.

The two women looked up at him.

"*Lok'-ti*," he said to them, pounding his own chest. It was as close as he could say "escape." He hoped his meaning was understood. It seemed oddly comforting, that the word was so close to the name of the Norse God Loki, whose mischief would vex the dark idols these people worshipped. Sweyn was surrounded by false gods.

The women looked at one another, the smallest glimmer of hope entering their eyes for the first time since he had seen them.

"You are crazy," Cualtzin smirked. "There is no escape."

"A storm is approaching, bringing unimaginable winds and rain," Sweyn told her.

"Then the gods are appeased and *tipahapaqui*—we are happy. The land will bloom because we die."

"The land will be devastated, and your death at the foot of a false god will save nothing." He felt better than he had for years. The storm tasted of the fury of the sea, and his blood was ignited with old passions.

An hour or so passed, as the horizon began to decay into dark blues and grays. The clouds began to tumble across the sky, broad bolts of lightning crossing between them. The thunder rolled across the treetops, shaking the rainforest canopy.

Guards came in as twilight began. They took Cualtzin out of the cell.

He watched them take her up a few of the stairs. When they got to the step that corresponded to Venus's current position in the sky, they stopped.

The women in the cell stepped back, covering their eyes.

Sweyn strained to understand the priest as he spoke, catching odd phrases. "God of Zero, receive our supplications."

Assistants pushed her down on a small stone stool, balanced neatly on three legs. They held her tightly, while a man dressed like a brilliant bird held her head. Another, dressed in a beautiful cloak made of feathers designed into a serpent pattern, grasped Cualtzin's mandible with his right hand. With a strong, jerking motion, he ripped the woman's jaw off.

Her screams melted into horrible, stifled, liquid groans.

With what amounted to mercy in a place like that, the man picked up his blade and thrust it deeply into her chest, killing her.

Her body was left on the stool, propped up grotesquely against the stone steps.

On the very top of the pyramid, Sweyn glanced at his ordained destination. The gruesome grinning figure of the Chac Mool, his stone hands cradling the flat stone bowl. Ready to hold Sweyn's eviscerated, still beating heart.

Four smaller bowls sat at the corners of the altar.

He did not want to know what those were for.

***

The priests obviously understood mathematics.

As Venus rose, more captives were paraded out, many with their hands tied behind their backs. Some wore necklaces made of bones, with human mandibles attached as horrific pendants.

After Cualtzin, two men were executed, one on either side of the pyramid.

After them, four men were taken to the next station Venus seemed to rest at, two on either side. They were executed, their hearts ripped out, like the men before them.

The bodies were kicked to the bottom of the pyramid.

A small river of blood formed down the center of the steps.

Sweyn wondered why the people were so docile in the face of such horror. He could only reason that they truly believed that the sacrifices enticed the gods to bring rain.

But he sensed discontent brewing among them.

Eight men were killed a while later, while the clouds billowed ominously in the night sky.

The sacrifices were growing in exponential value.

Until only he and four others would procure special indulgences from the gods above and the gods below, killed at the apex of the sacred stone building.

The two women were wretchedly nervous. The pregnant woman held her belly with horrible urgency.

Sweyn watched everything carefully.

The priests were breathing in a vapor that burned in small dishes at the top of the pyramid. The more the priests and guards inhaled the vapor, the more ecstatic they seemed. There was an obvious perception altering property to the smoke.

Sweyn was pleased: Intoxicated men fought poorly.

Now he needed to be armed, and to move fast.

It was not wise to fight inside the prison. There were too many sober reinforcements readily available among the jailors.

Once on the pyramid steps it would be too late to escape. The incline of the steps was treacherous, and they were narrow. With his large feet, he would have to tiptoe down them. In addition, the steps were now slippery with blood.

The best place to fight was between the jail and the pyramid.

Sweyn also could not afford to be bound; he watched the next set of prisoners pulled up the steep steps, trying to ascertain if there was any logic to who was tied and who was not.

Those who struggled were bound; those who seemed resigned to their hideous fate were free.

It would be a great struggle to keep himself calm when they came for him.

***

The winds whipped in, massive black clouds beginning to occlude the night sky. The torches were repetitively blown out, and novitiates spent time running up and down the steps rekindling them.

The guards were lining up the next groups to be marched up the pyramid. The task was becoming more strenuous, as the number of prisoners was increasing. Now hundreds of men and women were being readied for death.

Cualtzin had spoken of tens of thousands being sacrificed on a single day. Now Sweyn believed her gruesome story.

The victims seemed to know each other, and Sweyn could gather that they had been captured in battle for this purpose.

The cell doors opened for him and the two women. He started to walk slowly, without being prodded. The women imitated him, sensing he had some plan.

The guards seemed satisfied with their cooperation, wearied by moving up and down the steps and managing the increasing number of sacrifices.

As they were placed in the final line behind the wave of prisoners that would precede them, Sweyn noted that two guards came beside them, bearing two infants each.

The four small bowls near the Chac Mool made awful sense.

He remembered the boys, croaking like frogs. To catch the attention of the gods with their cries.

The babies were already screaming.

The guards did not seem affected.

Sweyn looked at 11 Kimi 14 Sotz and Kib Yaxk'in. Kib Yaxk'in glanced down at her own pregnant abdomen. He directed their attention to the babies. "*Mach, tzak*," he said softly, hoping he was conveying that they were to grab the infants.

They indicated that they understood.

Sweyn noted that many of the men and women in front of him were unbound. He wondered if any of them would seize an opportunity to rebel against their captors.

The wind was picking up speed, and its gusts began to push the guards off balance. The first sharp shards of rain were in the wind's spit.

Sweyn watched a guard come near them, armed only with a spear. Sweyn stepped back, as if pushed by the wind.

His intentions were hidden to the last moment: he lunged towards the guard with lightning speed and grabbed the spear out of the man's grasp.

With a quick stab to the throat, Sweyn killed the guard. He motioned to the women.

11 Kimi 14 Sotz and Kib Yaxk'in followed Sweyn's orders.

He may have been a stranger, but he was not dedicated to killing them.

He grabbed the infants out the arms of the guards, handing them to the women.

As he removed the infants from the first guard and 11 Kimi 14 Sotz gathered them in her own arms, Sweyn pulled a club off the startled man, smashing the stone weapon into the man's skull. It cracked with a sharp noise.

Sweyn felt his berserker spirit rise, freed after years of subjugation. The sea scent in the air revitalized long dormant fighting skills. He wielded the club effectively, his Viking fury directing well-aimed strikes.

As the disturbance rippled through the lines, the other prisoners began to react, some sensing an opportunity for freedom from their grisly fate. A man yelled out a word Sweyn had not learned; it seemed to be a battle cry.

The sacrificial throng began to surge, attacking the guards and grabbing weapons.

Others unbound their cohorts, adding to the confusion.

The priests and guards began to come down of the pyramid, their sacred rites disrupted.

The wind began to howl. The tropical winds, fearsomely sustained even this far inland, began to wreck devastation.

"We don't have much time," Sweyn said, guiding the women and their crying cargo towards him. "We need to escape the city and the storm."

Now he feared the storm more.

It was a force of nature, not likely to deviate from its course. It was a massive storm, like those he had seen on the distant horizon out at sea. There was no option to engage in a quick fight to resolve the destructive power of a hurricane. Pieces of thatched roof and stalks of maize plants were already flying through the air.

"You have forgotten Chac Ix Chel!" a man called out to his fellow priests. "The goddess of the flood grows jealous of your devotions to her brothers! She is coming to claim us all!"

"The maize is ruined in the fields!" another called out, bearing stalks destroyed by the approaching tumult.

Sweyn pushed the women along. "Now is a good time to leave," he urged. He didn't want to know what sacrifices the goddess of floods demanded.

The unrest and the tempest united, storming into the city as a destructive bride and bridegroom.

As he left, he found he had no sympathy for the people who had been prepared to eviscerate him. *They brought this destruction upon themselves*, he considered, *worshipping false idols and practicing such wickedness.*

As a Christian, his lack of sympathy for them disturbed him; as a survivor, he had few regrets.

***

The winds picked up even more. The force of the storm shocked him.

He had seen hurricanes on the horizon, churning in warm water while his people gingerly explored alien coastlines.

Nothing seemed to be slowing this monstrous weather system down. It was the type of storm that wiped cities away.

He hurried the women along, clutching the infants. A woman broke ranks from the lines of the condemned, running as best as she could to catch up with them. Her hands were bound; her garments were bloodied, as if she had recently given birth and her garments had not been changed. She had struggled greatly to avoid her fate. One of the babies lightened up, its eyes happy to see the woman. Sweyn untied her and motioned her to follow them.

She clutched her child in joy.

Two men likewise caught sight of the party and joined them. They regarded Sweyn with fear and appreciation, but he seemed to have a plan beyond instant death.

Sweyn moved them quickly away from the city center, hoping that one of the small stone buildings he had seen on the way in was close by.

He saw the outline of one of the buildings halfway up a small hill.

"One of the storehouses!" he said, pointing. He had reverted to his native Norse, but it did not really matter. The howling winds made communication a matter of hand signals.

They followed, somewhat hesitant. These were sacred spaces to them.

The wind noticed no piety, Sweyn thought as he broke the door open.

It smelled of scented wood and feathers. Sweyn grabbed a feathered cloak to keep himself dry.

"Get inside!" he ordered.

Garbed in the priestly robe, speaking in tongues, with the wind swirling around him, he marshaled them inside the small shelter.

Sweyn closed the door.

The hurricane still bore horrendous strength, even this far inland. Its winds howled, the rain horizontal in the sky.

Branches crackled, and trees fell loudly around them. The wind hissed through small cracks in the walls. The sound of water rushing below the little hillside was disconcerting.

Blessedly, the babies settled into fitful sleeps, their infant minds too overwhelmed to witness anything more.

After hours of bombardment, the winds began to slow.

Sweyn tried to tell them this was God's mercy, that no flood would ever destroy all mankind again.

They did not understand.

As the storm passed, they all succumbed to sleep, each wary to the sounds around them.

***

In the morning, the sun shone as if nothing had happened.

Once towering trees littered the forest floor. Water had flooded the low-lying areas around them.

Sweyn could smell water trapped in the stone city, not so far away. The flood and winds would have killed many and destroyed buildings and crops. The diseases and lawlessness that would follow might destroy the civilization itself.

With their failure, the priests had brought calamity upon themselves. With the destruction of the crops, the people had reason for rebellion. The prisoners, now freed, would very likely extract a high price for their imprisonment.

No matter how carefully the astronomers plotted the heavens, they would not find it so easy a task now to assert their authority over any immediate matters, in heaven, hell, or on Earth.

Sweyn moved the group quietly away from the authority of the city, before they were found.

They walked for weeks. The babies calmed down, the two women forming affection for their new charges.

As he walked past the great ceiba trees, Sweyn remembered the native creation story, the Popol Vuh.

Grandmother and Grandfather, Xmucane and Xpiyacoc, had made people from the maize. But the first people they made did not multiply, and so they were destroyed.

Xmucane and Xpiyacoc tried again, but the second people they created did not respect of the Heart of the Sky and neglected to worship the deities who had created them. These people were destroyed with a great flood; only a few escaped, to become the monkeys that sung in the trees.

On the third attempt, man was created.

Sweyn was happy he was a man: content not to be a god, thankful not to be a slave, and overjoyed not to be a sacrifice.

As he led his small band, finding new paths in the forest, he listened to the monkeys, those descendants of the second man. Sweyn heard both joy and despair in their howls, as the monkeys chanted in the great ceiba trees.

But they too, were not gods, not slaves, and not sacrifices.

A part of him understood their ancient song.

416175

This story won the 2007 Baker Award for best short story. Conspiracy theories, alien contact. What would you do if they came for you?

The old man was barely breathing.

Lynn pulled him from his car, dialing emergency on her cell phone.

"This is 9-1-1," the operator answered.

"I've found an old man. He's barely alive. Send an ambulance."

"Where are you?"

"Philadelphia Street. Near the park."

"The ambulance is on the way."

Lynn kept her phone on while she checked on the old man. He was coughing, his throat rattling gravely with every spasm.

She had been lucky to see the car parked in the distance. Jogging by, she noticed the black tube that had carried the exhaust to the driver's side window.

She had broken open the door and pulled him out.

He was in bad shape. He kept asking her, "Do you believe?"

"Believe in what?" she asked.

"Something bigger than yourself."

"Sure," she replied.

He smiled a weak plaintive smile. "Can you keep a secret for me? Something you promise not to tell."

Lynn nodded. The old man's eyes were dying. "I promise." She felt the need to humor him, to keep him hoping.

He slipped something into her hand. "Put it in your pocket. Now!"

She did as he requested.

"If you don't do anything, then destroy the envelope," he said. He looked heavier for a moment, then infinitely lighter.

Lynn knew he was gone.

An ambulance pulled up. Lynn had not heard it; its sirens were not on.

A paramedic jumped out and rushed to the man. He felt for a pulse.

"Is he dead?" Lynn asked.

"Yes, ma'am," the paramedic said.

Another man got out of the ambulance, wearing over-starched blue jeans and a crisp polo shirt. He approached Lynn.

"Did he say anything to you?" he asked her.

The first paramedic pulled a gurney out of the truck.

"No, not really."

"Nothing?" the man asked.

The questions were not normal for the circumstances. There was no inquiry about how the old man had died. That disturbed her.

"He asked me if I believed in God," Lynn replied. It was not quite the truth, but she had read somewhere that the more truth there was in a lie, the more believable the lie was.

"Bill must have gotten religion," the paramedic said, wrapping the body up on the gurney.

The man in the starched blue jeans looked at Lynn. "We have some questions. Perhaps you could come with us."

A small crowd was gathering.

"I have an appointment this morning," Lynn lied. "Why don't you give me your card? I can call you later."

"I'm all out," he replied. "Can I see your ID? I could copy your information down." He pulled out a weathered pocket-sized spiral notebook.

"I left my ID at home. I was just out for a quick jog." Lynn felt that she had suddenly become involved in a game she didn't know all the rules to.

"You should always carry ID. It's the law. Name and address?"

It was an order, phrased to compel information blindly.

Lynn's father had told her a story about captured Allied pilots in World War II. The Germans had an easy ploy to extract intelligence from them, giving the prisoners forms to fill out. All categories of forbidden information were included on the form alongside seemingly innocuous questions; it was the type of benignly bureaucratic information-gathering people became insensitive to. Name, date of birth, rank, duties, social security number, names of two relatives, city of birth, how many men are in your squadron, where are you based...

The man waited.

"Cynthia Garrett," Lynn said. Cynthia had sat next to her in high school chemistry; Garrett was an ex-fiancé's surname. "I 7878 Spirillia." The address was for a new condo tower currently being leased out.

The man nodded and then got back into the ambulance. It left without any fanfare. No lights, no siren, Lynn noticed.

"Ma'am? Ma'am?" Lynn heard a voice on her cell phone.

"Yes?"

"We have an ambulance on the way to your location," the woman advised.

"The ambulance just left," Lynn said.

There was the sound of computer keys clicking. "We show no arrival yet."

"They just took the guy's body away."

There was silence, followed by a sudden exclamation. "That's so weird. The entry just came in. I'll cancel the other truck."

Then it suddenly occurred to her. The paramedic had called the old man "Bill." As if he knew whom the old man was before they got there.

The little voice inside told her she was already part of something bigger than she was.

***

Lynn checked out of her motel, paying in cash. When the drunken desk clerk turned back to watching televised women's beach volleyball, she tore the page with her information out of the registry.

She was spooked by the man in the blue jeans. He had been too muscular and too efficient for any entirely wholesome job. He had the lean, heartless look of a predator.

It made her uncomfortable to think he had gotten her scent.

The old man had given her an envelope. Inside, she found an old Easter card containing a key, an address, some cash, and an index card with two circles drawn on it.

Make sure no one follows you, was written inside.

It struck her as a strange suicide note. Because it wasn't one.

It took half a day to drive out into the low mountains, where the address was located. Concrete highways gave way to asphalt roads, and eventually gravel-strewn dirt roads. She was glad her father had taught her how to use a compass and a map.

Lynn made a quick grocery and supply run on the way out, noting the lack of businesses along the road. She had packed her laptop and a few other personal items.

Once at the address the old man's note specified, she stopped the car. It was a secluded cabin, tucked away beneath tall pines. Little brown needles littered the drive.

She pulled the car beside the cabin and went into the house. The key provided with the Easter card worked, which amazed her.

Once inside, she locked the doors and took stock of her new home. The electricity and water worked, which implied that someone was paying the bills. She put her groceries away, noting how spotless the refrigerator was.

It was a small building, one large room with a separate bathroom. The main room was divided using furniture and screens into a bedroom, a living area complete with television, and a work area.

The latter area included a very modern computer. Next to it, in almost time-warping juxtaposition, were old electronics. A radio, transmitter/receiver, and a synthesizer out of a 1980s catalog. Quite a few of the machines were analog.

Lynn noticed how clean the place was; the scent of cleaning fluids lingered in the air.

Someone had been expecting someone to show up here.

Lynn hoped she was an acceptable guest.

She turned on the computer, the envelope the old man gave her resting in her lap. The computer greeted her, a voice-pattern program and artificial intelligence coursing through the machine's wiring.

"Enter pass code," a man's voice said.

It almost sounded like the old man.

Lynn thought for a moment. The only thing she had been given resembling a code was the number written on the old Easter card. She entered it, carefully typing "416715," and the machine dialed a number.

"Hello," a man's voice said over the connection.

"Hello?" Lynn replied.

"You the new operator?" he asked.

"I guess. You the new boss?"

"Not quite the same as the old boss," the man replied.

Lynn could hear the leather upholstery of his chair squeak. She could also hear an echo. He had a large office, surrounded by walls of glass or solid concrete.

"Where's the old man?" he asked.

"Dead. Carbon monoxide poisoning. He hooked the exhaust pipe of his car up to the inside. Did you expect that?"

"In a way," the man replied, without emotion. "Not that he was suicidal. But there were parties that wanted him to be that way. They must have finally made his mind up for him."

"So, the old man kicked the bucket. Where does that leave you?"

"Looking for a new bucket. You seem game enough to be here."

"You're very lucky, me being here. What do I call you?" Lynn had picked up a deliberate poise on the part of the man, like he was accustomed to getting his way and giving orders.

"Mr. Allen."

"No General Allen? Is Allen a first name or a surname?"

"Not in your need-to-know packet." There was a pause. "You did get the packet, right?"

The concern that trailed his question was the first chink in the armor Lynn had sensed. "I got an old Easter card, a set of keys and a map, and a few odds and ends."

"Who knows you're there?"

"No one. Should someone?"

"Privacy is next to godliness for you right now."

"I'll skip my next shower, since cleanliness is out, then."

Lynn could almost hear him smile. "Did anyone else approach you?"

"A stuffed suit in blue jeans pretending to be riding shotgun with the worst paramedic in the country." Lynn paused. "How dangerous are they?"

"Dangerous enough with a tailpipe and some hose."

"Noted."

"Lynn?"

"Yes, sir?"

"What do you think about UFOs?"

***

"Lynn?"

It was three hours later. Mr. Allen had been interrupted and had left to take care of more urgent business.

Lynn suspected there were many other things on his plate.

I'm the pet project's new manager, she thought. Not that she minded free accommodation, a small expense account, and something to do. It beat counting out nickels and dimes at the burger place before heading home to an empty hotel room.

The project gave her something to do. A sudden purpose in an emptying life. She could understand the old man that way. So much inside and nowhere to give it.

It had been serendipity for her, the old man, and Mr. Allen. Lynn had heard of luck, destiny, and even pre-destination. She liked the fewest syllables and silent letters a word had, so she thought of luck. It was the kind of convergence of events that her mathematical mind liked to classify as "elegant."

With no family, no job, and no direction in her life, the adventure had needed no further justification.

"Lynn?"

"I'm here."

"You savvy with computers?"

"Smart enough. I'm a math genius, so all the tests told me. But I have a discipline problem, always engrossed in the chapter, *not* on the test."

"You'll need to grow some discipline. Some housekeeping tips, Lynn. Stay low profile and stay inside as much as possible. There's a security system. It's pretty self-explanatory. The code is 416715."

"Like the computer. What's the significance of the number?"

"It was the old man's social security number, without the middle numbers. Now, what do you think about UFOs?"

Lynn had thought about that for a while. "Unidentified flying objects. Could be anything from the mundane to the freaky-deaky. Simplest explanation is that the observer simply doesn't know what they're looking at. My grandfather told a story about seeing a jet plane in England in World War II, before they were supposed to exist. That must have spooked a soul or two."

"Next level?"

"Classified stuff. We can't show the world every card we're holding. Next would be natural phenomena. Ball lightning or something like that. I once saw a flock of geese fly over a parking lot at night; their wings and bodies reflected the parking lot lights back an eerie white glow. A few more drinks, I might have imagined something else." Lynn paused. "Fourth category would be anything that doesn't fit into the above sets."

"Little green men?"

"Why not? The universe is a big place. It's hard to imagine that God built a master planned community and then stuck all the sentient beings in one little isolated house hidden in a back cul-de-sac."

"I like you, Lynn," Mr. Allen assessed. "You seem adjusted. Your predecessor saw too many boogey men."

"Just because you're paranoid doesn't mean everyone isn't after you."

"Can you guess what category of UFO this project you've stepped into concerns?"

"I'm going to go with door number four."

"Bright girl. You'll notice your computer has a unique screen saver."

"SETI at home," Lynn replied.

The program helped crunch the enormous data field being collected by the Search for Extra Terrestrial Life project, large technical ears eavesdropping on the universe for any sign of communication.

The waveforms stacked up over one another, filling the screen with a techno-rainbow of peaks and valleys. These were the sounds of outer space, being scrutinized for any organization that might indicate intelligence or purpose.

"You're on board, Lynn." Mr. Allen said. It was a statement of fact, her acquiescence immaterial.

"Mr. Allen, we search for extraterrestrial intelligence while we beam old *I Love Lucy*s into the cosmos. Perhaps they think we'd be better off cultivating our own intelligence here."

"You work on this puzzle, harder than you've ever worked," Mr. Allen ordered, ignoring her observation. "This project depends on you applying yourself to the chapter the test is covering. I don't take kindly to little Air Force O-4s telling me what they think at budget time. There's no way I'm letting an undisciplined Army brat with a knack for numbers put any brakes on my project—you do your job. We need the right answers on this one."

Lynn stopped to think his words over, considering them past his authoritative outrage. He seemed a few steps up the ladder, and not Air Force or Army. *Navy?* she thought. They had their finger in the space program pie. He could also be civilian agency brass, with a sky-high GS coding to his official job title.

One other thing stuck out to Lynn: She had never mentioned being the daughter of Army parents. Yet he had the knowledge to call her an Army brat.

"I'm in, Mr. Allen. I appreciate the opportunity." *Now,* she thought candidly to herself, *I'm thinking there's long-term strategic career planning in being a UFO chaser?*

"Good, because if I'm going to spend resources protecting you, I want you to be aware of how the world works."

"Protecting me?" Lynn asked.

"Yes, Lynn. People are trying to find you. I've already seen the pre-prepared press release announcing your death." She heard Mr. Allen lean back in his squeaky chair. "All it needs is a date."

***

It is an opportunity, Lynn realized. One of those that looked more daunting when it was really considered.

A quick thought flashed across her mind: *What would I say to the aliens if they were real? I might be the first person to talk to them, the person who makes the first impression for the whole damn planet.* The first to figure out what beings from someplace other than Earth think, believe, intend.

What would I say? She pondered. *Hi. I'm Lynn, an in-between jobs math geek with a jogging problem.*

It had never worked for her on the dating scene; she wondered why she thought it would work as an opening introduction to an intergalactic communications officer.

Mr. Allen had his own doubts to add to the stew.

"There may not even be aliens," he said ruefully. "You and I will just grow fat off a miscellaneous line-item expenditure in a classified budget report. But just in case, start with the notebooks by the computer. They'll bring you up to speed. Every abduction we know about is in there. Try to figure out if any of those are real. Why fly across a galaxy to tip cows?"

Lynn was alone in the small cabin, hidden away in a darkness of night she had never experienced before. A thousand stars she had never seen before peppered the night sky.

She opened a beer and started reading the notebooks. *Abductions always seemed to involve beer somehow*, she thought.

And Mr. Allen seemed intent on her exchanging her efforts for his generous donation to the "Save-the-Lynn" fund.

Every abduction file was neatly wrapped, notated, and catalogued. The old man had been a fastidious recordkeeper.

She took out a large map of the world and pinned it to a corkboard hanging on the wall. In the trunk of her car she pulled out skeins of yarn, remnants from an attempt to learn how to knit.

Mr. Allen called after she had been working for a few hours.

"What you got for me?" he asked her.

"I'm reading the files and color coding them. I'll hook a camera up to the computer later so you can see what I've done."

"Good," he said. "In the top drawer next to the computer is a bank card. I put some money on it this morning and changed the name on the account to yours."

"No need to fill out a W-2?"

"This is where your tax money goes," he replied. "How are you categorizing the cases?"

"I put a bit of yarn down on the map marking the place the abduction occurred. Red yarn for the tabloid stuff—anal probes, sex with the alien, or 'the baby is an alien.' All those file under 'I got paid by someone for telling my story' accounts. Orange yarn goes to spots where drugs or alcohol seem to have been consumed. There's a lot of orange up there so far."

"That's the world," Mr. Allen said. "Continue."

"Yellow is for frustrated teenagers and lonely adults. Green yarn is assigned to those cases where the details seem too rehearsed, or there is a bed-and-breakfast ghost."

"A what?"

"You know: Come stay at our place because it's haunted! Really!"

"You're much more cynical than the old man."

"I have a suspicion about supernatural things that lead to profit. Sometimes you have to witness, like the Southern preachers say, but other times the entire exercise seems designed to take in the Yankee dollar."

"And blue yarn?" he asked.

"That's for the most believable stories." Lynn paused. "Funny how it turned out to be blue for those."

"How so?"

"Project Bluebook, the UFO chaser's Bible."

"You believe in that?"

"It's big, boring, and incomplete. A believable government text."

"You're one of us now, Lynn. Technically a government employee."

"Ah, the government, who vote on if we go to war with Alpha Centauri and whether to continue carrying cheesy fries on the cafeteria menu in the same session."

"Anything else, Lynn?"

"Mr. Allen, do you ever wonder what color yarn connects you to the world?"

***

When she was done, Lynn was pleased with the work.

The yarn seemed bundled up primarily in the United States. Maybe, she thought, that was a lack of information from anywhere else. Maybe that was the way it was.

There really was no reason to keep legitimate alien contact a secret, Lynn thought. There would be a tremendous advantage in the mutual annihilation game to let on that you had access to alien technology.

Maybe that was the pathetic truth of the Roswell incident. *Everyone, pretend you saw something you can't talk about, in order to freak the other side out.*

Lynn remembered stories about a U.S. Navy vessel using alien cloaking technology. The idea of a stealth United States Navy would have been upsetting to the Warsaw Pact.

She rigged a camera up to the computer, very carefully defining the area it showed.

Mr. Allen contacted her over the computer, and she waved at him.

"We have Lynn-cam," he acknowledged. "Good. I always liked visuals in a presentation. You look just like your file photo."

She showed him the map with its string. "I hope the photo is better than the one on my driver's license."

"It's the same one," he informed her. "I like your Big Board approach to the data."

"Yeah. Lots of abduction stuff going down in zip codes where having a full set of teeth is an oddity."

"Be kinder to the locals," he scolded.

"My question is why would aliens pick people up in the middle of nowhere?" Lynn ran her finger along I-10. "You can see all major cities and most major interstates from outer space at night. An intelligent alien would notice where we were concentrated."

"Maybe you don't want to draw attention to yourself."

"Then why return anyone abducted? You could just keep them or pop them out of the airlock. Once back, people tend to talk."

"Maybe they think these people are easily discredited. You just dismissed many of them out of hand."

"Our faith still rests in alien life being out there," Lynn said. "It's a scientific machine with a religious operating system. We want to *believe*. If we didn't, SETI wouldn't exist, your funding would disappear, and H.G. Wells would have written the final treatise regarding alien interactions."

"So, the cynic believes?"

"I'm going to reread some of the creepier files," Lynn replied. "I'll talk with you later."

"I'll check in," Mr. Allen said.

She took a picture of the world map and transferred the image into the computer. Then she played with the colors, eliminating some, enhancing others. The world looked like it had a weird rash.

Nothing suggested an organized pattern to her.

She decided to let the mathematical side of her brain relax, while the philosophical part played.

***

It made no sense to Lynn that intelligent beings who could navigate interstellar space would be haphazard in anything.

Unless that was their intention.

She figured they had access to television and radio signals, at the very least. Anyone watching would quickly figure out who was who. The President, 1600

Pennsylvania Avenue. The Prime Minister, 10 Downing Street.

Corporate headquarters and military bases were usually obvious. The aliens would spot places with lots of satellite uplinks. If they wanted to make contact, they could just land on the roof of CNN in Atlanta and be done with it.

Lynn remembered a line from *Jesus Christ Superstar*. Something about why choose this backwards time and place? *Maybe the preachers were right*, she thought. Maybe the extraterrestrials wanted witnessing, not analyzing.

She sat back, looking at the screen.

The set looked arbitrary. She wondered about the aliens, mutilating cattle, screwing the locals, playing with anal probes. It seemed like senseless acts of violence, the type bumper stickers decried.

What if they aren't senseless? she wondered. Maybe they were intentional. A slap in the face.

When she was preparing for her Ph.D. defense, Lynn had known a law school student. They had lunch together in the campus commons, quizzing each other.

Lynn had learned about livery of seisin that way. A parcel of land moved in fee simply from one owner to another. But in the days before big books of deeds, people needed a way to record the event. The solution was to take a child, usually the son of the new owner, to the land itself. In the field, the old owner would hand a stick over to the new owner, symbolizing the transaction. As the ceremony was performed, the kid would get a sharp slap upside the head, completely out of the blue.

The end result was that the kid would remember the event.

Maybe that's why Planet Q puts anal probes on every departing flight, she mused.

She regarded the abduction sites. She couldn't help but feel they were a set. If they were, it might be possible to project them, using Lipschitz mapping, Lebesgue measures, Borel sets, and Hausdorff equations. It was the type of fractal geometry Lynn excelled at, taking seemingly random numbers and producing meaningful patterns.

She printed out the map, giving the picture an X- and Y-axis. Determined to figure out what the drunken Morse code was saying.

"A mass distribution μ," she mumbled to herself, "on my set F, with $0 < \mu(F) < \infty$."

It was the sort of thing she lived for, even if she did feel drafted into a one o'clock in the morning show on the Discovery Channel, some smooth voice narrating her clandestine story.

She manipulated and projected, turning the locations into a more manageable set of dots and dashes.

In time, she had a picture, something that looked ordered and deliberate. From chaos, something was taking form.

She sat back, amazed.

Now all she had to do was figure out what was the question she had asked to get her answer.

***

Lynn didn't believe in coincidences. She believed the laws of physics influenced all things, even when their operation was not apparent.

As she pondered her work, it occurred to her how fortunate Mr. Allen was that she had been the one to find the old man.

But it wasn't luck, she decided. *They knew I would be along.* They set the old man up for me to find. I jogged that route every morning. Or the old man managed to be where she would find him.

She wasn't sure if Mr. Allen and Mr. Blue Jeans were working together or were the fiercest of rivals.

The new boss was the same as the old boss; but the new employee was different from the old employee.

It really didn't matter: She sensed a trap around her.

"Any news?" Mr. Allen asked, in his customary afternoon call.

"I've been searching leads. The old five W approach. Who, when, what, where and how. Starting with where."

"And?"

"The beings who pilot hyperspace and monitor our transmissions would know we're just beginning to get technologically savvy. I figure they're testing us, seeing if we're puzzle solvers. I guess they want to know if there's intelligent life here. Can we answer the Sphinx's riddle yet?"

"Can you?" Mr. Allen asked.

"The four legs, two legs, three legs piece I know; it's the five tentacles bit that scares me."

"You'll let me know if you solve it, right? I'd like to advise you through any delicate next steps."

"I need to validate my theory and my approach. I don't want to hand you a piece of coal while calling it a diamond."

He let her go for the evening.

Lynn was happy he seemed to buy that she was less efficient than she really was. She remembered the man in the polo shirt and the jeans, pressed to a formal crispness.

He had been in uniform, even in civvies.

She watched the computer screen processing the SETI data. The graphs piled up on top of one another.

There had only been one close hit on SETI, when a team thought they saw a regularity in the data. One of them had said "Wow!", and that was what the data set was known as.

Lynn took out tracing paper and pens, wanting to work away from any keystroke surveillance.

The lines looked like a Cantor set. *But not quite*, she thought to herself. Fractal geometry was not going to solve the whole puzzle.

Lynn could sense a sequence. She remembered biology, complex globs of DNA unraveling to allow themselves to reveal the recipes for making proteins.

She held up tracing paper sheets with her sets on them.

How did that work? she thought. RNA went up to the DNA. The RNA read the code, making complimentary strands, mirror reflections of nucleotides. Then other types of RNA stepped up to the plate, retranslating the code and making the target protein.

But the relevant code was hidden inside a longer string of data. There were introns, pieces of DNA not read. And alternate splicing: depending on what fragments the RNA read, different proteins could be produced, depending on tissue type or need.

Lynn remembered a visual aid from class. A bunch of random letters—the letters S-W-I-N-G-I-N-G—random letters. The RNA knows to go to the correct section, and then what "letters" to select, depending on what "word" was needed. Swinging. Winging. Wing. Swing. Sin. Win. In. I. Wig. Sing.

What if the location projection and the garbled text from outer space were like that? Lynn pondered. *A key to tell us when to read and when to skip over signals? A little test to see if we were smart enough to observe, decipher, think, and translate?*

It might be a way to pick up the pertinent sounds out of chaos. Pull order out of entropy.

It was the kind of test she would devise if she was an alien.

She pulled her laptop out, deciding to use its lesser capacity for the most critical work. She picked up a secured wireless signal and opened her browser.

The search engine spewed weather conditions, entertainment news, and headlines.

She scrolled down, out of idle curiosity.

Down towards the bottom, one headline caught her attention: *California woman still missing; believed dead.*

She clicked on the link.

Lynn Kelsey has been missing two weeks. Now park rangers believe human remains found in the mountains may be hers. Kelsey was jogging in the region, known for occasional mountain lion attacks.

Lynn read her obituary with interest.

Whoever wrote it knew everything about her.

***

Officially dead, Lynn felt an impetus to work even harder. She had to make herself valuable enough to someone, to keep herself alive.

The morning was cool, and she made herself coffee and started a small fire in the cabin's fireplace.

She overlaid the set she had devised on various SETI printouts. She was looking for something that matched something, a kind of cosmic mah-jongg game.

She tried placing the tracing paper along the horizontal peaks, and along the vertical values. She rotated the paper along the diagonal, trying to match the points to anything.

The pattern of dots and dashes played inside her eyelids.

Days passed, and she humored Mr. Allen.

"There is a deadline," he suddenly announced.

"What do you mean 'deadline?' When?"

"You're not on that need-to-know list. How close are you to having anything?"

"Hard to tell. It could be the next five minutes, it could be decades. Science doesn't schedule its eureka moments."

"Well, work faster."

That afternoon she found a match. It was the sort of coincidence Lynn believed in.

At first, she disbelieved her own observation. Rechecking her work, she found she had something that lined up neatly, along a diagonal. She took note of the frequencies and durations of the noises represented.

In a sublime moment she basked in the possibility that she was alone on the planet, holding the key to communicating with something out there.

Lynn also wondered how far out there. Maybe Mr. Allen was seeing something she didn't.

Why would he suddenly worry about her timetable? Her predecessor had worked on the project for years, judging from the old man's notes.

But if something was passing by now, close to Earth...

Mr. Allen would want to have a greeting prepared by then.

Lynn pulled out the old man's transmitter and synthesizer. She hooked her laptop up. She started running a bogus program on the official computer, sensitive that her online work might be monitored.

"May as well have some fun while the computer is working for me," she said aloud, for the benefit of any bugs that might be planted in the room.

She programmed the sound date from the SETI points into the offline computer, guiding it to output the information as sound on the old synthesizer. She hooked it up to the transmitter, connecting her laptop microphone to her headset. She discreetly placed the card from the packet the old man had given her on her lap, hiding it slightly beneath her laptop.

The two circles drawn on the card each bore a line crossing their circumferences. Looking at the transmitter, Lynn realized there were two knobs, and the lines corresponded to settings.

She hit the on switches and sent the signal generated by the number set out into space.

It sounded almost like an old phonograph record being played backwards. Lynn half expected to hear the words "Paul is Dead" coming out of her headset.

Silence replied.

She hoped she hadn't said anything rude.

There was a fuzzy, crackling noise, and across her earphones she heard a word: "Happy."

She sat very still, trying not to look excited.

"Happy." It reiterated, the sound slightly different.

It wasn't a recording. It was something, somewhere, looking for a particular response to one word: "Happy."

It was the Sphinx's new riddle.

Lynn squirmed slightly. Happy what? It says "happy", I say "birthday?" That's too obvious. *What else is happy?* Anniversaries, Halloween, children, puppies, sailing, trails, Hanukah, dreams, faces, retirements, graduations?

She looked at her lap, noting the card the old man had bequeathed her.

The card, Lynn realized, the one with the access code 416715 written on it. A bunny adorned the card's cover, carrying a basket of multi-colored eggs.

She moved the microphone close to her lips and said one word back:

"Easter."

"Happy Easter," a voice replied, heavily distorted by background noise and thick with a strange accent.

"Do you speak English?" she asked, amazed. It was like a bad science fiction movie, where the entire universe spoke the Queen's English. Unless the movie was made in Tokyo, and then every sentient being out there understood Japanese.

"I have learned," the voice replied.

This is first contact, Lynn thought. She had no idea who or what she was talking to, but at least they hadn't already written her obituary.

She felt a queasy panic in her gut.

"Do not respond to anyone who does not give you the code 416175 first. Do you understand?"

"We understand," the voice said. There was an almost clicking subtext to its speech.

"I am in danger," Lynn said. She figured that whoever had decided a mountain lion should get her was the type of person who thought the Geneva Convention referred to a gathering of girls named after a city in Switzerland.

"In danger. Like Bill?"

"Like Bill," Lynn replied.

Her computer screen flickered, and a small map appeared. There was a spot highlighted.

"Bill said to go there," the voice said. "We will raise you up."

Lynn paused. She figured she had time to get there if she made the escape look like an overdue jog.

"Okay," she said.

There was silence again, and she turned off the machines.

"Back to work," she sighed to herself, for the benefit of anyone still watching.

She installed a few algorithms into the official computer, acting as normal as possible.

She discreetly burned the data sets and the old man's cards in the fire, under the pretense of putting another log on to burn.

"You keep working," she tapped the computer.

She quietly slipped out of the cabin, her laptop hidden under her track jacket. Going to the appointed location.

Sitting in the small clearing nearby, the sky rearranged itself before her eyes and a bright beam of light bathed her body.

It occurred to her that she was probably one of the few people to request an alien abduction.

She felt something from the ship pull her up towards the metal belly.

In the distance, she heard helicopters landing around the isolated cabin, people barking orders back and forth.

As she was lifted above the tree line, she could see the front door give way to the men smashing it in.

A man in a clean polo shirt and hyper-starched jeans walked around the grounds, a mountain lion at the end of his leash.

All things considered, Lynn hoped her future would entail explaining the old *I Love Lucy* episodes to enquiring alien minds.

Those question were easier to answer than anything any Sphinx would ever ask.

The Rainy Season

Know what surrounds you. Know what fills you. Know what you may fulfill.

1.
"Take it seriously"

At first, the rain had been scattered and light. By mid-afternoon it had become ferocious funeral weather. Rain fell from the sky in angry sheets; the wind howled like a wounded beast. Small, stinging pellets of hail crashed against the tent over the grave.

Karen was quickly commended to the ground, her closed casket strewn with pretty little flowers. Inside she was serene and peaceful, her long blonde hair framing her quiet face.

That was one advantage of swallowing sleeping pills by the fistful and washing them down with a bottle of sour mash whiskey: she still looked fine on the outside.

Rachel stayed until the end of the funeral. She and Karen had been college roommates; in the end, Rachel was the only person like family Karen had.

They could have been sisters, they looked so alike. Both were Texan blonde, with bright blue eyes and strong smiles. They used to joke with one another: The big difference between Texas blondes and California blondes was that while California girls kept spending money to try and make themselves better, Texas girls knew they were already more than good enough—the money needed to be spent *on* them, not by them.

The happy, carefree frivolity was a façade for Karen's depression. When the man she had being dating for six months—the man she loved with self-destroying intensity—announced he was marrying a childhood friend he had just reconnected with after seventeen years, Karen's heart snapped.

Rachel had intentionally not called Karen's recent ex-boyfriend. He knew nothing about the suicide or the service. It was the one manipulation Rachel allowed her grief as she arranged Karen's funeral.

The rain was still heaving droplets when Rachel got home from Karen's interment. The winds crashed them into her as she stood under the covering of her carport.

She looked around as she turned to enter her new house.

The young man who lived next door waved to her.

He wore a heavy black raincoat, sitting on a tired lawn chair, whittling a piece of white wood. He was looking at her, bright blue eyes the color of blue topaz.

He waved again. "Real gully washer," he chimed. His short, bleached goatee caught the reflection of a stab of lightning.

"Are you locked out?" she asked above the thunder.

He looked to his house's back door. "Nope."

She hadn't prepared an answer for that response.

"How was the funeral?" he asked.

"Fine, I guess," she replied. It had gone according to the order of service.

He whittled, bouncing his head back and forth to a rhythm only he heard.

"What are you doing out here? You're getting soaked." She took her house key out of her purse. The wet wind made her shiver.

"Watching."

"Watching for what?"

"Ghosts." He rotated the piece of wood, admiring it. "You believe in them?"

She shook her head. It was a cruel joke on a day like this. "No. Dead is dead."

"And buried."

She opened her back door and locked it behind her when she entered.

Perhaps she was being rude, but she was still angry about Karen's death.

The rain splattered against her windows.

The young man continued to whittle in the downpour, humming to himself.

2.
"It is a cry for help."

"Sorry I seemed blasé the other day," he said. He held out his hand in greeting and apology.

She shook it. "I was a little wrecked."

"My name's Barb," he said. He was tall, heavy set. His short-cropped hair was brightly bleached. Little chains and silver jewelry rattled on him as he moved.

"I'm Rachel. I inherited the house from my friend, Karen. She had no family."

"Karen. The suicide?"

"She killed herself in the parking garage where she worked." Rachel paused, summoning the courage to continue the conversation. "Is Barb a nickname?"

"Smart lady who lives next door," he grinned. "I play in a band and Barb is my stage name. My given name is Patrick. But I took 'Barbara' as a confirmation name. She's a cool saint. The patron saint of artillery. Big guns and a strong woman." He smiled; his teeth were big and white with furrows between them.

"You chose a female saint's name?"

"Mom and Dad wanted a girl. They were planning on naming her Barbara. They got four boys. I figured I'd do something to make them happy."

"That's sweet." Rachel took a small stack of mail out of her mailbox: all forwarded bills.

"Does it bug you that you inherited the house through suicide?" he asked. He stared right into her with a penetrating gaze. "I didn't know Karen well, but I heard what happened."

"She applied a permanent solution to a very temporary problem." Rachel replied bitterly.

"Guess you fit in now," he replied.

"How so?"

"Every house on this street had at least one suicide to its history, except for yours. Now your house has one." His strong jaw was stretched tight with dark glee. "At least it keeps the property values affordable. This is prime real estate, sitting in the shadows of the skyscrapers. A ten-minute commute to downtown. But you get a bargain moving into Suicide Central."

Karen's estate attorney had not mentioned that the neighborhood was plagued with suicides. The omission was probably not legally actionable: no death had actually occurred in the house Rachel inherited.

"Time to go," he said. "I have a rehearsal. We got a gig."

"Congratulations," she replied.

He turned away, humming to himself. It was a rambling tune in a minor key, with no real beginning or end.

Rachel looked down the long street after he had left. It was lined with old, wooden houses sitting on pilings and weed-etched concrete.

A dozen skyscrapers were visible above the old treetops. The soft buzz of the freeway was ever present in the background.

Bright paint covered most of the homes.

Rachel's was the only yellow house on the street. The only one without a suicide within its walls, she thought. There was sadness to the bright houses around her, as if she could see beyond their clown-like colors.

She was glad she had beer in the fridge.

3.
"Give, and receive, help quickly."

Barb was moving a small lawnmower along his front lawn when she saw him next. He was dressed in baggy black pants, a black bandana, and a black t-shirt. The t-shirt had a picture on it: an old woman, decaying in a noose. The words "Nine Tab" were written beneath her gruesome visage.

Rachel dragged a bag of potting soil around the corner of her house.

"Didn't mean to freak you out or anything," Barb apologized. "About the suicides. It's all the violence we get, if that helps. If you're safe from yourself, you're probably okay."

"It's all right. I just didn't know."

Rachel wasn't going to stop locking her doors anytime soon.

"My cousin killed herself in this house, two years ago." he said, gesturing back towards the blue trimmed house he lived in. "I'm staying with my aunt, helping her out."

"That's very nice of you."

"She's out of town a lot. Keeps herself in denial with work. I get a great place to crash, rent-free. Helps to have no bills when you're in a band."

"You had a gig?"

"Paying work," he replied. "You know, my cousin wasn't the first to do herself in, in this house. There was an old lady, Mrs. Gotsehr, fifty-four years ago, killed herself in the kitchen. But she had serious medical problems, so I really don't count her as a true suicide. She was just choosing her own time."

"That's morbid."

"You believe in the usufructuary use of the body?"

"Pardon?"

"Your body is yours to use, but not to destroy."

"I never really thought about it in those terms."

"You learn shit like that, talking to shrinks and counselors." Barb paused, pouring gasoline into the mower. "They all want to be heroes."

4.
"Listen!"

It rained in the morning.

As the day grew hot and humid, mist rose from the streets, the sidewalks, and the roofs.

More storms were moving into the area, dark gray clouds beginning to claim the sky.

Barb sat outside, whittling. His figure was taking an hourglass type shape. Rachel could see three similar figurines through the kitchen window of his house. Distaff statues made of ivory wood, sitting on the harvest-gold-painted windowsill.

The languid golden light splashed against them.

She half-dreaded seeing him. He gave her a weird feeling, like there was more than one of him watching her with those animated cerulean eyes.

She took her washed recyclables to the green plastic box at the curb.

"Better man than me," he called out, whittling away. "I can't keep up with all rules on saving the world."

"I have a little time on my hands," she explained. She was trying to hurry inside.

"Come sit with me. I want to show you something." He sported a manipulative grin. "The ghosts."

He motioned to a chair, a respectable distance from his. She accepted the invitation with queasy hesitation.

They looked at the corner of his house, beneath the kitchen window with the little handmade figurines.

The light of the sun danced behind the heavy wet clouds. The illumination mocked structures and landscape. Things looked like they were stage props.

"Do you see them?" he asked.

She was looked where he pointed.

The mist was rising from the ground, swirling and climbing. It clawed at the sky, wanting to dissolve into nothing.

Light traveled through the air, refracted by the water, the heavier medium. Little rainbows and sunbeams carved the atmosphere.

"There!" he said. He got up and grasped her face with his heavy hands. His calloused fingers felt rough against her cool, moist cheeks.

Her eyes looked, and fighting her own involuntary gaze, *she did see them.*

The forms were scarcely there. They twitched at the boundaries of Rachel's vision.

There were three figures, outlined in a rainbow-like aura. One was larger and yellow, jaundiced and static. Another was smaller, with azure light dancing around its outline. A third was fresher, enshrouded with a pale white light. They looked like an old woman, a young woman, and a girl.

They barely moved, and as the storm passed the sun, they disappeared.

"They're still there," he said. "But you can only see them immediately after the rain, when the sun comes out quickly."

"I have to go," she said, bolting up.

"Now you believe; now you see," he proclaimed. "There are phantoms in the air all around us." He stretched out his arms, the whittling knife gleaming in the angry sunlight.

5.
"Ask."

"I'm going away, on a small tour," Barb told Rachel the next time he saw her. He was placing outgoing mail in his aunt's mailbox.

Don't mention anything about the ghosts, she ordered herself. *Everything will be sane again.*

"Will you be gone long?" she asked, relieved he would be away for a while.

"A few weeks."

"What's your band's name?" She asked. Perhaps she could track them on the Internet, make sure that he was still far away.

"Nine Tab."

"Like your shirt?"

"It's a clever word game."

She didn't reply.

"Ixtab is the Mayan goddess of suicide. We made the 'Ix' the Roman numeral, IX, and then translated it as 'Nine.' Then we added T-A-B to complete the goddess's name. All of us in the band, we've all got suicide in the family. Figured we'd make it pay."

"You don't think that's unlucky? Like tempting fate?"

He laughed, cheeks cherry with glee. "I don't think so." He gave her a wicked stare, enjoying it playing across his face. "The counselors would tell you not to say things like that. Suggesting someone is manipulative or sinful or foolish. You'd make a bad shrink."

She found herself unable to quickly respond to his insinuations.

"You can pick the mail up while I'm gone?" he asked.

"Sure," she nodded, as he walked back into his little blue house.

6.
"Do not leave him alone."

"How long will you be gone?" she asked as he gave her a set of keys to the house. She had agreed to pick up the mail, water the inside plants, and feed the fish.

"Three weeks. College circuit. Chicks, beer, and rock 'n roll. Gotta live while I'm young."

She began to say something. He stopped her.

"Don't worry about me. I'm not the type to do myself in. Only the good die young. I'm going to live forever."

"I wasn't..."

"Insinuating anything? Sure you were. You've been reading books. Getting a little knowledge, a dangerous thing." He pressed a small wad of money into her hands. "For helping out."

She nodded. He was right. She had been reading a psychology text on suicide.

Rachel remained silent. The books said that listening was good.

Barb got into his car and rolled down the window. "Don't touch my cousin's—Lisa's—room, by the way. My Aunt Veronica has left it just the way it was. You know. The way it was on the day."

He rolled the window up and drove away.

7.
"Suggest professional help."

The second week he was away Barb sent Rachel a post card.

Rach –
Having a great time. Wish you were here! Seriously, thanks for taking care

of the beasties and throwing the lights on and off. Bet you always go in the
front door. You're afraid of the ghosts that live out back.
IX-TAB,
Barb

She left the post card on the dining room table in his house. She felt strangeness associated with it that she did not want to bring into her own home.

Its words haunted her all night.

The next day she went over to water the plants. The pothos ivy climbed against its trellis, the violets flourished in the kitchen.

She paused, looking at the little white whittled forms on the windowsill.

She picked one up.

It was much lighter than she anticipated, the soft wood like solid velvet against her palm. She turned it over, admiring the smoothness he had achieved in his working on the form.

He had signed the work, his name and the date of its completion written in indelible ink on the bottom.

It read *Lisa*, and was dated a little over two years ago.

Rachel put it back. She picked up the next figure, more crumpled in form than the lithe figurine that sat next to it.

Mrs. Gotsehr, it read, along with two dates. One was within the last four years; the other was over fifty years ago.

Rachel was almost trembling as she picked up the third figurine: its title was most familiar to Rachel. The name it had been given was *Karen*. It had been carved just prior to Karen's death.

She placed them back meticulously, as if it had been a grave sin to examine them.

She wondered what denials, angers, and grief hid inside the shadow of Barb's wide smile.

Why would he carve such evil little things?

8.
"Keep no secrets."

When he came back, Barb was busy.

A moving crew arrived and took things from the little blue house.

A couple of men in suits also dropped by. They held black briefcases importantly in hand, like onyx oracles.

After they left, Rachel saw Barb place the figurine he had been whittling next to the other three. The pale, bleached wood was shaped and sanded into a distinctly female figure.

He looked older, she thought.

She went over to return the keys.

"How are things?" she asked.

"Tour went great."

"*And?*"

"Smart lady who lives next door."

She waited, patiently.

"My aunt strung herself up in a hotel room while attending her last business conference. Cleaning staff found her two days ago." He walked to the kitchen, putting cleaning solutions back under the sink.

"Oh!" she exclaimed. It was such a weak response. Words had not presented themselves to express her shock.

He took the keys. His jaw was set firm; his cerulean eyes hid something inside his brain. He left for a moment, to go outside and place boxes in the storage shed in his back yard.

While he was gone, Rachel's curiosity claimed her imagination. She quickly picked up the new figurine.

On its base Barb had scrawled the words *Aunt Veronica*. He had dated it just a few days ago.

She saw his shadow cross where the ghosts lingered; she replaced the figurine quickly.

"Well, one more for the books," he sighed at her as he entered. "Do you feel all right?"

"Fine," she replied, feigning brightness she did not feel. "I feel fine."

9.
"Arrange for Recovery."

Barb knocked at Rachel's door, dressed in black, a small black cloth bag slung over his shoulder.

This time he meant it by dressing entirely in black. He was in mourning clothes.

The sky was gloomy. Cumulonimbus clouds rode warm air that fueled their instability. They were beginning to tower precipitously. Soon, they would rain, and die, and be no more. Tomorrow afternoon, more clouds would take their place.

"Thanks," he said, as Rachel exited her house. She locked the door.

"No problem," she said. "I brought an extra umbrella. Just in case the sprinkles turn to rain too soon."

They got into her car to go to his Aunt Veronica's funeral. Rachel had volunteered driving, hoping that by helping she would feel better. Perhaps a part of her had questions waiting to seize an opportunity to be asked.

It was like the empathetic ethos phase of romance, but twisted into a strangeness she could not decipher. Her emotions played around in her like a sickness with no origin.

She concentrated on the road, preoccupied with the weather.

"Are you angry?" she asked.

He opened the top of his black cloth bag, just enough to glance inside. "No. Suicide runs in my family. I'm ashamed."

"You shouldn't be," she said. She hoped she was doing no harm, having read only one book on the topic of suicide.

"Our bodies are given to us to use. We don't own them. We have no right to destroy them," Barb said. There was a new rectangular cube of bleached, soft wood in his bag. He looked at it meaningfully.

Rachel saw the cube and eyed it with curiosity.

"Are you okay?" Rachel asked. She meant: *Are you suicidal?*

"I have my ways to keep myself from destroying my own body," he said. "I'm not going to piss off any god. I took Saint Barbara's name for a reason."

"I thought she was the patron saint of artillery."

"And against suicide," he said. He caressed the edge of the wood. "But Ixtab has a surer way. She showed me how to make sure I never lose my body or my soul."

"You're upset," Rachel comforted, feeling intellectually and emotionally superior. *He's such a fragile young man*, she applauded herself, even as her sympathy made her feel oddly empty inside.

"I'm protecting my body, like I'm supposed to." Barb said.

He studied the wood as if it was begging to be given form. He looked at Rachel, as if his eyes were guiding where he would begin to whittle her form into the pliable wood.

He looked towards the back of his house as they turned away and searched the new rain at the back porch. Rachel glanced in the rear view to see what he was looking at.

The quartet of ghosts wavered slightly in the veil of falling water.

10.
"No more"

Rachel stopped the car on the way back from the funeral. Barb seemed satisfied, more than grieved.

"Thanks," he said, as he began to get out of the car.

His bag lay on the floor of her car.

Rachel reached into its open flap and pulled out the cube of soft wood.

He stopped, astounded.

"It's pretty," she said. "What do the figures mean to you?"

"Deliverance," he said. "Can I have that back?"

She rotated it in her hand. On its base he had already etched a name: *Rachel.*

"It has my name on it," she smiled. "Can I keep it? I might like to try working it into a figure myself."

Barb was uneasy. "I do the sculpting."

"You have yourself to take care of," she replied. "I think it would be a kind reminder of today."

He was caught without a reply.

Rachel felt an odd power returning to her bones; she wasn't going to relinquish the block of wood.

"I'll keep it," she said resolutely.

"You are the smart lady who lives next door," he said. "No matter. There are other women I can sculpt."

11.
"A new solution"

It had taken Rachel a while to find a block of wood of the same kind. The wood was from a fig tree, soft and not useful for bearing load. She had been cautioned to handle it with care, as the wood's sap was potentially toxic.

She had a few pieces cut for her, of the same dimensions of the one Barb had carried around.

She knocked on his door.

"Rachel," he greeted.

He seemed oddly frightened of her now.

"I felt bad taking your project away from you. I got you something to replace it with." She handed him the block of wood.

He turned it over. On the base Rachel had written *Barb/Patrick*.

"Usufruct means you use it," she said coolly. "Life is given to us to live. Death isn't our endpoint."

"You don't understand."

"I *do* understand. You have been misled. Live your life, Barb. Play your music and carve your niche." She turned to walk away, then stopped. She pulled another piece of wood out of her bag, one with his name likewise inscribed upon its base. "And if I ever see you carving anyone else's form into another block of wood, I'm going to whittle *your* form into this piece of lifeless cord. Do you understand that?"

He nodded and closed the door.

As she walked back to her house, she passed the ghosts.

They seemed to wave at her as she passed by. She ignored them, happy to walk away from any death.

Mr. Highjinks

Sometimes the rules really shouldn't be broken.

Roger Rincot finally had a house.

He had not earned it, never having "lived up to his potential" as his sister so lovingly wrote in a letter to him, happy venom in her tone. He had not even had to risk a dollar on the lottery, a vice he considered himself too intelligent for.

He had come by his new abode in that most blessed of circumstances: His aunt had bequeathed it to him.

The house came paid for, with a deed already made out in his name, and specific instructions that by accepting the property he was consenting to the terms of the Homeowners' Association Deed Restrictions and would abide by all Association rules.

"No matter how odd the request may appear to be," his aunt had stressed in her Last Will and Testament.

Tired of living in a crumbling apartment building, fighting cockroaches, and smelling the foreign cooking spices of his neighbors, Roger did not care what requirements accompanied the house.

It was a house.

He inspected his new home on a delightful Houston day: December 28, 74 degrees Fahrenheit outside, with the faintest touch of a cool breeze. The colorful leaves tumbled off the tree branches, carpeting the ground in pretty yellows, robust oranges, and shameless reds.

Tomorrow the Mexican gardeners would come by, with their truck full of yard keeping equipment. Using loud leaf blowers, they would move the matted cacophony of color off Roger's new lawn and into the street, where it would become someone else's problem.

He had to keep the yard maintained; it was in the Homeowners' Agreement. A covenant with his new neighbors.

Roger had never had the occasion to covenant anything before, just covet, and he was happy to have finally crossed that boundary.

He drove his car down the street, pulling into the driveway. Little pebbles—*his* little pebbles, crackled beneath the weight of the car. He owned a house now, and the first few inches of soil it sat on. The mineral rights belonged to a large oil company by some operation of law Roger did not fully appreciate.

As he walked to his house, key proudly in hand, he could see the neighbors regarding him with curiosity.

A woman with a sour face peered out from behind net curtains. Children paused from riding their bicycles to consider him with concerned expressions. A man down the street peeped up from pulling weeds to examine Roger.

"You the new owner?" a voice asked, deep and dusty, like his throat was a mineshaft that gave up sound instead of gemstones.

Roger turned around to see an old man. He had an authoritative posture.

"Yes," Roger said. "My aunt Violet left me the house."

"Sorry about her passing," the man said. "She was a good woman." He was old, perhaps about seventy, with the leathery skin that Roger always associated with people who had spent too much time outdoors. "She knew the rules."

"I have a copy of the Homeowner's Agreement," Roger beamed. "I haven't read it yet."

"Then hop to it," the man said. "We give newcomers thirty days. Then we have to expect them to pull their weight. You don't pull your weight, you don't belong here. Oh, and welcome to Sweet Plum Street."

He had no humor in his voice, and he left quickly, tightening his jacket against a wind Roger did not feel.

***

Roger moved his possessions into the house the following Sunday. It was early in the New Year, and the champagne headache from New Year's Eve still lingered.

At 83 degrees it hardly seemed like winter, but that was Houston.

Roger had moved to the Bayou City a few years prior, enticed by a job that lasted just long enough for him to decide that this boss, like every employer before him, was an idiot. *You work, they make the bigger paycheck*, he complained.

Roger knew could do better on his own.

So, he quit.

Aunt Violet had supported him, much to the dismay of his siblings. They had a dim view of him spending money they felt would be better left to her estate for equal distribution amongst them all.

When she died it was even more obvious he was, for no apparent reason, her favorite. It was surmised he resembled an old boyfriend who had fallen to German machine gun fire in World War II, going over a trench wall in France.

She had occasionally called Roger "Elliott," which added to the family mythology.

Roger did not have a lot to move in. The contents of a 600-square-foot apartment easily disappeared into an 1,800-square-foot house. Even his car was hidden in the little detached garage, after years of braving the outside elements parked on the street.

The house was normal in its design, except for one odd aspect that it shared with every other house on a street. A small room was attached to the back of the house, distinct from the main body of the house. A small door was on the outside with a window in it, with no lock, as if it were an attached, upgraded shed. It was like a mudroom that lacked an entrance to the abode itself.

Aunt Violet's Will had been very particular on the little room.

Do not decorate the small room at the back. The neighbors will show you what it is for.

Roger didn't have anything to put back there anyway.

By mid-morning, he noted a small crowd of people heading his way. They moved silently down the street, somber and serious.

The old man carried a lamp. The sour-faced woman from across the street bore a small table. Others carried chairs, crystal bowls, books, or small rugs.

The odd parade made its way toward him, silent and steady. The old, tired faces looked worried.

The old man knocked at the door.

"Howdy," he said, as Roger opened the door.

"Hi," Roger replied. He had tried not to pick up the Texan speech, nevertheless catching himself saying things like "fixin' to" even when he worked very hard against it.

"We're here for the back room," the old man said.

"Come on in," Roger said.

"Not in," the old man replied. "Round back. You haven't added a door into the house, have you?" Worry laced his query.

Roger shook his head.

The small silent mob moved around back, shuffling with their cargo.

A woman remained out front, thin and graying at the temples. She opened a small glass chamber at the top of a post at the front of the house and placed a candle inside. She looked mournfully at Roger.

He glanced down the street.

He had not noticed it before, but every house had a similar post, each equipped with a candle. The Deed Restrictions, he had noted, very specifically forbade gaslights.

She joined the others around back.

Roger walked around, to see what they were doing.

The small crowd had fitted out the back room quite nicely.

An armchair sat next to a table, over a woven wool rug. A lamp sat on the table next to a silver serving platter and a crystal bowl. A hand-painted ceramic mug was turned upside down on a doily. Books and magazines were neatly fitted into a little bookcase.

"Thanks," Roger said, eying their handiwork.

"Isn't for you," the old man said. "You haven't read the Agreement yet?"

"I started it."

The sour-faced lady got close to Roger. "You don't mess with nothing," she said harshly. "This is for Mr. Highjinks, and you'd best stay away from his stuff."

Roger was taken aback.

"Mr. Highjinks?"

The crowd looked at him with odd apprehension.

"Read the Agreement," the old man said. "You have thirty days. Thirty days until you either step up to the plate, or one way or another you're likely to be out of here."

The small group left, as quiet as they had come.

Standing in his back yard, Roger could see over the rows of low hurricane fences into his neighbors' yards.

Every house had a similar small room, tucked at the back of the house. Each was similar in its outfitting, with a chair and a table and a lamp.

"What a bunch of weirdoes," Roger said to himself.

***

In the evening Roger was carelessly flipping through the channels on the television. Even with cable and a good three hundred stations to choose from, his boredom was not assuaged by any of them.

He saw the thin woman with her graying hair, making her way down the street. The other neighbors watched her.

She stopped by a house across the street and a half-a-dozen doors down. Roger could see the house well enough.

Taking out a long lighter, the thin woman lit the candle in the little lamppost at the front of the house.

The old man, across the street, seemed to sigh to himself before disappearing again behind thick, velvety curtains.

The woman inside the house that had been selected worriedly made the Sign of the Cross over herself. She pensively stepped back, letting her own curtains fall back into place.

Roger watched her shadow curiously.

The woman sat down, her body silhouetted by the blue glare of her television, the flickering light oscillating inside her front room.

Roger wasn't entirely sure, but he thought he recognized the shadow of a rifle, sitting ready across the old woman's lap.

***

Eventually you will be the chosen one, Aunt Violet wrote in her will. *Abide by the Association.*

Houston had evolved without zoning; it had made up its own rules in its rapid expansion. The Homeowners' Associations made up the covenants of the neighborhoods and subdivisions. The agreements carried significant weight; violations could result in eviction.

In one neighborhood, Roger had heard you could not even trim your own trees without first obtaining the permission of the Association and the assent of your neighbors.

It was a power of necessity.

Without zoning, industrial business and home sites were not delegated to defined areas. A concrete factory, a small grocery, or a family dwelling could theoretically be built upon any ground.

In some areas the results were quaint and convenient, such as a small hairdresser's salon nestled amid homes, providing a local business that did not interfere with the morals of the community.

In other examples, the results were less attractive: a rowdy ice-house could be located next door to a small apartment complex, where drunken patrons urinating against a residential wall was not so endearing to the parents of small children who played in the same courtyard by day.

Still, the odd conformity of Sweet Plum Street seemed disturbing to Roger. The lampposts, the little rooms, the lady who carried the ceremonial flame to different homes each night.

The Association's Agreement provided a lot of "thou shalts" in regard to those items. The provisions spelled out the requirements for the room, for the furnishing, for the lamppost, and the acquiescence to having the candle lit in one's own yard once a month.

And the Agreement forbade going into the back yard when the light was lit in front of your own house or any house you could see into the back yard of.

For any reason.

Roger sniffed. The little Gestapo of neighbors seemed to be flexing too much muscle for his liking. The didactic tone of the Agreement seemed overblown and arbitrary.

He was amazed that no lawyer had challenged the terms.

It may seem unreasonable, Aunt Violet had written in the margins, *but follow the rules faithfully. As if your life depends upon it.*

***

Two teenagers were talking outside, skateboards tucked under their arms. They looked appropriately sloppy, with plaid flannel shirts over baggy cutoff shorts.

Roger went outside, under the guise of checking his curbside mailbox.

The boys eyed him from across the street, one more accusingly than the other. They turned away, but Roger could still hear them.

"New guy really messed up your family this month," one said.

Roger could just hear their words.

"Yeah," the other replied, "Thanks to him, we had to host Mr. Highjinks twice this month. Gives me the creeps every time."

"Think the new guy will fit in?"

"His aunt was decent enough. Let's hope he's from the good side of the family."

"He seems like a bum. Doesn't work, doesn't do anything around his own place."

They moved away, until Roger couldn't hear anything else.

He turned around.

The old man walked up to him. "You read your responsibilities?" he asked.

Roger was taken aback by the old man's ability to suddenly appear. "I did. Seems weird. Strange no one's challenged the agreement in court."

"Like a lawyer?"

"Yeah. This town is lousy with them."

"Son, I am one. I was a Texas Super Lawyer twenty-two years in a row. I specialized in homeowner's disputes."

"You should have challenged your own deed restrictions."

"For your information, neighbor, I was the one who wrote our Association's Agreement. Take it to court and I'll bury you myself."

**

A month had passed. The thin woman came down the street, wielding her lighter. She paused in front of Roger's house, eying him sternly. She lit the candle.

"You know the rules!" she called out.

Roger watched her through his curtains. He noted the other neighbors, nervously eying his house from their own living rooms.

His telephone rang.

It was the old man. "Stay inside, don't go outside. No matter what you hear. You got a gun?"

"What damn fool has a gun?"

"Damn fool who wants to defend himself," the old man said. "Gun may not help, but it might buy you some time to get away. Stay away from the room."

He hung up.

Roger placed the phone down.

There must be something in the water here, some toxic craziness bubbling up from the ground, Roger thought.

He sat down, guzzling down a cheap beer and munching on potato chips. He flipped channels, searching for something worth paying the cable bill each month. For all the hoopla, there were never enough tits on television for Roger's liking.

He found an old action movie, uncut, on a three-digit channel.

A noise interrupted his pleasant inactivity. The sound of the door on the little back room being opened.

He stood up, unusually alert.

Probably those teenaged punks playing around, he thought.

The punctuation of the telephone ringing interrupted his suspicions.

He picked up the phone.

"Sit down, son," the old man said. "I can see you standing. Sit back down. Keep your ears open, if you must. We all did the first time. But you need to stay put."

"What? Are you watching me?"

"It's your first night hosting Mr. Highjinks. We're all watching you."

Roger peeped through his curtains. Every house bore testimony to the eyes scrutinizing him, peering out from a dozen living room windows.

The woman with the sour face, the thin woman who lit the candles, the teenagers in their respective houses: Everyone was watching him.

"Mr. Highjinks visits us all, and we play good hosts. Provide him a place to shelter for the night. A little food. I brought a plate of fruit and cheese and some of my best port wine over this afternoon while you were out."

"What? Isn't that trespassing?"

"Your Agreement with us says we can enter the back room to maintain it. It's important. Mr. Highjinks is a shared responsibility."

"Who the hell is Mr. Highjinks? Is there some nut in my back room?"

"It's *our* back room," the old man corrected firmly. "Says so in the deed. The community as a whole owns the back rooms: Don't separate yourself from the community."

Roger felt his blood heat up. "What does that mean?"

"Mr. Highjinks doesn't like to be denied. Or seen. He has been here longer than any of us. His property rights go behind the soil, beyond the minerals. You don't mind the oil company owning the rights to any oil beneath your ground, do you?"

"I do, as a matter of fact. But there wasn't anything I could do about that."

"Same with Mr. Highjinks, son. His claims go back before you or I were born. We owe him a reasonable accommodation."

"What does this nut do if one of us stands up and says no?"

"Then," the old man said solemnly, "someone dies."

Roger stood for a moment, hearing the sounds of a body settle into the chair in the back room, the floorboards creaking with someone's weight.

There was a subtle musical noise, an old phonograph playing mournful blues.

"The Hell with this, I'm going back there," Roger said.

"Individual defiance is not the way," the old man warned. "You can't win. You don't even have a gun."

"I got a good enough steak knife. Anyway, what's it to you? You let this maniac sleep in your back rooms, feeding him fancy fruits. He's probably just a stupid vagrant who can't believe he's gotten away with this sweet scam this long." He hung up the telephone.

The telephone began to ring again, but Roger ignored it.

He was in his kitchen, plucking a large, sharp knife out of the knife block.

He stepped out of a side door and opened the back gate. The low wattage bulb in the lamp in the back room dimly illuminated the back yard.

Roger could hear the phonograph playing the blues, the distinctive scratchy, silky noise softly filling the mild night air.

He looked in the window, to confront his uninvited responsibility.

There was no one immediately visible in the small, strange room. Only a half-empty glass of port wine, some gnawed cheese, and a plate of crackers and crumbs.

"Sonofabitch," Roger snarled. *Probably the damned teenagers.* He prepared more for a verbal assault on them than an attack with a steak knife.

As his hand touched the doorknob, the door rattled violently.

A shadow thrust itself against the window. Something scratched long, claw-like nails against the inner glass. The sound was like a giant axe scraping against a blackboard.

The room began to rattle, fueled by a fierce wind that initiated from inside the neatly decorated walls.

The neighbors closed their curtains tightly, wanting no association with the defiant one.

***

Oina Rincot-Beltrán sat down across the table from the old man. He handed her a neat portfolio of papers.

"We're happy you're signing the house over to the Homeowner's Association," he said.

"I have a house in Flagstaff," she said. "I couldn't take on the responsibility of keeping this house up. And you're offering me more than a fair price. Saves me having to find a Realtor."

"We were awful sorry about your brother."

"He was prone to depression," she replied. She was uncomfortable, sitting at the same table her brother had died at.

Roger had been found the morning after he went out back. He had slit his wrists, the red puddles still warm on the linoleum when the police arrived. He had also plunged the thick steak knife deep into his throat. The police knew Sweet Plum Street: they didn't ask how Roger had managed that feat.

Only Roger's fingerprints were in the house, although it appeared he had been dragged from the back yard in through the side door.

That didn't get noted, either.

The street had a history of odd suicides, a string of tragic accidents, and a good set of unsolved murders. That was Sweet Plum.

Oina signed the papers. "You're using the house as some kind of community center?"

The old man nodded. "We're interested in preserving the neighborhood's traditions and institutions."

"You're not the average cookie cutter development," she said, happy to have relinquished her rights to the house both her brother and her aunt had died in.

Roger and Aunty Violet had been so alike in at least one regard: they were so ultimately curious about everything. And neither of them had ever listened to Oina.

The old man watched her drive away when they were done.

The thin woman approached him after Oina was gone. "It's done?"

"The house is ours," he reported. "When do the workmen arrive?"

"This afternoon," she said. "They say they'll have the light up by early evening."

The Association had met, deciding to buy the house rather than risk another uninitiated homeowner.

And they had passed a resolution, to allow the one and only gaslight on Sweet Plum Street.

Right outside Roger Rincot's old house. One light that would burn every night. Lighting the way for Mr. Highjinks.

Kryptos

The Laws of Physics. Those laws cannot be broken, even if you try.

The *Helen of Troy* was two months overdue for its return date. She had not communicated with any other ship, colony, or planet for over fifteen months.

An anxious message traveled through the developing network of communications that was being established in space: The *Helen of Troy* is missing.

***

"The *Helen of Troy* was a diplomatic vessel, carrying Annette Senti, then Ambassador to Varsara, back to Earth. The ship was commanded by Captain George May." Lieutenant Abigail Santomero briefed the core command group. That she spoke of the *Helen*, her crew, and her passengers in the past tense belied her fears for the vessel.

Santomero stood tall, her body bulked by months of having nothing better to do with her free time than work out.

By that same token, all the crew of the *Kryptos* was in good shape, even though extended space flight, even in an artificial gravity environment, still caused malformations in the human body. The crew, although it intellectually knew of the side-effects of space travel, would not truly notice how they had become more squared in shape until they arrived home again on Earth, years from now.

The *Kryptos* had been on a mission to establish locations for deep-space communications beacons. Now, the Earth-born laws of known sea replaced the laws of unknown space: A potentially imperiled vessel had priority.

"Everything was normal according to their last report. Their course had them returning along El Camino Royal," Lieutenant Santomero continued.

"That's a rare route back home," Mary Brewer replied. "Not much matter to skim along that course." She was a deep space astronomer, aboard the *Kryptos* as a specialist support. Her résumé included a Presidential recommendation for the mission.

"Most ships choose El Dorado, or the Space Center route. Those are more direct courses to Earth from that quadrant," Brewer added.

"They had a politician on board. Anything could have gone fubar," said Lieutenant Junior Grade Richard Pool.

"Lieutenant," Captain Lautenberg Hector countered.

"Sir. Apologies, sir." Lieutenant Pool returned.

The captain addressed his team, his face pale and puffy after nearly four decades of space service. "The beacons will have to wait. Our mission now is to find the *Helen of Troy.*"

"It's funny in a way," Brewer noted. "Them sending a Captain Hector after the *Helen of Troy.*"

"Space is full of ironic moments," he replied. Mary Brewer unnerved him, the way she could look into people, like they were just another set of puzzles for her to figure out. Despite Brewer only being middle aged, her hair was pure white; it was not the result of natural aging. Likewise, her eyes were unnaturally black, to the point that her pupils and her irises were indistinguishable. "Do you have anything to add, rabbi?"

The ship's chaplain shook his head. "We can pray for the ship's crew, and for ourselves. Until we get there, we cannot imagine what form our prayers need to take."

Every ship carried at least one military-trained chaplain aboard to minister to the spiritual needs of all the crewmembers. With his sandy hair and sinewy muscles, Rabbi Franklyn looked like a surfer who had ridden a wave into his vocation.

"Amen," Lieutenant Pool added.

"On that note, you are dismissed," the Captain said.

The team dispersed, other duties always beckoning.

Lieutenant Santomero started to close down the briefing room. "Anything else I should know, sir?"

"The *Helen of Troy* was a standard diplomatic vessel. It had some intelligence gathering capacity, but nothing more sinister. Ambassador Senti had already beaconed her reports ahead or given her information to ships that departed ahead of hers." He was thinking aloud, hoping that explanations would fall out between the words he spoke.

"So, no one had any reason to make the *Helen* disappear."

"No."

"You think they had an accident?" Santomero asked; it was clear that she was slightly agitated. Something beyond the mission disturbed her.

"You seem nervous, lieutenant."

"I don't like what Brewer said, focusing on you being Captain Hector."

"You've served with me fifteen years. My name never bothered you before."

"I just remember my English classes, sir. Reading the *Iliad.* Hector was a decent guy, serving his country, serving his king. He didn't run around stealing women." She paused. "I never liked the way he ended up."

"Let's just hope the *Helen of Troy* didn't run into a Paris, then."

"Or an Achilles."

Captain Hector thought about that for a moment.

"I'm banning that book on any future voyages," he replied.

***

Mary Brewer sat at her terminal, running through data even though her duty shift had ended hours before.

"For Jerusalem's sake, I will not rest," a voice said, entering the room.

"Jeff," she greeted, as the Rabbi sat down.

"May I join you?"

"Of course. The data set is for you."

"Thank you for agreeing to help me. I know it's not in your job description."

"Job descriptions go out the back end of a spaceship with the first blast of exhaust," she replied.

He placed a cup of coffee next to her. "Thought this might help."

"Ah, caffeine. The best thing on this ship. I would die for a piece of chocolate."

"We had some in stores when we left."

"Ten years' supply. We ate it in the first two," she replied. "There are thirty-eight women on board this ship. Mission Coordination has no clue."

"It's amazing to think how fast we're traveling," he said. "With or without chocolate on board."

"Almost 90 percent the speed of light. They didn't think that was possible a hundred years ago." She stopped, looking out the heavily-reinforced window. "I still have Alan Bean moments."

"Pardon?"

"Alan Bean was a twentieth century astronaut. On a trip to the moon, he noted how absolutely dark it was outside. He was right." She sipped her coffee and pivoted the screen towards him. "These are the new star maps. I hope they help."

"You've meticulously mapped every new star system we've passed through, including a reference for Earth's position, and an Earth day and month duration ratio. Thank you!"

"Why is it so important?" The glow of the screen cast a blue-gray tinge against the uninterrupted whiteness of her hair.

The Rabbi examined the maps, their images reflected in the dark, polished tabletop. The ship's symbol was painted into the table, a Greek hoplite's helmet surrounded by stars painted in gold, against a dark blue background. The ship's flag was surrounded by the words "Starship *Kryptos*" on top, and the ship's motto, "*Pro Patria Vigilans*," on bottom.

"The Jewish people have a lunar calendar," he replied, "which guides our ongoing pattern of growth, as individuals and as a community. God's will is that we follow the cycles of the heavens, and apply them to our lives. In interstellar space, our point of reference shifts. We need the maps to determine the seasons."

"It's quite a mission," she replied. "To find your identity written in moons you don't even know exist. Far away star systems guiding your coming and your going."

"Many times my people have faced foes that would destroy us. In the end, knowing who we are and trusting God's plans have been the only things that preserved us." He smiled quickly, trying to lighten the tone. "This data will help us figure out when to schedule our holidays in each respective system."

"I could never keep up with all the Jewish holidays."

"In essence they're all the same: Someone tried to kill us all, God saved us, now let's eat."

"I just remembered someone telling me that Hanukah happened at Christmastime, Passover coincided with Easter, and Jewish New Year happened about the same time as the baseball World Series."

"See, the symmetry of the universe."

He worked the data, the screen projecting star patterns between him and Mary Brewer. "I know you're not technically part of the regular crew," he said gently, "but I am chaplain for everybody aboard. I am here, should you ever need to talk to me."

"I believe I don't know enough to say what I believe," she replied. "My life story is complicated. But you'll put a good word in for me when I cross over, right?"

He paused before answering, feeling tassels he did not currently wear.

Mary eyed the computer's clock. "We're due on the bridge. No rest for the wicked, or the holy, in space."

***

The *Kryptos* was a large ship. It had been built in space, part of a military-corporate collaboration established after first contact with the Varsarans.

Aside from his core command crew, Hector had three more sets of junior officers training under his command, among a crew complement of one-hundred-and-forty-seven. All personnel were paid for every hour off Earth, into accounts that would greet them upon their return. Their space pay was tax-free. That was one of the incentives of space duty: One ten-year trip was the equivalent of a lifetime's work on Earth.

The duty was not easy.

Even when off-duty, they were still ship-bound. A disease called Vista sickness struck every space traveler with some degree of symptoms; simply not being able to experience wide-open areas caused a claustrophobic, cabin fever like malady. Deep space travelers missed the warming rays Earth's sun on their shoulders. They missed the rain; they missed snow. Most people adjusted; the ship's recreation rooms were designed to help the brain think it wasn't constrained by vessel walls.

The vessel itself was six floors of crew decks, thrust forward at sub-light speeds. The entire ship was encased in neutron and gamma shielding, as well as a reactive outer armor known as an *Estrella* shield which deflected space debris and prevented catastrophic damage to vessels going at sub-relativistic velocities.

Captain Hector was on his third tour, close to celebrating his thirty-eighth year in space.

"Captain?" Mary asked, reaching the bridge.

The captain sat in a solitary chair perched in its own miniature mezzanine deck. From his vantage point he could see all operations going on before him.

"Mr. Veify has received some information from the last ship to contact the *Helen* before she went dark," Captain Hector informed them.

Chebi Veify nodded. He was older than anyone else in the crew. Even serving as a civilian specialist, his service experience was evident in his bearing. "We have updated data about where the *Helen* was. Their last message mentioned that Ambassador Senti wanted to investigate an unknown object."

"The data gives us a more clearly defined search area. You're the astronomer, Miss Brewer. Look at the area and see if you can narrow the field down for us even more. I want the *Helen* found."

***

Customarily, all ships officially launched under an Earth flag were required to maintain a location beacon. The *Helen of Troy's* mandatory beacon could not be detected.

Mary Brewer sat at a computer, plotting out possible courses. She turned to Abigail Santomero. "Based on their last known position, their destination, and gravitational forces known in the system, the ship should be here." She pointed to a triangle that graphed a significant portion of open space.

"There's nothing in that area," the lieutenant said. "It will be like finding a needle in a haystack."

"Not quite as bad," Mary Brewer replied. "Finding a needle in a big nothing is a little easier than trying to find it in a mess of something. The ship will be the only solid thing around."

"If it's still solid and it's still around," Santomero noted.

"You're so pessimistic. See space as a little more filled with matter," Mary urged.

"Civilians."

The door opened. Captain Hector, Rabbi Franklyn, and Lieutenant Pool joined them.

"Mr. Veify has rigged a detection system, designed to find the *Helen* once we get closer to her," Captain Hector looked at the screen. "That's a big lot of nothing. That's our search area?"

Lieutenant Santomero gestured toward Brewer. "If our mission specialist says so—it's going to be like finding a ball bearing on the bottom of the Atlantic."

"Why so large an area?" Lieutenant Pool asked.

"There's nothing around to exert any force on the ship or attract it if it was in trouble," Brewer explained.

"Their last transmission said they had picked up an object and were going to take a quick survey before continuing home," Lieutenant Pool recalled. "Maybe we'll get lucky and find the same object and it will lead us to them."

Mary Brewer laughed softly. "Lieutenants. Such optimistic souls."

Santomero shot her an ugly glance.

***

Mr. Veify scrutinized his instruments.

"Anything?" Captain Hector asked.

"Nothing, Captain. My mind is going to start hallucinating soon. If we ever want to find nothing, this is the place to go. I'm happy for the dust that settles on the screen: It gives me something to look at."

Mary sat down next Veify. She handed him a cup of coffee. "Take a break. I'll watch for a spell."

Mr. Veify looked back at the captain.

"It's a good idea," Captain Hector said. "You've been hunched over that screen for hours, Chebi. Take a break."

"Civilians," Lieutenant Pool whispered, just loud enough for Santomero to hear him.

"We haven't seen any debris, at least," Mary said, ignoring the words she could easily overhear, settling into the chair. "That's a good sign."

***

Hours passed. Mary and Veify took turns watching the screen. Eventually they sat side-by-side, intent on the blank image.

Then they exchanged quick glances.

Mr. Veify carefully wiped a corner of the screen, removing imaginary dust off it.

She nodded to him.

"Captain," he said. "We have something. Something that shouldn't be there."

***

The *Kryptos* used its magnetic field's drag to slow down as it approached its mark. The approach used no extra fuel, and the effect was a graceful arc through nothingness as the ship pulled alongside the object Brewer and Veify had identified.

Captain Hector examined the view, confirming what his immediate crew knew. "It's the *Helen*."

"It's a miracle we found it," Lieutenant Pool observed.

Rabbi Franklyn smiled. "Miracles occur every day."

"Santomero—you, Pool, the rabbi, and Miss Brewer go over," Captain Hector ordered. "I want the rabbi there in case he's needed in his professional capacity. Brewer, you know the stars and systems in this section better than anyone. See if you can figure out what they were looking at. Santomero, you're in charge. Take a security officer and a medic. Pool—you do whatever is requested of you. I want constant contact. Let me know who else you need once you've assessed the situation."

Lieutenant Santomero stood at attention. "Yes, sir!"

***

No alarms had been sounded on The *Helen of Troy* and she was silent as the squad from the *Kryptos* boarded her. She still had power, keeping the lights on at their lowest level. It gave the interior a sterile, gray tinge. The ship's emblem, a beautiful woman in a tunic surrounded by stars, cast odd shadows in the dim light. Life support, set up to run long past the mission's duration, maintained a livable environment.

"Life support and communications still operable," Santomero reported back to the *Kryptos.*

"Keep your heads up," Hector ordered.

"You know," Mary Brewer said, her black eyes drinking in the scene, "When I was a little girl, I used to watch horror movies with my great-grandfather Alex. He had three rules for situations like this."

"What were they?" Rabbi Franklyn asked.

"One, never go onto the abandoned ship."

"Looks like it's too late for that rule," Santomero said, calibrating her instruments, assuring herself that she had enough power and signal to keep in contact with the *Kryptos.*

"What were the other two?" the rabbi asked.

"Never touch any idols you find aboard, and never read the diary with the forbidden knowledge written in it."

The rabbi smiled. "Good advice."

"Are we alone?" Pool asked.

"Looks like it," Santomero reported. "The *Helen of Troy* had a crew of nearly two hundred. I'm not picking up any signs of life outside our group."

"Nor any signs of death?" Mary asked.

"Let's take a walk," Santomero suggested. "See what we can find. Keep your eyes open. A whole ship's crew doesn't just vanish."

They climbed the staircase, entering the bridge. Occasionally there was a scorch mark on the wall, but nothing to suggest overwhelming violence. Months of residual dust had settled on the ship's surfaces.

Santomero paused next to an alcove. Inside it a withered plant sat dead in its pot.

"Not a good sign," she mumbled. "Their cactus is dead."

"Every ship carries one of those, even ours," the rabbi noted. "My mission training didn't mention why."

"It's a good luck charm," Brewer replied. "When Hillman, Hayashi, and Cohen did the original total conversion engine experiments—pre-antimatter drive—they put cacti in the control capsules to see if biological tissue could withstand the stresses of the early models. In the first experiments the plant material went splat against the walls of the capsule. When they finally got it right there was a cactus in the hot seat they had nicknamed 'George.' Since then, it's been good luck to have a genetic descent of George on the bridge."

He looked at her quizzically.

"We are a species that still puts trees on the top of buildings during construction," Brewer reminded him.

The group fanned out, cautious, but almost optimistic in their trepidation. Each secretly wanted to find something, no matter how terrible, to explain the fate of the crew of the *Helen of Troy*.

The medic paused at the navigation desk. "Lieutenant," he said, pointing to a small sheet of heavily worked metal, neatly placed at the helm. It had a peculiarly worked surface, almost like a metallic cantaloupe rind machined with arcane patterns.

Santomero picked it up with a pair of tongs and placed it in a bag. "We'll take it back for analysis. I want to get back to the *Kryptos*. An investigation team can take this thing apart later. Let the pros handle it. I don't want to mess up any evidence. Leave everything exactly as it is."

Mary Brewer retrieved a book as she passed the captain's chair.

"What's that?" the rabbi asked her.

Brewer thumbed through the handwritten pages. "Rough draft of the captain's log. Captain May was old-fashioned. He wrote everything out long-hand first, then dictated it into the computer."

"You realize that now we've managed to pick up an unknown item and you're reading the diary. We've broken all three of your Grandpa Alex's rules," Rabbi Franklyn said.

"Let's hope he wasn't on to something," Mary answered.

"Enough of the fairy tales. Everyone back to ship," Santomero ordered. She took one last look at the abandoned bridge, hating the unknown. It was difficult to devise strategy when all you had to work with was silence.

***

"Report," Captain Hector ordered.

"It looked fine inside. Aside from the entire crew missing," Santomero replied.

"Did you find the log?" the Captain asked. In space, as at sea, the Captain's log was often the most trustworthy eyewitness to the ship's life.

Mary Brewer handed him the handwritten log.

"A book?"

"We couldn't find the last data on the computer. It had been wiped clean, sir. No memory chips in the files. Brewer located some hidden data just as we were leaving," Santomero reported. "Something went very wrong on that ship."

The captain flipped to its last pages. A handful had been ripped out; some intriguing notes filled the last remaining pages.

"It lists their last position as quite a way from here. They were investigating an object. Then nothing. They must have drifted from that position," the captain said.

Drawings of odd shapes filled the last pages. Herringbone patterns collided with circles within circles. Triangles fell over each other, surrounded by shapes of regular and distorted character.

Mary peered at the pages. "That's not Captain May's handwriting," she noted. "See—the handwriting changes."

The captain flipped back a few pages, then returned to the last entries; the mission specialist was correct. A different hand had filled out the final pages.

"While you were on board the *Helen*, Mr. Veify found something else out there," the captain said. "As it's the only other object within reasonable distance, I want to look at it. It might be what the *Helen* was investigating."

"What did Mr. Veify find?" the rabbi asked.

"He located a large, spherical object. It's the size of a very small moon. But it's out here in the big nothing on its own," Hector replied. "It will take about two weeks to get to."

"Captain Hector," Mary began, unusually formal, "The log reported finding a spherical object that seemed to have life support when the *Helen of Troy* approached it. And the ship's data banks still had a few external images of the object, located in a cached file I found just before we left the *Helen*. I suggest we consider that data carefully before we get to our destination."

Hector nodded. "The object is currently putting out a weak signal. You have two weeks to use your powers of acumen to figure out some options. Forearm us, Miss Brewer."

"I'll get to work," she replied.

She left the briefing room to join Mr. Veify and the data they had managed to collect. The remaining members of the group were dismissed.

Lieutenant Santomero walked slowly away from the rest, joining Captain Hector. "Miss Brewer seems to have a flair for recognizing things. I've never met an astronomer like her before." Mary's altered appearance disturbed her.

"Not all civilians are as civilian as others," the captain said. "Beware translators, authors, dancers, diplomats, and astronomers. TAD-DA is what you say when the spy is revealed."

"I remember that day in class," Santomero replied coldly. "I hadn't caught on, I'm ashamed to say."

"Miss Brewer went out on a celestial mapping mission to Varsara twelve years ago, as a guest of Ambassador Senti. My suspicion is that she was the good ambassador's handler. The President himself seemed to think that our astronomer being on board would greatly aid our revised mission. Of course, he put her on my command staff to begin with." He paused, lowering his voice. "If she wasn't one of us, I would be tempted to push her out an airlock."

"Spies. No one loves a spook."

"That's because no one wants their ship haunted," Captain Hector replied.

***

"The signal is a directional beacon," Mary Brewer said, giving the briefing. The rest of the core crew sat around the table.

"How long until you figure out the message?" Lieutenant Santomero asked. She sat awkwardly on Mary Brewer's secret, disliking the woman who could so calmly hide her real identity.

"Perhaps a day, perhaps never. One of the Nazi World War II codes wasn't deciphered until 2006, and that was with a lot of people crunching data." Brewer's black eyes sparkled. "This signal looks to be a true message—not an urgent, short 'SOS' type of transmission. It's saying something."

"Perhaps the *Helen of Troy's* crew is sending out a distress signal on an alien beacon as best they can," Lieutenant Pool suggested.

"All we can figure out right now is that there is a big, spherical object out there, probably with an unsophisticated communications system," Mr. Veify said.

"Nothing in deep space is unsophisticated," Lieutenant Pool returned.

The captain put the piece of metal retrieved from the *Helen of Troy's* helm on the table. "Any thoughts on this?"

"It's an unknown alloy," Mr. Veify said. "Malleable, impervious, incredibly strong. It's a perfect space-faring metal. I'm excited to have it aboard. If we can reverse engineer it, we can greatly enhance our space vessel construction."

"It has an image," Mary Brewer pointed out. She traced a figure above the metal. "If you look only at the triangular markings, squinting your eyes, you can make out an outline, like a hidden connect-the-dots."

"I see a wicked looking bull," Santomero said, viewing it out-of-focus as Mary had suggested. The image was difficult to concentrate on; the other decorations distracted the eye. "A bull with sharp horns and huge balls. Something not afraid to let everyone know what it is."

She looked meaningfully at Brewer.

"It looks like money, knowledge, and progress to me," Veify corrected.

"I see a bull, as well," the rabbi said. "Money, by the way, is something a man makes for himself; knowledge, a thing he makes for others; progress, a thing he cannot make on his own."

"What comes to mind, Jeff?" Mary Brewer asked. He was thinking something.

"*What profiteth the graven image, That the maker thereof hath given it, Even the molten image, and the teacher of lies; That the maker of his work trusteth therein, To make dumb idols? Woe unto him that saith to the wood: 'Awake.' To the dumb stone: 'Arise!' Can this teach? Behold, it is overlaid with gold and silver, and there is no breath at all in the midst of it,"* Rabbi Franklyn replied.

"I don't need a surfer with a divinity degree quoting obscure poetry at me," Santomero returned.

"Habakkuk," Mary Brewer interjected. "The rabbi was quoting Hebrew scripture."

"You sure have a range of knowledge for an astronomer," Santomero said. She couldn't resist. "You a believer in things we don't know about? A faithful follower with a hidden allegiance?"

"You have nothing but doubt for the beliefs of others, lieutenant? Couldn't you find something else to question? Like who made this thing and what it means?" Brewer picked up the object.

"All I know is that you found the pattern easily," Santomero replied.

"I'm an exploratory deep space astronomer. Part of my job is to recognize patterns of matter and energy. It's easy for me to find patterns in artistic and ritual objects. The Varsarans, for example, are more than just artistic in their decoration. They hide secrets and unspoken history in their art."

"Is that why you went to Varsara? To help your puppet Senti decipher hidden Varsaran communications?" Santomero asked.

Captain Hector did not interfere, curious to see how the spy foisted upon him interacted with his most trusted officer.

"Ambassador Senti didn't need me to interpret Varsaran crypto-art. She was adept at that herself. And I was there to catalog new stars and their characteristics."

"You're always figuring out secrets," Santomero observed. "The Universe's, other people's. Almost like that's what you're trained to do."

"Finding out secrets is a science; keeping them is an art," Mary Brewer returned.

"You seemed comfortable on the *Helen of Troy*," Santomero said. "You knew right where to find the hidden cache of data, just before we returned to the *Kryptos*."

"If I had been that comfortable on board the *Helen of Troy*, I would have suggested raiding their stores for chocolate."

"Something bothers me," Lieutenant Pool interjected. He had not followed the subtext of the exchange. "Why is the *Helen* still here?"

"Pardon, lieutenant?" Captain Hector asked, glad of the distraction.

"Someone went aboard the *Helen*. Whoever it was ripped certain pages out of Captain May's log and took some time to put that item where we would find it. They didn't destroy the ship. In fact, they seem to have made sure it would be operational when they left it," Pool said.

Hector looked around the table. "Your thoughts?"

"Captain?" a voice sounded over an intercom, before any of them could reply.
"Yes, ensign?"

"We're at the object, sir. Ahead of schedule. It seems to have drifted towards us. We've also detected a personal beacon transmitting from inside the object. One of ours."

There were grim implications in the announcement: All star-faring personnel bore their own personal identification beacon, inserted beneath the skin in their left shoulder. It was there as a location device, detectable over short distances. In its default setting the device was dormant, due to lobbying by privacy advocates. It was only activated in an emergency.

"Whose beacon?" the captain asked.

"Ambassador Senti's, sir."

He looked over the collected group. "Get suited up for an EVA. You're going over there to find out what the Hell is going on. If Senti activated her beacon, we may have survivors in that thing."

***

Rabbi Franklyn put on his helmet. They had arrived at the object and had cataloged its surface features.

"You seem unusually tense," Captain Hector observed.

"The patterns on the metal plate found onboard the *Helen of Troy*—and the patterns on the object—are unsettling. They remind me of some decorations used by ancient cultures on Earth. The Assyrians. The Sumerians. The Hittites. The Carthaginians. People to be wary of," the rabbi replied. "This object is inscribed with similar motifs to those used by some very brutal peoples."

"I'm beginning to think I missed a lot not taking more art classes," Captain Hector said.

"It doesn't look friendly," the rabbi asserted.

"I'll agree with you there."

The object in space glowed with a subtle light. Its rind-like husk was riddled with dots, dashes, triangles, herringbone designs, and spirals, crudely machined into the external surface. Mr. Veify had plotted the roughly hewn symbols into graphs, connecting the triangles as Mary Brewer had on the smaller piece of metal. Images emerged, mythical chimeras of humanoid and non-humanoid features.

There were other images, when the other symbols on the object's surface were examined: figures cruelly torn apart, heads ripped from bodies, skeletons hung upside down from beams.

"They almost look like constellations," Mary Brewer said, fitted into her space gear, looking at the patterns of shapes and bumps.

"Yeah, the entrails of constellations," Santomero replied.

Hector interrupted to give them their orders: "Mr. Veify has found what looks like an entrance to that thing. Find the *Troy's* crew."

The small party prepared for the extra-vehicular mission. There was no evidence of a life support system operating inside the object. A thermal scan had managed to penetrate it satisfactorily; there were no signs of any living life forms. They were going in on nothing more than baseless hope.

Captain Hector issued weapons to his EVA squad. He had initially hesitated about assigning the rabbi to the mission, but the rabbi balanced out Mary Brewer's hidden agenda, as he worked for a clearly identified higher authority. Franklyn's knowledge of history and gut feel were also good assets. Most importantly, however, the rabbi had the highest level of expertise using short-range energy weaponry of all the *Kryptos's* crew. Hector wanted his best shooter on the exploratory team.

The small group went into what the crew affectionately called "The Tube." Someone had pasted a London Underground poster that declared "Mind the Gap" to the wall. Hector recognized the sign as a morale booster and allowed the non-regulation poster to remain in place.

The vault-like doors to the corridor closed, sealing the tube from the ship. Blue lights flickered on.

The EVA team walked slowly, each adjusting to the discomfort of the suits. Once in zero gravity, the suits would not be so burdensome.

At the end of the tube a sensor read the systems integrated into the suits, turning green as each self-contained environment passed its assessment. The tube behind them closed as they entered a square room. They strapped themselves into seats located around the room. Santomero punched in a code on a device on her seat.

The green lights turned to red, and a panel in the room opened onto the expanse of space. The vacuum drew the air out in perfect silence. Once the atmospheric evacuation was over, they unlocked themselves from the seats, which remained tethered to the *Kryptos*.

"Make very small, deliberate movements," Santomero reminded them, the EVA equivalent of telling them to 'drive safe.' "Isaac Newton is with you in no other place like he is on an EVA. You'll bounce around like a ping-pong ball if you bump into anything."

They followed her lead out of the air lock, popping like weightless feathers into a bottomless well. Starlight littered the sky around them, near and distant lights playing on their imaginations with false perceptions of brightness and proximity.

"It's so beautiful," the rabbi gasped. He had never been in open space before. "It's like being dust on the face of God."

"Mr. Veify?" Santomero asked. She nodded towards the rind of the object.

He carefully looked at them, checking a graph he had drawn up on the ship. "we should be able to access here," he said, pointing to a small odd-shaped section surrounded with spirals.

Lieutenant Pool looked up, as far as he could see. Three scorched panels spaced at regular intervals occluded some of the symbols.

Lieutenant Santomero carefully approached the area Mr. Veify indicated. Mindful of the laws of physics—and the military concerns of entering unknown territory—she gently nudged the door, using leverage that directed her against the surface of the object and not towards open space.

If things went very wrong for the small party, there would be no escaping the disaster without external help, and any chance of rescue was still sitting on board the *Kryptos*.

The panel gave way.

Inside there was a disjointed tube-like corridor, lit with little blue and purple lights. Its levels and angles changed with no apparent function or meaning.

"It's like a crazy house, the type they used to have at amusement parks," Brewer noted.

They floated in space contained inside the corridor, temporarily defined by the corridor's structure.

Mr. Veify quickly jotted things down into a computer located in his suit's sleeve. His pale azure eyes were like purple crystals in light.

They were surrounded by alien artwork, etched and worked into the metal of the walls and decorated with tiny lights still powered from an unidentified energy source. The figures were more carefully drawn inside, as if something had time to concentrate on the effort.

The images were of squat, almost human figures, pursuing various unknown creatures. The humanoids ripped off limbs from their quarry and tore skin from fallen victims.

"These are the symbols of a terrible culture," the rabbi said as he took notes on the images. Something inside him revolted with a visceral distrust and wariness of the unidentified artists.

Spirals overflowed out from the borders of the pictures, intermingling with more small lights. The spirals fell upon one another, until they exploded into a myriad of shapes, many distorted. Dashes led from the symbols, temporarily forming little sets of spheres. From those, the odd symbols drifted outwards, toward other spheres.

Santomero led the team inward. She pushed in a small interior door, Pool covering her. The rabbi had his weapon drawn, his hand steadier than Pool's.

Pool's breathing grew fast.

Brewer floated next to him. "Don't hyperventilate," she said. "Regular breaths. You've got plenty of air."

"Bloody spy," Santomero uttered beneath her breath, her microphone off, as she entered the room.

The rabbi read her lips and followed her closely. "Mary Brewer's been in space longer than you've been alive," he told Santomero.

"You seem to know her pretty well," Santomero said. There was accusation in her tone.

"I knew her when she was a brunette with brown eyes," the Rabbi replied. "Then something happened. She doesn't talk about it."

"She doesn't seem to be an open person," Santomero said.

"Perhaps she says little because she cannot reveal much," the Rabbi said.

Brewer, Pool, Veify, and Henderson, the medic, entered the room.

A small piece of fabric stained with black floated past the Rabbi. He grabbed it with his gloves and examined it carefully.

"Bloodstains," Santomero said. "Any droplets of blood would have boiled off, but the heme stains on the fabric remain."

The team looked around them; their suit-mounted lights illuminated the dark walls, revealing terrible truths.

Human bodies served as gruesome decoration on all six walls surrounding them.

The humans had been disemboweled, their flesh nailed to the surfaces of the room, forming a swirling pattern. The victims' features had been distorted by the action of the vacuum of space, the residual air inside their bodies sucked out long ago.

"Shit," Santomero said. She tapped her communications portal in her sleeve unit. "*Kryptos*, we have bodies."

"The *Helen's* crew?" Hector asked.

"We're not sure. We're going to examine," she said. "Fan out and try to ID," she ordered.

The group started to spread out, expect for Pool, who remained motionless. His eyes rested on the tangled net of naked human forms, tied together with their own intestines and nailed into the walls. Another blood-stained scrap of fabric floated by, landing on his faceplate. Pool spasmodically wiped it off. His breathing was rapid again, as his eyes fought the impact of the gruesome sight that surrounded them.

"Pool!" Santomero ordered. "Move while we're young! You waiting for an embossed invitation?"

He remained in place, quivering oddly.

"He's going to vomit," Brewer said, moving towards him, recognizing his body's contorted language. "Put pressure on the inside of your wrist," she told him.

"What the hell's that for?" Santomero said.

"It may quell the nausea—there's a pressure point on the inside of the wrist," Brewer said. "Henderson!"

The medic moved in beside Brewer. "I can't give him anything here—we're in space."

"I'm aware of that," Brewer returned. "Get him back to the ship."

"I'm in command," Santomero interjected.

"Then see to the welfare of your men," Brewer snapped.

Pool quavered oddly, and his body lurched. The inside of his helmet was suddenly covered with vomit. Little bits of stomach contents and hydrochloric acid circled weightless inside the helmet.

The smell caused him to retch a second time.

"The ship!" Brewer said. "He'll die here!"

"Now!" Santomero confirmed.

The medic moved Pool away, exiting the room and arranging the details of an emergency reception on board the *Kryptos.*

"Lieutenant?" the rabbi said, floating up to where the two women and Mr. Veify hovered. He held out his gloved hand; he had picked a piece of metal out from between the bodies.

It was a crew medallion; a beautiful woman in a tunic, surrounded by stars.

Santomero pressed her communications button. "Sir, I think we can confirm that we have found some of the *Helen's* crew."

***

Having accounted for fifty-two of the *Helen of Troy's* one-hundred-and-eighty-nine crew members, the team needed to account for the others. They could do nothing more for Pool and knew that Captain Hector would not tell them anything about his condition until they returned.

They followed a series of low-intensity yellow lights.

The lights and the symbols on the walls and ceilings picked up a rhythm, seeming to repeat in certain places.

"What do you make of it, Mary?" Rabbi Franklyn asked.

"I think it's a story," she replied.

The rabbi looked at the sharp series of lines that terminated most of the pathways of symbols and lights. "A story with many endings and very few new beginnings," he said.

They floated down the corridor until it widened into a large, open room. All the segments of symbols collected together until they formed one large image on an enormous wall.

Little chips of colored, glass-like crystal were fitted into the dark gray wall covering. Scribbles were written into the wall, barely scratching the surface. Some of the inset lights were steady, others blinked in a curious pattern.

"What story are these bastards telling?" Santomero asked.

Brewer stopped and contemplated the image made by the lights. "My God," she whispered.

"What do you see?" Rabbi Franklyn asked.

Brewer floated up to the wall; her black eyes were wide with recognition.

A lone dot of orange crystal sat in the upper left corner. It was largely unornamented. Below it, a yellow light glimmered dimly. Broken lines connected it to two dots roughly southeast of it. One was orange, the other red. Towards the right edge of the plate another yellow light shone brightly.

Towards the middle there was a rough triangle of dots, two orange-red, and one blue.

The little blue lights emanated from the blue spherical shape, surrounded by a variety of polygons and spheres; shallow writing was etched into that area of the picture.

In the very middle of the mural an intense yellow light burned.

"It's a star map," Brewer said. She dared to touch the yellow light at the center. "This is us—this is our sun."

"What are you talking about?" Santomero asked.

"I am an astronomer, remember?" Brewer said. "This is almost our current path, following from where we found the *Helen of Troy*." She moved her hand from open space directly towards the yellow light.

The rabbi looked at the lights. "I see it. From your star charts, the ones you were making."

Mr. Veify joined Brewer. "So we're looking down, from between Sirius and Epsilon Eridani?"

"The El Camino Royal route to Earth," Brewer noted. "The most unused star route we have. It's in the middle of nothing for almost twenty-seven light years." She hovered in space, moving from dot to dot. "This star is Epsilon Eridani," she said. She floated to the yellow crystal to its southwest. "This is Tau Ceti. Up there." She pointed to the orange sphere in the upper left-hand corner of the gray plate. "That's Cygni 2. The lower stars are Epsilon Indi and Ross 154. This—" She bounced to a low light coming out of a broken piece of vermilion glass— "is Alpha Centauri. The blue light is Sirius."

"Almost all roads lead from Sirius," Veify noted. Lines converged and diverged from the azure light.

"The map is from beyond Sirius," Brewer said.

"So, Sirius isn't the origin?" Santomero asked.

Brewer shook her head.

"It's a staging area," Santomero suddenly recognized, remembering drills from her military training. "All these courses lead to Sol."

"To *Earth*," the Rabbi realized.

"Mr. Veify, get back to the ship with this data." Santomero ordered.

He nodded and left the remaining three members of the EVA group aboard the alien craft.

"What about Ambassador Senti?" Brewer asked.

"She'll be dead," Santomero replied matter-of-factly.

"I know that," Brewer replied. "But it would be informative to determine the fate of the leader on board the *Helen*. Sorry, Jeff. Not much you can do for the dead, I suppose."

"God can attend to the dead without us. But we do need to find them to bury them," the rabbi replied. "And we are under orders to account for *all* of the *Helen's* crew."

"At least someone around here remembers how to the drill works," Santomero said.

They floated from the room with the star map, passing through a narrow, low-ceilinged opening.

"It's amazing that their lights still work," Brewer noted. "Whoever made this thing intended for it to endure."

"There's no life support," Santomero said.

"There's no life left to support," the Rabbi replied bleakly.

They had to arrange themselves in single file and travel through the next corridor. Santomero went first, popping out of the narrow passageway. She gasped.

If it were not zero gravity, she would have fallen two hundred feet to her death.

Instead, she floated in a vast room of darkness and silence. Brewer and the rabbi followed. They paused in awe of the surreal chamber, each readying their weapon.

The chamber was covered in black, obsidian-like glass. Little red lights filled the room. It was pitted, like honeycomb, with multiple chambers. At what would have been the top of the room there was a dome; within its belly a large red disc glowed, filling the room with a dark crimson light. A convoluted shape superimposed on the light cast odd shadows in the vast nothingness that surrounded them.

Brewer checked her instruments. "Senti's emergency signal is coming from there," she said, pointing to a side room carved into the wall.

The group adjusted the nozzles on their suits, maneuvering themselves to the signal's source.

Then they found the missing.

At the center of the antechamber Ambassador Senti lay, clad inside her spacesuit. A man's body was propped up next to hers, impaled with a sharp metal spike; three other men were likewise pierced with stakes, completing a square around her. The stakes secured the bodies to the structure of the room and kept them from floating.

Around them were more members of the *Helen of Troy's* crew, connected with crude metallic rope to anchor points in the room's walls and floors. Every crewmember was badly bruised, and many bore obviously broken bones. In the end, each had been strangled, a rope still tightly notched around every neck.

"They were put in their suits after death," Brewer noted.

"How can you tell?" the rabbi asked.

"Their internal harnesses, connections, and hoses are unattached. They were killed, and then dressed."

"By something on board this object?" the rabbi asked.

"Something that isn't here anymore," Santomero replied. "Something that went back on the *Helen of Troy* to fix its logs."

"And forgot to water the cactus," Brewer added. "It was weird, about the logs. There was enough information left to tell someone something. But I don't think it's a coincidence that what information we would really need was removed."

"The message in the last pages of the log—those symbols. It was intended for others like these creatures to find?" the rabbi asked.

"Why arrange the crew like this?" Santomero said. She looked around at the morbid scene, the crimson light and steady black shadows making the scene grotesquely surreal.

"Something that would appease dark gods before undertaking a great journey," Brewer replied. "We have a lot of questions. So far all of the answers have been tragic."

Ambassador Senti had been severely beaten. Her face was covered in large, dark welts. A sharp stick had been driven through her head, entering one ear and exiting the other. Stuffed above her head in the spacesuit were a handful of plants. The rough handling of Senti's body had activated her personal locator beacon onto its emergency setting.

"They brought their own sticks and special plants," Brewer said, inspecting the body of Senti as best she could. "I've never seen this type of vegetation before. And these are specialized killing sticks, brought from someplace other than Earth or Varsara. Whoever did this is beyond creepy."

A variety of objects were tethered to the bodies. Personal items like combs and coffee mugs floated on the ropes in the vacuum, alongside weapons and rank badges.

"They're all dead," Santomero surveyed.

The rabbi had moved out of the room, wary of the discovery. He glided effortlessly over the obsidian crypts in the main chamber.

"Miss Brewer, Lieutenant Santomero," he called. There was urgency to his tone. The two women joined him quickly.

He pointed inside a honeycomb-like chamber. "That's not one of ours."

Inside the obsidian crypt there was a skeleton, but it was not human in form. Its skull was larger, its ribcage more compact and fused.

A metal rope garroted its neck.

"All of these chambers are filled with the dead. Ours and those of other alien races," the rabbi observed. "This is a tomb."

"Which leads us to perhaps the most important of our questions," Mary Brewer replied. "Where are the tomb builders now?"

***

Santomero, Mary Brewer and Rabbi Franklyn quickly went through decontamination and got back into ship attire.

"Pool is dead," Hector told them, as they convened in his small conference room onboard the *Kryptos*. "It was close, but there was nothing the doctor could do. His lungs filled with fluid. Death was due to asphyxiation. You all did what you could. I'm sorry, Abigail."

Santomero hit the wall with her fist, uttering curses.

"The funeral is at 2100 hours. Until then, Mr. Veify informs me we may have more pressing issues to attend to. What did we discover, Miss Brewer?" Hector said.

"We accounted for one-hundred-and-seventy-eight of the *Helen's* crew. I checked against the *Helen's* manifest," Mary replied. "Captain May and ten crew members are unaccounted for."

"And no sign of what happened to them?" Hector asked.

"None, Captain," Brewer replied.

"Then we have a lot of major problems," Hector said. He projected an image of the star map they had found in the object.

"Tell me what you know. No bullshit. No secrets," he said to Brewer. "Was Senti sent to make contact with this object?"

"The *Helen of Troy* was on a standard diplomatic mission."

"Meaning Senti was a spy. Just like you," Santomero said.

"Senti was a political hack who liked the perks of diplomatic service. She wasn't a spy," Brewer replied.

"So, you were just visiting, what, an old college roommate, when you stopped by Varsara?" Santomero asked.

"I was on a legitimate astronomical mission," Brewer said. "But if you wanted to dig up meaningful trivia, you would find that I journeyed out and back on another diplomatic vessel: The *Cleopatra*."

"That was George May's command before they finished constructing The *Helen of Troy*," Hector recognized.

"George May was a good man," Brewer said. "One of the best. He could pick up a speck of dust floating through a volcanic ash plume if it was following an odd course. He wouldn't have initiated an investigation of an object like this. He would have reported it and left it for those trained to investigate unknown objects."

"And the object?" Captain Hector asked. "Was there any previous hint that it existed?"

"My orders were to find May. I had no knowledge of any object. I doubt May did, either."

"So, this thing is a fluke of discovery?" Santomero asked.

"Like many archaeological finds," she replied. "It was there, we found it."

"But this isn't archaic," the Rabbi noted. "It's still ticking."

"And its builders are heading towards Earth," Hector added. He touched a button on the computer. A dot flashed within the projected star map, its trajectory heading for Earth. "Mr. Veify found something ahead of us, massively red-shifted. It's not Earth or Varsaran technology."

"The vessel is moving faster than anything we've ever built. It's within a cat's whisker of c, the speed of light itself," Mr. Veify confirmed.

Mary watched the replaying video loop of the star map from the object. The lights twinkled in their odd pattern.

"Captain?" she asked suddenly. "Could you play the audio file of the beacon signal we picked up as we approached the object?"

Hector punched a button, the staccato signal broadcast over a speaker.

"Your cantor skills still up to par, Jeff?" Mary Brewer asked the Rabbi.

"They get me through the Yom Kippur service."

"Tap out the rhythm of the signal the object was transmitting, when I say start," she requested.

She waited for the light pattern to repeat itself.

"Start," she whispered.

The rabbi tapped out the beats of the signal. The rhythm kept time with the pattern of the lights as they waxed and waned.

"They match," Santomero observed.

"Interpretation?" Hector asked. "And no feigned humility. You're probably top of your class to have the President pulling strings to send you all over the universe."

Brewer watched the pattern of lights twinkle on the video feed, gaining intensity and tempo as they wove a way through the spirals towards the yellow light shining steadily in the center.

"My gut instinct says it's a message to those who will follow, those who are the same as the beings of the object," Brewer said. "I think the most immediate interpretation is: *Go there.*"

Every eye fell upon the light representing Sol, understanding that the light may as well be labeled "Earth."

***

"Anything?" Captain Hector asked.

Mary looked up from her computer. "A few things."

"Meaning?"

"We have something in common with these people."

She scrolled up an image of a black-and-white photograph on her computer. "This is seriously obscure. I ended up in the ancient history files, literally."

The picture was of a woman's body garbed in an elaborate gown closely surrounded by four dead figures. Other bodies encircled them. "Earth has a less than entirely savory past."

"It has a less than savory anytime," he reminded her.

"At least we're consistent, then. The newcomers will appreciate ancient Ur."

"That where we are?" Hector asked, gesturing to the photograph.

"Ritual burial," Brewer replied. "Thousands of years ago. A queen entombed; her court drank poison to accompany her on her journey beyond our space. I think the similarities end there."

Captain Hector nodded solemnly. "The scene on the object we found was more violent. And Senti wasn't their queen. Furthermore, the others were not voluntary participants in a commonly held ritual."

"Are you planning on destroying the object?" Brewer asked.

"I'm not sure yet. It points right towards Earth. I don't want it to lead others to us."

"That would let them know we know about them. It would be revealing our rudimentary intelligence," she said. "And then there are the bodies aboard. The rabbi will argue for taking our own home for proper burial; the scientists will want the alien bodies for study. And Mr. Veify is correct: The substance that makes up the object would greatly advance our own technology. We may need to bring ourselves up to their speed as fast as we can."

"What else did you find?" the captain said, silently noting that all her points had already run through his own mind.

"I put in the key words: sacrifice, burial, and impaling." She queued up her results. "That led to a lot of fun Earth history."

"I bet." He settled back in the chair. "Are we projecting our own cultural biases too much?"

"The brutality of life is universal," she replied. "It is mercy, honor, and grace that are learned and cultivated."

"And the first against the wall when the revolution comes. Let's hope we can keep what we've learned from dying under the latest threat."

"You need to speak to the rabbi," she recommended. "There's a reason every ship has a chaplain aboard." She returned to her research. "Do you remember studying Huns or Mongols?"

"Military science makes mention of them."

"Sorry."

"No offense taken. Continue."

"Before them there was a group called the Scythians. A fierce warrior race with a knack for stealing technology and making it their own. They also took a fancy to beautiful metalwork. They buried their nobles in massive mound-like graves called kurgans."

She brought up a computer-generated image of a mound surrounded by horsemen still in the saddle on war-ready steppe ponies. All the mounts and riders had been impaled around the mound.

"Fifty men and fifty horses, impaled around the burial of a king, set there to guard the tomb," she said. She sat back, her still black eyes looking into things he could not see. "I think the object we found serves many purposes."

"I have a feeling I'm not going to like any of them."

"I would like to suggest my conclusions to the group. I think their insight would be important."

"I will arrange that."

***

"The object still had power when we found it. Enough to light their star map," Santomero stated.

The group in the briefing room was glum. Simply knowing that they were still likely the only ones aware that something evil was heading towards Earth was devastating.

"The object still had power because it is designed to be found," Mary Brewer said. "It is a communications point and a place of ritual."

"It's a grave," Santomero pointed out. "Why put a grave in the middle of nowhere?"

"It marks territory," Brewer replied quietly. "When I ran through the history files investigating human burial patterns, I found an interesting article on Mesolithic man."

"Dawn of human history stuff right there," Veify noted.

"Mesolithic man started burying their dead in the area of their homes and settlements," Brewer continued. "It was a way of claiming the land, of saying *we're here, and we're here to stay.*"

"So, these creatures place their claim on space by burying their dead in space?" Captain Hector asked. "Why kill the crew of the *Helen of Troy*? They weren't these beings; how would burying them assert an alien claim to territory?"

"Burying their own dead holds their claim to space, probably to entire regions of it," Mary hypothesized. "But they also practice brutal sacrificial rites. The *Helen's* crew was most likely sacrificed to bring about some sort of result. A magic, if you will."

"Magic? In space?" Mr. Veify asked. "Seriously, Miss Brewer."

"You throw salt over your shoulder when you spill it, Mr. Veify. I've seen you do it," she returned. "And not everything in the universe is science. There are other subjects of study worth pursuing. You're losing the trees for the sake of trying to grasp the concepts of the forest."

"So, this belief, this ritual, this magic, this superstition—whatever it is—what does it mean?" Captain Hector asked. He looked from face to face. "Project yourselves on these people—what do you think they are seeking? What would you light a candle for if you were on the object?"

"Safe passage," Santomero whispered. She looked with a suddenly pale face at Captain Hector.

"Lieutenant?" he asked. "You look like you've seen a ghost."

"The *Iliad*," she replied. "To provide safe passage for the Greek fleet, Agamemnon sacrificed his daughter, Iphigenia, to the goddess Artemis. One fleet, one girl. A full crew might be what is required to grant safe passage for an entire race of beings."

"The *Helen's* crew were not alone in being sacrificed," Veify added. "We found evidence of fifteen types of unknown aliens dead in those chambers."

"They bring their sacrifices with them, or capture them," Brewer suggested. "Like the ancient Aztecs perhaps."

"Okay, people, I think we're losing ourselves in our own morbid history here," Hector cautioned.

"The object sent out the signal that we detected. The *Helen of Troy* could have heard a similar signal and decided to investigate. All Earth vessels carry the discretionary order to identify and contact alien beings they might encounter," Mr. Veify mentioned. "Perhaps the aliens wanted to stop the *Helen* from interfering with their rituals. Or stop the *Helen* from alerting those along their planned route of invasion. The *Helen* had seen too much, heard too much. The *Helen* had to be destroyed."

"Why? The aliens are faster. Even if the *Helen* saw them leaving for Earth, there's nothing it could have done to stop them, or warn Earth in time," the rabbi said.

"The aliens didn't know that," Hector reminded him.

"They knew it was a ship from Earth," Santomero said grimly.

"Why do you say that?" the rabbi asked.

"They know space pretty well," she replied. "Their star maps, their scribbling on the wall. All data they've collected. Our sun is the center of their designs. They've been watching for us. Waiting."

"For what?" the rabbi said.

"These are bastards on the move," Santomero said. "They have all the signs of people that systematically vanquish, subjugate, and annihilate others. They recognized the *Helen* as an Earth ship. A ship from the next intended conquest."

"So they lured it in?" Brewer asked.

"Artemis was very specific about who she wanted sacrificed," Santomero said. "I'm betting that their detection of the *Helen* was like a divine sign."

***

Captain Hector sat at his desk in his private office, watching the stars as they Doppler blended outside, forming little ribbons of lights.

Rabbi Franklyn entered. "You asked for me?"

"I need someone around who thinks non-militarily," the captain said. Music played in the background.

"Brahms," the rabbi noted, sitting down. "Symphony Number Three in F Major, Opus 90, third movement."

"You know music as well as religion, art, and expert marksmanship, I see," Captain Hector said. "It's funny how we carry so much knowledge with us everywhere we go. As if it will save us."

"What was it they taught me in my space military science courses? *We learn so that we may outthink an opponent, we anticipate in order to outsmart our opponent, and we adapt in order to outfight our opponent?* Learning is the root of survival, Captain."

The captain projected the moving dot that represented the alien vessel on his wall. "It moves inexorably towards an unsuspecting planet. Bearing a species that claims empty space by slaughtering people amidst the stars. Bearing a species that already views our planet as their own to claim. Like Assyrians with warp drive."

"You have warned everyone you could."

"I sent a message to Varsara. I sent messages to all the colonies, and to any Earth ship I could locate."

The rabbi picked up the piece of metal they had found on the *Helen of Troy* from the captain's desk. "This was a calling card," the rabbi said. "Something to say we've been here."

"We are four light years from home, rabbi. Mr. Veify estimates the alien ship ahead of us, the one from the tomb, is going 0.99c—nearly the speed of light. It has a fifteen-month head start. Even allowing for deceleration time that means the aliens will reach Earth in about three and a half years. Moving at the speed of light, our radio messages will take a smidge over four years to get home."

"Six months too late," the rabbi said.

"We may not have a planet to go home to," Hector added.

***

Brewer was ordered to Captain Hector's personal briefing room. She sat next to the rabbi.

"I need your thoughts," the captain told her.

"I think those creatures may be in for a rude awakening if they think Earth is all soft and diplomatic," Mary said. "We are the species that produced the Assyrians, Scythians, Huns, Mongols, and Aztecs. The aliens may find out the hard way that we're better at ruthless violence than they are."

"That's your comforting thought?" the rabbi asked. "Don't ever consider becoming a rabbi."

"It is legitimate data," Hector said, "You're our Cassandra, now, Brewer. Keep on talking, even when the rabbi thinks it sounds crazy." A well-managed anger tinged his voice. "We can't get to Earth before the aliens, and we can't send a transmission that will get there any faster, either. We're in an intergalactic spacecraft loaded with the most advanced weaponry our species has ever produced, and we are completely unable to help the people back home."

"What are your plans?" Brewer asked, intrigued by the composure slipping away from the captain.

"I'm taking us back to Varsara. We can accumulate resources there. I want these other alien life forms identified. If there are other pissed off people out there looking to settle a score with these creatures, they may be a big help."

"When the big fight breaks out," the rabbi observed. "Grant, these allies may be like us Earthlings, first in glory among those who oppose this terrible threat."

"I like the evolution of Hector's words from the *Iliad*," Brewer noted.

"I am seriously banning that book from all future missions," Hector said.

"Jeff is just looking forward to another victory; another event to celebrate with eating," Mary said, nearly smiling for a moment. She hoped her levity would bolster morale.

"Amen," the rabbi replied.

Captain Hector sat in his chair, looking at Franklyn and Brewer. "I'm a combat arms man, all hoo-ah, hoo-ah. I never really respected support services—not before meeting you two. Things like the Chaplain Corps and civilian intelligence were always less than real fighting men in my book."

"I've met that sentiment," the rabbi replied. "We forgive you."

"This force is more overwhelming than anything humanity has ever faced before. The slap in the seat of my pants is that the threat we face needs *your* skills even more than mine to fight." Hector shook his head. "And we may soon be the only humans left to fight these things."

"You have an able and well-trained crew," Mary said.

"But in this fight, their training won't save them." Hector surveyed them, his eyes quiet and cold. "We aren't fast enough, we don't have enough ammunition. From this point forward, you two are now the front line. Mindfulness is the key to this victory; spirit and stealth will be our greatest weapons. "

"Then we need to run silent and deep, sir, so the aliens don't find us," Brewer replied, already in her new role.

"Your suggestion?" Hector asked.

"We break off all communications until we're safe on Varsara," she returned. "And we don't stop for anything. Not like the *Helen of Troy*."

Hector nodded. "Then it's time for the *Kryptos* to go missing."

His eyes rested coldly on the red dot, moving through the stars.

The House Across the Street

The secrets you don't know may be more jolting than the secrets you do know.

Eric watched them work on the old house across the street. It wasn't a very old house, but he heard people looking at it, saying words like "tired" and "dated," as if the dwelling made the lookers themselves older.

Mrs. McVicker, whose husband had left her years before to move back to Ireland, had died, and now the old house was up for sale.

Eric did not think the house deserved to have its very soul ripped from it.

The workmen came in dirty pickup trucks, fueled by visions of renovation. Remaking homes was so popular now. Even if the home didn't need the facelift, it was subjected to the surgery anyway.

An old house didn't stand a chance against the redecorators.

But the old house across the street was a special house, Eric knew.

It was haunted.

He worried terribly about the spirit that prowled the old home.

The workmen never noticed the phantom, even when their tools moved seemingly on their own or their papers were rearranged. They were the type who scratched their heads much less frequently than they scratched their rear ends.

The workers ripped things out, sanding and sawing and melting. Hammering in new bookshelves and cabinets. Eviscerating the old home, then putting in new plumbing and new lights. Ripping up the yard and laying down fresh sod.

The innards of the old house were lain to rest in a large, rusting garbage bin. Discarded and rejected, they were taken away by the refuse company, as if they had never witnessed any memories worth saving.

At nights, when the workmen went home, the ghost would come out, each night later than the night before. And he would leave earlier. As his habitat was being destroyed, his walks were growing briefer.

Eric watched the ghost every night, with peculiar interest.

The spirit of an old man, with a rumbling laugh, graying hair, and a rounded belly, haunted the old structure.

Eric did not remember seeing the ghost when Mrs. McVicker lived in the house. Perhaps the workmen had roused the ghost, as they began to destroy the old boards that bore his imprint.

Perhaps he had lived there before the McVickers. Eric did not know.

But he did know a ghost when he saw one. And this ghost walked across the living room, pausing once every night, before the fireplace. He would push phantom spectacles back up his nose, then walk some more until he disappeared.

Eric could see the stones of the fireplace through the ghostly form.

Then one day, the workman started destroying the old living room, smashing the old fireplace into rough pebbles. They were putting in a new floor, building a new mantle. Moving the walls, so that the room had new dimensions.

The new stones reminded Eric of warm vanilla candy. He could almost taste their color.

Down the hall of his own house, Eric heard Mom calling to the other kids. She looked out at the activity across the way. Modestly inspired by the work on the old house, she plastered and painted her walls responsively, covering the walls with pretty colors like warm wassail and sparkling sand.

One day, she paused in her sprucing to take the baby to the doctor. She told the baby she had to have shots. Eric was frightened at first, fearing the baby would *be shot*, but Mom continued. She explained to the baby that they were only called shots, and these immunizations would keep the baby safe from diseases and fevers.

Eric drank the knowledge in.

Mom and the baby came back. The baby looked contented and happy. Mom nursed her, and they both took an afternoon nap, the gentle sunlight filtering through the blinds.

Eric wondered about the shots. Maybe if they had them when he was a baby, he wouldn't have died of the fever. He remembered drifting groggily away, exhausted and parched. When he woke up, his body was locked away from his mind, and he drifted, his form unseen and unheard. His mother had cried so much he thought even he would die again from her pain.

His mother left one day, years ago. To move, along with his father and siblings, some born after his death, to someplace else. But Eric stayed put, not wanting to hazard leaving the spot. When he was smaller his mother always told him to stay put, or he'd get lost more.

So, he stayed. Waiting for her to find him.

He was thankful that the Mom who lived in his house now hadn't caught the redecorating bug too bad.

Eric needed the integrity of the house maintained. He needed something tangible from his living days to help him maintain his presence between worlds. Something his energy had gone into, in life. All spirits needed an imprinted physical resonance, something that would guide them back. A whisper of something familiar on a path lost in fog.

Remove the structure, and the spirit could only linger, formless and isolated.

So Eric waited in his old spaces, and watched the living while he did. There was a boredom to eternity that even timelessness did not remedy.

Now even the distraction of watching the other ghost was lost to Eric as an activity. The old man's ghost had not walked the night before.

Eric wondered. Was the spirit still able to manifest in the changing structure? Or had the workmen torn too much of the old house out to sustain his presence any longer?

The house was well lit from within this evening, its bare windows allowing easy viewing of the house's interior. Eric was curious, never having been afforded such a glimpse of the inside of the old house before. The workmen were working inside, late into the clement evening.

Then there was an unexpected flurry of activity across the street. A workman came sprinting out of the living room, his eyes as wide as two fried eggs cooked and ready for the plate.

Before Eric could absorb himself in the new drama, something else caught his attention.

A voice, calling his name.

"Eric! Eric! Oh, my baby! Where are you?"

"Momma?" Eric cried, moving towards her lovely, lovely voice. He had not heard her voice for decades, but time melted away the moment he recognized her call.

And she was there, just as he remembered her from the last time he saw her. Tears flowing down her face. She held him close, her ethereal body hugging his.

"Oh, my baby!" she moaned.

"I didn't move, Momma! I stayed put, like you always told me to."

"I know, baby, I know," Momma cried.

"How did you find me?" Eric asked.

"Mr. McVicker told me," Momma said. "He was finally freed, and he told me where you were. He's been keeping an eye out for you all these years."

"Mr. McVicker?"

"The man who lived across the street. His wife said he'd gone back to Ireland."

"That was his home?" Eric asked, thinking of the old house.

The workmen were now running out of the old house with odd urgency, gasping and swearing as they spilled onto the fresh new lawn.

"Oh, baby!" Momma smiled through the tears, "That was just his house. Now he's truly going home, just like we are."

She held his little hand in his and led Eric out of the old structure. He felt his body drift painlessly through the old boards, past the other Mom and her baby, playing in the sun-drenched yard.

Eric didn't look back.

He didn't see the workman hysterical on the yard across the street, and the foreman on the telephone, serious and pale. He didn't see inside the house across the street, where the last drywall of the living room had been smashed out and after all these years they had finally found out where Mr. McVicker had truly gone.

Not Ireland, after all.

His walled-up bones tumbled out into a neat pile on the fresh new tiles, in the house across the street.

It wasn't Mr. McVicker's house anymore. It was no longer the house across the street from Eric. The little boy who had died of the terrible influenza, the same day Mrs. McVicker declared herself a merry widow.

Lyra Sacra

Traditions die hard.

Keaton O'Brien lived down the hall in Apartment B. Emma rarely heard him, although she often heard the heavy footsteps of Mr. Uzick who lived in the apartment above hers.

Keaton had moved in a month ago, and Emma had kept an interested eye out for any female visitors. To her delight, none had appeared.

It took a few tries, but eventually Emma engineered a way to pick her mail up at the same time Keaton approached his box.

"Hi, I'm Emma," she said, introducing herself.

"I'm Keaton," he replied. It was simple intelligence to exchange. Their names were written on the mailbox bank, after all. A: Emma Holder. B: Keaton O'Brien. C: Abraham Uzick. D: Vacant.

The landlord had divided an old house into four apartments. There was a small pool in the courtyard, usually less than sparkling turquoise. The property was aged, but the rent was affordable.

"You just moved in." Emma said.

"A month ago," he replied, shuffling bills.

"I've been here a year," she added quickly, sensing he was losing interest in the mundane conversation. "I'm a med student. I'm going to be a doctor." Why did that line work better for her male classmates? They always got laid using it; she just looked desperate.

"That's a lot of work," he said. "I'm getting my master's in music."

"What do you play?"

"I sing," he replied. "I've been adding some education classes lately. Enough of my friends are having a hard time finding paying work. I might try to teach."

"I'm planning Ear, Nose, and Throat as a specialty. I guess that's close."

"Pipes are pipes."

"We should get together some time. I know the city pretty well. I could show you some of the sites."

"That would be nice."

Emma frowned as he left. *Nice?* That was almost as bad a direct rejection.

She would have to work on her lines better, for next time.

***

Houston had been miserably hot all September. Emma remembered hearing that no one scheduled interviews in Houston in the summer months, so prospective employees and students were not driven away by the sweltering, blast furnace like heat.

By October, the first cold fronts had drifted lazily down, causing the temperatures to fall into the eighties. That was cool for a Houstonian. The evenings sometimes dropping into the fifties, which was almost downright frigid.

Emma had the windows open in the afternoon but closed and locked them at night. While the temperature was inviting, there was still crime in the large city, and she didn't want to invite any of it in.

She finished studying, her head aching from words and diagrams. She had sworn off coffee after six in the evening, so her mind slowed down to useless speed.

Flipping channels on her television had proven fruitless. The programming offered little that seemed interesting, notwithstanding things she had already seen a dozen times before. Then there were the advertisements. She wondered if anyone ever noticed that three easy payments of nineteen ninety-nine(!) was actually more than the one-time payment of fifty dollars. Maybe the target audience was not expected to have arithmetic skills. They certainly seemed to be deemed unable to properly use paper towels, buy herbs at a local shop, work a mop, or use regular epoxy.

She heard Mr. Uzick go to bed about 10:50 p.m. Other than that, the evening was still and quiet.

In the distance she could hear the continuous whoosh of cars circulating on the 610 Loop. Traffic never stopped on the freeways. When asked to evacuate in the approach of Hurricane Rita, she had left early, managing to avoid the dreadful traffic jams. She had left even earlier for Hurricane Ike and returned to the blanket of low-level devastation Ike had left everyplace in his wake. She spent six days without electricity, picking up branches and a seemingly endless supply of debris.

While Emma slept, the next cold front arrived, bringing swift, strong winds as its heralds. Rain pelted against the window, the musty smell of moist earth rising in the air. It had a name, Emma knew: petrichor. That delicious smell of soil being infused by fresh rain.

Emma stirred in her sleep, thinking she heard a woman's voice.

Singing? she thought. The sound was hardly musical. It sounded like a woman, straining to hit high soprano notes and shrieking as she failed spectacularly to make them.

The lease called for no loud noises after ten p.m. on weekday nights.

But Emma was willing to let the noise go. It was probably a coworker of Keaton's, helping him prepare for one of his few paying jobs. She hoped Keaston was better than his female colleague.

"How did your practice go last night?" Emma asked the following morning, passing Keaton in the building's common hallway.

"I didn't have practice last night," Keaton said.

"I heard a woman singing. I thought perhaps you had a rehearsal at your place."

Keaton shook his head. "No. I went out for dinner with some friends last night. Tonight, I have a rehearsal. I got a job singing at a synagogue Friday nights. I need to learn quite a bit before I start next month. You keeping busy, doc?"

"Very busy. I have labs to do, exams to study for. The usual. I'm counting down to the end of the semester. Exams are in early December."

"Well, best of luck."

"Yeah," Emma said quietly. "You, too."

She wondered if he was lying about the singing woman. After all, the woman had been garishly bad.

Emma encountered Mr. Uzick in the common hallway.

"How are your studies?" he asked.

"Good," she smiled.

"I see we have a new neighbor."

"Keaton."

"A nice looking young man. He seems to have a steady friend, a young man who stops by quite frequently. How is that grandmother of yours?"

"Still planning to climb Everest."

"You tell her to stop by here on her way to Nepal."

"I'm seeing her tomorrow. I'll tell her you said so."

Mr. Uzick moved on to his home.

Emma could hear Keaton singing in his apartment. His rich voice filled the hallway. She also heard him talking, another man's voice responding.

She stepped closer and placed her ear on the wall; the dampness in the air lingered on the plaster, tickling her ear.

"So, love," Keaton asked, "Where do you want to eat? When I start work, we'll lose Friday nights."

"But gain another paycheck," the other man pointed out, playful humor in his voice.

Emma peeled her cheek off the wall. A sudden wave of embarrassment covered her, and she retreated to her own apartment.

Once inside, she put on her headphones and tuned into a local radio station. She had exams to study for.

How could I have been so blind? Her mind couldn't let go of the intimacy in the two men's voices. *And how the Hell am I supposed to pass my labs if I can't even figure out the cute guy down the hall is gay?* She scolded herself.

The tunes in her headphones drowned out any other music that might have been playing around her.

***

By December, the weather was alternating between cold and clement. It had even snowed, albeit a Houston snow, which sufficed to dust the cars with a single layer of snowflakes. It delighted the children, and everyone came out in heavy coats with digital cameras and video recorders to document the miracle.

It was two a.m., and Emma swore she heard something stepping on the cold ground outside: footsteps in the back yard, soft and feminine. It was too late for Mr. Uzick to be awake. No one was living in the long vacant Apartment D. Keaton and his companion were still out.

Emma tiptoed out of bed and gently pulled back the curtains. There was nothing outside but trees gently swaying in the light breeze. The security lights were on; no odd shadows fell across the sidewalk.

She shrugged and sat on her sofa, picking up a novel. Waking up had disturbed her sleep cycle, and Emma was now too awake to reclaim her rest. She was in no mood to memorize acronyms and biochemical pathways. It had taken her half a semester to realize that "AAA" wasn't the automobile club, or an eager extension of Alcoholics Anonymous. *Abdominal aortic aneurysm*, she had overheard two upper classmen talking in the hallway, when the light bulb went off in her mind. *I hope someone famous dies of one of those before I have to know that for a class*, she found herself thinking, *then some improbably beautiful anchorman can explain the symptoms and causes to me—before some hopelessly obtuse professor that we're all afraid of tries to.*

Outside, the wind rustled the leaves.

Hidden among the sound, Emma heard it again: A shivering, shrieking noise, a little louder in volume than before.

She put down her book.

It wasn't the neighing sound of a screech owl, although the sound was similar in some ways.

It was more of a wailing noise, like a woman crying a discordant serenade.

Emma checked outside again. She could not see anyone, and that disturbed her almost as much as if she could see the source to the horribly mesmerizing tune.

She really needed the semester to be over. The singing was already disturbing her sleep.

***

Keaton was picking up the Saturday mail. He looked at Emma oddly.

"Morning," she said, politely.

"Morning," he replied. "Hey, were you singing last night?" he blurted it out in that way that suggested he had thought of no other way to ask.

Emma shook her head. "No. I don't sing."

"I heard a woman singing."

"I heard it, too. I looked outside but couldn't see anybody. Maybe we have another diva in the courtyard."

She regretted her choice of words, feeling insensitive. "I mean, other than me singing in my shower from time to time. Well, they say sing like no one's listening." That suddenly struck her as a stupid thing to say, too. *My bedside manner is going to rock*, she thought sarcastically to herself. *Is it too late to go to law school? Lawyers get paid good money to say stupid, insensitive things. I might be a natural for that.*

***

"Emma!" Grandmother Holder greeted. Despite strained relations between Grandmother Holder and Emma's mother, the family matriarch always had time for Emma.

Emma hugged the healthy old lady.

"You look great," Emma said.

"I'm working out at the Y."

"Better than I've been doing."

"You have to work and study so many hours. You'd think being in medical school, they'd teach you to take better care of yourself."

Emma took a seat in her grandmother's small suite at the assisted living complex. "How are things here?"

"It's quiet." She sat down opposite her granddaughter. "You look very tired."

"There's been some woman singing around the building. It's woken me up twice."

"You should report her to management. That's against the lease, isn't it?"

"Yeah. But I don't know whom to report. When I look around, there's no one there."

"Well, I'm sure you'll catch her sooner or later. She sounds flamboyant."

"That's one word for it," Emma replied. "So, where do we do lunch today?"

"You should be out with younger people more, not always taking me out to lunch."

"You're young at heart. Anyway, you'll listen to my stories. Even the very boring ones."

"Well, I am especially interested in the story about this mysterious lady singer," Grandmother said, gathering her coat and purse.

"That is precisely the story that I'm most interested in telling you."

***

Saturday night, Emma sat watching television while studying. She saw Keaton and his boyfriend depart for another evening out.

Mr. Uzick was also out. He had met a lady at Bingo.

Apparently, everybody but her was hooking up.

She felt oddly alone without the footsteps and chatter of her neighbors.

At about ten thirty p.m., the singing started again. It sounded like a tuning fork being grated against a washing board.

Emma stood up quickly, determined to stop the noise.

She saw no one outside. She opened the back door and stepped out.

The singing persisted, high and shrieking one moment, low and moaning the next, alternating with terrible unpredictability.

Emma listened, following the noise to its source. She looked up the back staircase, to where the odd voice wove its bizarre hymn.

A woman stood at the top of the stairway, stately and middle-aged. Her hair was graying, but long and red at the ends. She bore a sad, noble expression.

The notes dripped, now sour and echoing, from her lips.

She looked down, and as Emma started to speak, the woman's figure dissipated, turning into empty air, leaving only the lilting harmonic of an interrupted note.

Emma froze.

The leaves whirled quietly around her.

***

It was Saturday again, a week later, and Emma looked like Hell. Her eyes boasted bloated, reddened bags beneath them. Her face was pale and thinner.

"Goodness, child!" Grandmother Holder said. "You look awful."

"I feel awful. I haven't been sleeping," Emma said, without vigor. "At least finals are over. If only the singing would stop."

"The singing is still going on?"

Emma sat down.

Grandmother Holder put the kettle on. "I'll make some tea. Did you find out who was making the racket?"

"Sort of."

"Well?"

"There's a woman who sings on the back stairwell, every night. Her songs are getting louder and longer."

"Have you complained?"

"To who?"

"To the apartment management. You need to have her evicted."

"I need to have her exorcised."

"How do you mean?" Grandmother Holder asked.

"She disappears every time I look at her. Standing there, with her solemn look, her mournful eyes. Not that she hangs around after she knows I've seen her."

"Is she young or old?" Grandmother Holder asked. It was a thoughtful and probing question.

"Middle aged. She's very respectable looking—her posture is so perfect. She wears a drab gray cloak and carries dead flowers. It's a charming thing to see. Her singing is even worse than she looks."

The kettle boiled. Grandmother Holder got up and made tea. "Who is in your building?" she inquired, dunking tea bags and adding milk.

"Mr. Uzick, who always asks after you."

"He's a sweet man. Who else?"

"The new guy, Keaton O'Brien."

Grandmother Holder stopped what she was doing. "O'Brien?"

"He's a musician. I don't think the woman is part of his musician friend crowd, though. He's as miffed by the noise as me."

"I want you to listen to me," Grandmother Holder said. "And don't think I'm a crazy old lady."

"You're one of the few sane people left on the planet."

Grandmother Holder held Emma's hands in her own. "You have a banshee."

"A banshee? Like in the old Irish fairy tales? Please, Grandma. This woman is real. Except for the disappearing into thin air part."

"The banshee is a creature that portends death. It can appear with three faces, as it chooses—as the young girl Badhbh, the matron Macha, or the old hag Mor-Rioghain. The banshee keeps faith with the five old families of Ireland: the O'Neills, the O'Connors, the O'Gradys, the Kavanaghs, and Clan O'Brien."

"O'Brien? Like Keaton?"

"Is your friend a healthy man?"

"He looks fine. I guess he has some lifestyle risk factors, but we all have those, when you really think about it."

"You should tell him to take care of himself," Grandmother Holder said. She sipped her tea.

"Should I tell him? About the banshee part?"

"Just in case he doesn't know," Grandmother Holder replied. "While the banshee keeps its faith with the clans, not everyone keeps faith with the old ghosts anymore."

"It was hard enough figuring out how to say 'hello' to Keaton," Emma said. "Now I've got to figure out a way to tell him a banshee is singing for him and that his death may be approaching?"

"You're a bright girl, Emma. You'll figure out a way. After all, you want to be a doctor—people will expect you to know how to bear bad news as much as good."

***

"Mr. O'Brien?" Emma asked, as she purposefully bumped into him, picking up the Monday mail.

"No one calls me Mr. O'Brien." He laughed. "What's on your mind, Emma?"

"Are you doing okay?"

"Fine," he replied. "Why do you ask?"

"Just wanted to make sure everything was okay." Emma paused, awkwardly. "Have you heard that woman singing?"

"Every damn night. I never see her, though."

"I have."

"Did you tell her to shut up?"

"It isn't quite that straightforward." Emma shuffled nervously. "Do you remember the tales of the banshee from Ireland? Your family's old country?"

Keaton laughed. "Not really. Keaton O'Brien is my stage name. My real name is Polish. It has every consonant invented in it. They'd run out of Zs long before they'd finish putting my birth name up on any marquee. There isn't a drop of Irish blood in me."

"Oh," Emma said, feeling insensitive and stupid again.

"What about a banshee? All I know about those is that one of my former choir directors used to accuse the sopranos of sounding like banshees when they got too much vibrato going."

"Just that the woman... she sounds like one."

"Yeah, I guess she does," Keaton replied, grinning. "You're pretty funny for a science geek. I'm having a small get together at my place weekend after this. Why don't you come over?"

"I'll try to be there," she offered.

He hurried off to his ever-vibrant life.

She opened her mailbox. Picking out the envelopes, she noted their origins. Bills, advertising circulars, and an offer for life insurance addressed to Keaton and accidentally put into her box.

She slipped it into the crack in his mailbox.

"You still may want to look into that," she said quietly.

***

The singing continued all week long.

By Friday night, Emma was sick of it. The lack of sleep was disrupting her concentration. She was drunk with fatigue.

She stepped outside, fully prepared to face the ghastly attendant of the five old families.

The figure stood at the top of the stairs, wailing her pitiful song. It screamed sharp, discordant notes, sending them whirling in the cool night air.

"He's not a real O'Brien!" Emma yelled up at the figure, finding courage in hearing her own voice. "He's Polish. Lots of Zs in his name. Just like the Zs I'm not getting. Surely you're needed someplace else! The phone book is full of O'Briens."

The figure turned sharply, and with a searing, blasting scream, it made itself disappear. It seemed to study Emma's face closely as it left, peering into her soul.

"Hopefully that will do it," Emma consoled herself.

***

Grandmother Holder looked pleased when she saw Emma on Saturday.

"You look rested!" she beamed.

"I finally got some decent sleep last night. And I needed it," Emma reported, putting the kettle on. "This banshee thing really screwed with my routine."

Grandmother Holder was concerned. "Don't speak so lightly of dark fairies. They wield powerful magic."

"I told it to take its warnings elsewhere." Emma smiled.

"What!"

"I spoke to it. Told it to go away. Stop bothering the neighborhood. It turns out," she said as she finished making the tea, thoughtfully stirring in the milk, "That Keaton isn't really an O'Brien."

"What do you mean?"

"I spoke to him. Turns out he's Polish. O'Brien is his stage name. The big ole melting pot at work." Emma placed the teas on a table. "Why do you look worried? The banshee should be gone. Keaton isn't really Irish."

Grandmother Holder's expression was not relieved. "Has her song been getting longer, getting more powerful? The song gets more intense as death comes closer. It is a holy deed the banshee does, Emma, intended to give the soon-to-be-dead time to prepare for the world to come. To do the work necessary before entering eternal rest."

Emma noted her grandmother's increased concern. "I don't like how upset you look. This is how you used to look when you and Mom had a big fight and didn't tell me anything about it. Which was about every time you and Mom met."

"Did your mother ever tell you why she and I had such a falling out?"

"No."

"Now might be the time to tell you," Grandmother Holder said. "Twenty-four years ago, your father and your mother were going through a rough patch. He was drinking and not working; she was working and not having any time to drink. He had an affair."

"I knew they had problems. They resolved them."

"Before they reconciled, your mother decided to get back at your father. I cautioned her not to. She had a one-night stand, with a man she met at an airport lounge."

"I never knew that."

"Your mother and I kept it secret. We saw no reason to upset your father. I was terribly upset with her. Your mother and I were never the same after that. Carrying that secret strained our relationship."

"Why tell me now?"

"You were born nine months later. Your mother and I were never sure."

"Sure about what?" Emma asked, sensing an unpleasant speculation.

"Sure if you were your father's daughter. He was my son, Emma. I didn't want to ever suggest he was raising another man's child."

"And why tell this to me now?"

"The man your mother had the affair with matters."

"Why does that matter? Who was he?"

"Sean Michael Kavanagh, on a business trip from Dublin."

"Kavanagh?"

"That would make you Emma Kavanagh. Not Emma Holder."

"Kavanagh is one of the five old families."

Grandmother Holder had tiny tears brimming on her lower lids. "The banshee hasn't been singing for your Mr. O'Brien. Oh, sweet Emma—the banshee has been singing for *you.*"

The Woven

When you want something to watch over you, wouldn't eight eyes be better than two?

The younger policeman seemed nervous, very much a messenger uncomfortable with the news he carried. He fidgeted in his uniform, brushing himself off with agitated hands.

Rashi approached the house, splashed with rotating flashes of red and blue light. The younger officer intercepted him.

"Good morning, sir." Uneasy nerves didn't suit the young man; they made him look a bit the imbecile.

"Yes?" Rashi asked.

"You're not afraid of anything, are you, sir?"

Rashi paused and raised an eyebrow. "Unemployment," he replied.

That put the young man even more ill at ease. "It's just that... this is an unusual crime scene. You sure you don't have any phobias?"

Rashi grunted. He was a long-term veteran of the police force. He had seen almost everything. Some images stuck with him, often striking him at unexpected moments, but he had learned various methods of coping over the years. His memories were often triggered by smell.

There was a smell here, an olfactory link to a half-forgotten event. There was a damp, peculiar animal scent in the air. It reminded him of a theater trip when he was a boy. His mother's faux fur coat soaked with rainwater as she got him and his brother into the dry car. She stood in her high heels, rainwater pouring off her, making sure her sons were attended to first.

Dad was not there.

He had been a cop, too.

As Rashi approached the crime scene he saw a young policewoman standing restlessly outside the residence. Yellow tape fenced in the little green lawn around her.

Rashi considered the uniformed officer critically. "Aren't you on body watch?"

"Yes, sir," the young woman replied.

"Shouldn't you be in *there*? With the body? Unless you have x-ray vision, you can't keep an eye on it out here."

"I don't think anyone will mess with it in there," she hazarded.

Rashi shook his head. He wasn't sure about what they were teaching at the Academy now. He had an old school mind: *Be speedy to obey a superior, be dignified before the young.*

Neither junior officer seemed speedy. They didn't look dignified either as they shuffled, scratched, and swatted at themselves.

Rashi stepped up to the door. *There was the smell again.* Damp hair, like wet bristles.

Something moved in the window and caught his attention. He glanced over and saw what made the movement.

Jumping spiders. About two-dozen of them crawled on the inside of the windowpane. They pivoted about, their little eyes attentively looking out of the window. Rashi looked at them closely, through the glass.

They paused, their little furry legs balanced oddly on the dusty glass. It was almost as if they were looking back at him.

Rashi had a few vices, and a few fears. Luckily arachnophobia wasn't among the latter.

He pushed out the tip of the ballpoint pen—pen and paper were still his most valuable tools. *Old school, again*, he thought. He felt his age, watching a nearby technician from the crime lab enter notes on an electronic tablet.

The technician looked up. "You don't have a palm computer?" he asked.

Rashi shook his head.

"I don't know how you can operate without the latest technology," the young man said, typing away. "I don't know how people got by before the twenty-first century. Heck, I can't imagine how I lived before last week."

Rashi frowned. He had been working homicide for longer than he cared to remember. The tools of the trade changed, mostly for the cops. Sometimes for the killers who used new weapons, but that was rare. Murder had remained fundamentally unchanged since Cain slew Abel. A club had worked then; a club still worked now.

Rashi took a breath and entered the house.

It smelled of old death.

Jeremy Houston, Rashi's partner, was already there. Bits of fluff floated in the bright morning air.

"What has the uniforms spooked?"

"The crime scene." Houston smiled evilly.

Rashi looked over his shoulder at the young woman who quavered slightly as she stood outside the door. "She'll have to get over that. Why isn't she in here with the body?"

"I don't think it's the body that's spooking her."

Rashi shrugged. There was a lingering rotting chicken smell in the air. That meant it had been a while since the crime had been committed. "How long has the vic been dead?"

"No definite idea yet. A local busybody called it in. Hadn't seen the old gal who lives—lived—here for a while. The witness was babbling something about the spiders on the windows alerting her." He gestured, "We were waiting for you to get the party started."

Rashi moved farther into the house.

In the living room, fierce light fought to get in between old velveteen curtains. An end table was upset, and a few things had been thrown around.

The body was in the middle of the room. Its form was discernable: a small, female figure. It was wrapped in a shroud of silk.

The webbed shroud reflected the light as almost pure white. Webbed lines wrapped around the feet and head, forming strong bundles; the webbed ropes then formed a woven hammock that was attached to the walls, suspending the body in mid-air. The body was in effect on a silken burial platform, as if a venerated mummy.

"Good Lord," Rashi said. Little shadows scattered across the floor. The damp hairy smell was very perceptible now. He smelled spiders. *Lots and lots of spiders.*

Houston pulled out his own notebook, reading aloud. "Ellen Mation, aged seventy-eight. The ME says it looks like she was attacked."

"By what?" Rashi asked. It was an eerily legitimate question.

"An intruder. Forced entry through the rear door. Some items removed from the mantle. She probably surprised a burglar. Struggle ensued. She was hit with something heavy, from what the ME could gather."

Rashi looked at the suspended body. The walls were crawling with spiders now. They crawled out from dark corners, from behind the couch, from the folds of the curtains. They seemed fearless, oblivious to the size difference between them and the humans. Attentive, they focused on Rashi and Houston.

"The ME could only get a quick look," Houston explained. "Then the little guys convinced him to back off."

"How poisonous are these things?" Rashi asked.

"Venomous," Houston corrected. "If you bite it and get poisoned, it's poisonous. If it bites you and you get poisoned, it's venomous."

"Okay, then. How *venomous* are these things?"

"Individually, not very. Not like your black widow or funnel web. And, in case you're wondering, there's no evidence they tried to make the old lady dinner. They just wrapped her up and lifted her body off the floor." He shrugged. "Sounds crazy, but it's like they're protecting her. Or trying to."

A spider bungeed down in front of Rashi's face. It stopped, eyes to eyes with Rashi; he brushed it away. It fell the rest of the distance to the floor and scampered off quickly.

Rashi looked at the floor around the suspended body. He squatted down, pulled out a flashlight. In the sideways-directed light he saw something glistening.

"What do you make of that?" he asked his partner.

Jeremy Houston maneuvered his girth, observed the glittering fragments in the carpet. "Glass. The back window was broken."

"How did it get in here?" Rashi asked. He moved the light around. The glass had not only been moved, but it had been organized. The fragments made up a perfect circle on the floor, surrounding the body.

Houston shook his head, mystified, as he straightened up.

Rashi put a small piece of glass in a tiny clear plastic evidence bag.

The spiders moved, in a concerted wave, looking up. They scattered as the police detectives walked around the body of Mrs. Mation.

"There are enough of them," Houston noted, side stepping out of a spider's way. "I don't know how many angels dance on the head of a pin, but I think we're about to figure out how many spiders can live in a thousand-square-foot house."

A gentle sawing noise filtered in behind them.

"What's that?" Rashi inquired.

"There's a sealed door down the hall. I have some uniforms trying to pry it open. Want to take a peek?"

Rashi nodded and walked towards the sound. There three uniformed police officers were sawing through the perimeter of a closed door with hacksaws.

Rashi inspected the seal around the doorway. It was white and silken. There was a lot of it. "Web?" he asked.

One of the uniformed men shuddered.

Houston arrived in the hallway, escorting a woman to meet Rashi. She was about forty-five years old, with long black hair. She wore a black shawl that jingled with little bells every time she moved.

"This is Ms. Vogel," Houston introduced. "She's the one who called it in."

"Ms. Vogel," Rashi greeted. "So, you hadn't seen your neighbor in a while?"

"A few months."

"That wasn't unusual?"

"We kept different hours." Ms. Vogel smiled secretively. "I'm a night person. She was a morning one. Sometimes it would be a while between meetings. But this was *too* long. I came over, and then I saw them." She wrapped her finger around a blue glass bead necklace she wore as she spoke, little eyes painted in black and white on each bead.

"By 'them' you mean the spiders."

"The weavers," Ms. Vogel corrected.

There was a little wave of spiders that crawled around the corner. They dropped out of the air vents. They sat on the wall, clung to the ceiling, and crouched at the floorboards. The spiders focused on Rashi and the woman, as if watching the interview intently.

The largest spider took the prime position. She sat on the wall and raised her front legs. She was closer than Rashi wanted any spider to be. There was an unnerving penetration to the arachnid's gaze. Like its miniature brain held much more information than how to spin webs, catch flies, and make little spiders.

Ms. Vogel eyed it cautiously. "They were everywhere," she stated. "The window was almost black with their bodies. They tapped on the glass, like Morse code. They wanted me to come in. They wanted me to find her."

"They wanted you to find Mrs. Mation?"

"She was the sweetest woman. A vegetarian. She gave generously to charity. She was always looking for a way to help others and never hurt a soul. She even left the spiders alone. Said they had their place in the world."

"A real saint," Rashi noted, writing something less exalted in his notebook.

Ms. Vogel gave him a scornful look. "Good people still exist," she said. "The Fates know that. They see everything."

"Fates," Rashi echoed, an interrogation technique, to keep her talking.

"Fates," Ms. Vogel reiterated. The large spider, the intelligently poised one, peered into Ms. Vogel's face. "They weave our lives. Clotho, who spins." Ms. Vogel made a spinning motion with her hands, the bells on her shawl jingling. "Lachesis, who gives us our destiny, and Atropos, the Inexorable, who cuts the thread." She snipped the imaginary thread with fingers imitating shears.

"The Inexorable," Rashi wrote down. It wasn't a word he had ever envisioned himself writing down in his evidence notebook.

"You know, fate," Houston piped in, dark humor in his tone. He brushed his pants leg, a spider falling off. He swore, and tried to crush it underfoot, but it scurried away with graceful speed. The other spiders eyed him hatefully.

"I'm going to take a break," Houston said. There was a little single file of spiders lining up on the wall, moving in angry dance, agitated at the big policeman.

Rashi could smell their aggravation. Furry, damp, like dog hair whipped about on an open sea. He looked at a few of the spiders in the line. Some of them clutched small pieces of glass, and others clutched little golden chips of something he couldn't identify.

The big spider turned to them and wriggled her forelegs in the air. They dispersed at her commands, going in separate directions. The spiders that carried the glass fragments navigated towards the body; the one with the golden chips arched over him, crawling back into an air vent above the sealed door. He could see their little silken trails behind them, catching the sunlight.

He redirected his attention to the witness with two eyes and two legs.

"Not even the Gods could change what the Fates decreed," Ms. Vogel was saying sadly, shaking her head.

"Good thing we don't live in a Greek mythology world," Rashi summarized.

Ms. Vogel smiled, a peculiarly self-satisfying smile. "But the Fates still watch us," she whispered. "They watch everyone, everywhere. They send eyes among us. You never know whose eyes they are looking through. They watch me. They watch you."

Rashi raised both eyebrows.

There was a cessation to the sawing.

"Sir, we have the door open," an officer announced.

Rashi nodded; at his command they pushed the door in.

The smell of rotten human flesh rushed out in a sickening wave. "I think we found our burglar," the younger officer assessed grimly.

Inside the room, the perpetrator's hands still gripped a fistful of Mrs. Mation's jewelry.

The criminal has been strapped to the wall with silken web. More webbing crossed him haphazardly, binding him, tying him. His skin had been bruised, as if he had hit things, trying to get out of the room—or trying to crush little bodies.

There were hundreds of little discarded exoskeletons on the floor. They crackled crisply underfoot.

The criminal's flesh bore the marks of a multitude of bites. Tiny pieces of torn flesh bore witness to hundreds of small injections of minute doses of venom. Summed together, the bites had taken their toll. The burglar's eyes were frozen open, cloudy and horrified.

At his feet there was a piece of jewelry that had dropped from his hands, a small golden broach. Little chips of the gold had been carefully scraped off.

On the floor, against the hardwood, the light caught the glitter of the metal. It had been carefully arranged into a pentagram, pointing towards the dead thief.

The spiders surged into the room, pressing past Rashi. He could feel them as they crawled over him to get into the room, jumping off his head, struggling though his hair. He jumped back, as they used him to gain access to the room. Their legs felt like little pipe cleaners prickling on his skin.

They stopped in the shadow of the dead man, proud in their victory. Their little bodies mingled, fore limbs going up and down. The large spider dropped down from the ceiling, her eyes on her sisters. She stood in the middle of the thinly rendered symbol and pivoted around. *She is the leader*, Rashi recognized, admiring the power in the spider's little body.

The uniformed officers behind him reacted very differently. They did not appreciate the arachnid's perception. One vomited, another ran, and the third gasped in revulsion. Ms. Vogel smiled.

"They know justice," she said, walking slowly away. "Little packets of justice."

The room smelled fiercely of musty fur now, packed with little furry jumping spiders, dancing excitedly.

Rashi pulled out his walkie-talkie. "I need the medical examiner back here." He said, happy for the distraction to have something to do.

The large spider seemed to rest. Her eyes locked on Rashi.

*****

Rashi had written up his notes and set up his case file. He transcribed written words into the database, filled the template with ordinary looking notations. Then he began to write about the spiders.

That was something he was not ready to do.

He went home and showered. It was a long shower, and he rinsed himself more times than usual. His skin still writhed, as if he could still feel the spiders crawling on him.

It took a while, but eventually he managed to fall asleep.

In the night, while he slept, they watched. They came crawling out of the corners, from behind his books, from under his counters.

Their little eyes weighing his actions and his inactions, assessing him in the darkness of his room while he slept. They were fulfilling their mission.

They considered his fitful breathing and the words he mumbled in his sleep, when no conscious filter operated to disguise the truth of his inner thoughts. And they remained unseen, yet ever present.

They were watching, ever watching, as they and all their kind did: Watching with their many eyes.

Their eight tiny, little eyes.

Candy Lace

Be aware of your surroundings. If you don't pay attention, you never know what you may miss.

She sat by the roadside, on the gentle slope of a green hill, almost hidden by the tall green grasses. Her face was just a little sunburned. Her features, young and happy, shone with the light of innocence and the illumination of promise. Her pretty, long hair, the color of straw, glittered in the sunlight. She wore a simple cotton dress, a print dress, with pictures of apples and honey and happy bees on it. The dress was hemmed with lace the color of candied apples. It matched the bright blush in her cheeks. She sat, with her knees up under her chin, her arms wrapped around her legs, smiling at the bright, beautiful sunny day.

He had been driving all night. He had watched the sun rise as the city surrendered to the suburbs, and the suburbs melted into small farms, and the small farms disappeared into the seemingly endless expanse of open land. Some land held lonely houses, with pools and brick carports. Other plots supported only small, dilapidated barns, their wood withering and roofs rusting, as time marched over them.

Verdant land, he noted, overpoweringly green, dotted with milk cows and small groves of trees. Turkey buzzards flew high on the thermals. Always looking, looking below.

It was gorgeous. Springtime had arrived, and wildflowers looked up from the roadside at the bright, shining sun. Sparrows darted about in the air, singing their pretty songs. Hawks rested on poles and fence posts, leisurely in their predation. They looked as if they almost considered it too beautiful a day to hunt.

It had been very windy in the area the night before, but now gentler breezes caressed the land. There was an occasional gust, which flattened the grasses like waves.

He didn't care about that. It was a glorious day to have nothing but open road and a sweet convertible to conquer it with.

The trouble was that he was completely lost.

He had taken a wrong turn somewhere and now he was on a farm-to-market road, with ribbons of asphalt snaking across the concrete paving. He had not seen many cars and few road signs. There weren't many places to go to, so there weren't many markers. Those signs he did see always seemed to point to a local road, frequently unpaved, with names that indicated the celebrity status of the local gentry. Every now and then he came across orange traffic cones and saw county workers fixing up little stretches of this backwater thoroughfare.

He needed to get back to the main highway, find a gas station, and stretch his legs. He regretted forgetting his map at the last motel and regretted even more allowing his cellphone battery to lose its charge. His phone seemed to have a sense of when was the most inconvenient time for it to die on him.

Several orange cones sat by the roadside, along with a sign telling him to reduce his speed. There were a few orange cones lying flat on the ground, occasionally pivoting back and forth on their points as the breeze passed by. The winds had tipped them in the night, like little bright orange city cows. He wondered if people really did that out here—tipped cows. It could be an urban legend. He wouldn't know.

He was wary of rural speed traps and obeyed the reduced speed limit posting. If it had been the city—his own element—he would have ignored them. He enjoyed racing his sporty little car among the skyscrapers, seeing the sky only as reflections in the mirrored glass windows. But here he knew the local constabulary would consider speeding tickets a major source of revenue, so he slowed down.

If he had not done so he might have never seen her at all. A girl, in a pretty candy apple colored dress, sitting on an upcoming hillside. She sat alone, watching the landscape. She kept a very intrigued eye on him.

A local, he thought happily. *Maybe she can tell me how to get out of this middle of nowhere and get me back on a real road.*

He pulled his car onto the soft shoulder as he approached the hill and turned off the ignition. He put on his suit jacket, pulling a pack of cigarettes out his pocket. He lit a cigarette with a slim silver lighter.

"Hi." He waved.

"Howdy!" She waved back. There was an incredible lightness in her voice.

"Quiet day," he said, just to get the conversation started.

"Quieter than usual," she replied. "But all days are beautiful."

"A philosopher, huh?"

She smiled. "You lost?"

"Yeah," he admitted, scratching the back of his head.

A stiff breeze tossed the tall grasses about, making them sway like a great green sea. The bluebonnets and Indian paint brushes bobbed bright blue and red. She picked out a little purple evening primrose and stroked it gently.

"The Interstate is just around the corner," she told him, anticipating his question. "You have to take the next exit. Carson-Kimball Road, it'll say. Be careful, though. It curves as you exit—there's a big blind spot. Then it straightens out. Keep on the exit road about a mile, and it will hook you up to the freeway."

She looked up at him, smiling so brightly and freshly that he thought he must have seen her before, perhaps on a television commercial for one of the local dairies. He took a long drag off his cigarette.

"You shouldn't smoke," she said.

He was mildly annoyed at her. "I'll stop when it kills me," he returned, a bit harshly. He hated being nagged about his habit. Smoking cigarettes was one of the few things in life he enjoyed.

He got back in his car, started it up, and traveled towards the exit, traveling considerably faster than before. He was a little angry about the smoking comment, and more than a little eager to get back to civilization. And he could see the flat road ahead, no place for cops to hide with their speed guns.

He pressed the accelerator, dragging tobacco-flavored air into his lungs.

How could anyone live out here in the middle of nowhere? he wondered.

***

As she sat there, the hours passed. No shadows fell on the ground, as the sun was directly overhead, and the little sparrows sought refuge from its rays in the branches of the trees. She didn't feel the heat, so it didn't bother her.

A workman came by, adding more orange cones. He stopped his truck with the big orange water jug mounted on the back. He didn't see her, even though he was parked right below her.

"Oh, Jeez..." he exclaimed suddenly. Something had upset him.

She leaned forward, resting her chest on her thighs. Listening closer.

He muttered to himself, picking a board up off the road. He inserted it into a holder, which had failed against the previous night's gusts.

She strained her neck to look at the board's writing. *Carson-Kimball Exit Closed*, it read. *Danger! Do not exit! Take next exit, Frye-Bennings Avenue.*

"Carson-Kimball shut off at that bend, too," the workman thought aloud. "Big pile of construction materials just sitting there. Almost waiting for someone to slam into it. Hopefully no one's tried to go that way yet." He patted the top of the board, as if to secure it a crucial millimeter more into the holder. Shaking his head, he muttered some more at the orange cones as he picked them up, placing them back into position. "You guys stay put," he ordered, as if the inanimate could comprehend him.

It must be a lonely job, she thought.

He got into his municipal vehicle, turning on the ignition. "Guess I better go check on the other warning signs," he said to the now visible board. "If you fell down, I bet they did, too."

There was a sense of purpose to his driving.

She watched him go down the flat, black road, little bits of asphalt kicked up by the truck's big tires.

***

She sat by the roadside, on the gentle slope of a green hill, almost hidden by the tall green grasses. Her face was just a little sunburned. Her features, young and happy, shone with the light of innocence and the illumination of promise. Her pretty long hair, the color of straw, glittered in the sunlight. She wore a simple cotton dress, a print dress, with pictures of apples and honey and happy bees on it. The dress was hemmed with lace the color of candied apples. It matched the bright blush in her cheeks. She sat, with her knees up under her chin, her arms wrapped around her legs, smiling at the bright, beautiful sunny day.

"I don't suppose you could have told me about that?" he asked, flapping his jacket over his shoulder. He took out a cigarette and lit it.

He walked from over the top of the hill, crossed over the lush swaying grasses and sat down next to her. Little wispy white clouds blew gently across the blue sky.

"I didn't know," she offered.

"Carson-Kimball." He snorted. "Should have named it Blind's Man's Curve." He puffed on the cigarette, agitated.

She looked at him, trying to be happy. "Still, you have to admit. It's a beautiful sunny day."

"Yeah, just beautiful," he replied sarcastically.

"Don't be upset with me," she pleaded, her big, youthful blue eyes shimmering. "I didn't know. I swear! The winds blew the warning sign..."

He nodded, reluctantly. "Yeah, I know." He paused, watching the breeze ripple across the grasses. "How long am I stuck here, now?"

She shrugged. "A few days," she said sadly. "'Until they give you a proper burial."

He raised an eyebrow.

"The workman's probably already found your wreck. Usually with other folks who pass through here it only takes a few days. I figure they find the body, dress it up, and have the funeral." She paused; embarrassed by something that brought her joy. "I don't mind the delays too much," she confessed. "Gives me company for a little while. I get lonely out here sometimes, just waving to the cars as they go by."

He was suddenly curious. "Why are you still here?" he asked.

"They still haven't found my body. The mean man put it over there, past the trees." She looked scared, concerned. "The mean man still comes out here sometimes," she whispered. "Looks to where he buried me. Stands there, does things. He's the only one who knows where my body is."

He felt a sudden wave of guilt, revulsion, and anger. All mixed like a wicked emotional cocktail. "I wish I could help you." He paused. "Why didn't anyone see you sitting up here? I mean, people must have searched the area." He was beginning to think he knew why she seemed so familiar. Death had added clarity to his memory. A photograph on a little card enclosed with some junk mail, years ago. *Have you seen me?*

She looked awkwardly at her feet, feeling bad for him. "No one ever made it here to look for me," she said. "My killer hid me where he knew no one would find me. It's been a while, from what I can tell. People must have forgotten about me by now." She bit her lower lip, guilt etched on her buttercup brow.

"And?" he prodded.

"Not everyone can see me," she confessed. "Only those who will die soon, one way or another. Only they can see me. Sometimes they die in a matter of minutes, sometimes in a few months. That's what I've been able to piece together, talking with my visitors. That's why I told you not to smoke—I figured it was slowly killing you."

He sighed, looking across the verdant fields and endless expanse of land. "So, what do we do?" he asked, genuinely curious.

"We sit and wave at the cars that go by." She smiled again, like a girl discussing her favorite birthday gifts. "Folks are real friendly in these parts."

Those about to die, we salute you, he thought, with less bitterness than he thought he would feel. Walking away from his body had begun to do strange things to his perspective.

The winds rushed quickly by them, but he didn't feel anything. Not even the hot noon sun, blazing overhead.

A car drove by. The driver did not see them, but his passenger looked up at them and waved.

He and the girl waved back.

He took another puff on the cigarette. "At least know I know I'll never have to give up smoking."

Then he wondered about the passenger in the car who had just driven by. About what the girl had said about those who could see her. *We're all going to die sometime*, he recollected, exhaling a smoke ring into the air. It hovered a long time, immune to the breezes that would have ripped it to pieces before. *I didn't believe it, though. Even if she had told me, I'd have thought she was just a creepy little kid.*

He felt sympathy for her, as she sat on the hillside in her pretty print dress. No one seeing her who could really help her, either.

The sky offered up a quick breeze, and it rushed through the verdant grasses next to where they sat. By the roadside, on the gentle slope of a green hill. Almost hidden by the tall swaying grasses.

She gave him a quick kiss on the cheek, an impulsive gesture, and then she sat back in her own space. He didn't mind; she probably didn't get much opportunity to interact with anyone while she waited.

He put his arm protectively about her shoulders; she rested her weary head on his chest and closed her eyes.

He watched the cars go by, sitting on the hill with the girl in the dress with the candy apple lace.

For the Love of Rachel

Be careful what you wish for.

R achel had taken a lover. Jeremiah knew it, deep in his bones.

He never saw a man walking in or out of her house, which sat neatly across the street from his, but he *knew*. He sensed it in the way she walked, as if her belly were still on fire from rapturous passion. When he passed her in the street, he could smell her sweet sensual odor mingled with the musky smell of a man's fluids warm within her.

Jeremiah despaired, for he had always planned that he would be her lover. He even hoped for more, planning to marry her one day.

She had filled his thoughts since the first time he saw her silhouetted upon her bedroom window, peeping out of his own home late one night.

Brian, her husband, and Rachel had hosted a housewarming party, inviting old friends and new neighbors. Their house, small and inviting, encouraged guests to disperse into every room.

As she circulated through with drinks and casual conversation, he sat on the bed—her bed—and imagined himself laying her down upon it, spreading her legs apart, and entering her with delirious, yearning force.

He found it hard to concentrate in church when he followed Rachel there. He spent his time meditating upon her, and not the scriptures.

When her husband died, Jeremiah stopped going to church altogether.

It felt wrong to pretend to be a man of God when he knew he had been the one who killed Rachel's husband.

Rachel stopped going, too. She seemed to have developed other interests.

***

Brian had proved to be an easily manipulated man. Charitable aspirations had always tempted him beyond his own common sense.

It didn't take much to lead him into danger.

Jeremiah had waited, dressed in decent but slightly dirty clothing. He looked respectable, trustworthy, and yet ill-treated by fortune. He had picked a wig and some eyeglasses up at a party costume store, just in case Brian recognized him. Which was unlikely, as Brian was seldom home to observe his neighbors.

Brian walked out of his office at precisely nine forty-five p.m., as he did every night. He locked the building door, glancing about nervously.

Jeremiah approached. "Excuse me, sir?" he asked.

Brian seemed to pride himself on putting others ahead of himself and his wife. "Yes?"

"My car won't start, and I need a tow. The cellphone company says I owe them money, so they turned off my phone. Could you please use yours to call my motor club? I'm worried that my wife and children will miss me if I get much later."

Brian drank it in. "Sure. Where is your car?" He had pulled out his phone, his fingers ready on the keypad.

"It's over there. I'm not sure about the street names—I'm in town interviewing for a job. I pulled it off the street to avoid getting a ticket. I can't afford one of those."

Brian was overjoyed to help in the face of such adversity. He did not seem to mind at all that he was delaying his own drive home to such a beautiful wife.

They walked together, and Jeremiah pointed down an infrequently used alley between two buildings abandoned to the dream of urban renewal. Jeremiah's car was parked there, meticulously backed in.

"Are you out of gas?" Brian asked. "Maybe you could try turning it over once. I could always come down here with my car. I have jumper cables if you need your battery sparked."

Jeremiah let Brian approach the vehicle.

From behind Brian, Jeremiah hoisted a brick, and forcefully struck Brian's head. The blow made an oozing, thud-like sound as it hit the back of Brian's skull.

The blood splattered all over the red bricks that gave the derelict buildings their faux Federal façades.

In a flurry of blows, Jeremiah made sure he got the job done. When he was satisfied Brian was dead, he took Brian's watch and wallet, and left the body there.

Jeremiah was elated. His plan to win Rachel for himself was in motion. When he got home, he locked his doors and celebrated with a stiff gin and tonic.

That night he masturbated with a delectable rush of freedom and joy. The release was magical. As he climaxed, he thought of Rachel and dared to dream that the next time he came, it would be inside her.

***

Jeremiah gazed longingly upon Rachel at Brian's funeral. She wore black, appropriate to the occasion, but she did not appear to him to be unduly aggrieved. She looked more tired, as arranging the funeral had taken considerable effort. Brian had left no particular instructions on what to do in the event of his death.

He had not anticipated so early a demise.

Jeremiah considered that an oversight, given so gorgeous a wife.

A wife who was now a glorious widow.

Jeremiah had an unusual angle of sight as he watched Rachel approach the ivory-colored coffin.

Was it his imagination, or did she truly smile as she bent down and placed a white rose on the alabaster coffin lid?

***

Jeremiah could not understand how another love could have claimed Rachel so quickly.

He had closely followed Rachel, ever since she first moved in. No man had ever lingered near her door. She had been alone most of the time, while Brian worked ever-lengthening hours and took more and more frequent trips away from home.

Jeremiah stalked her with affection, enabled by a programming job that allowed him time to sit in his parlor and work at a keyboard while gazing at her through net curtains.

She did not employ any man—or woman—for that matter, to attend to her chores. She took out her own garbage, picked up her own mail, and kept to herself when she went out.

In the evenings, she would put on music that would seep out of her house. It was harder music than Jeremiah would have anticipated, full of deep rhythm and delicious dark rage.

When she was ready to retire, she would go, perfectly alone, to her bedroom. He would watch the light in the front bedroom illuminate and gaze upon her shadow through the blinds.

Jeremiah could often see the soft, muted glow of candlelight against the windowpanes, its illumination lovely through the thin curtains and blinds.

He would leave his house and creep up, as close as he dared. He would sit in the shade of the oleander and crepe myrtles and strain his neck to see inside her room. But the blinds, while allowing shadows form, prevented him from obtaining a perfect vision of his sleeping love.

How he ached to go inside and relieve her of her loneliness.

Yet, oddly, now that she was free of her matrimonial bond, she seemed farther away from him than ever.

He returned to his room, night after night. Frustrated, and wondering who he would have to kill now to gain access to Rachel's affections.

***

Rachel's house was eclectically decorated inside. She had gathered odd knick-knacks from all the corners of the world.

She had renovated the aging rooms of her home herself.

Jeremiah remembered noticing, at her housewarming soirée, that she had a dramatic flair for painting the walls with a wide palette of colors. Bold geometric designs swept across the walls, unifying the whole house in a wave of energy and illusions.

There were little quadrangles of odd color in almost every room. She smiled when asked about them.

"That," she explained, secret joy in her eyes, "is where I would run out of the main color I was painting with. Rather than leave an unpainted spot, I squared off the areas with painter's tape, and used the leftover remnants of other colors that I had on hand. You will see that a major color in one room forms a minor color in another. That way, nothing is wasted, and I don't spend extra money on paint I will never use. It also creates a visually interesting effect."

Jeremiah admired his love for her savvy and her resourcefulness.

There, once again, he noted, *Rachel took care of her own business.* She hired no painters. She entertained no decorators.

Jeremiah was perplexed.

Who had somehow snuck into her heart?

***

Jeremiah burned Brian's wallet and buried Brian's watch. He carefully dug a small hole in his back yard, next to his patio. He bricked over the small grave he had dug for the timepiece and placed a potted plant on the pavers.

He changed his tires, slightly ahead of schedule, to prevent anyone ever matching his tire tracks to anything found at the scene of Brian's death.

In his mind he was thinking ahead. He was worried that perhaps someday someone might grow suspicious of his glorious marriage to Rachel. Someone might suspect that he, and not a maniacal transient, had slain Brian.

But before any of that could truly worry him, he had to find a way to court and seduce his love.

Jeremiah sat on the back porch, next to the buried watch, and dreamed up well-orchestrated encounters, plotting his words, and practicing his expressions.

How he would beguile her with his wit and win her over with his passion! His concerns about her ever being his evaporated when he thought about her naked body lying next to his, her soft breasts against his chest.

He had to disregard any possibility of competition and apply himself in earnest to capturing her attentions.

He had killed to win her for himself.

It made no sense to surrender in his pursuit of her now.

Obsession had a lovely way of making itself its own driving, pounding force.

***

Jeremiah visited Rachel on a Saturday afternoon.

She opened the door sheepishly, as if he had caught her in the middle of some delicate encounter. He looked around as she admitted him.

There was no hint of another lover to be discerned.

"I was just coming by to see if you were all right," he said, "to see if you needed anything. Anything at all."

"You're very sweet," she replied.

"I just look that way," he answered, feigning innuendo. His penis rose in a strong erection, being so close to her.

Rachel had been reading and sipping iced tea when he arrived. She put her books away, tidying her parlor.

"What are you reading?" he asked, feigning interest. His whole body ached for her.

"Just some old stories," she replied. "Do you want some coffee? Maybe some tea?"

Or me? he fantasized her adding.

"No," he said instead. "I was just stopping by. It's been a while since the funeral."

She sat down on her large sofa. The walls of the room were painted a light copper color. A square of gold-brown paint, perhaps two-by-three feet, was set in the wall just behind her. The gold-brown paint dominated the entire length of the hallway that led away from the room.

"I'm getting by just fine," Rachel beamed. "Brian left a sizeable inheritance, believe it or not. His insurance policies were quite generous."

Jeremiah nodded, feeling oddly inadequate.

If he could not entice her with his wealth, his battle for her attentions might prove more difficult than he had initially imagined.

"Are you up for dinner, with a friend?" he asked hopefully.

She shook her head. "I'm not interested in going out," she answered. "Perhaps lunch, sometime in the future. I'm very busy right now."

"Oh. What projects do you have going on?"

"Things," she said, vaguely. She arose from the chair, her body language screaming that the audience was over.

He admired her form as she got up. The sunlight streamed in from the windows, making her dress a diaphanous delight. He could see her body silhouetted, her figure an arousing shadow on the wall.

As he turned his eyes from staring at her, his attention was drawn to a peculiarity in her shadow.

Did she cast two shadows on the wall?

He looked, intrigued by the illusion. The other shadow was not his. His shadow fell across her carefully cleaned hardwood floors.

"I have things planned," Rachel said, speeding him up in his departure. "Not that it hasn't been good seeing you. You should stop by again sometime. I'll give you a call."

She escorted him to the door.

He hugged her awkwardly, as a friend who wished to be a lover did. Not wanting her to feel the stiffened member bulging in his trousers.

***

Jeremiah went home. To ease his longings with his own hands.

When he was done, he went outside, to sit on his patio and drink a rum and cola. The ice jiggled in the glass, and he watched the droplets of condensation fall on to the bricks.

He regarded the well-concealed place where the moist dark dirt embraced Brian's still undoubtedly ticking watch.

Jeremiah thought about Brian, considering those months he kept pace with Rachel's husband. Jeremiah had learned Brian's routines, kept up with his schedule. Determining when and how he should strike his rival.

Reflecting back, Jeremiah contemplated Brian's actions and motions those last few months of Brian's life.

At the time Jeremiah had thought the doomed man obsessive and distant.

Brian had altered his habits, spending more and more time away from home.

Jeremiah sipped his drink, hearing the dull pounding of Rachel's hypnotic music drift from her house through the skies.

***

Jeremiah passed Rachel's house, on his way to pick up his mail from the communal bank of mailboxes that served the street. He had worked late, and the moon was already placed high in the night sky.

He glanced at her windows, the evening air swirling around him. The taste of autumn was upon the wind. Foretelling chilly weather and spiced desserts, the breeze kissed his lips as it blew past, tossing dead leaves in its wake.

The candlelight glowed softly from within her bedroom.

He paused, watching her shadow move across the blinds.

Her back was suggestively arched, and she removed her camisole, seductively and playfully. Her form swayed, voluptuous and sweet with passion; her comely shape inspired Jeremiah's own lust for her, and he found himself mesmerized by the dance-like eroticism of her movements.

She is posing for someone, he thought angrily. Working up someone else's desire.

Irritated, he moved closer, hiding himself among the oleanders and crepe myrtles just outside her bower. The angle gave him a unique clarity of vision, the shadows cast like Polynesian puppets towards him. He could never have seen the detail of their movements so clearly from the street.

He could hear two voices from inside: Rachel's voice, and a man's. The latter voice was deep and resonant, and his accent was one that Jeremiah had never heard before. The tone was archaic, as if speaking from a great depth.

Rachel's shadow crawled on top of the man's, straddling him. Her head bent down, and her tongue touched the man's abdomen, licking the course of his body up to his throat.

When their shadows kissed, Jeremiah could see their tongues plunging hungrily into one another. Rachel's hands reached down, towards the man's groin, her sensuous fingers massaging his shaft.

The man's shadow groaned, and he pulled Rachel on top of him, entering her with breathtaking force.

She gasped in ecstasy.

Jeremiah sunk down in despair.

Who was this rival? How had he snuck into Rachel's life? Jeremiah never witnessed anyone other than Rachel enter or leave her home.

As Jeremiah contemplated Rachel's clandestine lover, he moved inadvertently, his body breaking some small branches in the trees. They crackled and broke with a brazen sound.

Jeremiah froze, the noise distressingly loud. He felt his gut tighten.

Rachel's form moved, in response to the sound. Jeremiah could see her get up and throw her robe around her slender shoulders.

In an instant she was on her doorstep, with a flashlight in her hand.

She swung the beam around. When the light found him, crouching in the darkness, she smiled.

"Jeremiah," she greeted. "I had no idea you were stopping by here tonight. Why don't you come in? It's not very comfortable in my front yard so late at night."

Trapped in his voyeurism, Jeremiah felt compelled to humor her. He had to explain, somehow, why he was spying on her. And he had to find out who his rival was. He smiled weakly and stepped inside her house.

She closed the door, bolting it.

Rachel smelled of the man, his strong commanding odor all over her soft skin.

"Are you alone?" Jeremiah asked. "I wouldn't want to interrupt anything. I could come by tomorrow."

"No," Rachel reassured him, her voice smooth and cajoling, "Tonight is as good as any."

She had a bottle of wine out. Two glasses sat by it. One contained the residue of the rich, red vintage. The other glass remained crystal clear.

She took out a third glass from her cabinet and poured the wine for Jeremiah. She offered it to him.

He took it, watching her shadow on the wall. The flickering golden candlelight in the parlor captured her long, lean body. Her gorgeous image slinked across her peculiar paintwork.

Jeremiah concentrated, and in the low darkness of the room, he saw something else. In the corner of the golden-brown square painted onto the copper hued wall, a dark umber moved.

It was not her shadow, nor his. Nor did it represent the form of anything solid in the room.

He sipped the intoxicating wine, paying closer attention to the shape within the painted square. The shadow moved of its own direction, and it began to take form before his eyes.

A man's hand emerged clearly, darkly grabbing the edge of the square. Strong, opaque fingers tensed around the odd painting's perimeter.

Jeremiah's erection faded quickly, as the shape molded itself out of the darkness. His skin became clammy and chilled.

He turned and handed the glass to Rachel. "I'm sorry I dropped by unannounced," he stuttered quickly.

She followed his transfixed eyes to the square, watching the shadow emerge, its black form stepping out of the wall.

Jeremiah looked frantically around, as the shadow of the man, tall and barbaric in its proportions, stood up straight. He focused his eyes, trying to find a third person in the room.

Perhaps someone is behind me? He hoped, trying to discern the focal points of shadow and light.

The third shadow moved menacingly. Jeremiah could see that it was still aroused from Rachel's touch, and that in its hands it held the shadow of a sword.

Jeremiah's blood froze. Fear brimmed in his eyes. He turned, in anguish, to Rachel. "I should go," he said, the words tumbling out.

Rachel smiled, and put her hands on Jeremiah's shoulders.

"No," she said, as she looked lovingly upon the haughty, hulking shadow beast. Wicked delight danced in her eyes.

She held Jeremiah tight in her grip. "We think you should stay."

Jeremiah closed his eyes, his body cold with fear. For some reason, he remembered Brian's watch buried in the back yard, still keeping perfect time.

As he thought about it, Jeremiah realized something he had not understood before: Brian was not neglecting his wife.

He had been afraid of her.

Dashboard

We get so accustomed to the technology and information flow that surrounds us. But do we always understand the signals we are being given?

In the small coastal community of Esse-by-the-Sea, you could either consult the haphazard predictions of the local meteorologist regarding the weather forecast, or you could simply call Erin Cruz and ask if she was driving into town. Because it rained every time Erin had business in Esse. *Every. Single. Time.*

And if it was a nighttime meeting? Then there was going to be a deluge.

This evening was no different. Erin was paused at a red light, the rain assaulting the windshield. She had the wipers turned up as high as they could go. They merely swished the sheets of water back and forth; visibility was scarcely enhanced.

She had been called to present at the most distant of the hospital system's member hospital locations. Erin worked a desk job fifty miles away from Esse; her duties included providing guidance to hospital personnel on how to stay compliant with the mangled web of federal, state, and local laws and regulations that governed healthcare. When necessary, she drove out to the member hospitals of the healthcare system, educating on important changes in the law. A recent set of regulations demanded changes to some patient care practices, so here she was, committed to a schedule of visiting hospitals strewn across four counties—and addressing every shift in each hospital. To accommodate schedules, the education would require multiple meetings at each hospital in order to give all pertinent personnel an opportunity to attend a session.

The first night shift meeting at the Esse location hospital had gone well, but now Erin faced an hour's journey home in a torrential downpour. The streets were retaining water, the storm sewers filling quickly. Water was beginning to bubble out of the manhole covers. Erin had driven in rain many times before, but this was exceptionally bad weather.

"This isn't good," she said to herself, watching the water begin to pool in the middle of the main road she usually took to gain access to the freeway. She turned her phone's map app on. "Recalculate route," she requested. People died in floods every year, whisked away by rapidly rising water, or even being sucked into storm drains ravenously swallowing the rising waters. She wanted to find a drier route. She wanted to find that route now.

Erin was directed to turn onto a dark side road named Berkeley Road, the app indicating it was higher ground. She had never noted the side road before, and it was difficult to see the new route due to the storm and the darkness. There were very few lights of any kind on the road; those few lights that did line the street were occluded by tree branches and leaves. But the road was on higher ground, Erin could tell, as she felt the subtle climbing slope of the asphalt.

"Take it easy, slow, and smart," Erin told herself. *Don't drown, turn around*, was the Gulf Coast mantra about flooding streets. She believed it.

She took a sip of hot coffee from her travel mug to keep her senses alert. As she sipped, the car tire hit a pothole. A little splash of coffee splattered out of the top of the mug.

It took Erin a moment to regain her composure. She instinctively checked the car's dashboard. These tires on her German import car were exceptionally prone to going flat, and a change in tire pressure would register on her dashboard. The only light on after the sharp hit was the light that alerted her when a passenger had not buckled themselves in.

She looked to the seat beside her. There was nothing in it to trigger the light; sometimes her purse weighed enough to trigger the sensor, but her purse was on the floor of the passenger side.

"It could be water in the electrical system," she worried aloud. That was even more incentive to get onto higher ground quickly.

She turned on her radio, partially to find relaxing music and partially to catch the weather forecasts that were broadcast between song sets. They were playing "Rainy Days and Mondays," because the deejay thought that playing rain-themed music during torrential downpours was somehow hilarious.

"In four hundred feet, turn right on Raynham Drive," the map app voice said soothingly. The app had no idea how difficult it was to see in the storm and the darkness.

Erin slowed down, her eyes intent on the road surface. She saw the intersection and took the turn, wary of water ponding on the side of the road.

"In five hundred feet, turn left on Tulip Way," the map app commanded.

Once again, Erin obeyed. She could see lights from the frontage road for the freeway. She sighed in relief. The roadway became more defined; the rain was letting up a little and she was on definitively higher ground. The radio crackled slightly as a bolt of lightning raced across the sky.

She checked her car gauges; the passenger seat belt light had turned off. "We're already drying out," Erin noted. She made it to the frontage road, working her way home.

The deejay put on "It Can't Rain All the Time" from *The Crow* soundtrack.

"At least you're well versed in your precipitation-themed music," Erin mused aloud. The radio crackled, as if it had heard her and approved of her message.

***

"How was the meeting?" Colleen Cruz asked the following morning. Like her older sister, she had dark auburn hair and bright green eyes; their skin was smooth and olive. They looked almost like twins, but they weren't.

"Meeting was good," Erin said. "Getting home was a bear."

"At least it was a Friday night," Colleen noted as they walked towards Erin's car. "Now we have a weekend. Even if the storms are supposed to persist all weekend long."

"Retail therapy is in order," Erin agreed.

Colleen sat down in the passenger seat. She reached down to the base of the seat and found the bar that adjusted the seat's position and slid the seat slightly forward. "Oh, I found something," she said as her hands felt the floor beneath the seat. She pulled up two copper pennies. "Guess I'm giving you my two cents worth," she smiled, putting the coins into the center console cup holder.

"Yay, I'm rich," Erin smiled. "They probably fell out of my purse. I've got to clean that thing out."

"Don't spend it all in one place," Colleen said, buckling herself in. "Do you have to go back to Esse anytime soon?"

"Monday night, believe it or not," Erin said. "Follow up to Friday night's meeting. And probably Tuesday night, as well."

"Can't they have the meetings during the day?"

"I work for a hospital system. Sometimes the night shifters need my guidance. I accommodate their schedules. Those folks work hard. I can adjust my cozy office timetable to keep from interrupting their sleep cycles. I'm not the one sitting up with dying patients in the Emergency Department." Erin yawned, just thinking about the late nights. "I don't know how they do it every night."

"Coffee time for Erin," Colleen urged.

Erin agreed, and they drove towards the nearest coffee shop.

***

Monday night was another late night. Erin noted that it was close to midnight when she was finished. She was thankful for the enclosed crosswalk to the parking garage, which kept her protected from the ferocious rain that was plummeting down from the pitch-black skies.

"Be safe out there," the security guard said as she walked by him.

"I will, Rick," she replied. "You have a pleasant evening."

"I get to stay inside," he noted. "You've become a frequent visitor. They'll have to find a broom closet to office you in if you show up any more frequently. You finished with your assignment?"

"Tomorrow night should wrap it up," Erin replied. "It's a different place out here at night."

"Yes, ma'am," he said. "They have a flash flood warning in effect from midnight until two a.m. Drive safely."

"I will," she promised as she exited the building. She navigated the parking garage and drove out onto the dark roads. The ground, saturated with water from three days of rainfall, offered little drainage to the deluge.

Erin looked at the water pooling again in the streets that served as her customary route home. That route was a straight shot to the frontage road, but she knew there were dips in the road; those would already be filled with water. The alternate route had served its purpose a few nights before; she decided to opt for that route again.

She turned onto Berkeley.

The visibility was even worse than on Friday night. She kept her eyes intent on the road surface, watching the water as it collected on the street's surface and keeping track of the lane-marking stripes. She flipped on the radio, Peter Gabriel's "Red Rain" playing. "Seriously, deejay dude," she uttered. "We get it—it's raining."

The car tire bumped again in the same spot it had a few nights prior. The radio crackled for a moment, then resumed with The Who's "Rain on Me."

"Stupid potholes," Erin muttered to herself. She checked the gauges. The passenger seat belt light was on again.

Erin shook her head. "I need to have that looked at," she resolved. "The wires probably aren't drying out completely." The radio crackled, as well; that further indicated possible electrical issues.

She guided herself onto Raynham and then Tulip, reaching the frontage road and the freeway. The rain stopped momentarily as she drove home. Erin turned off the wipers and noted that the seatbelt alert light had turned off sometime during the journey.

She parked under the carport at her house and reached over to pick her purse up from the floorboards. Two gleaming pennies sat beneath the purse. Erin picked them up and put them in the center console cup holder. She noted the four pennies. "Few hundred more potholes knocking my purse over and I'll have enough loose change to buy myself a cup of coffee," she said to herself.

***

Tuesday night at eleven forty-five p.m., Erin passed by the security guard.

"You all done?" he asked.

"For now. I have a regular daytime meeting next week. No more late nights for a while." She looked at the sheets of rain falling outside. "Does it ever stop raining down here?" she asked.

"Not when you're here. Storms seem to like you," he answered.

"Fabulous," she said. "I should invest in a boat to float down here."

"Be safe," he said, as she left the confines of the building and entered the parking garage.

The water, with no place to run off to, was already building at the lip of the parking garage exit.

The main road had turned into a small river while she was in her meeting. Erin was apprehensive about the flooding, so she made the turn onto Berkeley. The street was covered in about an inch of water, but her car could handle that.

"Where is this pothole?" she reminded herself, as she drove. She got to the spot she had driven over it twice before and veered slightly to the left, to take advantage of the highest point of the road. There was no bump.

"Missed you, Mr. Pothole," she said. There was flash of brilliant lightning and a crack of immediate thunder.

The passenger seat belt light came on. "I really need to get you into the shop," she told her car.

The radio crackled for a few moments, until the upbeat silliness of "It's Raining Men" resumed.

"And at least you chose a lively song, Mr. Deejay," she said.

Erin made her turns onto Raynham and Tulip. The light turned off. The radio uttered a little staccato burst of sound, and "Purple Rain" began to play. "How many rain songs are there?" Erin pondered aloud.

The rain became a light drizzle as she drove home. The deejay put on "Raindrops Keep Falling on My Head," as if he enjoyed annoying Erin.

***

The following Monday, Erin had a daytime presentation at the Esse campus, summarizing her work from the previous week. The project had gone well, and the daytime staff felt they could benefit from her observations and conclusions. In fact, she had been given a small office at the Esse-by-the-Sea campus, with a directive that she spend one day every week attending to that hospital's business. *Never dismiss the insight of the security guard*, she thought to herself. At least her Esse office was bigger than a broom closet, and she could see the bay from her office window. It was a pleasant enough new assignment.

As she left the main hospital building after the meeting, Erin noted that there was a light rain. That was okay. A day shower was nothing compared to the diluvial nighttime rainfall she had driven through recently. There was plenty more rain predicted for the remainder of the day. The deejay was showing his anime chops by playing "Rain" from the *Cowboy Bebop* soundtrack; Erin was reconciled to his commitment to finding weather-based tunes from every musical genre.

As she put her purse into the passenger seat of her car, she noted a copper glimmer from beneath the seat. She felt the floor and picked up two gleaming new pennies.

She put them with the others in the console. "The wages of keeping a messy purse," she said, as half-a-dozen shiny copper coins now sat in the cup holder.

She drove out of the garage, curious about how the alternate route looked in daylight. "Time to see you, Mr. Pothole," she announced. With her trip likely to become more regular, she wanted to know her alternate routes in and out of the campus.

She turned onto Berkeley. The sides of the road were edged with tall oaks and thick shrubs. Wild flowering vines grew with uncultivated abundance. They formed walls around the street.

Erin noted a small crater in the asphalt. "There you are," she said, making a mental note of the pothole's precise location as she veered around it.

The passenger fasten seatbelt light illuminated.

Erin looked at the light briefly before disregarding it. She recommitted herself to having the faulty light fixed.

She turned onto Raynham.

The trees began to clear, allowing Erin to see an aged wrought iron fence. Beyond the boundary of the fence, there was an old cemetery filled with ornate statues of grieving angels gripped by ravenous vines. The double-door gate to the cemetery entrance was located off Raynham; one door of the gate was open, leading to a gravel roadway that entered the heart of the graveyard.

Erin marveled at the cemetery's beauty and its neglect. It had been invisible in the darkness and the deluge.

She turned onto to Tulip.

The passenger seat belt light turned itself off.

Her peripheral vision sensed motion. In her rear-view mirror, she saw the open gate of the cemetery close.

Erin stopped the car. She looked back.

The gate was now indeed closed. The light winds of the afternoon shower were too weak to account for moving the heavy gate.

The rain fell gently on her car. The sun was peeping through the clouds, casting bright rays of yellow light through the towering gray cumulonimbus clouds.

The tones of the Grateful Dead's "Looks like Rain" disappeared as a crackling sound emanated from the radio speakers. But unlike the times before, this time Erin could discern words lurking in the choppy noise.

The remark was garbled, but it was undeniable: a voice uttering the words, "Thank you."

She looked back at the gate; it had opened invitingly again.

Erin looked down reactively towards the floorboard; there were two shiny new pennies waiting for her to find them.

They were not spilled loose change; her purse was fully closed and sitting upright.

These were new coins. These were payment.

The deejay put on Johnny Cash's "Five Feet High and Rising."

"Two pennies for the ferryman," Erin remembered her mother saying when she was little. Two pennies to pay Charon to guide the dead across the River Styx.

She looked at the cup, accumulating pennies.

An ambulance passed by, its lights glaring but its siren off. She could see the crew member in the back, sitting back in dutiful resignation.

The passenger seat light illuminated.

Erin circled the block, out of morbid curiosity. Surely everything was coincidental. The rain, the light, the crackle on the radio, the pennies.

As she passed the cemetery, the passenger seatbelt light extinguished.

Erin heard two pennies gently hit the inside of the cup.

Her phone buzzed, indicating an incoming text. It was from Colleen: "*How's the latest assignment going?*"

Erin wasn't quite sure how to respond. She seemed to have filled a position she had no recollection of applying for.

The deejay put on Jasmine Thompson's haunting cover of "You Are My Sunshine."

"I liked the rain music better," Erin whispered.

The rain began to fall in earnest, as the chorus sung at Erin.

***

Erin got off the elevator in the basement of the Esse campus hospital. There was a mail drop box located in the basement, and she dutifully deposited a stamped envelope, paying one of her bills, into the mail slot.

As she went to get back onto the public elevators and go up to the hospital's main floors, she noticed a man wheel a gurney onto one of the freight-only elevators. The gurney was covered in a black velvet shroud, the outline of a body bag evident from underneath the velvet sheet.

She made the Sign of the Cross. Her elevator took her back upstairs and she went to her car.

In the loading dock she could see the man push the gurney into the back of a black SUV with heavily tinted windows. The modern-day hearse bore metal S-shaped scroll landau bars on its body. The man got into the modified SUV and started the ignition. He drove out slowly, passing behind her as she got into her car and started the engine.

The radio in her car was already on; Axl Rose and Guns N' Roses churning out how even with cold November rain, nothing will last forever.

She sighed. More rain songs, more rain. In the distance she heard a clap of thunder. "Of course," she said to herself.

She noted that the hearse was on the road leading directly to the freeway.

She felt weird following it, so she turned onto Berkeley. The rain was starting in earnest; she flipped on her windshield wipers.

It was then that the passenger seat light snapped on.

Erin stopped the car. She looked over at the passenger seat.

The cushion bore the imprint of a person, as if an invisible body was sitting next to her.

The radio crackled.

The command, "Drive!" Came over the radio, between the static crackles and the straining rifts of Slash's guitar wailing in the song's emotive conclusion.

Erin obeyed. She started driving, keeping her eyes focused on the road. But in her peripheral vision, she could see the imprint on the seat cushion squirm anxiously.

She turned onto Raynham. There was a sound, the soft clinking of two pennies falling into the cup holder. The imprint on the seat disappeared.

The passenger seat light went off.

It felt frozen inside her vehicle. Erin turned up the heater, despite it being warm outside.

She turned restlessly on to Tulip.

"Please don't be two more pennies in the cup holder," she said, forcing herself to look.

Beside her, in the cup holder, were two new pennies. With fibers of black velvet floating on their shiny surfaces.

She drove, just wanting to get away. Away from the cemetery, away from the rain.

The hearse was paused, waiting for her at the intersection. The man in the driver's seat looked at her and smiled. He gave her a curt nod, then drove on.

"She Brings the Rain" by Can started playing on the radio.

"This one goes out to someone," the deejay spoke, as the gloomy chords started to align themselves. "I don't know who. But I know she's out there.

"She brings the rain."

Erin didn't immediately merge onto the freeway. She let the hearse with its spiritless body get an exit or two ahead of her.

Then the inevitable had happened; the rain began to fall out of the gray sky in heaving sheets of precipitation.

It was raining. Just like it did every time Erin had business in Esse.

Every. Single. Time.

But now she knew.

The rain was waiting for her before it could fall.

There were a lot of things waiting for her in Esse-by-the-Sea.

Beyond Valhalla

Are you home, Dean?

Dean stood in the observation lobby watching the monstrous doors open. It was like being in the belly of a great space-faring beast. The metal heaved outwards, the darkness of nothingness lurking outside the carefully crafted landing deck.

Dean's mother stood beside him, still in her uniform, squeezing his hand. It was *his* eighth birthday, he remembered thinking. *Why did Allison have to have a field trip today? Couldn't she just leave one day, just for him?*

The field trip was a routine excursion. A quick look at the stars outside as part of the deep space astronomy lessons, then a return to the safety of the *Estrella*. It was the sort of thing that large spaceships did almost every day.

Dean popped bubble gum in his mouth. It had been in a birthday card he had received earlier in the day, before they had to go and pick up Allison from the landing bay. He could hear the hum of the ship in his ears. Usually he did not notice the omnipresent white noise, but as he popped the gum, he changed the dynamics of his eardrums. The sound ebbed and flowed with increased clarity, a slow, steady, almost pounding beat.

It was not too bad, being a kid on a space-faring vessel. There were less responsibilities than on Earth, certainly less than on the colonies. It was comfortable, with his father as an interstellar cartographer, his mother as a senior terra-forming officer. He just wished he had them all to himself sometimes, not having to share them with brilliant sister Allison, who already showed great promise in alien geology studies.

Not like him. No one was quite sure what to do with Dean.

He watched the shuttle approach, its small size dwarfed by the landing bay. It was moving very slowly, aiming towards the plate-like dock.

Then Dean saw it.

He was sure he saw it first.

Just outside the bay, as the shuttle slipped from the oblivion of space back towards the *Estrella's* womb, a small fireball exploded on the outside of the shuttle's skin.

All Hell instantly broke loose.

Unlike the fortified *Estrella* with its advanced reactive armored hull, the shuttle was not designed to take much of a hit. It was designed for near ship excursions, or atmospheric transfer.

The unanticipated space debris pierced the shuttle's armor almost instantly. It began to erratically wobble. Security personnel flooded the observation deck, herding the waiting observers together.

Dean resisted, pressing his nose against the cold glass, watching. Black screens fell between the glass planes, cloaking the events from his witness.

An investigation and a few years later, the rules would be changed. Every shuttle would have fully reactive armored hulls. That would be because of the *Estrella*.

But on that day, it did not matter to Allison and the others aboard.

And it did not matter to Dean.

He would always remember his sister dying on his eighth birthday. It was the sort of memory that would not fade.

***

Fifteen Years post Estrella Incident

Dean sat across from the Academy official. He supposed other people might sweat an event like this, but the conclusion was already so neatly drawn it no longer concerned him.

The man placed a plastic box filled with brightly colored tablets and pills in front of Dean. "Are these yours?"

"Sure," Dean replied. It was his birthday today and he was remembering again. His self-medication helped stop that usually, but they had found his contraband in his locker. Now the memories danced in his mind.

The little flame on the shuttle, like his own firework on his birthday. He remembered his mother, usually so calm and sensible, screaming as the alarms went off. He imagined, as he had pressed his face up to the unforgiving glass, that he could see Allison's pretty, bright blue eyes fill with confusion as the vacuum of space ripped the life from her lungs.

"Son?" the man asked. "I've tried to help you. Anyone else would have been kicked out on the first offense. But because you are an *Estrella* family, we gave you three strikes. This time, son, you're out."

Dean nodded, his mind overwhelmed by the memories. His mother had never believed they did not suffer on the shuttle. She had taped a photograph of Allison up on the wall, alongside the twenty-three others, to commemorate the dead. Dean remembered the picture. It had been of him and Allison, but his mother had cut him out of the photograph and pasted the remainder on the wall.

Sometimes Dean would go with her when she went to cry and whisper Allison's name. Dean would put his ear next to the cold metal of the wall, imagining that he heard them outside. Knocking on the hull. Wanting to get back inside the *Estrella*.

"I could almost understand amphetamines," the official droned on. "Something to keep you up, help you study. But hallucinogens make no sense.

And you've failed your psych evaluation. They don't let unstable pill poppers run interstellar hyperdrives. You do understand that, don't you, son?"

Dean had no emotions to offer the man. "I probably never really wanted to go back into space anyway," he answered.

***

Twenty Years post Estrella Incident

Dean's hands were in cuffs. He was wearing a garish orange uniform, the convicted criminal's costume. It had been five years since they had thrown him out of the Academy. Five years that hadn't gone well.

"Dean Yallis?" the transfer judge asked. She looked him square in the eye. "You have been found guilty of felony murder. This court has sentenced you to lifetime confinement on the penal colony on 2002LM60. Therefore, you are ordered aboard the prison vessel *Resolution* for transport." She cracked the gavel against the bench. The sound echoed in Dean's ears.

Dean's lawyer moved him along.

Dean breathed the air in with a purpose. It would probably be his last breaths of real air. From now on it would be recirculated manufactured atmosphere, generated on board ship or by the penal facility.

"Not much we could do," the lawyer said, walking Dean to the ramp. "You were bound for Quaoar the moment you stepped foot in that bank."

Dean declined to shake the attorney's hand. "Well, thanks for nothing."

"You made your own bed," the lawyer replied.

"Now I get to go lie in it."

He stepped into the airlock. The doors slid down, cloaking him from the world.

***

Twenty Years, Three Hours post Estrella Incident

The process was bureaucratically slow.

As Prisoner UXB22224fm10QL, Dean moved in a slow line, along with the other prisoners. A woman at a doorway pressed a small, gun-like utensil against his shoulder, injecting a locator chip.

A muscular man walked up beside Dean.

Dean recognized him. From the Academy.

Back then, the man had been qualifying for security. Now he sported a large scar, weaving its way around his bald head.

Forbidden to talk in the line, they nodded recognition.

The larger man moved on.

Dean shuffled, happy for the distraction. His mind was filling with the sound of the *Resolution*, its propulsion system humming lowly.

It had been a long time since Dean had heard the incessant hum of engines. It was almost like returning to the womb.

***

Twenty Years, Four Hours post Estrella Incident

The guard paused outside Dean's cell. "It will take a day or two for your mind to learn to subtract out the noise," he said. The guard's body was plopped into the wheelchair like a scoop of flesh-colored ice cream. "The noise is worse back here, near the lifer cells. You ever been in space before?"

"I was in space, as a kid. My folks were part of the early Titan development team." He remembered Titan, with its orange soda sky, the rings of Saturn barely visible through the gauzy atmosphere. The terra forming had gone faster than scheduled.

"That was good work," the guard said. His body was ill defined and atrophied. It was uncomfortable to look at him.

"I guess," Dean answered. "It took their minds of my sister's death. They worked all the time. We were on the *Estrella* right before then."

"The *Estrella?*" the guard said, awe brimming in his dark eyes. He said the ship's name correctly, melodically rolling the double L into a lyrical Y sound.

Dean nodded. All things dated back to that day. Not just for him. The papers still used it as a benchmark. *Pre-Estrella. Post-Estrella.*

Dean didn't like the noise of this ship's engines, the peculiar oily smell of the vessel. He didn't belong here, in space. *This is where Allison and the others live.*

The guard's reaction was expected. Dean was used to the sanctity the *Estrella* accident inspired. He supposed it was like the *Titanic* in the twentieth century, or the 9-11 terrorist attack of the twenty-first. There was an aura to the *Estrella*.

He had borrowed very heavily against the line of sentimental credit it afforded.

"My sister died on my birthday," Dean said, "So I don't have much opportunity to forget." *It wasn't her fault*, a voice in his mind whispered. *She didn't schedule the field trip on your birthday. Remember how you found her gift to you when you got home? The headphones and the music chips? So you wouldn't have to always hear the hum of the engines?*

"I am sorry, *señor*."

"You speak Spanish? I had to learn, in the Academy." *Voices, go away!*

"*Sí*," the crippled guard replied. "It is my native language. I was an engineering officer in beyond systems exploration, for the Regnas Corporation. Before it became the huge company it is today. We had to speak five languages back then to qualify for flight status. English. Spanish. Russian. Japanese. Hebrew."

"Beyond system? Is that how you got like that?"

The man's body had been reduced to rubber. It was a well-documented consequence of long-term zero gravity exposure. The guard looked old enough to have flown in the days before artificial gravity had been fully developed.

"'No G does a man no good,' they say. Now all I can do is work the prison ships. By the way, call me Galvéz."

"I'm Dean, Dean Yallis."

"Well, Dean, I must be attending to my duties. *¡Adios!*"

Dean watched the guard wheel himself away. "Yeah. I'm Dean. Always just one letter away from dead."

***

Twenty Years, Three Days post Estrella Incident

The life sentence prisoners were located near the back of the ship. The death sentence inmates were located towards the middle. Crew and operations comprised the front end of the vessel.

Once on the prison asteroid, the death row inmates would be separated from the life sentence prisoners by a barren, frigid, uninhabitable landscape, incarcerated in two distinct facilities. On board the *Resolution* they were permitted to mingle, more out of logistic simplicity than any sense of shared community.

During morning recreation, Dean sat on a bench. Humming to himself. Trying desperately not to hear the engines. The large man from the Academy sat next to him.

"You a killer now?" he asked.

"Felony murder," Dean replied, surprisingly casual. "You?"

"I settled a family quarrel in a dramatic way," the bald man responded.

"Your lawyer didn't go for diminished capacity? Moment of passion? I hear about that on television all the time."

"Helps to be a celebrity for that to work," the man replied. "And my targets were sleeping when I had my moments of fame. The prosecutor argued I had time to cool off before going over there with a new gun and extra bullets in my pocket. His argument ended up being the more persuasive one."

"Sorry to hear that, Gustar." Dean reached out and shook the man's hand, using the handshake they were taught during their senior year at the Academy. When it looked like they were set to graduate.

Gustar remembered the handshake. "Long time since those days," he said. "I heard you got a life sentence, Dean."

"At least I don't need to worry about what I'll be doing for the next sixty years."

"I'm not so willing to go to a fucking hunk of ice at the edge of nowhere." Gustar paused, cautious for eavesdroppers. "I have a plan."

"Really?" Dean asked, hiding his doubts.

"Some other Academy rejects got a small ship together. They make delivery runs to the nearer colonies. I've coordinated a rendezvous."

"How do you intend to transfer? I doubt our captain will just let you hop off this ship and onto another."

"I have plans." Gustar paused again. "I want you to be one of us. I need someone who can get the engines under my control. That was the only thing I didn't have planned when I got on board. Then I saw you, and my wishes were answered. An engine man."

"I trained on relativistic drives, long-range hyperspace propulsion. This thing only has fusion. Short solar system jaunts, maybe nearby colonies."

"In other words, a piece of cake for you."

"If it'll get me someplace where I can breathe real air and not have to listen to the damn engines, I'm in."

"Welcome aboard, brother," Gustar said, getting up.

They shook hands the secret way. Dean watched Gustar walk away, back to the death row cells in the forward prison bays.

***

Twenty Years, Three Days, Six Hours post Estrella Incident

There was a small monitor in each cell. It provided a real-time visual of the outside space. Civil liberties activists had lobbied for the devices, arguing the screens humanized the prison transport system.

Dean watched, hearing the squeaky wheels of Galvéz's chair approach.

"*Buenos días,*" Dean greeted.

"*Habla muy bien en español,*" Galvéz complimented.

"I speak Spanish okay," Dean replied. "You been to Quaoar before?"

"Only to transfer prisoners. It is no tourist destination. It is a ball of ice, *amigo*, floating in a debris field with the rest of the crap that never made the cut to being part of a planet. It is dark all the time."

Dean watched his video screen. A thin streak of light shot access the dark expanse of space.

"Meteor?" Dean asked.

"Human remains launch," Galvéz replied.

"On its way to Valhalla," Dean surmised. Human remains were frequently transported to Valhalla, commonly called the tenth planet. The remains were either jettisoned from ships or placed in capsules on guided rockets and fired towards the planet.

Dean remembered Allison's internment there. She and the other *Estrella* victims, their lead coffins placed on the icy surface. The cemetery crew working the Valhalla shift had carefully arranged the boxes on a sculpted mound. Dean remembered the first nine measures of Beethoven's *Andante* from Sonata 25 playing as the metal crypt was placed on the viscous glair.

"My whole family is on Valhalla," Dean commented casually. "My sister. My father—he died on a mapping mission. My mother—she died when an atmospheric conversion unit exploded. They all got a hero's funeral. It's an efficient ritual. A place to put bodies without polluting space with our debris. And it keeps the population back home happy, not knowing exactly how many people died setting up those profitable colonies."

The guard was silent and only the hum of the engines filled the air. The other prisoners in the bay were sleeping or didn't care to make any noise.

"Yep. No normal people die in space," Dean remarked coldly. "Only saints and the damned."

Galvéz made the Sign of the Cross with a shriveled hand, as best he could, over his sunken chest. "You should be careful what you say about the dead," he warned.

"The dead never talk back," Dean replied. "Trust me. I've been listening for years."

***

Twenty Years, Three Days, Sixteen Hours post Estrella Incident

Dean sat out again during the next recreation hour. He didn't see the point in maintaining muscle mass. He would never be the strongest; and even in artificial gravity, his musculature and bone structure would eventually start to whittle down. His skeleton would warp, his limbs shorten.

Gustar, soaked in sweat from a vigorous workout, sat next to him.

"I heard you were on the *Estrella*," Gustar said solemnly. "I didn't know that."

"My sister died. They say she didn't suffer."

"You don't believe them."

"Governments live off telling us what they want us to want to hear. How often does the truth fall into that category?" Dean fidgeted. "I saw the particle that compromised the shuttle hull. *It was beautiful.* It was my birthday and the thing sparkled like a candle lit in space itself. Just for me."

Dean paused, swallowing and clearing his ears. "My sister had been the center of attention all morning, getting ready for her first trip off the main ship. I was pissed. It was *my* birthday, and everyone was fussing over *her*. How brilliant she was, how far she was going to go in life. I made a birthday wish: I wished that she would die. Then I could have all the attention and never have to share anything with her ever again. What kind of god answers a prayer like that?"

"The kind of god a man creates to grant such prayers. We get the god we deserve, engineer. That's why I don't believe in one. It keeps me safe from my own wishes."

"By the way, no one kills the guard—Galvéz," Dean said abruptly. "That's part of my payment in your scheme."

"The platypus? Why protect him?"

"He's like us. The people who matter regard his life as nothing. He has spent lifetimes at the edge of nothingness."

"He's your problem, then," Gustar replied. "I'll come back and get you when the time comes. By then we should have control of the bridge. I'll spring you and you run the damned engines until we get to our rendezvous point. Understood?"

Gustar left, wary of being seen talking to anyone for too long.

Dean leaned back, feeling the vibration of the engines in the wall. He looked at the monitor. It was empty space, the mind-numbing emptiness that no one on Earth could possibly fathom.

Somewhere out there his family lay, frozen in the ice on Valhalla.

He remembered his fourth grade astronomy: *2003UB313, commonly called Valhalla. The planet's discovers had tried to name it Xena or Planet X, as in the Roman numeral for ten. But references to twentieth-century television characters faded centuries later, quickly replaced by the name the planet's purpose suggested.*

Valhalla was the last stop of the way out of the solar system and the first stop on the way in. Ships departing for deep space fired up their relativistic engines; those arriving cut back to less than relativistic speeds. It was like an old wake zone back on Earth.

Those who die in space are buried on Valhalla, hence the colloquial name. They are placed in lead-lined burial chambers and sent to the surface, where transient cemetery crews attend to the remains by placing coffins and marking gravesites at the edge of the solar system, among the gravitationally-collected debris of creation.

It had been so romantically taught—almost to encourage children to imagine a glorious burial there and sacrificing their lives for the exploration of space.

Dean had never bought into it.

Perhaps that was why he never applied himself to his studies the way Allison did.

He remembered seeing one of the inspirations for Valhalla on a field trip to Earth when he was thirteen. Traveling in an old bus on a tour of Cape Kennedy, they passed by a large mound of dirt covered with grass to make it look inconspicuous. His mother had told him what it was even when the tour guide failed to.

"That's the remains of the *Challenger* craft," she said quietly. "It exploded shortly after liftoff, late in the twentieth century. They used *huge* rockets to launch in those days."

Dean had looked at her coldly. "More people died on the *Estrella*," he had said. "I know. I was there."

More people had also died at his own hands during the bank robbery. They would never be buried at Cape Kennedy or Valhalla.

He walked back to his cell early. Galvéz locked him in.

Sleep took Dean, plunging him into the old nightmares. The distant stars became Allison's blue eyes. He missed her more than he would permit himself to acknowledge. In his dreams, she greeted him as she had in life.

Allison was always the first to say hello when he came back home. She would rap her soft knuckle playfully on his forehead. *Knock! Knock! Dean, are you home?*

Then the knocking seemed to come from outside, from outside the cell—from outside of the ship. *Allison rapping on the hull, begging to be let back in.* Crying to be released from the cold.

***

Twenty Years, Three Days, Twenty-Three Hours post Estrella Incident

There was a wild rapping on the walls. Men's voices were joined in a frantic chorus. Dean roused uneasily from his nightmares.

Galvéz was wheeling by quickly, taking up a defensive position with two other guards. Their weapons were drawn; their faces grim and gray like the metal skin of the ship—cold, colorless, and made to bear stress.

Dean pressed his face to the bars of the little window in the door of his cell. "*¿Qué ha sucedido?*" he asked. *What has happened?*

"Riot," Galvéz reported.

"So Gustar went for it."

"You knew?" There was a taste of betrayal in the old man's voice.

"He talked big," Dean replied. "But you never know with a guy like him."

"They are being fought back," the guard told him. "Away from the bridge. Most of your friends are dead, *señor*. We are going over Enceladus now. Only ice volcanoes down there."

The noises grew louder. Dean could hear the peculiar report of line-threaded shells, little charges attached to cords. The tow weapons allowed aimed shots of energy without risking compromising the internal walls of the vessel.

"Gustar will have a plan," Dean said. "I doubt he wants to hit the Kuiper Belt without his shadow crew up and running."

"What do you not understand?" Galvéz asked. "There is nowhere to go."

"*Amigo*," Dean replied. "Some of us were going nowhere to begin with."

***

Twenty Years, Four Days, Four Hours post Estrella Incident

Galvéz and the two other guards huddled together like a tiny ancient phalanx set accidently in space. The noise outside the lifer unit was unnerving. The ship rattled with the sound of combat. Screams and yells and pounding filtered through the barrier doors.

Dean checked his video monitor. They had passed Saturn; Neptune was barely visible as an unfaltering star in the sky, distant in its orbit.

The fight is taking too long, Dean thought. *We are picking up speed. The captain is hurrying to get us to Quaoar.*

He closed his eyes and the stars became Allison's eyes again. Begging him to come outside and rescue her. *To save her from his wish.*

"Your friends will not capture the bridge," Galvéz said. "It is compartmentalized within the ship."

The banging and knocking within the walls were increasing. Dean felt uneasy. It did not sound like the herald of liberation, but the staccato moaning of the besieged.

He could hear Gustar just the other side of the door, calling out a minor victory cry. The metal door began to lift, clicking into an open position.

Knock! Knock! Dean heard Allison say, buried deep inside his mind. *Is Dean home?*

Why did I choose that moment to wish her dead? Dean wondered, watching his monitor aimlessly.

Why does she choose this moment to haunt me?

***

Twenty Years, Four Days, Five Hours post Estrella Incident

The *Resolution* passed Pluto, a little bone-ivory marble in a sea of velvety blackness, three small dots just visible around it, awkwardly shepherded by the object that had once been catalogued as a distant planet.

Gustar, bloodied and limping, tumbled into the lifer bay. Ten other men accompanied him, most having fared worse than he had.

The other lifers clamored forwarded, demanding to be released from their cells.

Gustar handed a small box to a man next to him. "Figure out which button does what," he ordered. "I want the engineer out first. We need him to slow this bitch down."

The rioters moved forward on a signal from Gustar. *Many hands to one beast.*

Fresher and better armed, the guards moved quickly. Galvéz directed targeted shots from his wheelchair with a tow weapon equipped to respond to nerve impulses from within his withered arms. His shots were unexpectantly accurate. Four rioters fell dead to the floor before his lethality was recognized.

Gustar staggered towards Dean's cell. He grabbed the box back from his appointed right-hand man. Gustar bled from multiple wounds on his arms and chest.

Trench knife wounds, Dean noted.

Bladed weapons had enjoyed a comeback as spacefaring opened up. The fear of internal hull breach dissuaded most energy or projectile based armaments.

The rioters were tiring and becoming demoralized. Dean sensed there had been heavy casualties.

"We can't get to the damned bridge," Gustar yelled out, still trying to decipher the electronic box he held.

"The bridge is contained in what amounts to being a cocoon. It is nearly impervious. If we can get to the engines, maybe we'll have some bargaining power."

The guards pulled out their knives as the rioters moved forward. There was fierce hand-to-hand combat, but the guards had trained together and offered a coordinated defense against weakened and disorganized adversaries. Three more rioters fell, blood beginning to pool on the black metal floor.

Galvéz was left with clear shots, picking off two more.

The remaining rioter was outflanked and one of the guards gutted him like an unwanted fish. Moving in, the guards slit the throats of everyone on the floor.

Coup de grâce, Dean noted sourly.

Gustar frantically pushed buttons. Dean heard cell doors in the adjacent bay open, the jubilant cries of the over-eager echoing off the metal walls.

Galvéz motioned the other guards forward to assist their cohorts in quelling the insurgency in the adjacent cell bay. He shot Dean an ugly glance as he left. "You'll get death row now," he said as he slid between the bays. The separating doors came crashing down again, leaving Gustar frozen against the wall. He pushed one button on the box, calculating the schematic.

Dean's cell door opened.

Gustar slid down, blood rupturing from wounds he did not even know he had. Red gore oozed between his fingers.

"We're still in the game," Gustar said.

Dean shook his head. "No. They'll contain the adjacent cell block soon, and we can't access engineering from here." He grimaced. "I'm not going to death row for your failures."

Gustar was too injured to reply. He gripped a tow weapon in his hands. "You have another plan?"

"There's an escape pod in this bay for emergency evacuation. It was designed with just enough room for the guards—three people. It won't go far, but it will get us somewhere other than here."

"It's too early for my rendezvous ship, and an escape pod doesn't have the ability to stay in orbit," Gustar objected.

"We'll get another ride to the rendezvous ship. Something we can launch when the time is right."

"Where do we get that from, engineer?"

"Valhalla."

"Nothing but dead people there."

"Not entirely. The cemetery has a small short-range ship stationed there, used for near-space access to pick up coffins from passing ships. They call them

Valkyries because someone won a 'what-to-name-them' contest. Real imagination at work there." Dean smiled, trusting in his own plan. "My whole family is down there—I'm well acquainted with how Valhalla works. We can launch the Valkyrie and meet your rendezvous when it passes."

"Better than what awaits us on Quaoar," Gustar said weakly.

***

Twenty Years, Four Days, Six Hours post Estrella Incident

Dean dragged Gustar into the escape pod.

He had not trained on this particular model but was familiar enough with the class of craft to figure out how to disengage it and chart a course. He got them off the damned prison ship.

Gustar clutched his short-range weapon and closed his eyes as they fell away from the belly of the *Resolution*. Dean watched as the course he plotted appeared as a yellow line on a view screen; a white line, indicating their actual course, tracked it faithfully.

"Two hours," Dean said. "Two hours and we're on a Valkyrie. Three hours and we're being picked up by your contact."

Gustar was silent. His weapon slid from his hands, discharging a short-range charge as it fell. The charge slammed into the control panel behind him.

"Fuck!" Dean screamed, jumping up. He raced to the panel, fire extinguisher in hand. "What the hell are you doing?"

There was no fire and the panel appeared only cosmetically damaged.

He turned to Gustar. The bald man's head pivoted in an unnatural way. His chest did not rise and fall with the rhythms of inhalation and exhalation.

Blood soaked his chair.

"Crap," Dean assessed, pushing the dead man's face away from him.

Now he had to hope he'd recognize his ride when it came by.

***

Twenty Years, Four Days, Seven Hours post Estrella Incident

An hour later, Dean noted the way the white line deviated from the yellow. He activated the navigation system, attempting to correct the wayward course.

The computer examined the pod's operations. Navigation had been damaged; the stray weapon discharge had upset the gimbals and dislodging wiring. Worse, it had caused oxygen to be vented from the craft, diminishing the supply of available breathable air. Dean had an hour of oxygen left.

He was glad Gustar had died early and was no longer using any portion of the tiny atmosphere.

The deviation in course was critical. At the current trajectory, the pod was bound for open space.

Dean sat beneath the panel, attempting to locate the damaged components. If he could correct the physical damage, there was a chance he could correct the course.

He worked frantically, realizing the pod offered little in the way of emergency repair supplies. Pods weren't required to carry much in terms of tools and extra parts. Undoubtedly it would take someone else's future tragedy to correct that oversight.

The sweat poured off him as he attempted to reconnect frayed wiring without electrocuting himself. His breathing became shallow as the oxygen diminished.

He could hear little fragments of ice knock against the outside of ship, glancing off the reactive hull. It sounded like rain falling in space. He could see Valhalla, its icy surface a dimly lit diamond set against the blackness of space.

The knocking continued.

The ghosts want in.

"Stop it!" he yelled at himself, wrestling with the visions. He had to keep *her* out of his thoughts. He had to concentrate on the repairs.

He told himself that oxygen deprivation and stress were taking their toll. He looked out at the immortal expanse of space. Valhalla emitted an odd blue tinge the closer he came towards it.

Knock! Knock!

Dean recoiled in desperation as Valhalla slipped beneath him. He struggled to attempt repairs he could no longer comprehend. His mind filled with voices liberated by exhaustion and despair.

Dean. Are you coming home?

He sank into the belly of the pod, the hum of the small engine filling the void.

You came back for me! I knew you would. Happy birthday, Dean!

The lights turned themselves off. The oxygen supply was nearing depletion.

In his delirium, Dean was back on the *Estrella*, letting the ghosts inside.

Space rushed into the opened pod, eager to embrace him.

The knocking at the hull finally stopped.

Lake Salida

Tranquility can be an indicator of peace. Or it can be the repose of discord. Interpret it wisely.

"You have to stop wishing people dead," the old man told her sternly.

"Pardon?" Suzie asked, startled. She wasn't supposed to be here; she had passed numerous NO ENTRANCE/NO TRESSPASSING signs all the way to the edge of the lake. The old man had snuck up on her; she hadn't heard him coming up.

The man was thin and aged. He wasn't threatening; he just seemed disappointed in her.

"Only one reason people step up to the edge of Lake Salida," he said knowingly. "And that is because they have wished people dead as they saw the lake. And now they're curious. Because the people they wished dead—*died.*"

"I don't know what you're talking about," Suzie replied.

He extended his hand in greeting. "I'm Gilmore League, owner of this property. And you—you're both a murderess and trespasser. You got a name, woman?"

"Susan Miles," Suzie replied. "But everybody calls me Suzie." She shook his hand, not knowing how to respond to his accusations.

"You're pretty and young," he noted. "The type who has time for repentance and penance. Maybe you can get out of this web you've woven. You religious, Miss Suzie?"

"Not really."

"About time you became religious," he instructed her. His eyes were crystal blue and glistened like pure glacier ice. It was almost impossible to guess his race. His skin was so weathered and tanned by decades of sunlight that its original color was indistinguishable. His teeth were impeccably white. His hair was long and silver, braided, and tied back. There was a Southern twang to his accent, but his voice also had hints of Connecticut Yankee and Newcastle British. He could be from anywhere, anytime.

"What do you mean about the lake?" Suzie asked. She found a tree stump to sit on. Her face reflected at the edge of the lake's waters: curly auburn hair, hazel-amber eyes, impeccably dressed in quality outdoors wear. She even wore golden jewelry and an expensive watch in the woods.

"The first time you flew over this lake," he asked, "What were you thinking?"

"How do you know I flew over?"

"My property has no paved roads leading to this spot," he told her. "I make sure of that. You had to hike in from the rest stop, about three miles away, to get here.

People can only see this siren water by flying over it—usually on one of the airplane routes to Las Vegas from the south or the east. I've heard the story hundreds of times, believe me. Don't think you're special."

"I was on my way to Vegas" she admitted. "I travel there frequently."

He pulled out two bottles of water, handing one to her.

"And?" he prodded. "Who was vexing a pretty little thing like you? Who did you think ill of while you flew over this mesmerizing little spot of water? Let me guess. I am sensing that you are squared away financially. You don't seem distressed. Must be romantic troubles."

"The husband's mistress," Suzie confirmed. He seemed to know her story before she told it.

"Good old-fashioned reason to wish somebody dead, I suppose," he acknowledged. "*The mistress.* I've heard that one—the lover or the mistress rationale—dozens of times before. I keep hoping for something more original. Occasionally I get a different twist. Does your story have a different twist?"

"Well, she was a cyber-mistress, if that counts." Suzie replied. "They were dirty texting, having phone sex. She would send photographs of her floppy tits to him. He would send her, well, how do I say this delicately? He would in return send photos of himself. In particular, parts of himself. Private parts. She would tell him how she wanted him to flick his tongue..."

"I don't need all the tawdry details," he said, stopping her. "I get the picture. I'll give you that most people see dirty texting as adultery. And jerking off to the floozy crosses a line, I suppose."

"He created a fake online profile, so she and he could like one another's stuff without me knowing about it."

"But you did know about it."

"They weren't as smart as they thought they were. I played dumb. Pretended to have no idea."

"So, you're on the plane to Las Vegas, cyber-stalking the cyber-adulterers, and you look out of the window."

"And I saw this lake," she continued, oddly knowing that he could seamlessly enter into her story.

"Tell me about the lake. How it looked to you from all the way up there in the heavens."

"The lake looked like a blue sunny-side-up egg. Its fringe was a crystal-clear turquoise, its 'yolk' an incredibly vibrant blue depth of water. From 20,000 feet in the air it looked... magical. So remote. So untouched. Situated in a clearing, surrounded by tall trees. A single path leading to it. A small house nearby. What looked to be a small parking lot a few miles away."

"The Lakota called this Lake Ayusta," he said. "An interesting word that has different meanings. Ayusta means 'abandon,' 'give up,' 'leave alone,' or 'let.' You get the drift. I call it Lake Salida, because this lake is all about exits."

"Are you Lakota?"

"One-sixteenth," he answered. "I'm about one-sixteenth everything. Or at least I was. Now I'm just old." He paused, taking a drink of water. "You looked at the lake, as it flew beneath you, and you felt its power. Then you thought about that woman—that rival for your husband's affections, for his time, for his wasted sperm. And you wished her dead."

"Yes," Suzie confessed.

"And what happened?"

"After I got back home, about two weeks later, she was dead."

"There was something odd about her death," he reminded her. "The lake signs its work."

Susie felt very uncomfortable, realizing that the conversation had progressed from conversation to confession. "One of her kids found her as she was dying. Her eight-year-old son. She was lying on the floor, convulsing. Looking at the ceiling, saying, 'They have no eyes. They have no eyes.' Repeatedly. Until she died."

"How did that make you feel?"

"It creeped me out. I felt sorry for the kid."

"But a coincidence, right? You only *wished* she were dead. We all say bad things all the time that we don't really mean. Even though we're taught our words have power. You uttered the words under your breath. Didn't think anybody would hear you."

"Yes."

"Makes a difference when *something* is out there to hear us, doesn't it?"

She took a sip of the water from the bottle. "It's completely quiet out here." She wanted to talk about something—anything—else.

"Nothing lives in the lake, no animal comes near it," Gilmore said. "They know better than us. They don't even look at this water. The golden silk orb weaver spiders make large webs between the trees at night, so the critters can feel the webs in the darkness and turn around."

"You make it sound like some sort of mythical bad magic lives in the lake. That would be like a fairy tale. Fairy tales aren't true."

"Then let's tell another true story," he prompted. "Tell me about the next one. The *second* one. You didn't hike three miles to see dead water for nothing. One time is coincidence; the second time is evidence."

"A woman named Serendipity," Suzie said, slightly unnerved that he seemed to know her stories before she told them. "And, yes, that is her real name. She was visiting from out of town, staying at our house for a few days while she was traveling from one place to the next. I was getting ready for a business trip to Vegas, again. I had to run out to the store for a few minutes. I came home earlier than expected and I heard laughter through the walls of the house. My husband had her pressed up against the bar, from behind. When they saw me, they made some excuse about him critiquing her flabby triceps."

"On that next plane trip, you thought about how you wanted her dead, too. You summoned that fate for her, as you looked outside the plane window down towards the lake."

"Yes."

"How did that work out for you?"

"A few weeks later she went out for a walk, listening to music. She always had ear buds in her ears, listening to music. The people who witnessed the accident said that they saw her crossing the street—she was jaywalking, but she was apparently attentive. Then she stopped suddenly, looked straight ahead of her as if she saw something, and started mumbling, 'They have no eyes! They have no eyes!' She stopped right there in the middle of a busy intersection. A small utility truck hit her. It had the right-of-way. She was dead upon arrival at the hospital."

"And you began to wonder," Gilmore League said. He looked suddenly agitated. "We've been here a while," he explained. "Too long, really. We need to be walking back."

He pulled a small bundle of leaves and twigs out of his pocket and lit it with a match. It smoldered, and he wafted the vapors around them. He took out a rattle and rattled it as they began to walk away from the lake.

She followed him, sensing his urgency.

"The thing they both said—'They have no eyes,'" Suzie explained. "It seemed too odd. Like the deaths were connected."

"Why are you here?" Gilmore asked. "You have questions. Start answering them."

"The only other apparent connection between their deaths was my wishing them dead when I flew over this lake. I wanted to see the lake up close. I just felt that I had to. Compelled, really."

"Truth is, *the lake wanted to see you.*"

"I don't understand."

"Becoming preoccupied with the sins of others is a great way to become trapped in your own," he said. He shook the rattle rhythmically, moving the burning smudge of herbs around them. "Vengeance isn't ours for a reason. That prohibition is meant to protect us."

She followed him as he traveled down the well-trodden pathway away from the lake. "Protect us from what?"

"Things like this lake," he replied. He nodded to a spider spinning a web between two trees near them. "We're leaving just in time."

"I'm not following your meaning," she said.

He walked fast. She was forced to put considerable effort into keeping up with him, both with regards to his stride and in deciphering his ramblings. He seemed to have every step memorized, every point cued. It was as if he had done this dozens—maybe hundreds—of times before.

"Dogs chase cars every day, darling," he told her. "With no intention of doing anything if they catch them. Your hubby is like that dog. Way I understand it, you are a beautiful woman with a good job that puts you into expensive clothes and seductive perfumes, then flies you to and from Las Vegas all the time. Your hubby is probably concerned that *you* might leave *him*. That Sin City will seduce you. Or that someone in Sin City will. All this extra-marital chatter of his is probably him just keeping his romancing skills intact in case you leave him.

"You thought about just talking to the man? Maybe he is a piece of shit, but I suggest you look in the mirror and consider that you may not be acting right as well. You seem to have an odd way of dealing with your petty frustrations and conjectures, straight up wishing people dead. Seems disproportionate to me. But what do I know? Like I said, maybe I'm just old."

"Why does the lake want me to visit it?" she asked. "You said that it wanted to see me."

"Because it needs voluntary consent now. It needs you to bind you to it," he said. "Those two times before—you didn't truly know what you were doing. *But now you do.* You're smart; you have connected the dots. Are you going to wish every woman your husband bats his eyelashes at dead? Start taking intentional trips over the lake just to rid yourself of potential rivals and perceived enemies? All sorts of people piss us off from time to time. Doesn't mean they deserve to die, much less that we have a right to kill them. Even if we know we can get away with it."

"I don't think I'll be wishing things like that anymore."

"Sure about that?"

"Yes."

"Plenty of others been here, saying the same thing," he told her. "Hundreds of other men and women have trespassed on my land. You drove up here because you had to see that font of unholy water up close. And I made sure to meet up with you, just like I have every other one before you. Kept you talking so you couldn't be wishing things by that pretty poisoned well."

A spider glided behind them, connecting to two tree trunks with a long strand of silk.

"You are going on another trip soon," Gilmore guessed. "You have a third candidate. The lake wouldn't have drawn you here if you didn't. The lake is like a drug dealer: it gives you a few free hits to get you hooked. Then it will own you. Now that you have seen the lake, you will have to start paying for your wishes. Who vexes you now? A competitor for your business? Your whore husband's next cyber conquest? You have somebody in mind. The lake wants to know. I want to know."

"My husband checks his computer in front of a picture on his nightstand. The glass in the picture frame reflects the screen. I can read backwards—you learn how to read all sorts of ways, doing business in Vegas. One night he was arguing by text with the first one—the one who convulsed to death. I could read their text thread in the reflection. She had gotten a boyfriend, a real man in her life. He told her to stop bothering him then, and that it didn't matter because he had already found another. That she had been replaced. Then there were some mysterious calls from New Hampshire after that. I don't know much more."

"But you and the lake know enough. It can find her. Send its servants after her," Gilmore stated.

He slowed down, so she could catch up to him. "The lake feeds off vengeance, Suzie-Q. It feeds off grief. You've heard of a wishing *well*? That lake is a wishing *ill*. It can drown those who never even see its waters."

"You said that there were others," Suzie noted. She glanced behind them at the spiders forming a barricade of silken fence around the entry paths to the lake. "Other people who realized their wishes... their curses... were becoming reality?"

"Quite a few."

"You said you talked to them."

"Every one," he replied. "I know when someone comes onto my property. I feel it."

"Why not cover the lake? Or drain it?"

"Tried both, multiple times," he answered. "Just so you know, the damned are very persistent. And it's not easy to kill something that isn't technically alive. Way I understand it, my duty is the people who cross my land, not to the pit that pollutes it."

"Do any of them ever contact you after they've left?" Suzie asked. "The ones before me? Tell you how they're doing? If they've resisted temptation or not?"

"Some do," he replied. "To tell me they have gained control over the thoughts of their minds and hearts. Others... others I find out about."

"And?"

"The lake always turns on those who use it," he warned her. "Sooner or later. You will reap what you sow."

"Do they die?" she asked. "The ones who don't stop wishing?"

"They die."

"How do they die?"

"Many different ways," Gilmore assured her. "But their deaths all share one thing in common."

"Which is?"

"When their bodies are found," he answered, "They have no eyes."

A spider slid out onto its anchor line, dangling in front of Suzie. Its gaze engaged her momentarily and then it threw itself across the chasm between the trees, to continue its task.

They were at a fork in the path, one way leading to his little house, the other to the parking lot where Suzie's corporate-fleet black Mercedes-Benz AMG was parked.

"Get back to your car and don't trespass on my land again," Gilmore ordered, gesturing towards the direction of the distant parking lot. "You can visit, but next time come to my front door and have the decency to knock. Don't ever go near that lake again. Never even fly over it again. No matter how tempted you may be. Find yourself a different route to Vegas. This is your only warning."

"How do I avoid the temptation?" she asked.

"Simple." He chugged a mouthful of water and shook the rattle violently. "Open your own damned eyes. While you still have them."

***

Back at his house, Gilmore League sensed a golden orb weaver fly between the framing posts of his porch. More spiders dropped down, eager to form their protective web around his house.

He sat down on an old rocking chair and listened to them, appreciative of their labor. He rocked in the chair and remembered. He knew the temptation the others felt; he had answered the Lake's malignant promises himself, a long time ago. But Gilmore League had been given a singular opportunity to atone, by guiding others off the path he had once followed himself.

But that salvation had not been earned until he after had paid the lake what he owed it.

As he rocked in his chair, he touched his face, feeling the glass eyes implanted in his orbits. Knowing he could never see the lake again, to be tempted by its promises.

Knowing he had seen to it that he had no eyes for a reason.

About the Author

Laura J. Campbell lives and writes in Houston, Texas. She grew up in the coastal community of El Lago, Texas, Home of the Astronauts. Her career has included taking care of venomous snakes, medical research, and health law. She has published over forty-five short stories and two novels. Mrs. Campbell won the 2007 James B. Baker Award for short story for her science fiction tale, "416175", included in this collection. When she is not writing, Mrs. Campbell can be found running, weight training, or attending good old-fashioned rock-and-roll shows. She is encouraged in her writing by her husband, Patrick, and children, Alexander and Samantha. Many of Mrs. Campbell's more recent works are available through Amazon at https://www.amazon.com/Laura-J.-Campbell/e/B07K6SZJJ9.

Editor's Note

The font used for the body text in this collection is called Maiola. It was created by Veronika Burian, who founded TypeTogether with José Scaglione. Their goal, per the information on the Adobe Fonts website, is to create "innovative and stylish solutions to the greatest problems in the global, professional typography market. The foundry focuses on text typography for intensive editorial use, both digital and in print."

Laura and I chose this font because we wanted a sophisticated and feminine touch to her collection. There are thousands of fonts available for commercial use, but I was thrilled to see Adobe had gathered fonts by women in a package. Some of Laura's themes speak of the female experience, so this font seemed to really fit her style and unique voice.

You can learn more about TypeTogether at www.type-together.com.

Andrea Thomas, Editor
Arizona, 2021

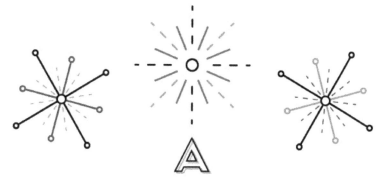

A CELEBRATION OF STORYTELLING

The Anthological Festival of Tales

58 stories by 39 authors designed to honor the art of writing by
including a fair, festival, or celebration in each telling.
From fantasy to sci-fi, from thrillers to mysteries,
we know readers will truly enjoy this feast of fables.

THE DARK

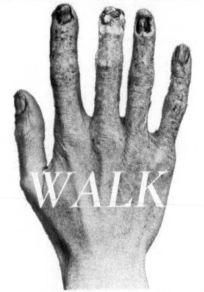

WALK

FORWARD

A HARROWING COLLECTION BY
JOHN S. MCFARLAND

Available in paperback and on Kindle from
DARK OWL PUBLISHING, LLC
www.darkowlpublishing.com

SOMETHING WICKED THIS WAY RIDES

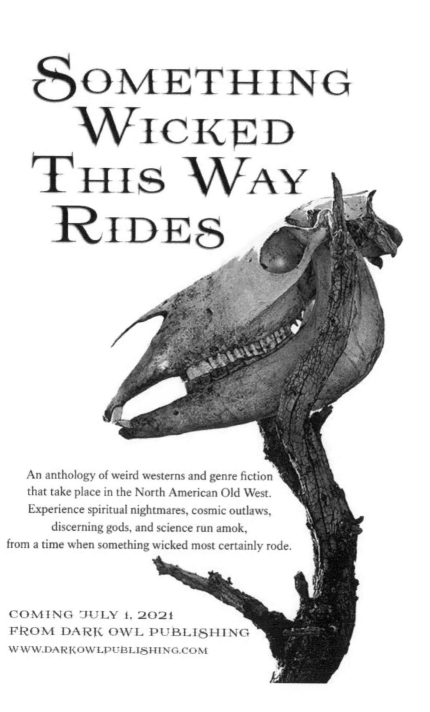

An anthology of weird westerns and genre fiction
that take place in the North American Old West.
Experience spiritual nightmares, cosmic outlaws,
discerning gods, and science run amok,
from a time when something wicked most certainly rode.

COMING JULY 1, 2021
FROM DARK OWL PUBLISHING
WWW.DARKOWLPUBLISHING.COM

The king is dead! Long live... um...

It's now up to a wizard and a witch to pick
the next ruler, in a long line or rulers,
all no longer in possession of anything
to put a crown on.

They figure something has to change.
Aside from being messy, beheadings by the subjects
don't help anyone.
So what can this unlikely - or perhaps quite likely -
pair do to end the streak of regicide
and make such unhappy humans happy?

And then it hits them: the perfect solution.
Or, at least, it better be perfect.
It just *has* to be.

Just About Anyone

Carl R. Jennings

Coming September 1, 2021
in paperback and on Kindle
www.darkowlpublishing.com